THE LEGEND OF
DEV CAMERON

From what she'd heard, both from her mother and from the official accounts uploaded onto the New American Net, his personal contacts with the alien Naga had made him something of an alien himself—a being capable of melding with Naga and DalRiss alike in a symbiosis that no one in human space really even understood yet. He'd been linked with both during the battle when he'd been killed.

Interesting datum, that. Dev Cameron had died in the last big battle against the Empire in the revolution . . .

And Kara was going to die in the first battle of the new war.

The thought bit, cold and hard-edged. *No!* She was *not* going to die . . . not like this!

WARSTRIDER

NETLINK

WILLIAM H. KEITH, JR.

AVON BOOKS • NEW YORK

The poem "Fire and Ice" by Robert Frost is from *The Poetry of Robert Frost* edited by Edward Connery Lathem. Copyright © 1951 by Robert Frost. Copyright © 1923, 1969 by Henry Holt and Co., Inc. Reprinted by permission of Henry Holt and Co., Inc.

WARSTRIDER: NETLINK is an original publication of Avon Books. This work has never before appeared in book form. This work is a novel. Any similarity to actual persons or events is purely coincidental.

AVON BOOKS
A division of
The Hearst Corporation
1350 Avenue of the Americas
New York, New York 10019

Copyright © 1995 by William H. Keith, Jr.
Cover art by Dorian Vallejo
Published by arrangement with the author
Library of Congress Catalog Card Number: 95-94491
ISBN: 0-380-77968-4

First AvoNova Printing: December 1995

AVONOVA TRADEMARK REG. U.S. PAT. OFF. AND IN OTHER COUNTRIES, MARCA REGISTRADA, HECHO EN U.S.A.

Printed in the U.S.A.

RA   10   9   8   7   6   5   4   3   2   1

Prologue

The most beautiful thing we can experience is the mysterious. It is the source of all true art and science. He to whom this emotion is a stranger, who can no longer pause to wonder and stand wrapt in awe, is as good as dead.

—ALBERT EINSTEIN
mid–twentieth century C.E.

Star stuff spiraled into emptiness, the thunder of its passage a shrill keening in his mind. >>DEVCAMERON<< watched that ruby-glowing cataract . . . and wondered.

He was no longer human, not entirely, anyway. He retained his memories of being human, certainly; and much of the intelligence and adaptability, the lust for *knowing*, the self-deprecating wit that had shaped his personality when he'd been alive remained intact, but his physical body had been lost . . . how long ago? Twenty standard years? . . . thirty?

It was hard to know with any certainty. His internal RAM, the nanogrown hardware with its highly accurate timekeeper function, had been vaporized along with his physical brain at the Second Battle of Herakles, and he no longer knew how to measure the passage of time objectively.

It didn't matter much, one way or the other. The DalRiss had a somewhat different concept of time, more relaxed than that of humans, while the Naga experienced time by events, an alien way of thinking that guaranteed they would never be bored. >>DEVCAMERON<<, in his new incarnation, tended to use the subjective time-measuring faculties of his hosts.

There were times when he brooded about the loss. The human mind and the human body went together, interlinked, interdependent in ways that even the best human somatic engineers and medical AIs didn't yet fully understand, and he had lost that link. He was a ghost, mind alone without body. The mind could be pictured as a self-correcting program running on an organic computer. When the DalRiss-Naga starship to which he'd been physically connected at Herakles had been destroyed, the program had continued to run on the interlinked nodes of the other living DalRiss ships. Same software, different hardware. Existence . . . *awareness* continued.

In countless ways his senses were far more subtle than they'd been before, possessing both the keenness and the range of the far-flung sensory web of the DalRiss fleet. As his human-evolved programming interpreted the inflowing data, he *heard* the hiss of particulate radiations cascading along the Galaxy's magnetic fields and the symphonic tunings of distant radio sources, *felt* the tickle of dust motes adrift in emptiness, *tasted* the bite of gamma rays and X-rays announcing the long-ago deaths of suns. A planetoid, eight-billion-year-old relic of stellar birth and death, tumbled through blackness twenty million kilometers to the left of >>DEVCAMERON's<< disembodied point of view.

Straight ahead, two million kilometers distant now, lay Wonder . . . and a piercing, scintillating Beauty.

The stars, both of them, were tiny remnants of a vaster, ancient glory, degenerate suns larger and more luminous by far than traditional white dwarfs but shrunken nonetheless. >>DEVCAMERON's<< new brain registered that the two objects were separated from one another by just less than 800,000 kilometers—about twice the distance between Earth and Earth's moon—and that their mutual orbit had a period of three hours, twenty minutes.

So fast did they rotate about their common center of gravity that the movement was easily discernible to the eye; both suns generated visible shock waves in the mist of gases and churning star-stuff through which they moved. Mass was the secret behind their speed, of course; each semi-collapsed star still massed as much as Earth's sun, despite the fact that each was scarcely the size of the planet Neptune, a scant 48,000 kilometers in diameter or less.

The strange system, the twin dwarfs and the sea of churning stellar debris surrounding them, had a combined absolute luminosity of about twice that of Earth's sun. Human eyes would not have been able to make out any detail, but to >>DEVCAMERON's<< heightened senses it appeared as though those two radiant spheres were enmeshed deep within swirling shrouds of blue and ultraviolet light; each sun was ringed by an accretion disk, spiraling gasses glowing red and orange against the fierce blues and blue-whites of the parent.

Here, at least, was one area where >>DEVCAMERON<< knew that he'd not entirely lost his humanity. The two suns glowed with a haunting, a riveting splendor, sheer beauty in gas clouds, mass, and the outstretched hand of Newton. His hosts could not fully comprehend the feelings that moved him. The Alyan DalRiss thought of beauty solely in terms of efficiency and utility; the Naga were different enough that the very concept of beauty was as alien to them as was the concept of individuality.

>>DEVCAMERON<<, however, could look on those two tiny suns embedded in liquid currents of light and feel the old stirrings and appreciation of color and splendor that proved there was humanity in him yet.

"It's beautiful," he thought, directing the comment into the matrix of living machine and intelligence that surrounded him.

"It is impossible," the mind of his host replied. "The laws of physics are subverted here."

>>DEVCAMERON<< was amused by the bafflement he sensed in the host's thought. DalRiss and Naga both, he realized by now, had a more direct, less emotional response to puzzles than did most humans. Both, like humans, could feel awe, but mysteries, impossibilities, miracles were for them sources of frustration more than of wonder.

He could feel the trickle and splash of numbers moving at the fringes of his awareness, the host grappling with measurements that violated not only physical law but common sense. Something strange was at work here. There was mystery in those paired suns as well as beauty, and, for >>DEVCAMERON<<, at any rate, a special wonder born of awe.

Possibly there's more of the human left in me than I thought. . . .

In the face of such strangeness, the thought was oddly comforting.

Generally, accretion disks were the sweepings of dust and hot gas collected by an astronomical object with a respectable gravity and compacted into a spinning, flat wheel as they spiraled inward. This, however, was the reverse. Ultraviolet-hot plasma was spiraling *up* from each star's equator, arcing across empty space in a vast, S-shaped curve. Each dwarf and its thread of uncoiling star stuff mirrored the other in its reach; the ribbons, cooling to near invisibility halfway between the paired dwarf suns, grew hot and brilliant once more as they mutually spiraled into a tight, glowing pinpoint of dazzling light midway between the rapidly circling stars, a *something* that gave >>DEVCAMERON<< the uncanny feeling that it was devouring the substance of the dwarfs, a cannibal . . . a *vampire* feeding on the lifeblood of dying suns.

The DalRiss-Naga fleet was studying that *something* intently now with every sensor and instrument at its disposal—including >>DEVCAMERON's<< once-human intelligence. At first, the communal mind of the widespread fleet had assumed the devourer was some traditional astronomical object, a black hole or neutron star whose gravity outpulled that of both orbiting stars and dragged parts of their atmosphere into itself in stellar gluttony.

Now, though, as they moved cautiously closer, >>DEVCAMERON<< knew that the reality was not so simple . . . and was far stranger. They could sense mass down there at the cusp where the gravitational fields of the two stars balanced, but it was not the mass of a third star. The period of the two circling dwarf stars was precisely that expected of Sol-massed stars in an orbital embrace at that distance; had there been a black hole of stellar mass at the system's center, their period would have been shorter by far.

No, the mass they felt balanced between the stars was scarcely that of a single world, yet energies were being wielded there at the central focus of light sufficient to tear gigatons of material each second from the surfaces of each star, channeling them in vast and ever-tightening interwoven spirals into a maw of strangeness, of otherness where, silently and with no fuss whatsoever save that diamond-brilliant gleam of radiant energy, they simply disappeared.

Together with the intermingled consciousnesses that made up the DalRiss fleet, >>DEVCAMERON<< watched . . . and wondered.

Not until later was that wonder transformed to an emotion all three species—DalRiss, Naga, and human—could equally share.

Terror, it seemed, had always possessed more value as a survival trait than wonder. . . .

Chapter 1

By the early twenty-first century, the lines between the biological and the machine, between natural intelligence and artificial, between physics and chemistry, between life and lifelessness, were already becoming blurred.

—*The Golden Apples of the Stars*
SHELLY WESTEGREN
C.E. 2457

A flight of missiles shrieked in from the northwest, barely clearing a sand dune before plowing into ocher desert in a thunderous cascade of smoke and flame and dirt. Lieutenant Kara Hagan ducked and pivoted, leaning into the detonation's shock wave as stones and grit clattered across the outer hull of her warstrider.

"Air attack!" she yelled over the squadron's tactical channel. A threat warning winked at her from the lower right portion of her visual field, responding to the caress of hostile targeting radar and ladar sensors. Her strider's nanoflage coating was still absorbing most of the radiation, but the bad guys were close enough now that they almost certainly had the assault squadron pinpointed. "Kim! Daniels! Watch the sky!"

Seconds later, a pair of Imperial sky-ground attack drones screamed through an azure sky, banking sharply left above the sea at the warstriders' backs and vanishing behind a line of Martian palms along the beach.

"*Kuso!*" Sergeant Jack Hayden's voice said in her mind. "Where the gok did *those* come from?"

"They didn't tell us we'd be facing hunter hawks!" another voice added.

"Freeze it, people," Kara snapped. "Keep it iceworld! Nobody promised you *easy!*"

As if to underscore that thought, another barrage of explosions tore through the sandy soil to Kara's left as the two *ryoshitaka* attack craft reappeared, low above the horizon to the east. She rode with the blast, her combat machine's legs giving to absorb and distribute the impact. Before the dirt had stopped falling, her KS-1090 Cutlass had pivoted, its hivel cannon flipping out of its foldaway recess in the mirror-slick black shell, its sensors locking onto the nearer of the Imperial fighters and highlighting the machine in flashing red. The hivel screamed, slashing into the banking aircraft with a white-hot scythe of depleted uranium slugs. There was a blinding flash as the hunter hawk's fusion containment fields collapsed . . . followed an instant later by a second explosion as Warstrider Kim hivel-popped the other one.

She checked her systems readouts. Everything was still online, still well in the green. Warstriders were *tough. . . .*

Shrugging off the last of the gravel spilled across her back, she moved forward, cresting a low rise. The objective was in sight now, a sprawl of domes and fortress turrets several kilometers distant.

From Kara's point of view, she *was* the Cutlass, black-hulled, humming with power as she drifted over the mist-cloaked terrain. Just three meters long, the warstrider had an egg-sleek surface, with an organic look reminiscent of some living DalRiss machine. The only violation of its light-drinking nanoflage surface was the grinning shark's mouth on the prow, and the flyer's name in gold script—KARA'S MATIC. Earlier generations of warstriders had been ponderous, heavy-limbed, walking targets by comparison. The advent of Companions and Naga-DalRiss biotech had made possible new levels of control in the man-machine interface.

And advances in nanotechnology—the technology of the very small—had transformed the ancient art of war as well.

"Okay, boys and girls!" Kara snapped off the Companion-linked order. "Time to pick up your feet!"

She'd already loaded her warstrider's main grenade launchers with QEC projectiles. She extended her arm . . . and the strider's AI interpreted her thought as a command, cutting loose with a long, thumping staccato of rapid fire. White smoke exploded from a dozen points around and ahead of Kara's strider, a thick and heavy mist that refused to rise or billow, that flowed across the uneven ground more like a liquid than a gas. The other striders in Kara's squadron joined in, lacing the ground with the milky fog. In seconds, the entire area for kilometers around was covered, the fog swiftly seeping away into the ground. A green light winked against her vision, indicating the presence of an active floater field.

"I've got localized readings at ten to the seven gauss!" she reported over the tacnet, watching the flicker of numbers scrolling past the right side of her visual field. "Now ten to the eight! I'm floating . . ."

True antigravity remained one of the classic impossibilities of physics, one of those technological dreams that had teased at Man's imagination for centuries. The nano fired from Kara's strider and from the other striders of her squadron, however, was programmed to work its way down into the ground and begin reshaping itself and the dirt around it, creating uncounted trillions of quantum electron cages.

QECs were highly specialized molecules. Trapped within each buckyball cage was a single electron, its position balanced by the attitude of the atoms around it, its spin rigidly locked in a delicate and specialized violation of Heisenberg Uncertainty; the immediate result of so many electrons held with polarized spins was a magnetic field strong enough for a warstrider to grab hold of with its own maglev fields. At another thought from Kara, *Kara's Matic* retracted its spidery legs, folding them away into its body as the machine hovered two meters above the ground.

One by one, the other fifteen striders of the Black Phantoms' First Squadron folded their legs as well, drifting forward over the smoking ground in an open-V assault formation. Gausslev movement had the inevitable tradeoffs characteristic of all combat innovation. It made the machines faster and more maneuverable, but they would be restricted to the area blanketed by nano smoke, and the ground field would become increasingly patchy and intermittent as it degraded under the assault of surface explosions and enemy antinano countermeasures. The field would last, however, for several minutes—an age in this type of battle—and it was easy enough to replenish as long as the QEC-programmed nano held out.

Kara swiftly found the rhythm of thought and movement that matched her pace to that of the other drifting machines. A warstrider moved in response to the same signals a human brain generated to make its body walk; Kara was not piloting her warstrider so much as she was wearing it, the same way she wore her own body. *Kara's Matic* slid forward, accelerating rapidly until it was moving far more swiftly than legs could have carried it.

Ahead, light flared and strobed around their target, a sprawling, multiply domed structure on the horizon. Kara wished the assault team could have been dropped closer to the objective, but simulations trying on-site insertions had invariably been slashed to pieces by the fortress's defenses, usually before the warstriders could even deploy. The question now was whether they had any better chance deploying some kilometers away from the Imperial complex, then advancing through a wall of fire to reach it.

The technology of modern warfare was changing so rapidly it was becoming hard for any one person to keep up with it. The changes in warstriders alone in the past twenty-five years—as in the nanotechnic man-machine interface—were astonishing. Companions, for instance . . .

"I'm getting movement between us and the objective," Sergeant Lechenko's voice said quietly over her NCO command channel. "I make it eight . . . no, ten hostiles, in open deployment."

Between the Black Phantoms and the complex, shapes were moving . . . deploying in an unfolding pattern with the speed of thought. "I see them," she replied. "All units. Prepare to engage!"

Laser fire flicked out toward the assault team as they floated down the gentle slope into the open. Kara checked her sensor readouts and suppressed an inner twinge of dismay. Those warstriders were Imperial Tsurugis, large, powerful, and thoroughly nasty machines. The CMI—Confederation Military Intelligence—had reported the possibility that at least a squadron of Tsurugis was stationed in the Noctis Labyrinthus area of operations, and the raid had been planned with that possibility in mind.

Ten—no, twelve, now—twelve Imperial warstriders were blocking the way. Ten more were deploying closer to the fortress.

"Gok it, Lieutenant!" That was Warstrider Phil Dolan's mental voice on the tactical link. "We can't face that mob!"

"We can and we will," she replied. "Let them come to us. Defensive Plan Echo." That would put the burden on the hostiles and possibly even the odds a bit. The two sides were trading heavy fire now, with laser beams and particle cannon bolts lacing the air between them. Defensive formation or not, though, the Black Phantom assault force had to keep moving to avoid being pinned or cut off by the enemy movement.

Particle accelerator fire blossomed in blue-white lightnings. Lindsey Smeth's Cutlass took a direct hit that carved her machine open from prow to dorsal carapace, and Kara felt the inner shock as the other warstrider's mental link with the squadron snapped off. Damn . . . !

Her death left a hole in the Phantoms' right flank, and the enemy striders were pouring through. "Pivot right!" Kara yelled over the link. "Block them! Block them!"

"Block the gokers!" Sergeant Vasily Lechenko echoed. "Newbury! You heard the lieutenant! Move your tail!"

In seconds, Defensive Plan Echo was a swirling confusion of drifting, fire-spitting machines, both lines broken and the battle reduced to isolated pockets of one-on-one and two-on-one. Kara had a tac display of the battle up in a small corner window of her visual field, but there was little to discern there beyond an almost chaotic choreography of moving points of light.

No battle plan ever survives contact with the enemy. Who had said that, she wondered? She'd downloaded that bit of aphoristic military sentiment during her training at NAMA, the New American Military Academy, but she couldn't at the moment recall the author. The failure was irritating, a small proof that no technology was perfect. What else, she wondered, had been downloaded into her skull during those years that she'd somehow failed to retain?

Kara was twenty-two standard years old; most of her squadron mates were younger. Cephlink downloads made it possible for warriors to be fully programmed before they were eighteen, a fact that let the Confederation military take advantage of the peaks of their mental and physical strength and flexibility. A few—Sergeants Lechenko and Daniels, especially—were older, balancing the reflexes of youth with experience and seasoning. As in every army since the time of Nimrod, NCOs were the military's heart and backbone.

And like every good officer, Kara had learned to rely on her sergeants.

"Vasily!" she called over her NCO channel. "Take four or five people through *there*." She indicated a route with a set of thought symbols overlaid on the tac map. "See if you can get behind them!"

"Right," Lechenko replied. "Blasey! Pascoe! Newbury! Maslov! With me! *Move* it! *Move* it!"

On her map, five of the green blips representing her forces began sliding east, getting between the enemy units and the fortress. That threat might break the impetus of the Imperial attack. She found herself willing the strategy to work....

The problem was that the enemy had already won, simply by forcing the Phantoms to stop and duel with them. The objective of this raid was the fortress ahead, not battling Imperial warstriders.

Kuso! If those rear-end, fantasy-linked, nullbrained gokers in Ops Planning would just wake up to the possibilities of the Aresynch mission...

"I've got a problem here!"

That was Phil Dolan. On the map, it looked as though he'd managed to get himself cut off from the rest of the Phantoms, a single green blip surrounded by reds. Kara was closest; she urged her machine forward, swinging wide to the left to clear Dolan's stricken machine from her field of fire. There he was... the focus of three Tsurugis who were taking an intent and personal interest in his strider. With a thought, she targeted the nearest Imperial machine and opened up with her particle accelerator cannon. Blue lightnings flared, sun-brilliant and dazzling. One Tsurugi, its floater field failing and smoke spilling from a savage rip in its side, drifted unsteadily down a gentle slope, legs extending. The other two pivoted in midair, bringing their weapons to bear on Kara.

Her PAC was still recharging from the last burst so she switched weapons and triggered a volley of VR-89 rockets, tiny, texture-homing projectiles that sprayed the nearest Tsurugi in a rippling cascade of small, sharp explosions; the last Imperial machine fired a PAC bolt that grazed her starboard side, jolting her back on her floater field and sending a cascade of red warning indicators flashing across one side of her visual field. Spinning and drifting to the left, she returned fire with a burst of nano-D rounds, thumb-sized shells bearing disassembler nanoprogrammed to eat through warstrider armor.

The Tsurugi's black hull turned blotchy under the as-

sault, the damage chewing across its surface until its nanoflage layers could reprogram and stabilize under the assault.
By then Kara's PAC was recharged, and her full-powered
bolt of artificial lightning punched through weakened armor
like a hard-driven fist through cardboard. The Tsurugi tumbled backward, rolling on its gausslev field until the mags
failed and it smashed into the ground.

The other two had limped clear of the immediate area, so
Kara turned her attention to Dolan's crippled strider, which
was lying on its side in a shallow ravine. The machine's
name, *Philosopher*, had been almost entirely scoured away,
along with much of the outer, light-sensitive nanoflage layer.
Arms extended from *Kara's Matic*'s side, long and multiply
jointed; nanomorphic clamps grasped hold of *Philosopher*'s
hull, the nano of the clamp welding itself so completely to
Dolan's armor that the two became one. Leaning back
against the new weight, she began dragging Dolan's strider
out of the ravine.

"Dolan!" she called over the tacnet. "Are you okay?"

There was no response, but it was possible his com was
down. His machine felt dead, however, and he wasn't able
to help. Worse, her own magfields were failing. Red-
highlighted messages warned of damage to her gaussfield
generator couplings . . . and the local floater field was de-
grading as well, the nano-QEC alignments disrupted by the
violent electrical groundings of multiple PAC discharges.
She overrode a power-shutdown alert, then extended her
legs. An electrical failure in her stabilizer system threatened
to pitch her to the side, but she compensated with a burst of
new-grown circuitry and an emergency patch from her
power reserves.

Damn . . . she was leaking power, *bleeding* power like the
hemorrhage from a deep, slashing wound. Her fusorpack was
limping along at eighteen percent of capacity, and the warning
flags were coming at her faster than she could deal with. She
tugged harder at *Philosopher*'s fire-savaged bulk, struggling to
drag it back into an area where the floater fields were still
intact. Even if Dolan's self-repair systems were down, it might

be possible to give him a charge of circuitry nano or even send her own Companion across to recharge his systems and get his gausslev units back on-line. If—

The blast caught her from behind, a searing onslaught of gigajoule laser energy that overloaded her struggling external nano coating and melted its way through her hull like a blowtorch through polystyrene. Diacarb alloy vaporized at that deadly caress. Two of her four legs were sheared off in a flash of raw energy. Unbalanced, *Kara's Matic* pivoted around its attachment to *Philosopher*; Kara tried uploading the mental command to dissolve the nano bond with the other warstrider, but her systems were already in cascade failure, one tripping out the next in a dizzying collapse of all command and control functions. She had time only to glimpse her attackers, a pair of Tsurugis that had managed to slip behind her using the crest of the ridge for cover.

Then her visual field shattered in a burst of static and she was plunged into blackness absolute. She felt the shock as her strider struck the ground, and she wondered if the Imperials would finish her off immediately or leave her where she was, an easy pickup for their legger infantry.

Inside her body now turned coffin, Kara bit off a savage curse. She *hated* being helpless like this, unable to move, unable to defend herself or even see outside her near-dead warstrider.

Her only chance now was to wake up . . . and she quickly began uploading the commands that would make that possible. . . .

Chapter 2

It is now recognized that human technological development does not proceed in steady waves as was first assumed by the primitive models created at the dawn of modern sociohistory during the mid- to late-twentieth century. Instead, it advances in leaps interspersed with long periods of null growth. Technology feeds itself, one advance spawning others in quick succession, but such a pace cannot endure for long. Humans require time to assimilate the resultant changes to their environment.

A prime example of rapid advancement, of course, is the period immediately after the Confederation Rebellion when, in the space of a few decades, contact with alien species propelled Humanity into an entirely new technological milieu.

—Man and Immortality
DR. ROBERT FISK
C.E. 2567

At least, she thought of it as waking up. The sensations of a linkage disconnect were much the same, with a moment's disorientation as her brain adjusted itself to new input, similar to the groggy and somewhat confused *where am I* of waking from a dream that had seemed more real than reality.

Her surroundings were at once strange and familiar, a close, almost coffinlike enclosure lit solely by the wan gleam of a systems status board in the padding near her head. Now that her bodily sensations were no longer being filtered out by the link, she ached all over, as she always did after a long session piloting a strider. Had her strider been configured as a warflyer, her lifepod would have been filled with a gel to cushion her body against the brutal accelerations demanded by space combat. As it was, even strapped into the pod's liquid-filled rider couch, she had been left bruised and sore by the shocks and jolts of the past few moments.

Reaching up to her face she unstrapped her LS mask. Theoretically, both her life support needs and her physical connection with the warstrider's AI could be provided solely by her Companion, of course, but even the most rabid Nagaphiles rarely staked *everything* on a half kilogram of symbiotic alien nanogoo.

The status board gave light enough to see. Raising her left hand in front of her face, palm up, she concentrated. Her Companion, already sensing her purpose, began emerging almost at once.

Companions were the biotechnic descendents of the Nagalinks and comels of two decades before, living bits of Naga tissue that vastly extended the range of human-machine interfaces, generating an astonishing revolution in human societies from the Core Worlds to the Frontier. Kara's Companion formed a lump in the palm of her hand, tar-black in the uncertain red-tinted light. A larger mass flowed from the back of her skull onto her shoulder, connected to the first by a thread-slender strand emerging through the skin of her arm and the slick plastic fabric of her skinsuit. The process was painless, almost unfelt save for a feather-light brushing sensation against her skin; individual Companion cells were only slightly larger than the mitochondria of Kara's cells, so tiny and compactly organized that they could slip right through the skin, tissue, even bone of their human hosts and not disturb a single nerve.

The original Nagas encountered by humans had been huge, as massive as a good-sized planetoid. In their native state, they could be thought of as living nanotech, vast masses of specialized and interconnected cells that absorbed rock and broke it down virtually atom by atom. With human guidance, they could manufacture nearly anything. There were cases on record of inquisitive Nagas so completely patterning injured humans that they'd been able to rebuild them, literally molecule by molecule, and they'd vastly improved on the genetically engineered biotechnic links humans had used to communicate with the alien DalRiss.

A Naga was composed of uncountable trillions of individual "paracells," each massing a kilogram or two and, when free of its parent, bearing a disturbing resemblance to a shiny black slug the size of someone's head. "Domesticated" Nagas had learned to bud off smaller and more protean pieces of themselves, creating the Companions. Like their paracell precursors, Companions had no intelligence to speak of on their own; Kara found it convenient to think of them as non-AI computers, capable of storing and manipulating vast amounts of data and, when linked to her own brain, able to greatly extend her own intelligence and abilities.

Within moments, her Companion had left her body completely, save for a tiny percentage of itself still lodged within Kara's brain, connected to the rest by an almost invisible thread emerging from the back of her head and penetrating her skull unfelt, a lifeline to help it find its way home. The main body of the Companion, its orders already downloaded, reached with pulsing, amoebic ripplings up off her shoulder and slid into the red-lit console.

The warstrider had its own nano for damage control, but its programming wasn't up to this level of DC. Through her Companion, however, Kara could initiate repairs with more control and with a better understanding of just what was going on inside her vehicle.

An expansion of the idea of human-Naga symbiosis, Companions were fast proving to be the gateway to a radically new way of thinking about tools, about Man, about the universe itself. For centuries, human-machine interfaces had required one or more metal and ceramic receptacles surgically embedded in a person's head. Computers, ViReality feeds, and other cephlink technologies were accessed by jacking a plug into neck or head sockets. Low-level connections could be made through palm implants, nanogrown traceries of wires and contact plates usually embedded at the heel of the person's thumb on his nondominant hand.

Within the Hegemony—the Imperium-dominated collection of national and world governments that spanned most of human-colonized space—how many sockets a person had was a mark of status, since only three-socket jackers could be guaranteed full employment jacking equipment, vehicles, or spacecraft. As part of its welfare program, Earth's government provided free palm interfaces that allowed people to carry out monetary transactions and download government entertainment feeds. In the Frontier, though, things were a bit more freewheeling, but even there sockets were necessary if you wanted to get anywhere in life. And cephlink implants, grown by injections of specially programmed nano that plated out within the sulci of the brain and in the feeds to surgically implanted external sockets, were expensive.

Companions, however, were cheap, self-reproducing half-kilo lumps of living Naga tissue extruded by a planetary Naga that had already had contact with humans. Alive but almost certainly not intelligent or even self-aware, a Companion could slip through the tissues of its human host to achieve an intimate physical interconnectivity with the brain exactly as had the nanoplated layers of metal and plastic in the older style cephlink implants. Instead of having permanently attached sockets, a person with a Naga Companion could form as many sockets as necessary, of any size or capacity, simply by willing it; at a thought, part of the skin would refashion itself, in seconds extruding the necessary hardware.

Not everyone, of course, had embraced this new biotechnology. Too many still remembered the Naga as Xenophobes, the mindless destroyers of the colonies at An-Nur, Herakles, and Lung Chi. Others were simply unable to even consider opening their bodies to an alien life-form, a *parasite*, even if it resembled a lump of tar more than a living organism. Most Japanese, Kara understood, considered such symbiosis to be filthy, akin to rolling around in excrement.

But for those who weren't disgusted by the idea of forming a partnership with the things, Naga Companions were already transforming the way people did business, exchanged credit, or jacked in for entertainment, work, or education. If the Core Worlds were slow to accept Companions, the Confederation had adopted them with an almost passionate enthusiasm. Possibly, Kara thought, the fact that the Confederation had won its independence from the Imperial Shichiju only twenty-five years before—the two were still engaged in almost constant skirmishing and raiding—had something to do with it.

Already, the economies and the industrial infrastructures of New America and the other Confed worlds had been transformed. A new attitude was sweeping the Frontier, one due largely to the influx of alien biotechnology. B-tech, it was called, the blending of human nanotechnology—the manipulation of individual molecules and atoms on the nanometer scale—with the DalRiss understanding of biological systems and controlled evolution, and the Naga ability to pattern and change living materials literally atom by atom. A host of new products had appeared within the past few decades, products that had changed the way people looked at themselves . . . and the ways they presented themselves to others. Naga Companions had already changed nearly everything about how New Americans did business, from the use of information—bytes of data—as a currency base to the ability to transform their faces and bodies into things of pure fancy and fantasy.

Kara closed her eyes, concentrating on the information trickling back down the living thread from her Companion. Her fusorpack, as expected, was off-line and it would take time to build up power enough to recharge its containment fields, but there were substantial reserves yet in her batteries. A short circuit had melted the battery power feeds and fried the control circuitry. She uploaded a series of thoughts to her Companion, directing it to begin emergency repairs. With the bionanotechnological wizardry of its Naga parent, it would be able in a few seconds to regrow new circuitry from the carbonized remains of the old as easily as it could reshape Kara's skin texture and conductivity.

Repairs had only just begun, however, when her strider lurched hard, rolling to the side, and Kara clutched at the edge of her couch, staring with alarm at the padded inner curve of her life-support pod centimeters above her head. Had that been a near-miss, an explosion close beside her strider, or was one of the Tsurugis investigating her damaged machine? Damn, if she only had windows. . . .

Another lurch, a jolt that nearly tipped her over, but then the pod dropped back, rocking heavily before coming to rest, tilted nose-high. The insulation qualities of layered diacarb and ceramplast were superb, but she still could hear the faint rumble of thunder, the shriek of PAC bolts. It sounded like a pitched battle being waged, close by the ravine where Dolan's and her warstriders had fallen.

Who, she wondered, was going to win? Not just this battle, but this ongoing war between Confederation and Empire. The *chi*-war, the New American news medes were calling it, from *chiisai*, the Nihongo word for little. Little war it might have been, minor raids for the most part, with the occasional ship seizure or act of sabotage; certainly, though, it was large enough for the men and women it killed. This raid—Operation Sandstorm, some wit had dubbed it—was supposed to be of supreme importance, though no one had told Kara yet the why of the thing. This world was not exactly an easy mark; the Imperials called it Kasei, but most people on the Frontier knew it by its Anglic name.

Mars.

A Confederation raid against an Imperial research complex on old Mars, right next door to Earth itself, was bound to escalate the *chi*-war to something larger. She just hoped to hell that whatever the Phantoms were supposed to grab here was worth the cost.

And the *risk*.

The political situation was so damned confused just now. The Confederation had won its short, sharp war of independence with the Empire twenty-five years ago, but victory had not brought security. Confederation, Periphery, Frontier . . . names giving substance to a lie. A quarter of a century ago, perhaps, the Confederation had been unified, an alliance of frontier worlds fighting against the Shichiju, but even in victory that alliance had already been crumbling.

Theoretically—at least according to the history ViRsims—

New America, Rainbow, Liberty, and a handful of other worlds had forged a new government, one based on Libertarian ideals now virtually extinct among the crowded dependencies and nation states and Fukushi protectorate arcologies of old Earth. Under the leadership of Travis Sinclair and a few other visionaries, freedom had been wrested from the Empire by sheer grit, determination, and a will to be free of Earth and its heavy-handed Hegemonic bureaucracy.

Though raised and download-educated on New America, Kara knew that there was a certain amount of self-deceptive propaganda behind that version of history. To begin with, no handful of colonial worlds could have hoped to fight it out with Japan's military might or with the Japanese-backed government of the Terran Hegemony and long survive. Shichiju, the Nihongo word for Man's interstellar realm, meant "Seventy," and in fact, the Hegemony had ruled more than seventy worlds at its height. Only about twenty of those worlds—all thinly populated, possessing limited resources and few ships, and located far from the Shichiju's heart—had openly broken with Earth and joined the Confederation rebellion. Japan had held a ruthless monopoly over K-T drive technology and the techniques necessary for building large starships for too long for the newcomer upstarts of the Frontier to be able to challenge them in open war. For the most part, the Confederation's strategy had been to make Japan's inevitable victory too expensive to pursue. At that, luck had more to do with their independence than military prowess—luck . . . and their communication with two separate alien species, still the only nonhuman cultures known to Man.

The DalRiss had first been contacted by a Hegemony survey fleet in 2540, just before the Rebellion. Their technology had taken an odd turning down the path of biology; they *grew* cities and starships rather than building them. Humans had for much longer known of the Naga, entities stranger than the DalRiss by far. In an attempt to attach human motives to nonhuman perceptions and actions, they'd originally called them Xenophobes. Immense fluid or plastic creatures inhabiting the crusts of several worlds scattered across those reaches of the Shichiju toward the constellations Ophiuchus, Serpens, Aquila, and

Hercules, they possessed dizzyingly alien modes of thought and perception . . . and a control of their own internal chemistries far more precise and powerful than the crude nanotechnology of human science.

The Naga inhabiting the now-deserted world called Herakles, Mu Herculis III, had been instrumental in the defeat of an Imperial warfleet. Massing as much as a small moon and drawing its energy from the heat of a planet's core, it could wield incredible powers; while linked with the rebel commander Devis Cameron, it had manipulated powerful magnetic fields in such a way as to propel one-ton chunks of ferrous material at velocities approaching ten percent of the speed of light. The largest and most powerful of the Empire's dreadnoughts had crumpled and flared like moths in a blowtorch when subjected to the Naga's accurate and deadly fire.

Kara sighed. Devis Cameron. Now *there* was a name. She'd never known the man personally, of course, since he'd died during the Second Battle of Herakles almost three years before she'd been born. Still, Kara felt as though she had known him. He'd been the lover of her mother, Katya Alessandro, for a number of years during the war . . . and he'd fathered her half brother, Daren. A year after Cameron's death, Kara's mother had established a long-term contract with another rebel officer, Vic Hagan—like Katya, a New American.

Devis Cameron had been from Earth.

Kara knew her mother as well as anyone alive; she still didn't understand what the woman had seen in that man. For one thing, as an Earther, he'd started out owing his allegiance to the Terran Hegemony, which, of course, was little more than the Empire's puppet. The word was that he'd been loyal to the Empire for quite a while, that he'd even won the coveted *Teikokuno Hoshi*, the Star of the Empire, for his part in contacting the Naga at Alya A-VI. Later, while operating against rebels on Eridu, he'd been given an order he hadn't liked . . . and had joined the rebellion.

That told Kara quite a lot, that Cameron hadn't had much in the way of personal convictions, that he'd let himself be buffeted back and forth rather than setting a course and sticking to it. From what she'd heard, both from her mother and from the official accounts uploaded onto the New American net, his personal contacts with the alien Naga had made him something of an alien himself, a being capable of melding with Naga and DalRiss alike in a symbiosis that no one in human space really understood even yet. He'd been linked with both during the battle when he'd been killed.

It was quiet again outside her warstrider. Her emergency repairs were nearly done. Maybe she could get out of this fix yet. . . .

"Lieutenant Hagan," a new voice said inside her head. "We are terminating the simulation."

She blinked. "Wait a minute!" she said. "I'm not dead, am I?"

The voice chuckled. "Not quite. Our AI out here gives you a sixty percent-plus chance of completing your repairs. But I'm afraid the mission completion probability's only about twenty-eight percent."

Gok. "We should still play out the simulation."

"We will. But we're declaring *you* dead. A message just came through for you. They want you up in Ops Planning."

Kara stifled a groan. Normally, important messages would have been handled by her Companion, which either would have routed them through to her immediately or dealt with them according to program. Her messages were being handled now, however, by the AI running this simulation; apparently it had decided that this one was important enough to have her declared dead for the rest of this scenario.

"Who's it from?" she asked the voice.

"Double ID," was the reply. "General Hagan and Senator Alessandro. And it was coded urgent."

"Okay, okay," Kara said, closing her eyes. "I'm on my way."

Once again—and this time for real—she woke up, this time in the couch of a ViRcomm module in the Ops center of ConMilCom HQ. Warstrider Lindsey Smeth—"killed" moments before in the fighting on Mars—was there to help her unstrap. "Tough luck, Lieutenant," she said. "We almost had 'em that time."

"*Almost* doesn't cut it," Kara replied, standing up and

stretching stiff, sore muscles. Even ViRsimmed war could be rough on the body, when the body believed that what was happening to it was real. "That's what, fifteen tries against that base so far?"

"Sixteen," Smeth said. "But who's counting? I'd rather ViRdie than buy it for real."

Kara grinned. "Just so you stay in one piece when the show goes down. And, speaking of staying in one piece, I'd better go see what my brass-crested parents want."

"Good luck, Lieutenant."

"Thanks. I have a feeling I'm going to need it."

Chapter 3

Bella detestata matribus. (Wars are the dread of mothers.)
—*Odes, i*
HORACE
B.C.E. 20

Senator Katya Alessandro stood before the viewall in her husband's office, watching the city. Though his office was on the fifty-third level, his viewall was using a ground-floor pickup, set to show a realtime view of the building's transplas atrium and the broad, green expanse of Franklin Park beyond. It was just past Second Eclipse, and Columbia hung suspended in the west, filling nearly an octant of the sky, a pale, immense, crater-blotched crescent bowed away from the golden glare of 26 Draconis A.

Opposite, on the far side of the park just a kilometer away and rising eighty stories over Jefferson's government district, was the one-time headquarters for one of the larger Imperial corporations doing business on New America; even yet the locals called it the Sony Building. The holographic lettering above that gleaming facade, however, now read PEOPLE'S CONFEDERATION CONGRESS, marking it as home to the Confederation Free Senate and what passed for government on New America these days.

Government? Katya grimaced. Anarchy was closer to the mark.

Why, she wondered, had she ever left the Confederation military? She'd *thought* she would be able to make a difference by running for office. During the time she'd been a senator, though, she'd seen little evidence that she was doing much of anything worthwhile. Lately, most of her time was spent mindlooping—what an earlier age had called "paper shuffling," though that term was as dated now as "typewriter" or "videotape."

She glanced sideways at Vic, who was leaning back at his desk with the distracted, glazed-over look of someone tapping his internal RAM for a piece of squirreled-away data. He'd made the right choice, clearly. He was a general now, one of the senior officers in ConMilCom's Operations Center.

Katya Alessandro loved Vic Hagan dearly, though, as she sometimes tried to make herself forget, he'd been her *second* love. When Dev Cameron had . . . changed, his body destroyed at Second Herakles as his mind somehow became part of the group mind of the Naga-DalRiss fleet, any chance of a common physical ground between her and Dev had been wiped away. A year after Dev had left human space with the alien fleet-mind, she'd palmed an extended cohab contract with Vic. Daren—Dev's son—had already been born by then, and she'd needed . . . *somebody*. A year and a half later, Kara had been born, her daughter by Vic.

Eventually, she'd resigned her commission and gone into politics. As one of the heroes of the revolution, she still had good recognition on New America, and she'd won her seat in Congress with almost embarrassing ease.

She was, by anyone's standard, successful.

Why then, did she feel like such a failure?

The war, of course . . . She shook her head. She'd long ago decided that the politicians of human-explored space would get themselves into far fewer wars if more of them started off as warriors. Civilians, she'd found, were too likely to become caught up in the supposed glory of war. It took a soldier to remind people of why war was something to be avoided.

Central Jefferson, she thought as she watched the view-all, was crowded. The capital had always been bustling, but the congestion had been getting worse lately. During the war, its location, almost forty-nine light years from Sol, and its industrial base, in a system rich in raw materials, had combined to make it a good candidate for the capital of the fledgling Confederation. The sign in front of the Sony Building back then had read FIRST PEOPLE'S CONFEDERATION CONGRESS, a nod both toward the old-Earth North American model upon which the government had been based and to the fact that, in those far-off, pioneering days, at least, it had been assumed that the Congress would meet only intermittently, in times of crisis.

Like all governments, however, it had somehow put down roots and grown . . . though whether that growth had been more like that of a tree or a cancer, Katya hadn't yet decided. And in the meantime, the mingled cultures of New America and the Confederation were transforming as swiftly as the technology. It was becoming harder and harder to maintain any kind of unity even among the cultures resident just on New America.

And Katya was less and less sure that unity was something the government should—or *could*—impose. The Sinclair Doctrine applied here as well as to the scattered worlds of Confederation and Shichiju, didn't it?

She knew all of the arguments, of course. She'd invoked them plenty of times herself on the Senate floor. Unity was necessary now because the Imperials were pushing hard and would take advantage of any perceived weakness. Worse, things were changing so god-awfully fast. Technology was changing, the rate of change increasing at a pace that seemed totally out of control, and society itself was showing deep and troubling strains.

It was almost impossible to keep up with the shifts and reworkings of Confederation culture anymore. As she looked through the viewall into Franklin Park, she could see some of the bizarre shapes strolling there.

The Naga Revolution, it was called by some, especially by the younger generation, the kids born since 2550 or so. Most had personal Nagas, Companions, that fulfilled all of the functions of the old cephlinks and added a few more. It was curious, Katya thought, how a symbiosis that was changing the very way Man perceived himself was being manifested by New America's younger citizens primarily as fashion statements. It seemed unbalanced, somehow, almost sacrilegious, if such a term had any meaning anymore, something akin to using a quantum power tap to light a match.

There was a young couple riding a slidewalk just in front of her. The girl was nude, save for sandals and her Naga's skin expressions—patterns of green and silver opalescence that rippled up and down her legs and torso, alternately revealing and concealing as it shifted. Her companion was sheer fantasy, human in shape but patterned in a hallucinatory montage of scales, feathers, and tawny predator's hide, all fashioned through his Companion's alterations to the cells of his skin. She assumed the person was male; the only clue to his sex was the outsized genitalia dangling between his legs, though even that in itself was no guarantee. Many people routinely changed their sex as casually as they changed clothes; others changed only the *appearance*, and there was no way to be sure which was which.

The Naga Revolution had challenged old definitions not only of what sex you were, but of what it was to be human in the first place. There was an entire subculture given to experimenting with deliberately alien and outrageous body forms, humans in the guise of aliens born of fantasy. That sort of thing had long been common enough in ViReality links, where a person could assume any desired persona online. With Naga Companions as fashion accessories, however, the blurring of reality and fantasy had escaped the world of VR-communications and entered the real world.

What, Katya wondered, was going to be next? It didn't seem as though things *could* change much more, though she imagined that neolithic-hunter-gatherers must have felt the same way about cities, pottery, and agriculture.

Change, she knew, was the one constant of humanity.

A tone sounded and she turned from the viewall, just as a door slid aside and Kara entered the office. Katya felt a thrill of pride; her daughter looked so erect and sharp in her Confederation grays. The pride, though, was darkened somewhat by fear. *God, I don't want to lose her.*

"Hi, Dad, Mums," she said. "I got a flash you guys wanted to see me."

"Yes, Kara," Vic said. "Come in and sit yourself."

"You ought to know," Kara said as she took a seat, "that the simulation AI killed me in the last run-through just so I could check out and come up to see you. So I hope this is worth it!"

Katya heard the banter in Kara's voice but couldn't feel much in the way of amusement. Her daughter had "died" in a number of these operation ViRsims lately. She could so easily die for real in the actual mission. Especially with this new mission rewrite.

"Some new orders are coming through for you," Vic said. "Direct from Confederation Military Command itself."

"What . . . new orders?" Kara leaned forward, obviously interested.

"ConMilCom has accepted Skymaster. In full."

"Thank God! It took them long enough, didn't it?"

"There's more," Katya added. She felt curiously detached as she spoke the words, as though it were someone else entirely who was speaking. "They're asking you to volunteer for the slot."

"*Strictly* volunteer," Vic added. "And I for one wish you would turn it down cold."

"Gok, no!" Kara said. "This one's *my* baby! If anybody's going into the Kasei Net, it's going to be me!"

And Katya had been certain that Kara would say exactly that.

Every world inhabited by Man had its own computer Net, a meshing of all of the computer systems running all of the business, finances, data storage, and communications of an entire planet. Technically, each world's Net was linked to the other worlds, space stations, even ships in that system, though the time lag engendered by the speed of light could drastically slow the exchange of data over interplanetary distances. And across interstellar distances, of course, communication from Net to Net could only be through the physical transfer of data, by storage devices transported aboard starships. With typical interstellar travel times limited to about a light year per day, New America, for instance, was almost fifty days' travel time from Earth, and a single exchange in a conversation, there and back, took over three months.

For any given world, the local planetary Net was of supreme importance for everything from keeping track of trade balances to coordinating local defense forces. Usually, the system's principal military node was located at synchorbit, where it could tie directly into the traffic control systems that monitored and directed ship traffic arriving at and departing from orbit.

"Ops was assuming you'd want to go," Vic was telling Kara. "I must say, you were . . . eloquent."

"Your sim results on Operation Sandstorm were even more eloquent," Katya added. "Enough said?"

Kara grimaced. "If there's a way to pull Sandstorm off without sending in more striders . . . or without the Skymaster option, I sure as hell can't see it. We've tried, gok . . . every combination *I* can think of. And I've been beaten, killed, and sent running with my tail between my legs more times in the past month than I care to remember."

"We've already looked hard at sending in more than three squadrons and the leggers," Katya told her. "What we've got is the most we can pack into a Nighthawk. And we *can't* send in more than one."

Everything about Operation Sandstorm depended on getting the assault team to the surface more or less unnoticed. A single ascraft, it was believed, could make the orbit-to-surface insertion without attracting unwanted attention from the Imperial tracking systems; a fleet of air/space craft would set off every AI-monitored threat-tracking network from Mars to Tau Ceti. The mission's planners had secured an old Model

IV Artemis Nighthawk, a great, black, vaguely streamlined shape with a variable geometry to give it greater flexibility in atmospheric approaches and maneuvering and a mass of nearly eight thousand tons. Its cargo bay had been adapted from its original civilian configuration to haul three full warstrider squadrons, plus four neatly folded Gyrfalcons and a pair of assault/infantry transports. There were no heavy transports that could carry a larger load, and there was no way to squeeze anything more into the Nighthawk's bays. The only way to send more warstriders to Mars would be to send in more than one ascraft, and the computer sims they'd been running endlessly since Sandstorm's conception the previous month indicated that trying that would almost certainly alert the AIs monitoring near-Mars space for just such an attempt.

"Our preliminary sims," Vic continued, "suggest that Sandstorm has an eighty percent–plus chance of success *if* we jigger things at Aresynch."

Katya could sense her daughter's elation at the news. Ever since Operation Sandstorm had been suggested, Kara had been insisting that three squadrons of warstriders—a total of forty-eight machines—would not be able to crack the defenses of the objective, not when there were plenty of Imperial bases within easy reach from which reinforcements could be summoned. Kara had argued that only a ground assault coupled with a covert mission at Aresynch had any real chance of success.

Reluctantly, Katya agreed with her. Some missions were simply impossible, and hitting MilTech's Kasei complex without the added security of Skymaster was one of them.

"Let's see Mars and the sky-el," Vic said. "I'd like to look over the approach vectors again."

"They haven't changed, Vic," Katya told him.

"Maybe not. But the timing on this thing is going to be goking tight."

Mars materialized above Vic's desk, an ocher red ball smeared with patches of blue, green, and white. Oldest of the terraformed worlds, Mars had an Earth-like atmosphere and climate, albeit still a bit on the cold, dry side. *Kasei* might be the Japanese name for the place, but most New Americans still called it Mars, even though it was a much different, more hospitable world than it had been just a few centuries before. The Boreal Sea covered much of the northern latitudes, with the North Polar ice cap centered in a swirl of clouds. The Marineris Sea edged south of the equator, then ran due west for better than five thousand kilometers, stopping at Labyrinthus Bay against the rise of the Tharsis Shield, just a few hundred kilometers short of the Pavonis Mons sky-el.

At this scale in real life, a sky elevator would have been invisible, but the projection displayed it as a thread of white light, extending out from the Martian equator at Pavonis Mons into space. Synchorbit for Mars was just over seventeen thousand kilometers out, about two and a half planetary diameters, a point on the model marked by a spray of tiny lights. The thread of the sky-el continued outward beyond synchorbit and terminated at Deimos.

The Pavonis Mons sky-el was the first of all such structures raised—hung, rather—by Man. Its construction had begun at the end of the twenty-first century, shortly after the beginnings of the Mars terraforming project. Pavonis Mons was an extinct volcano, middle of the row-of-three volcanic peaks stretched across a thousand kilometers of the Martian surface southeast of towering Mons Olympus; by chance, it lay squarely on the Martian equator, making it an ideal anchor point. Phobos, Mars's old inner moon, had been sacrificed for the building materials, mostly carbon nanotechnically grown into pure, long-chain molecular diacarb woven into the sky-el's main cable. The tiny outer moon, Deimos, speeded up in its orbit, now served as the space-side anchor holding the entire structure rigid as it spun with Mars's twenty-four-hour rotation, a whirling rock on the end of a string.

Most populated worlds had sky-els, providing cheap and easy access to orbit via pods accelerating up the sky-el cable on precessing magnetic fields. New America was one of the few worlds lacking one, because of the disruptive tidal effects of Columbia and because the planet's rotational period was so long that synchorbit was impossibly distant.

"As you've been telling us all along, Kara," Vic was saying, "Aresynch is going to be the key to a successful ground op."

As Vic discussed the mission with Kara, Katya's attention wandered to a smaller holographic projection floating in space beneath the larger image of Mars, a detail of the orbital facility at Aresynch.

Because it had been in existence longer than any other synchorbital, Aresynch was huge and tangled, a steadily growing accretion of shipyards and docks, military base, civilian transport nexus, marketplace, storehouse, and computer center. Kara's target would be in *that* area... highlighted in blue.

Operation Sandstorm, according to the plan worked out by ConMilCom Ops, would now be a two-pronged mission. As originally planned, one Artemis Nighthawk, carrying forty-eight Confed warstriders and several hundred ground troops would land next to the bay at Noctis Labyrinthus, deploying to capture the MilTech facility. At the same time, a team of covert operatives would slip into Aresynch, enter Kasei Net's military node, and disrupt communications long enough for the ground forces to complete their operation.

Katya watched her daughter detailing the parameters of Skymaster, the covert Aresynch insertion. She seemed so self-assured, so confident. It was impossible for Katya to look at Kara and not feel a faint, uneasy echo of disappointment in Daren, her son. Close behind that thought came one closely related: would Daren have been different—less self-absorbed, less petulant—if Dev hadn't been changed, if he'd stayed with her instead of vanishing with the DalRiss among the stars? The question had no meaningful answer and she dismissed it. Still...

Dev always knew how to handle things, how to get things done, she thought. *Things* happened *around him.* I *wish—*

She stopped and glanced once again at Vic, feeling guilty. He returned her glance, his lips quirking back in a sad, I-love-you, it'll-be-okay smile. The man always had damn near been able to read her mind. . . .

As proud as she was of Kara, she couldn't help but fear what this change in orders meant. The Imperials were not known for the gentleness of their interrogation download techniques. It had been bad enough when Kara had been assigned to the assault team at Noctis Labyrinthus, where failure in all probability meant death. Now Kara would be going into the Aresynch military node, engaged in virtual combat rather than actual. Discovery in that environment meant, not death, but something to Katya's way of thinking much worse, the gradual and dehumanizing peeling of memory and mind and personality by the interrogators of the infamous Teikokuno Johokyoku, the Imperial Intelligence Bureau.

In her darker moments, Katya sometimes told herself that she would rather Kara died cleanly, in combat, than face the nanoprobes and ego uploads of the TJK.

Still, she'd kept her feelings to herself—had tried to, at any rate, knowing that Kara would be less than appreciative of any attempt by either Vic or herself to protect her or make things easier for her. In some ways, it had been harder on Vic than on Katya. Katya was just a Confederation senator and member of the military committee. Vic was squarely in the chain of command that passed orders down to Kara directly, and his decisions could mean her survival or her death.

"I still wish you would reconsider going on the Skymaster part of this op," Vic told Kara. Again, it was though he'd been following Katya's thoughts.

Kara shook her head. "Negative, father-dear. I worked it out. Nobody else knows the background I've downloaded on this as well as I do. Besides, I'm not sending people into a virtual environment that I'm not willing to face myself."

"We understand that," Vic said. "But it's not as though you're the only qualified person. That's why God invented download technology, after all. What you've learned, someone else can download through a comlink in a few seconds. Right?"

"Not right. I am the senior officer available on this." She began ticking off names on her fingers. "Lieutenants Herlehy, Ferris, and Markov," she said, listing the Second, Third, and Fourth Squadron Commanders. "They're all junior. Colonel Hastings . . . well, you know as well as I do that regimental commanders don't go on field ops."

"There's the Phantoms' First Company Commander," Vic pointed out.

"Captain Ogden is a biopurist," Katya reminded Vic. Biopurists disliked the notion of incorporating alien life forms—meaning Companions—into the human body. Ogden wasn't a fanatic about it, believing—unlike most Biopurists—that the choice was up to the individual, but he would not accept a Companion and probably wouldn't link directly with anyone who did.

"That's right," Kara said. "And without a Companion, he'd never even make it into Aresynch. So you see? I'm the only candidate left for the job."

"There's still time to find and train a special agent," Vic said.

Kara grinned. "I don't see what the big deal is. You and Mums were in the revolution together. You didn't try to keep her safe, did you?"

Hagan frowned. "Truth is, I couldn't. She was my commanding officer."

"I still am," Katya said. "Senators outrank generals."

They laughed. The joke helped break the uncomfortable tension.

"The worst part about being Skymaster," Kara said thoughtfully, "will be not being able to go in with my people on the ground."

"Only three strider squadrons can go in anyway," Katya said. "If you're Skymaster, we'll pull First Squadron out. Three can go in with Two and Four instead. We'll draw your security element from volunteers from One."

Kara's brow furrowed for a second, a tiny, brief shadow. Then she nodded. "Right. That makes sense."

"Problem?" Katya could tell Kara was concerned about something.

"No. It'll work. It *would* be nice if I knew what it was we're supposed to grab. In our training sims, we've just called it 'the package,' and I've been assured that it won't be larger than a warstrider could carry out. Sooner or later, you're going to have to tell us just what it is we're going to Mars to steal."

It was Katya's turn to grimace. "The Senate Military Committee hasn't decided when to release that information,'' she said. ''I haven't even been able to tell Vic yet.'' Security was extraordinarily tight on this op. It had to be. Sometimes it seemed as though the medes—the various online and ViRnews reporting services—could be as efficient at ferreting out information as TJK interrogators. It was not impossible that this room was bugged, and the nature of Sandstorm's objective was such that even a hint released over the New American Net could reveal to the Imperials that the Confederation was aware of *o-denwa*. They couldn't afford that risk. When Vic and Kara were brought fully into the picture, it would be at the last possible moment.

''Whatever this thing is,'' Vic said, ''it had better be damned important.''

Katya sobered. ''It is. It's a device so important that some of us consider it a threat to the whole Confederation.

''The Japanese Imperium is about to win its war against the Confederation once and for all. If they do, there will be no more independence movements. Not for us. Not for anyone.''

Chapter 4

Surprisingly, there proved to be numerous loopholes in the physics that stated that faster-than-light travel was a total impossibility. Perhaps most promising at the time were the "wormholes" that soon became the staple of romantic fiction. A special case of the wormhole was described by twentieth-century physicists who envisioned a super-dense cylinder many kilometers in length, rotating at relativistic speeds about its long axis. In theory, the space-time geometries created by these machines would open vast numbers of pathways bridging light years . . . or even traversing time itself into past or future.

Even after other means of traveling to the stars were found, however, such grand and large-scale solutions remained well beyond even the theoretical reach of human technology.

—A History of Star Flight
DR. CHASE RANDALL
C.E. 2451

It gleamed, a taut-stretched thread, a whisker of quicksilver set against the night, ruler-straight and so slender compared to its length that it seemed insubstantial, a scratch, perhaps, across the dark.

>>DEVCAMERON<< checked again the numbers overlaying his perception of the universe. That whisker was just over two kilometers thick and well over a thousand long. There was no way to know, of course, what units the thing's builders used, but it was interesting that the cylinder's length was *precisely* 512 times its width, which suggested the use of binary arithmetic.

In terms of sheer size, of course, >>DEVCAMERON<< had seen human-built structures outwardly much grander than this. The sky-els hanging from the skies of most of the Shichiju's colonized worlds were the largest artificial structures known, cables tens to hundreds of meters thick and towering forty thousand kilometers or more all the way to the planet's synchorbital. But the density of this artifact approached that of a neutron star, with the mass of a fair-sized world packed into that whisker's long and narrow volume. Too, it was rotating, rolling about its long axis so fast that a point on its circumference was moving at relativistic velocities . . . better than seven tenths the speed of light.

With a moderate amplification of his senses, >>DEVCAMERON<< could look into the surface of the cylinder, but the closest examination revealed nothing useful. Rotation wiped any detail into a mirror-silvered emptiness, too bright and perfect even to be called a blur. Though they could not sense it in such strangely distorted space, the watchers felt that some sort of force field was in play; without one, centrifugal force would have ripped the cylinder apart. Human technology routinely manufactured electromagnetic screens—necessary to protect crew and equipment aboard vessels from charged particles at relativistic speeds—but a true "force field" in the classical sense of an invisible and impenetrable wall remained as much a physical impossibility as moving suns or communicating instantly across the Galaxy.

No human technology—no DalRiss or Naga biotech, for that matter—could even approach the varied magics they were witnessing here. Even from a hundred thousand kilometers away, >>DEVCAMERON<< could sense the tug and twist of that thing as rotating gravitational mass reshaped the fabric of local space. According to theory, those reshapings opened paths, invisible slits in spacetime that led . . . elsewhere.

>>DEVCAMERON<< had downloaded what history he possessed that might have a bearing on the thing. Centuries before, human theorists had speculated that such a construct might be used to open pathways across the light years, though there was no substance to such speculations, nor had the thing ever even been given a name. For >>DEVCAMERON<<, as for the DalRiss and Naga intelligences he was linked with, it was simply the Device.

And it was hungry.

It hung suspended in space at the gravitational balance point of the two shrunken suns of Nova Aquila. A stream of crimson flame spiraled out from the equator of each spinning star, arcing across millions of kilometers of intervening space, the feathered tips dwindling as they were compressed and reshaped by forces beyond comprehension, then vanishing into empty space just beyond the ends of the cylinder.

They appeared to vanish into nothing, uncounted gigatons of star plasma whirling silently into emptiness each second. From a distance, the silvery thread appeared stretched tight between the tips of those fiery prominences. At closer ranges, it was clear the star stuff was being funneled away to someplace else, plunging into gateways opened outside of the normal dimensions of space and time.

The Device raised so many, many questions, all thus far

unanswerable. Foremost, however, were who had built it . . . and why.

"Humans have records of this star exploding," >>DEVCAMERON<< told the DalRiss-Naga fusion that was his host. "It was seen in the skies of Earth in pre-spaceflight times, in the spring of 1918, Current Era. It was the brightest ordinary nova ever witnessed, outshining every star in the skies of Earth's northern hemisphere except for Sirius."

"The DalRiss, too, have such records," a voice replied in his mind. "A bright star appeared in the night skies of GhegnuRish some forty sixes of seasons ago. We were involved with the *Gharku* at the time, however, and could pay scant attention to stars, however bright."

"I can imagine."

"Gharku" was what the Riss had called the Naga, before human contact with one of the entities had opened new possibilities in understanding and being. The name could be translated, roughly, as "The Chaos." Before peaceful contact, which the being that was now >>DEVCAMERON<< had first initiated almost by accident, humans had known the Naga as Xenophobes, an assumption about motives that later proved to be quite wrong.

"We're about twelve hundred light years from Earth," he thought. "Eleven hundred from GhegnuRish. The star went nova almost two thousand years ago, sometime around 700 C.E."

"What is the significance of the time?"

"Nothing, I guess. Except that I'm wondering if whoever made the Device also made Nova Aquila explode in the first place. If they did, it means the Device is two millennia old. Has it been eating these stars the whole time?"

"The designers could be opportunists who arrived long after the detonation. The date of the explosion does not logically fix their place in time."

"No."

But >>DEVCAMERON<< was being gnawed by a terrible fear.

Some of the information he'd downloaded included an interesting datum about novas seen on Earth, something he'd picked up long, long ago when he'd downloaded anything at all that he could find about the stars. It was basically a meaningless piece of trivia, not germane to affairs closer to home.

The appearance of a "new star," a nova, had always been cause for wonder . . . and occasionally fear. Some few, like the brilliant beacon that illuminated the skies in C.E. 1054, were spectacular stellar deaths, the supernovae that collapsed a sun into a tiny, fast-spinning neutron star at the heart of an expanding cloud of dust and gas. The vast majority were not so violent. Ordinary novae, like Nova Aquila, blew off vast amounts of their outer shells, leaving behind shrunken remnants, planet-sized white dwarfs. Most were double stars, as in this system; it was hypothesized that the novae were caused by the expansion of one star's atmosphere, launching a torrent of gases on the companion star and triggering a detonation, which either tore away the first star's substance or triggered a second explosion in turn.

That much, at least, was known about novae.

There was one mystery, though, that had dogged the subject for centuries, almost since the beginning of astronomy as a technical science. Novae *should* be more or less evenly distributed across the entire sky, with a slight clumping, perhaps, along the path of the Milky Way where the concentration of stars was thicker. Instead, a disproportionate number of stars had exploded all in the same general region of the heavens, toward the Earth-sky constellations of Aquila, Cygnus, Scutum, Serpens, Ophiuchus, coreward from Sol and slightly to spinward in the great wheel of the Galaxy.

This was far more than any statistical fluke. During one brief forty-year period early in the twentieth century, twenty-five percent of all of the novae seen on Earth had appeared in roughly two percent of the sky. Two of the brightest novae ever recorded had blazed forth in the same year—1936—and the nova of 1918 in Aquila had been the brightest ordinary nova ever recorded.

In the six centuries since, the percentage had fallen and the area of sky expanded, but the records still showed something like ten percent of all novae occurring in about five percent of the sky. The chances of that kind of clustering occurring randomly were in this case literally astronomical.

And here was possible proof that that apparent clumping was not an accident of statistics . . . but the result of deliberate and intelligent action.

What kind of intelligence would destroy a star?

What need would drive them to destruction on such a massive scale?

"Are there planets in this system?" he asked suddenly. If this star had once possessed worlds, even life . . .

"We need your help to determine that, >>DEVCAMERON<<," the host replied. "You will need to guide our Perceivers."

"Link me in. . . ."

The DalRiss had evolved with a very different set of senses and perceptions than humans. Their primary sense was one that felt the shape of electrochemical fields generated by living tissue. They "saw" life, while inorganic matter was a kind of emptiness, a void they were aware of only by its shape. The DalRiss had engineered other life forms to extend the range and clarity of their visual perception. "Perceivers" were small artificial creatures that were eye and brain and little else. When connected to the interwoven nervous systems of several DalRiss, they provided a kind of sight.

But little understanding. That was one reason the DalRiss had invited >>DEVCAMERON<< to join them, after he'd lost his body. >>DEVCAMERON's<< brain had evolved the ability to make sense of his surroundings through light-sensitive organs. The DalRiss fleet, numbering eighty of the huge living ships, was as dependent on Dev for his knowledge of what a star *was* as it was on the Perceivers who actually saw its light.

>>DEVCAMERON<< extended his optical senses, enhanced by the sensitive organic optics of the Perceivers. If this double star had been the center of a planetary system two thousand years ago, those worlds would be remote indeed from the tiny, planet-sized white dwarfs that circled one another today. Scored by nova's heat, then left to freeze in the icy wastes far beyond the reach of those wan dwarfs, if those worlds had ever been touched by life, they were dead now.

He searched for long minutes, sensing only emptiness beyond the wan light of the suns. That proved nothing, for any worlds out there would be dimly lit indeed. Leaving several Perceivers to continue an automatic search, he turned his attention back to the Device.

"How would such a thing work?" the DalRiss voice said in his mind.

"I don't understand all of the math," he replied. "But just as a rotating black hole could theoretically open up pathways—wormholes, we call them—to distant points in space or time, a cylindrical mass like this, rotating at relativistic speeds, should open up . . . gateways in the space around it. A number of these cylinders could have paths lined between them. Or you could send a ship through to a point in empty space, light years away."

His DalRiss hosts—and of course the Nagas who rode with them—had never imagined such a thing and could not follow the concept as he tried to explain it. If he'd had the math, possibly he could have done a better job, but as it was, all he could do was observe and try to describe what he was sensing to the others.

"You are saying, then," the DalRiss continued, "that this is a machine for traveling instantly from point to point. Like our Achievers."

"That's right," >>DEVCAMERON<< replied.

Achievers were artificial, DalRiss-grown life forms that could visualize a distant point in space and somehow—no one, not even the DalRiss themselves, was quite certain how it worked—move the ship in a blink across tens or even hundreds of light years, killing the Achiever in the process. When humans first contacted the DalRiss, there'd been speculation that their mode of travel through interstellar space was far superior to the slower, shorter-ranged abilities of human K-T ships, and there'd been discussion about how humans could adopt the DalRiss method.

That was unlikely, at least in the short term, no matter what the advantages might be. DalRiss starship-cities were immense living organisms grown for the purpose; so far as human experimentation had been able to determine in the years since

First Contact with the DalRiss, the process they used to move their ships from point to point required that the vessels be organic, their lives meshed symbiotically with those of the Achievers in ways human biotechnology didn't yet understand. Someday, living human ships might be grown as well, but in the meantime, the only way to use DalRiss technology was to get them to literally carry human ships inside the far larger DalRiss ship-creatures. And, for their own reasons, the DalRiss rarely agreed to do that. Humanity would have to learn how to grow its own ship-creatures.

The DalRiss themselves were the product of artificial symbiosis. The "Riss" portion of the joint creature was a roughly crescent-shaped, many-armed rider atop the bulky, six-legged starfish shape which was the "Dal." The two were extremely closely linked, sharing one another's sensory perceptions, a single organism in fact.

Something moved across >>DEVCAMERON's<< field of view—not in deep space but in close to the Device, a black shape flickering into existence some tens of kilometers above the spinning silver cylinder. "What is that?"

"We perceive nothing—"

"Quickly! On my scan! Enhance! *Enhance!*"

Two more shapes followed the first, as quick as thought. His first impression was that they were alive, so fast and agile were they . . . but the reality was swiftly apparent. The three were dissimilar in details of shape, yet alike, organic-smooth forms, jet black in color, with a line of wickedly curved blades down one side, like saw teeth, or the fins of some aquatic creature, but angled to stab forward instead of trailing behind.

"Ships!" >>DEVCAMERON<< announced. "I've never seen their like! They just materialized out of the space close to the Device."

He could sense more of the DalRiss hosts shifting linkages within the network, their equivalent of standing on tiptoe to see as they switched to their Perceiver arrays for primary input.

The alien ships were moving almost too quickly to follow, and once they were clear of the Device they were virtually impossible to see against the blackness of space. In seconds, however, they'd streaked toward the nearer of the two white dwarfs and were visible once again as dust-mote silhouettes against the raw, pearly white glare of the star's surface.

"They seek to end their existence," a voice said in >>DEVCAMERON's<< mind.

"I don't think so. Why would they come here, from wherever they came from in the first place, to do that? Can we signal them?"

"We are attempting to get their attention, using both radio and laser communications. There has been no response."

"Keep trying."

It was difficult to follow the alien vessels' descent into the stellar corona. The Perceivers' optics had not been designed to handle such light levels, and several of the creatures went off-line, their vision destroyed.

Then the mystery ships were gone, vanished into the star.

"Have they been destroyed?" a voice asked.

"I . . . I still can't believe they deliberately destroyed themselves," >>DEVCAMERON<< said, but his thoughts were unsteady, uncertain. Various possibilities occurred to him. They were probes of some sort, sent to plumb the star's depths. They were starminers, seeking energy or raw materials.

A third possibility was more chilling. If these were the people who'd once made a star explode, perhaps they were trying to do so again.

But minute followed minute, and there was no change in the white dwarf's complexion as it continued its swing about the Device, paired with its opposite number on the far side.

Were these the same people? The ones who'd destroyed a star? Were they the same as the builders of the Device?

So many questions and not answers enough by half.

"The Perceivers' scan has found planets," the voice announced. "Four. They are far beyond the star's zone for liquid water, however."

"They would be. These dwarfs don't shed much more than a few percent of the light and heat they used to. Where?"

A silent thought indicated direction and distance. Piggybacking himself onto the nervous system of a battery of

DalRiss and Perceivers, he focused on one world, then another. Three were gas giants, so distant that at the highest magnification they showed no detail at all.

A fourth was closer, about three astronomical units away. It was a rocky world, its surface a patchwork of ice and rock, without even a trace of atmosphere. But >>DEVCAMERON<< felt a stirring as he watched that distant world, for his DalRiss senses indicated that the planet possessed very nearly the mass of the Earth.

"I think," he said, "that that ice ball should be our next stop."

"There is no life."

"No. But I'd like to know if there was life there once."

"We go, then."

The host accelerated out from the enigmatic, rapidly spinning whisker and all of its hidden secrets.

Chapter 5

To a greater force, and to a better nature, you, free, are subject, and that creates the mind in you, which the heavens have not in their charge. Therefore, if the present world go astray, the cause is in you, in you it is to be sought.

—*The Divine Comedy,*
Inferno, Canto XVI, l. 79
DANTE ALIGHIERI
C.E. 1320

Dr. Daren Cameron stopped, pausing for breath as *kata* vines dripped scarlet beneath a lowering orange and green sky. On the horizon, beyond the swells of a shallow sea, a volcano rumbled, staining the sky with a pall of greasy blue-gray ash as lightning played and flickered about the mountain's crest. Sulfur tainted the air, giving it a burned, unpleasant taste.

He knew the world as Dante, though that was not its true name. The second world of a type K3 star cataloged as DM-58 5564, some thirty light years from Earth and over seventy-six from New America, it had originally been named Dantai, a Nihongo word meaning, roughly, social organization or group. Western survey team members, however, had twisted the name in literate wordplay, pointing to the world's sweltering heat, its sulfurous air, its bizarre and, at times, demonic inhabitants.

Dante was the more apt name, Daren thought, looking about at the raw, young landscape. He couldn't actually claim that he was experiencing any discomfort at the moment, but the sulfur-laden air, the evil-looking sky, the beach of black, volcanic sand, all contributed to the atmosphere of a place that Dante Alighieri or his Virgil might well have recognized as the gateway to hell.

Damn it, where was Taki?

The air was warm and humid, promising a storm, and a salt tang hung in the air. Boots crunching in the black sand, Daren strode across the beach, then scrambled to the top of a spray-slick boulder to get himself a better view of the land-and-seascape encircling him.

East was ocean, deep green-gray in color and patched with whitecaps. West, behind the tumble of breakwater rocks, the land was a low and fetid swamp, rising through tangled matari trees and traveler roots to higher ground. Beyond, the land moved higher still, rising through rolling blue-green foothills that vanished into the blue mist walling the Airy Mountains, white-streaked purple walls of granite so sheer they looked like a painted backdrop.

Daren was alone.

Frowning, he turned slowly on his boulder perch, scanning the coastline north and south. As a precaution, he set his Companion to recording the scene in full sensory detail. The world was slightly smaller than Earth, with eight tenths of Earth's gravity. It was younger, too, and with a hotter core; vulcanism was extensive, plate tectonics active. The Airy Mountains to the west topped twelve thousand meters; there were mountains at the equator half again taller.

At the same time, the atmosphere, at 1.2 bars, was slightly denser than Earth's and had a much higher carbon dioxide content, nearly two percent. The seas and air were warmer, the storms vaster, wetter, and longer-lived. Erosion proceeded at a faster rate, wearing down mountains and using them to thicken the coastal oceans with silt. There were eight rivers on Dante the length and breadth of Earth's Nile, four Amazons, five Mississippis. The seas, shallower, smaller, and more landlocked than Earth's, carried higher concentrations of sediments and dissolved chemicals washed down from the highlands.

North lay his destination, a clustered and interlocking series of gleaming white towers, rising stepwise from sea and beach, with curving sides and curiously twisted, angular faces, the tips of the highest fully a kilometer above the surf breaking at their feet. The cluster looked much like images of arcologies or large-scale hab units in one of the more modern cities on Earth.

And so they had looked to the planet's first explorers. The men and women of the initial Japanese survey team to visit Dante over two centuries before had been convinced they'd discovered another sapient species. Eighteen years of unrelenting work to establish communication had ended in frustration and failure. Private groups and foundations had continued the work, which was proceeding even today. After more than two hundred years, however, it still wasn't possible to know for sure whether the Communes, as they ultimately became known, were intelligent in any meaningful sense of the word. Like the ants and termites of Earth, the Communes were social creatures, living in vast lime-cement structures accreted out of seawater, rising like terraced buildings above the shores of Dante's shallow, brackish seas.

They appeared to be a littoral species, limited by their adaptation to their environment to the planet's coastal regions. Extensively researched by terrestrial xenozoologists, they carried the scientific name *Architectus communis*, the social builders, though individuals came in so many different shapes and sizes that the scientists were still arguing over whether the Communes were one species with hundreds of extreme variants or hundreds of different species living in close communal symbiosis.

Each of those towers enclosed thousands of kilometers of hollow tubes, and intricate nonmechanical valves and pumps driven by differences in temperature between air and sea. Seawater drawn in at the base was circulated throughout the tower; calcium carbonate and other dissolved chemicals were precipitated out along the way and used as building materials where needed. The towers were elegantly cast, their faces angled to take best advantage of the moving sun, the walls stronger than conventional concrete.

And yet the creatures that had built them were small, few larger than Daren's hand, most the size of his thumb, not counting the legs. They reminded most humans of insects—spindle-legged, spiny, and iridescently delicate—though most had but two body sections and they breathed with lungs. Warriors could be deadly; some were the length and breadth of a strong man's arm. With dozens of clawed legs and powerful tripartite jaws armed with acid sacs, they appeared by the millions when the nest was threatened, and they could strip a human to the bone and then dissolve the bones in something less than ten seconds.

The question remained: were they intelligent? They cooperated and they built; so did terrestrial ants, though perhaps not on so grand a scale. They communicated with one another, if not with human zoologists, using sophisticated pheromones and scents; so did Earth's social insects. They controlled their environment, adjusting the temperatures inside their towers with a precision measured in tenths of a degree; so did termites and, to a lesser extent, bees. At times they were capable of astonishing group collaborations, moving and acting like a single organism, extending immense pseudopodia across kilometers of open ground; the same could be said of Earth's driver and army ants.

There were many who continued to insist that the Communes were an intelligent and self-aware species, that they were simply too different for humans to find common ground sufficient for communications. Most now held that their monumental engineering achievements were purely instinctive, honed and polished by the hand of Darwin across some twenty million years.

Daren had been studying the Communes for only four years now, as part of his ongoing postdoctoral research at the University of Jefferson, and he was trying to keep an open mind. It was impossible to watch Commune activities closely, however, and not get the clear if subjective impression that they acted with a conscious and self-aware volition.

There'd been that time a year ago, for instance, as he'd been moving through the swamp west of the main group of towers, picking his way carefully across a narrow ribbon of solid ground, when he'd encountered the leading tip of a questing Commune pseudopod. For several moments, he'd stood there, unmoving, watching the writhing mass of tiny shapes a few meters in front of him. Abruptly, then, the pseudopod had heaved itself erect, forming a pillar two meters tall composed entirely of the interlocking, finger-sized creatures. For moments more, the two, human and colony, had regarded one another, each using senses indescribable to the other. For Daren, it had been a transcending moment, an instant of certainty that he was confronting intelligence.

Then the pillar had dissolved, the pseudopod had retreated, and he'd been alone in the swamp once more, with no solid proof at all, nothing, in fact, but his personal and highly subjective impressions.

The AI running that simulation had later informed him that lone encounters with Commune 'pods initiated such reactions some twelve percent of the time.

Someday, Daren told himself, he would have the money, the backing, and the status to organize an expedition of his *own* to Dante. He slid down off the rock; it *felt* hard and wet, and it scraped at his seat as he rode it, but then, these full ViRsimulations were designed to be as lifelike and as realistic as possible, right down to the whiff of sulfur in the breeze. All that was edited out were some of the more unpleasant consequences that would have accompanied standing on the real Dante—such as the fact that a two-percent CO_2 level in the air would have killed him in short order had he actually been breathing it.

But damn it, sims added nothing to the total of human knowledge. Every detail was there because it had been programmed into the AI running the show. It was a splendid training device, but it lacked the possibilities of broader discovery. You couldn't learn anything *new*.

Turning, he eyed the towers in the distance. There was so much to be learned yet, so many worlds to explore that couldn't be explored from inside a goking simulation.

At its greatest extent, before the Confederation Rebellion, the Shichiju had embraced a ragged-boundaried sphere a hundred light years across, seventy-eight worlds in seventy-two star systems so far terraformed and colonized by Man, as well as several hundred outposts, mining colonies, research stations, military bases. In all those worlds, Humankind had encountered three species showing behavior that might be interpreted as intelligence. There were the Nagas, of course; everyone knew about them. The other two were more mysterious—the enigmatic Maias of Zeta Doradus, and the Communes, and it still wasn't known for certain whether either of those was even self-aware. Beyond the Shichiju, one other intelligent species had been encountered, the undeniably intelligent and self-aware DalRiss, but they were in the process of leaving, abandoning their world in a great ongoing migration that humans still didn't fully understand.

Man needed to see a wider cross-sampling of intelligent species . . . needed more friends, a broader outlook on the cosmos.

"I'm sorry I'm late."

Daren started, then spun. "Taki! Where the gok have you been?"

The woman was tiny, her delicate frame turned small and masculine by the khaki bodysuit she wore. Dark eyes regarded Daren through a shuttered expression. "I have to be careful. You know that. It took more time to set up the shell than I expected."

His heart beat a bit faster. "Were . . . were you able to pull it off it then?"

She smiled, the expression dazzling. "Of course. You don't think I'd miss an opportunity like this! Of course, if I'd known you were going to bite my head off the moment I jacked in—"

"I'm sorry, Tak. I was just . . . worried."

Her smile widened. "It *is* hard, meeting like this."

Dr. Taki Oe was one of Daren's colleagues at Jefferson University, a professor of exobiology. She was twenty-six standard, with short, glossy black hair, a pixie's sense of humor, and an intelligence rating of at least eighty, maybe eighty-five, which gave her a healthy edge over Daren's seventy-eight.

She was also Japanese, and on New America, at times, that could be a problem.

Daren wiped his hands on his coveralls, then glanced down, embarrassed by the unthinking gesture. His hands were, of course, quite clean. It was impossible to actually get dirty in a simulation, unless the AI had been programmed to simulate dirt as well as the other more mundane aspects of a virtual reality. He held out his arms. "I'm awfully glad to see you, Tak."

"I'm happy to see you. I was in agony until I could get away."

She melted into his arms. They stood there on the black sand beach for a long time, savoring one anothers' touch.

ViRsims were often used for personal meetings like this, with the AI running the sim feeding the same environmental stimuli to both of their brains. Though their bodies were unconscious, jacked into separate ViRcom modules in the huge U of J comm center, their minds were here, sharing the same program. Taki's delay in joining him had been caused by her need to create a programming shell for herself, a false identity that masked her presence here. So far as the monitor AI was concerned—or anyone else who might be interested in a record of who Daren was simming with—she was Ann Gallsworth, an assistant xenogeneticist with the university staff. The shell wouldn't hold up under a close scrutiny, but there was no reason yet to think that they were under suspicion.

Daren detested the politics that made secrecy necessary. For himself, he would have contracted with Taki in an instant, broadcast their relationship on the planetary net, hell, made love to her on the front steps of the Sony Building . . . but for the unfortunate fact that his mother was a Confederation senator and his sister was a warjacker with a class Blue-one security rating. He didn't care what people thought of him, but he was well aware of how much trouble he could cause for the rest of his family, trouble that would *not* be appreciated.

He drew his lips back from hers. "Damn, I wish we didn't have to sneak around like this," he told her.

She shook her head. "It won't be forever, lover."

"No? Seems like it, sometimes."

"After we get our own survey, nobody'll care what we do together!"

"Maybe." He gnawed his lip. "Though the chances of that aren't looking so good now."

She drew back a little, her eyes dark, questioning. "You heard something? Your last proposal?"

He nodded. "Sanders downloaded a reply this morning. All deep space plans are on hold right now. 'The possibility of imminent hostilities,' " he said. He snorted, disgusted. "Staticjack! The whole goking Confederation is going nullhead!"

"Iceworld, Daren," Taki said. "Don't burn out your feeds. If there's a war, there's a war, and there's nothing we can do about it. When it's over, we'll have our survey."

"I hope so, Taki. I hope so. I worry about you a lot, though."

She grinned. "Don't stress-test to destruct, round-eyes. I can take care of myself!"

At the beginning of the twenty-first century, the Western powers, obsessed with social and economic problems, had abandoned space . . . this despite the fact that the old United States had been first to reach Earth's moon. The Japanese had never lost sight of their ultimate goal, however, and their domination of the Shichiju for the next six centuries was due almost entirely to the fact that they'd managed to secure the high ground of space, pioneering the technologies that had opened the stars to Man: nanotechnology, the quantum power tap, the cephlink, the K-T drive. As a result, the Terran Hegemony was little more than a puppet for Japan's Imperium, and sizable Nihonjin populations lived on most of the worlds of the Shichiju, whether they had anything to do directly with the Imperium or not.

During the revolution, large numbers of Nihonjin had fled the rebellious worlds of the frontier, seeking refuge among the safe worlds of the Shichiju's core. Those who stayed did so because they considered themselves New Americans—or Liberties, or Eriduans, or *humans*—first, and Japanese only by accident of birth and genome. Taki's traditionalist parents had fled New America during the war, returning several years after the Imperium's recognition of Confederation independence to work with Mitsubishi-Newamie Industries. They'd left once more two years ago, as tensions between the Imperium and the breakaways had continued to increase; Taki, however, had refused to go. She had her tenure at U of J to consider, for one thing . . . and for another, she, like Daren, was hoping for a chance at a slot on a survey expedition, and such chances were rare on Earth.

Galactic Survey, deep exploration, alien contact—*that* was where the future of mankind lay, so far as Daren was concerned. In the ten years since he'd begun high-level downloads, training to be a xenosophontologist, the need for new surveys into the dark beyond Man's handful of worlds in known space had become something of a crusade for him. For Taki, too; that was what had drawn them together in the first place. Both were convinced that Man's future, even his survival, depended on establishing communications with as wide a range of intelligent civilizations and cultures as possible.

Unfortunately, deep surveys were rather in short supply just now, and most xenologists on the Frontier had been reduced to training exercises and simulations, shuffling through old data. Known data.

When there was so much more to be learned through reality.

"I haven't given up, Taki," he said. "Sanders doesn't have the last word."

"He's head of the field research department."

"But Eileen Zhou is his boss."

"How can R&D help us?"

"For one thing, Madam Zhou controls Sanders's budget. For another, my mother knows her."

"Ah. That again."

"Yes. Again. She's a senator. If she pushes for this, we're going to get it."

"Your mother hasn't been willing to help so far."

"No. But there's got to be a way. If nothing else, I'll wear her down through damned stubborn persistence."

"You've been trying for three years."

"Then I'll try for three more! Damn it, Taki, something's going to give!"

She smiled, and held up her hand. "Pericles, Daren."

He took her hand, squeezed it, and drew her closer once more. "Pericles."

It was a kind of code phrase they used between themselves, a promise that what they were doing was right.

Ancient Greece had been a patchwork of tiny city states, each evolving on its own, isolated from its neighbors by Greece's rugged terrain. Once contact was established, however, and trade begun, the result was the flowering of the golden age of Pericles, the birth of democracy, and a worldview that postulated and discussed atoms, a round Earth, and life on other worlds. The crossing of cultures, of ideas, of worldviews and ways of thinking and looking at things led inexorably to synergy, with results that no one could guess at beforehand.

Communications with the Naga had first been made possible by contact with the DalRiss; soon after, exchanges with both species had resulted in an explosion of new understanding, new science, new technologies—especially in the fields of nanotechnology and biotechnics—leading to a genuine renaissance in the biological and linkage sciences. The Naga, with their literally inside-out worldview, had given Man a whole new way to look at the universe; the ability to link closely with pocket-sized Nagas was transforming the way Man looked at himself.

But Daren was seeking more than just new races, new ideas, or new ways of thinking, and he certainly had more in mind than new forms of Naga-expressions or more convenient ways of linking with machines. Misunderstanding and lack of communication had resulted in a fifty-year war with the Naga, a war fought with weapons that could devastate entire worlds. If each new contact brought with it the possibility of knowledge about still other races, an ever-widening web of contact and communication could be created. The fact that three species coexisted within a hundred light years or so of one another suggested that the galaxy must be positively teeming with life and Mind. Daren was convinced that it would be good to find out about those other near neighbors, and to do so before there were any more misunderstandings.

Wars could be avoided that way.

But the university was not willing to even consider organizing an expedition beyond known space. Nor were any of the usual science foundations and corporate R&D facilities. War with the Imperium was too real a possibility just now. It would be foolish to invest some tens of millions of yen in an expedition that might be canceled at any time because the ships were needed for conversion to military purposes.

And that was the worst of it. Compared to the DalRiss or the Naga or any other thinking, technic species that man might encounter out there, the differences between New American and Terran, between native Japanese and descendant of North American colonists were insignificant to the point of absurdity.

Sometimes Daren wondered if half of the reason behind his drive to meet new species wasn't the knowledge—the hope, really—that the problems and hatreds separating humans might be forgotten in the face of something, some*one* really different. He couldn't think of anything else that stood a chance in hell of making the human race unite.

"Well?" Taki said at last, looking up at him from within the circle of his arms. "We *are* scheduled to watch the Communes this afternoon."

"Um. Correlations of observed Commune behavior with physical expressions of Nakamura's Number," he said, reciting with distaste the title of their current research project. "Wonderful."

"Come on! You're not demonstrating the proper enthusiasm

requisite for an up-and-coming xenosophontologist!''

"I don't know, Taki," he said, letting his hand rove across her body. "I'm more interested in another kind of research right now. And so far as physical expressions go—"

She squealed and playfully batted his hand away. "You know, Daren, if I didn't know you better, I'd think you just might have had some ulterior motives when you suggested we share this sim."

"Who? Me?"

"You. Never mind giving me the mock innocent look and the big gray eyes. Come on. Let's try those rocks up the beach."

They found a sheltered niche walled by house-sized boulders, floored by soft sand. Their hands, moving with urgent, yearning haste, found the touch seals on one another's coveralls, and in another few moments they both were naked, exploring one another eagerly with hands and mouths. Their clothing spread out beneath them would keep the sand from irritating the more sensitive parts of their bodies, though Daren wasn't certain if the sim loaded that much reality. Most ViRsex subroutines boasted in being indistinguishable from the real thing, however, and he didn't want to take any chances.

There was reality enough for him in Taki's image, though, as he lowered her to the ground and eased himself down on top of her.

And the hell with what his family would think. . . .

Chapter 6

Contagious magic is based upon the assumption that substances which once were joined together possess a continuing linkage; thus an act carried out upon a smaller unit will affect the larger unit even though they are physically separated.

—*The Golden Bough*
SIR JAMES FRAZIER
C.E. 1923

The floater car hummed quietly, slipping through one impeller field after another as it flashed through the late evening sky toward Cascadia. Derived from the QEC nanofields first employed by the military, impeller fields were projected by stabilized clouds of nano spaced along the traffic routes to and from the various cities of New America.

The vehicle was controlled by its AI, interacting with the far larger artificial intelligence at the traffic control complex in Jefferson. Kara could have linked in with the machine if she'd wanted to exercise a measure of control over the flight—she nearly always did—but this time she had a passenger with her, and she was enjoying the conversation.

"You can't hate these affairs as much as you let on," he was telling her.

She gave her passenger a sidelong glance. Lieutenant Ran Ferris was the commanding officer of the Black Phantoms'

55

First Company, Third Squadron, the 1/3, as she was CO of the 1/1. He was tall, good-looking in a rough-hewn and crooked-grinned way, and he was smart. She'd found herself attracted to him almost from the first day he'd joined the Phantoms two years earlier. They'd enjoyed good, clean, recreational ViRsex together any number of times, using a link through the regiment's rec center com modules, and even shared the real thing four times . . . or was it five now? It hardly mattered. Kara preferred virtual sex to the groping and sweaty real-world article, though she had to admit that Ran was good, both in virtual reality and out.

"I can and I do," she said. "I suppose it's a necessary part of my mother's role as a senator. And it's not surprising that I'm . . . *expected* to make a showing at these things. But I gokking sure don't have to like it. Especially when she damn near makes the invite an order." She reached across the seat and touched his thigh. "I'd much rather spend the time with just you."

He grinned. "Well, I can't argue with that. I've been to a couple of these whirls of your mother's, remember. They're lots more boring than you are."

She arched one eyebrow. "Thanks a *lot!*"

He laughed, teasing. "I do wonder why you hate the things so much."

"I'm not sure, really. Somehow . . . well, especially when there's a mission coming up. The closer the op gets, the more tedious Mums's parties get. And the shallower and stupider her guests get."

"Sounds like the problem's in you, not the parties."

"Of course. But it doesn't mean I have to enjoy them."

"Well, all we have to do is put in a showing, right? Maybe we could odie someplace private afterward."

"I'd like that, Ran. I think I'm going to *need* it."

Conventional military wisdom insisted that sexual liaisons with other members of your unit weren't a good idea, and Kara was aware of any number of good reasons for that prohibition. Jealousy could wreck a unit's effectiveness . . . as worry about a sexual partner could wreck an individual's effectiveness. There were no rules against sex with someone else in your unit, though, and everybody did it. Her mother and Dev Cameron had been deeply involved with one another, Kara remembered, involved enough that her brother had been the result. As she'd been the product later on of Katya and Vic Hagan.

But Kara was beginning to understand the reasoning behind the nonrules. By accepting the Skymaster role in Operation Sandstorm, she'd taken the 1/1 out of the fight—and put the 1/3 into it. If she'd kept her mouth shut, if First Squadron was still riding the ascraft down to the shores of Noctis Labyrinthus, Ran and the 1/3 would still be slotted to stay in reserve. *Safe* . . .

She found herself fighting against the urge to use her influence to keep Ran out of the Kasei expedition. It was going to be a damned hairy op . . .

"I can't wait for this thing to get going, though," Ran told her. "We've been training long enough. It's time to go *do* it!"

"The opsims are coming back sixty- and seventy-percent plus success," Kara said. "Skymaster is going to make a difference, I think."

"I'm going to be worried about you up there," he told her.

She smiled, or tried to. "And I'll be worried about you. Damn, I wish the one-three wasn't being pulled into—"

"Whoa, there," he said in mock warning. "I thought you were the one who got mad when your parents tried to keep you out of the action, tried to keep you safe. You wouldn't be pulling the same stunt with me, would you?"

Kara laughed. "I don't think I'd dare. Not now. Just the same, I'll sure be glad when this is over."

"You and me both, Kara. You and me both."

Her parents lived in a somewhat remote estate in the forest Outback, looking across a lush valley to the ice-glint beauty of the Silverside Cascades. The region was dotted with the homes of other high-ranking military and government types. Vic Hagan had named the estate Cascadia.

The floater's AI banked the vehicle and extended its varigee wings. They were in free flight for several moments, and then Cascadia's gaussfield caught them and gentled them in to the estate's landing deck.

Guests had been arriving for some time. The parking area

was half full, and the approaches to the house were cluttered with small groups of people, some in formal dress or military uniform, others—the women especially—in displays of skin, holoprojection, and nano expression that managed simultaneously to be imaginative and to leave very little to the imagination.

It was well past Second Eclipse, and the long Newamie day was slowly fading into night. Gloglobes hung suspended on their magnetics, and radiant pools cast soft, pastel ripples across the stonework. Inside, the gathering room and the broad atrium were crowded, with people spilling out onto the back patio. Viewalls displayed shifting, abstract patterns, matched by the vividly glowing floor display. Servots floated on hidden maglev traces set into the floor, passing out drinks and food as quickly as people would take them. Animated conversation mingled with the soft tones of neural harmonics floating from hidden speakers. New America might still be a frontier society, lacking the more civilized amenities of old Earth and the Shakai—the upper-class society of the Imperium—but the people did appreciate a good party.

She identified herself and Ran to the servot greeting each new guest, and then they walked into the house's atrium. Her mother was there, literally radiant in pastel skin tones and holographic light. "Kara!" her mother cried, reaching out and hugging her. "Thanks for coming."

"Your invitation didn't leave a lot of options open," Kara replied. "Mums? You remember Lieutenant Ran Ferris."

"Of course, Lieutenant. How are you?"

"Fine, Senator." He gazed around the atrium. "A nice party."

"Thank you."

"So," Kara said. "Is Daren here tonight?"

"He should be." She sounded distracted. "He's working late at the university tonight, but he promised he'd be out as soon as he could get away."

"Mums? You okay? You seem preoccupied."

"No. No, I'm just tired." Katya looked at her daughter.

"I . . . know you'd rather be elsewhere tonight." A smile tugged at her lips. "Both of you."

Sometimes, Kara thought, her mother could be a little too observant. Or was it that Kara herself was too transparent? In an information-intensive culture, it became harder and harder to maintain a polite mask. Even after the Rebellion, many aspects of New American culture were still drawn from the Imperial Shakai, such as the need to present a neutral face. In Nihongo, the word for one's physical face, *men*, was the same as the word for "mask."

"I'm always glad to see you, Mums. You know that."

"Hey! Kara! Good to see you!"

Kara turned at the voice. At first she didn't recognize the speaker, though the voice was familiar. The nude man standing in front of her possessed skin that was a rich, light-drinking ebony, and she couldn't see his features well enough to be able to place the face.

"Hello, Senator!" the black-skinned man added cheerfully.

"Hello, Geoff," Katya said. "Enjoying yourself?"

A name and a position dropped into her mind, thanks to her mother's use of the name: Geoff Rawlins, one of her mother's executive assistants.

"Sure am." He looked Kara up and down appraisingly. "Still in uniform, huh? You should do something about that." He grinned at her, his teeth and the whites of his eyes startlingly bright against the black skin. It was hard to look at the man without staring. She could tell he wanted her to ask.

"Okay, I'll jack in," she said. "When did you become a worshipper?"

She'd heard about sun worshippers, of course. They wore yet another type of Naga expression, one that transformed the outer cells of their skin to jet black, the better to absorb every watt of sunlight that fell on their skin, then incorporated it into the worshipper's metabolism as additional energy. They still had to eat—sunlight couldn't provide enough energy even over a couple of square meters of skin to keep a human going long with no other input—but they claimed that taking a substantial part of their nourishment this way was more natural, and healthier, than old-fashioned eating.

"A couple months ago," he told her. He held one hand out and looked at it, turning it to admire its tone. "Nothing like it in the universe!"

"Mmm. What are you doing in here, then? I thought you people didn't like the 'taste' of artificial light?"

"Hey, until the sun comes up in another forty hours or so, we take our pleasure where we can. You should try it, sometime, Kara! You'd look fantastic in basic black!"

"Not my style, Geoff. Hard getting enough to eat inside a warstrider."

"Ah, yeah. Didn't think of that." He opened his other hand and extended it, revealing a smooth sphere of polished gold, glistening against the black of his palm. "Take a jolt? Either of you?"

"*Kuso*, no!" Kara said, making a face and turning away.

Katya, more diplomatic, shook her head. "Thank you, Geoff. No."

He grinned. "I'll be glad to wait while you reset."

"Listen," Ran said firmly. "Can't you see we're trying to talk?"

His bluntness didn't seem to bother Geoff. He simply shrugged. "Hey, suit yourselves. I'll be around if you change your minds."

There was nothing improper about senspheres . . . though public attitudes toward them had been changing somewhat since Naga Companions had started becoming popular. Held against the old-style nanogrown palm implants, senspheres generated a mildly stimulating, erotic tingle throughout the body. People with Companions, however, with their skin circuitry and artificial implants absorbed and reformed by their Naga, could set their body's interpretation of the sensphere's stimulation to be something considerably more than a euphoric tingle. Companion-linked people who used senspheres had the reputation of being wild and daring sexually.

"Kuso, Mums," Kara said. "Where did you download *him*?"

Instead of answering directly, Katya looked at Ran. "Lieutenant? I wonder if you could get us all something to drink? Icecaf for me."

"Certainly, Senator. Kara?"

"I'll have a Columbiarise."

"Be right back."

"Take your time," Katya said. "I need a quick private link with Kara."

"You know, Mums," Kara said as Ran walked away. "I really don't have a lot in common with all of this." She nodded toward Geoff and a young woman wearing a Companion-grown spray of scarlet feathers. The woman held out her hand, nodding, and Geoff passed the sensphere to her. "With all of *them*."

"I know. Sometimes I don't think I have much in common with them either. But it all comes with the job. Come on. Let's get comfortable."

Together, they walked out of the atrium and into the conversation room, a circular, comfortably furnished area with a three-step-down pit in the center ringed with soft sofafloor that wasn't occupied at the moment. Sitting side by side, the two women faced one another, extending their hands.

They touched, hands clasping hands. Katya could sense her Companion reforming part of itself, flowing out through both of her palms to make direct physical contact with Kara's Naga. With their Companions able to intermesh smoothly with the human CNS to the point of actually becoming part of it, they were, in effect, directly joining their brains.

"This is a lot better," Kara said in Katya's thoughts. It was like being in a com module with the words appearing in your mind, but closer, *warmer* somehow. Other people in the room would see them sitting together on the sofafloor, eyes closed, holding hands. Social protocol was specific about such things. They would not be disturbed.

"Yes . . . "

There was worry in her mother's thoughts. Kara could taste it, dark and smoky. There were no masks here, in the intimacy of linked minds.

"I should tell you first," Katya said in her mind. "I . . . I don't want you on this mission."

"Mother, we've been through this before. Many times, in

fact." She hesitated. "Damn it, you were in the military. You should understand what it all means if anybody can. The closeness. The *rapport* . . . ."

"I understand too well. Why do you think I'm so scared? I don't want to lose you. Like—" She stopped abruptly.

"Like Dev Cameron, you were going to say?"

"Sometimes, daughter, I think there's a lot of Dev in you, even if Vic was your father. Your humor reminds me of him sometimes." Katya gave the mental equivalent of a sigh. "Anyway, I needed you to come tonight because I wanted to let you know. Sandstorm is go. You'll be shipping out tomorrow."

Kara felt a flash of excitement, a leap behind her breastbone . . . but she reined it in when she sensed the answering pain in her mother's mind. "I am glad," she said. "We've been running those sims until I think we're going to wear out the AIs. We've been getting good success rates lately. And low casualties."

"I know. I've been keeping tabs. There's more. Would you like to know what it is you're going to Kasei to collect?"

"Of course! Most of the people in First Squadron are betting it's a prototype for some new Imperial warstrider." That had been Kara's guess as well, the only target that really made sense. A raid against Kasei—old Mars—itself was certain to escalate the long-standing chi-war between Empire and Confederation, could easily lead to the all-out conflagration of full-scale, planet-busting interstellar war. Whatever Sandstorm's objective was, it had to be of vital importance.

"The Imperials," Katya said, "have probably developed a prototype quantum-messaging device. Instant communication, across any distance."

Kara said nothing. She couldn't. The shock of her mother's words had momentarily stunned her. "An FTL com unit?" she managed at last.

"That's right. And if we don't catch up with them on that little piece of high-tech magic, the Confederation stands to lose everything it's won. *Everything.*"

"Mums . . ." It was difficult holding on to the link. "Mums, do you have any idea how *bad* this could be?"

"The raid? I think I do. Yes."

"I meant the FTL comm. I was thinking about the Sinclair Doctrine."

"I've been thinking of it too. So have most of the military committee people. That's why we've authorized this raid, why we're risking a much larger war. Our survival, as a people, as a culture, could be at stake."

The Declaration of Reason had been written during the war by General Travis Ewell Sinclair both as apologetic and as unifying inspiration for the Confederation's war of independence. Central to the Declaration was the concept that it was both impractical and immoral for any government to impose its will upon a subject people so far removed from the seat of that government that true representation was impossible. With K-T technology, New America was a three-month round trip from Earth. If an Imperial governor could dispatch a report—or a call for help—and have it acted upon the same day instead of three months later, that government and the power it wielded were suddenly much closer at hand . . . and far more dangerous.

"How close are they to developing this thing?" Kara wanted to know.

"Very. We're not sure, but we think the Imperials may already have some of their fleet units equipped with I2C already."

" 'I2C'?"

"Instantaneous Interstellar Communications. The latest in government-military acronyms."

"But . . . but *how*? I thought something like that was impossible."

"Apparently it's not. You're familiar with phase entanglement?"

Kara pulled a fast download from her RAM. "Twentieth-century quantum mechanics," she said. "The first experiments, anyway."

"That's right. It was demonstrated that if two particles interact—two quons, I should say, particles that act on a quantum level, photons or electrons—if they interact, they become . . . related. More than related. In some ways, it's as though the two particles are the *same* particle.''

In swift, concise thoughts, Katya described the concept. Two phase-entangled quantum particles acted as though they were connected, even when separated by light years. Early quantum physics investigators had focused on phase entanglement, hoping to disprove it because it suggested a faster-than-light connection, something thought at the time to be impossible. They never did, though. Phase entanglement was part of the mathematics of quantum mechanics, and eventually they were able to prove the fact in the laboratory.

And now nanotechnology had provided a way of dealing with this particular twist to the murkier side of physics. Machines small enough to manipulate individual atoms could literally build a cage a few atoms wide on a side, a cage designed to trap and hold a single quon, and to register such properties as spin. Quantum cages were routinely manufactured as a part of the nanofields projected ahead of warstriders when they were operating in floater mode, or in the projected impeller fields of private vehicles.

Presumably, the Imperials had found a means of using electron cages and quons to transmit data. In theory, the spin of an electron could represent one binary bit of data in a message—up spin for one, say, and down spin for zero. With an array of caged electrons, each paired with an identically caged twin at a distant site, data could be fed in at one end, and it would emerge at the other, instantaneously, no matter how many light years separated the two. More, it was a communications link that could never be tapped, never be jammed, and never be intercepted, since the data passed from transmitter to receiver without crossing the intervening space at all.

Their mental conversation slipped into the military aspects of the discovery. Communications were one of the key factors in any combat situation. Clearly, with I2C the Imperials would possess an overwhelming advantage if they faced the Confederation in any military showdown.

"Really!"

People linked directly with each other were not entirely cut off from the outside world; one of the reasons for using comm modules in long-distance linkages was to cut off external distractions in order to help build the virtual reality world within the participants' brains. In full linkage, of course, all external stimuli could be filtered out by the AI managing the session. In a simple one-to-one like this, however, a loud voice could still work its way into her perception, grating and annoying. Kara opened her eyes, blinking.

"Oh . . . *really!*" a woman standing with the group a few meters away exclaimed again, louder this time, loud enough that the murmur of conversation in the room momentarily faded away, and carrying a distinct edge of shock and unhappiness.

Arra Thornton was a substantial woman, the wife of a general on Vic's planning staff. She was wearing a diaphanous gown and a tasteful, golden halo holographically projected above her head. She was staring at the far side of the atrium with something akin to horror on her face.

"Arra?" Katya called sweetly. "Whatever is the matter?"

"Oh, Senator!" the woman said, turning. "I didn't see you there!"

"You sounded upset, dear."

"Oh, dear, I was just wondering who had invited *her*."

Kara looked toward the atrium. A woman was there, a *Japanese* woman, wearing a conservative gray sheath. Daren was at her side.

"That is my son and his guest, Ms. Thornton," Katya said, her voice a trifle chillier than liquid nitrogen. "Is there a problem?"

"Oh!" The woman's eyes bulged and the corners of her mouth worked soundlessly for a moment. "Oh, my, well, I mean, of *course* not! You can invite whatever you want to your party, dear, of *course* . . . ."

"I do, Ms. Thornton." *After all, I invited you.*

The big woman turned away hastily and began talking with the people near her in hushed, flustered tones.

Katya grinned at Kara. "You know, that was fun! I've always wanted to do something like that."

"I agree with her," Kara said. "How the hell could Daren bring—"

"Kara!" Katya's tone was sharp. "I take people one at a time, not as monolithic wholes."

She stood as her son approached them.

"Mother!" Daren said. "Sis! I didn't think you'd mind if I brought a guest. I've told you about my colleague from the University? Dr. Taki Oe."

"Dr. Oe," Katya said formally, bowing. "*Konichiwa.*"

"*Konichiwa*, Senator Alessandro," the woman replied, returning the bow. "Thank you so much for having me."

"Dr. Oe," Kara said, frowning, "I wonder if it was a good idea, your coming here tonight. There's a certain amount of tension—"

"Between the Japanese and the New Americans, lately. Yes, Lieutenant, I am very much aware." She looked at Katya. "And I assure you, Senator, that I am New American. Whatever shape my eyes might be."

Katya sighed. "You're welcome in this house. You should be aware, though, that some of my other guests may not draw the same distinction between nationality and phenotype." She looked pointedly at Kara. "But I will have my guests treated with hospitality."

Kara heard the anger just beneath her mother's *men*.

"We won't be staying long, in any case," Daren said, a bit hastily. "Mostly just wanted to drop by and link in. Nice party."

Kara was furious. *Damn* Daren, anyway! He could get so wrapped up in himself sometimes, completely oblivious to everyone and everything outside his immediate circle of awareness. Here she was getting psyched to go out and kick Nihonjin ass, and her brother had the nerve to bring one to the party! Insane! She scanned the room until she caught sight of Ran walking toward her with two drinks in his hands.

"Here's your icecaf, Mums. Ran and I have to go now," she told her mother. "It was nice to see you." She walked away without another word.

• • •

Katya watched her go with a sinking feeling inside.

"I'm sorry," Taki said. "Daren? Maybe we should go—"

"Nonsense," Katya said, addressing her son and his guest. "Stay as long as you like. You can at least have something to eat before you go."

"That's an idea," Daren said. "We haven't had much to eat today. I'll get something for us from that 'vot over there."

As her son walked away, Katya looked at Oe, unsure what to say. "So, Dr. Oe. Have you known my son long?"

"We've been working together on several projects for about a year and a half now, Senator. He is very good at research."

"I know." He *was* good, if a bit single-minded in his pursuit of his own interests and projects, sometimes.

Katya studied Taki Oe as they chatted, measuring her. Daren had introduced the woman as his colleague, but Katya was both a mother and a human being with an unusually fine-tuned set of perceptions. She could look at Daren and the Oe woman, look at the way they stood, the way their eyes made contact with one another, and in that moment she knew, that these two were more than friends, more even than partners in casual sex.

"Mother," Daren said brightly as he returned with two plates of food. "I was hoping to get some time with you tonight. I, I mean, *we* need to talk to you about the survey project."

Katya shook her head. "This is a bad time, Daren."

"I'm beginning to think there is no good time."

"I don't mean now, the party. I mean it's a bad time for the Confederation. I don't think you have a prayer of getting the appropriations you'd need. Or the ships."

"Yeah, but if you could just push a little for us. . . ."

"Damn it, Daren! Do you think my political career exists so that you can run surveys? Look for aliens? It doesn't work that way!"

He looked stricken. "If you just knew how important this was—"

"I've heard the arguments, Daren. Believe me. I even believe most of them. But there are political and economic realities, *mili-*

tary realities, too, that won't simply vanish because we want them to. I'm flattered that you think I possess so much power, but I don't, and I'm sick of hearing your whining!''

She was angry with herself for losing her temper, but the anger was tempered by the realization that she was already upset by the possibility of losing Kara.

Oh, Dev! she thought, a little wildly. *Where are you now, and why didn't you stay here with me, with us? I need you!*

It was all she could do to keep her *men* in place.

Some say the world will end in fire,
Some say in ice. . . .

—*Fire and Ice*
Robert Frost
c.e. 1923

Frost had it right, he thought. Some chance crossing of memories had led him to download the ancient poem during the flight toward Nova Aquila's orphaned, inner world. Now, standing on the ice plain beneath a black and star-strewn sky, >>DEVCAMERON<< recited the lines to himself once more.

Some say the world will end in fire . . .

The planet was as dead as he had expected. As his walker stepped off the grounded DalRiss ship, his upper body sensors took in a dim panorama of ice and broken, blackened rock. The two suns were only just visible, a close-set pair of bright but minute pinpoints close to the zenith. With a thousandth of the luminosity of Earth's sun, they were by far the brightest of the sky's stars, twin beacons casting eerie shimmers of light across the rolling plain of ice, with a radiance carrying no warmth at all. Though it was nearly local noon, the landscape was so poorly lit, only by the stars, that even with enhanced vision >>DEV-CAMERON<< found it difficult to penetrate the shadowy landscape.

The temperature, he estimated, was around minus two hundred Celsius.

He remembered a popular expression from his human life: *iceworld*. It meant . . . be calm. Be cold. Don't let it bother you. Standing here on an icy plain, impressed by the preternatural stillness of the place, he knew more than ever what that expression meant.

> *But if it had to perish twice,*
> *I think I know enough of hate*
> *To say that for destruction ice*
> *Is also great . . .*

This world had perished twice, first in fire as its twin suns exploded nearly two thousand years ago, then in ice as those stars dwindled away to hot but tiny fractions of their former light and warmth. The expanding shell of gas from the nova had probably widened the planet's orbit, but more, white dwarfs simply didn't have the surface area to provide the heat necessary for life.

He began moving away from the grounded DalRiss ship. The rest of the fleet remained in orbit over the planet or near the Device, watching for further appearances of the mysterious spacefarers who'd built—or who at least presumed to use—the Device for their own ends.

It always felt strange having a body, familiar but with odd and sometimes contradictory sensations. >>DEVCAME-RON<< took a cautious step on the ice and then another, still working to get the proper feel and balance for his radially symmetrical body. The ice was not as slippery as it looked; it was far too cold and was as hard as granite. Too, >>DEVCAMERON's<< new feet, all six of them, possessed stubby, rubbery projections that gripped even the smoothest surface and gave him excellent traction. He was aware of the cold through various sensors embedded in his skin, but his brain registered the temperature as chilly only and not as a cold bitter enough to liquefy oxygen.

The walker was a biological construct specially grown for him by the DalRiss's master biologists, but it was not even remotely human. It resembled one of the DalRiss themselves, a starfish shape two meters across, supported well off the ground by six blunt, spiny arms, and with a crescent-shaped sensory package and a forest of delicate manipulatory tendrils perched on top.

>>DEVCAMERON's<< original human brain and nervous system had evolved to handle only two legs, two arms, and two eyes; the DalRiss had written a special software package that let him handle six of everything, downloading it into his Naga-patterned brain.

The basic Dal form had been modified in several ways for his convenience, however. It possessed the visual sensors and nervous system of a Perceiver, giving >>DEVCAMERON<< sight, and it had been designed with a particularly thick and impermeable hide, one that would retain its metabolic warmth and internal pressure despite the frigid temperatures and hard vacuum of the world's surface. In a sense, it was a living environmental suit, capable of surviving for days at temperatures below minus two hundred Celsius, with oxygen stored as hyperoxygenated fatty tissue padding his legs.

The ice gave way to black and crumbling rock. "Frost," he said, transmitting on his inner radio circuit.

"The local conditions are considerably more severe than that," a voice responded in his head.

He turned, studying the speaker, the movement a trifle clumsy. The speaker also wore a temporary body, one grown specially to withstand cold and vacuum. A cold-adapted Perceiver had been grafted in with the sensor cluster; its eyes regarded him emotionlessly.

"Actually, I thought that would be a decent name for the planet," >>DEVCAMERON<< replied.

"The word 'frost' describes a meteorological condition in which a thin layer of ice forms on cold surfaces exposed to a particular gas, usually water vapor or carbon dioxide, in the atmosphere. There is no atmosphere here, save for the trace subliming from the surface ice, and—''

''Never mind,'' he interrupted. ''It was just a thought. Not important.''

''Thoughts give shape, content, and meaning to the universe,'' the DalRiss said. ''None are unimportant.''

>>DEVCAMERON<< didn't want to discuss it further. He'd not thought he would miss his own kind in this form of existence. He had plenty of sims stored in his replicated memory that he could relive at need, but there were times . . .

The DalRiss were good traveling companions, all in all, but they took things so damned literally. They understood wonder, certainly, but they were baffled by such a simple thing as poetry. Or . . . >>DEVCAMERON<< thought ruefully, perhaps poetry was not such a simple concept after all. Sometimes he marveled that he still appreciated the art, even now, after losing his humanity.

But the DalRiss were *so* different, and in so many ways. The Frost misunderstanding was a case in point. They didn't understand the human need to give names to places. Hell, they didn't even have names for one another . . . or if they did, they were names based on their individual life energies, as untranslatable as an EEG tracing, or a fingerprint. Their name for him was sort of a mentally shouted impression of being, one filtered through his Naga's brain—>>DEVCAMERON<<, a kind of instantly recognizable ''Hey, you!''

Trying to explain to the DalRiss that he was referring to a name, Robert Frost, that he wanted to have a name for the world instead of the vague, chilly impression of lifelessness they were using, that Frost had been a poet speaking of human emotions, that emotions were . . .

Just the thought of it made him tired, and there was still a lot to do.

For >>DEVCAMERON,<< though, this world would remain ''Frost,'' a memorial to the twentieth-century poet who'd pronounced the world's epitaph.

''There is nothing here alive,'' the DalRiss voice reminded him after a time. Was it impatient? ''This world is empty.''

He turned slowly, once again, facing the speaker. "Possibly. But I'm curious about whether anyone used to live here. It would . . . it would tell us about the beings who destroyed this world's suns."

"We are wondering about something, >>DEVCAMERON<<."

"Yes?"

"Why is it that you turn your body when you wish to speak with a Riss who is physically present? Are you having difficulty with your Perceivers?"

"No." >>DEVCAMERON<< chuckled to himself, deep within his thoughts. One of his problems in adjusting to these temporary bodies was the fact that, where real DalRiss rarely thought in terms of front or back, he retained a human preference for one direction which he still thought of as "forward."

For some time now, >>DEVCAMERON<< had not been a corporeal entity; and wearing a body again, even a strange one in a strange and hostile environment, was a relief, as if it reminded him of an anchor he'd mislaid.

His original human brain had been destroyed with his body, of course, at Herakles, but its patterns, including all of its memories, its identity of self, its perceptions and knowledge, had been retained by small communications-trained Nagas occupying other living ships of the DalRiss fleet. When the ship holding his physical body had been incinerated, his mind—the set of software running on his wetware that constituted his thoughts, his memories, his sense of *self*—had been resident in those other ships, riding in a Naga copy of his brain. Aboard ship, his "body" was the ship itself, or any of the multiple ships of the fleet, wherever Nagas were resident; during the fleet's rare planetfalls, one of the small Naga subsets that had patterned his brain flowed into a carefully designed niche inside his artificial and temporary skull. >>DEVCAMERON<< could not sense any real difference . . . save for the trouble he had navigating, or when he forgot and turned the radially symmetrical body without need.

There were other things as well, he was realizing. He missed intelligent human companionship. He missed conversations where he didn't have to explain concepts like "poetry" or "names." He missed specific people, individuals whose differences sparked and fired his own thoughts, generating new ideas that let him know that he was alive.

And, oh, *God* how he missed sex, despite the fact that he didn't have a body. He was no longer aroused by hormones triggered by thoughts, of course . . . but the thoughts remained, and the habit patterns of desire remained closely linked with them. Even a decent ViRsex simulation would have helped, but for that a sophisticated AI was needed, an AI with a better understanding of what it was to be human than these Nagas and DalRiss had.

Hell, even just the sensation of another human's touch, fingertip feather-light on skin, or hearty clap on the shoulder, or hand squeezing arm, with no thought of sex in the contact at all . . .

He'd lost so much. He'd thought that, given time enough, he would forget.

Resigned, he focused his attention on the task at hand. He was looking for some sign of intelligence.

Normally, such a search would have been doomed to failure, if only because a planet was immense, the indicators of intelligence tiny and scattered and, in the case of Frost, at least, flooded first by fire, then by ice. The DalRiss, even with the help of their Perceivers, still had trouble recognizing nonliving organization or artifacts; it had to be alive for them to understand it, to really *know* it in the sense that humans knew and understood something by seeing it.

But he had scanned the surface as they'd approached, absorbing the configurations of black rock and white ice, then feeding the patterns through a set of programs loaded onto his borrowed Naga brain that tested those shapes for fractals. In nature, most forms were either random, or they unfolded in repeating iterations that followed the mathematical language of fractal patterns. Shapes that showed order without the iterations of fractals were, most likely, artificial.

And he'd seen such. Even without the fractal detection routine, he'd seen certain regular spacings of rock on ice that had reminded him of photos of cities taken from orbit. There was no proof in that observation alone, of course. Lots of natural phenomena could mimic the regularity or the geometry of artificial structures.

But it was highly suspicious, and the fractal routine had agreed, returning a probability of eighty-two percent that what he'd glimpsed was not a natural formation. The DalRiss ship had landed close to what he suspected was an enormous structure mostly submerged in ice. Accompanied by the lone DalRiss, he walked toward an upthrust black cliff a few tens of meters distant. Behind him—he really could see it without turning with his all-round visual organs—the DalRiss ship rested where its Achievers had materialized it on blue-white ice, a black starfish shape the size of a small city.

He wasn't sure exactly what he was looking for, but he found it almost at once. The rock cliff, extending several meters above the ice, was rough-hewn and rugged, split in places by deep cracks, and could easily have been natural after all, *could* have been . . . except for the corroded, outstretched fingers of metal embedded in the rock's face.

Gently, he reached out one of his manipulatory tendrils, stroking the length of one of those bars. It felt like metal—bitterly cold, of course, and so brittle from millennia-old oxidation that parts of the surface flaked away at his touch. There were six curved, flat bars, appearing eerily like rust-brown human ribs protruding from the stone. What had they been like, the people who had built here once? Nothing remotely like humans, he was certain of that much. He wished they could take the time to excavate and explore, and knew it was impossible. He wanted to know them, know something concrete about them.

This much they'd had in common with the children of Earth, he knew already: they'd been builders, manipulators of their environment. And perhaps that was kinship enough, for it made them more like humans in at least that way than humans were like either the DalRiss or the Naga.

He wished there were some way of running an analysis on the metal. The ribs might be highly oxidized iron, or they could be the remnants of some more sophisticated alloy, but he couldn't tell by touch alone, and the DalRiss weren't very good with nonbiological assays or tests. A Naga might be able to tell—they were superb at chemical analysis—but a Naga unprotected in this environment would freeze solid in seconds. Perhaps he could break a piece off and give it to a one aboard ship later.

Breaking a chunk of the metal off, though, seemed like sacrilege, a defacing of a monument that had stood here unchanging for two millennia. There was no other way to tell what the things were, no way to even guess at what they might once have been a part of . . . but he didn't want to commit that desecration.

But there was no denying the fact that they were artificial.

"This is what you sought?" the voice said in his mind.

"Yes. Someone built here, once."

"I . . . don't understand what I am seeing."

He moved a tendril along one of the metal ribs. The DalRiss were at a serious handicap here. They could directly sense unliving metal only through their Perceivers, and their own experience did not include building large structures. They grew everything they needed, from houses to entire cities to starships. How to explain? "There is no natural process I know that could have caused this. I think it may be part of the framework of a building."

"Like a skeleton?"

"Like a skeleton, exactly."

"And those who grew it were native to this world?"

"I don't know. I suppose it could have been a colony, or an outpost. But the fractal images suggest that this planet was fairly heavily built up. Lots of very large structures. That means a large population."

A large population that had been incinerated.

Deliberately?

There were still too many unanswered questions. The builders of this structure on Frost might have been long gone by the time their stars exploded; there was even the possibility that they had been the builders of the Device, that the Device itself was unrelated to the nova.

But >>DEVCAMERON<< could not shake the feeling, as cold and as chilling and as bleak as the glacial landscape about him, that the double sun had been deliberately exploded to feed the

Device, that someone was feeding it now for reasons only its builders knew . . . and that whoever had done the deed had done so either in complete ignorance of, or with a complete lack of concern for, the beings living on Frost.

And >>DEVCAMERON<< wasn't sure which possibility was the more terrifying.

Chapter 8

Perhaps the most surprising discovery of the mid-twenty-sixth century was the incredible diversity of separate evolutionary systems. And this diversity was expressed not simply in alien biologies, but in mutually alien philosophical outlooks as well. Human, DalRiss, and Naga, it was clear, each possessed worldviews that diverged remarkably from one another, in part because of differences in their physical senses, in part because of their origins and their environments. And in some ways, the Web's picture of the universe proved more disparate still.

—*Reflections of Intelligence*
Dr. C. Nelson Bryce
c.e. 2575

>>DEVCAMERON<< had remained on Frost for the equivalent of several standard days, probing among those ruins that were free of the vast plains of encroaching ice. He'd found nothing that told him more about either the inhabitants of the dead world or the calamity that had overtaken them; and, in the end, he'd been glad to shed his artificial DalRiss body and return to the freer, more spacious life within the DalRiss city-ship.

An Achiever died; the immense vessel vanished from the ice plain, rematerializing in space a few thousand kilometers from the enigmatic Device.

The Device remained in space, midway between the two white dwarf suns, still funneling the infalling streams of glowing star stuff into nothingness. The other DalRiss cityships were where he'd left them, watching. There were no answers here, either, it seemed. Not yet.

"Five more spacecraft have emerged from an area close to the Device," a DalRiss voice said in >>DEVCAMERON's<< mind. "They traveled directly toward one or the other of the dwarf stars."

"Was there any reaction to your presence?"

"None. We tried again to communicate on a wide variety of channels. It is possible, however, that they use frequency bands unavailable to us."

"And no sign of life on the vessels themselves?"

"No. Of course, we would not be able to sense life hidden behind dead matter."

"I understand."

Still, it was curious. Surely those vessels could sense the strange fleet slowly orbiting the Device, eighty flat disks, each one hundreds of meters across, sprouting multiple arms and radiating energy signatures that spoke emphatically of life.

>>DEVCAMERON<< decided to do some research.

Each DalRiss vessel possessed a sizable fragment of a full-grown planetary Naga, a kind of organic communications network that invisibly bound the fleet together. When linked by radio or lasercom beams, each fragment became one node of a massively parallel organic computer with impressive stores of memories. He'd spent considerable time after his return interrogating that organism, which he thought of as the fleet Naga. While not nearly so massive as a planetary Naga, and with only a fraction of a planetary Naga's hand-me-down memories, the being possessed enough memory chains among its far-flung nodes to enable >>DEVCAMERON<< to trace back through several generations of the being, searching for some link between the Naga and the ships glimpsed traveling between the Device and the white dwarf suns.

Full understanding by Man of the life form once known as *Xenophobe* had come slowly and only through the communication made possible by DalRiss biotechnology. Nagas began as small lumps of compact and tightly organized cells, molecule-sized organic machines that penetrated a planet's crust, assimilating rocks and minerals and reorganizing them into more Naga cells. Debate still raged among human researchers as to whether the Nagas were a naturally evolved life form or the runaway end product of an evolving alien nanotechnology, and the Nagas themselves could not say. Certainly, Naga cells behaved much like a thinking version of human nanotech, able to sample, manipulate, pattern, and even replicate complex molecules at the atomic level.

With a metabolism driven by the planet's interior heat, the thermophilic being tunneled deeper and deeper into the crust, finding an ideal habitable zone several kilometers down, one balanced between the cold surface and the great deeps where the temperature was so high that even Nagas couldn't survive, and spreading out in all directions.

Eventually, the Naga occupied vast expanses of underground real estate, existing as concentrated pockets of tissue interconnected by vast networks of tendrils; the comparison to the interconnected neurons of a brain had not escaped the researchers studying Naga physiology. Ultimately, the entire Naga massed as much as a fair-sized planetoid and was spread throughout the planet's upper crust. Its tendency to detect and assimilate large concentrations of refined metals and alloys had led to the confrontations between Man and Xenophobe on a dozen Frontier worlds and to the assumption by humans that they were being attacked by a spacefaring race. Only after fifty years of sporadic ''war,'' the loss of several human colony worlds and tens of thousands of people, and the eradication of the planetary Naga infesting Loki, was the truth finally learned.

Each planetary Naga was an independent organism, completely unaware of the Nagas occupying other worlds. Its ''acquisitive phase'' might last tens of thousands or even hundreds of thousands of years as it grew, permeating its planet's crust. Eventually, however, as its nodes became more closely interconnected and parts began overrunning the planetary surface, the Naga shifted modes, becoming quiescent—entering its "contemplative phase." Using its ability to draw on enormous reserves of energy and to produce and manipulate powerful magnetic fields, the Naga hurled tiny packets of itself into the interstellar deeps at high velocities. Most of these packets were lost in the immensities of space; some few, guided by a primitive kind of programming that recognized the heat and magnetic fields of suitable planets, fell onto the worlds of other, nearby suns . . . and the cycle was begun anew.

Perhaps strangest from Man's limited point of view, however, was the curious way the Naga had of looking at the world around them. Restricted by their underground isolation from the rest of the universe, the Nagas perceived the cosmos as endless rock. Outward the rock grew hotter, providing life; inward, at the center of all, was a vast, hollow cave, a yawning blank emptiness that the Naga, in its binary logic, thought of as *not-rock*. Pods of new life launched into space crossed not outer but *inner* space, the gulf at the center of all.

From the human perspective, the Nagas literally saw the universe inside-out. Their perceptions of humans were just as skewed; if Nagas divided their cosmos into *rock* and *not-rock*, they separated their awareness into *self* and *not-self*. Wild Nagas were always astonished to learn that it was possible for *not-self* to think and reason, just like *self*.

But communication was possible. Once contact had been achieved with one Naga, through DalRiss biotech, it had been learned that fragments of that Naga could pass on what it had learned to wild Nagas. If human culture had been undergoing a revolution thanks to peaceful contact with the Naga, it was nothing like the revolution in individual Naga thought and understanding. Though their feelings, if they had any, couldn't be expressed in words, it seemed as though they were allowing themselves to be integrated into the DalRiss fleet through a simple lust for wonder, for input on a cosmic scale.

And that, after all, was much of the reason >>DEVCAMERON<< was here as well.

"I need to see the past," he said in his mind, focusing on the matrix of the interlinked Naga's flickering, eldritch thoughts. "I need to know if you've been here before."

"I do not understand what you mean by 'here'...."

>>DEVCAMERON<< uploaded images of the Device, a thread-thin needle of brilliant silver rotating about its long axis beneath the light of two shrunken suns.

He received a blurred storm of warped and fragmentary images in return.

Despite the differences both in their perceptions and in their way of reasoning, humans linked with Nagas had managed to secure tantalizing glimpses of the beings' remote past. Given that Naga reproduction was essentially asexual fission on an enormous scale, it was no surprise to find that one Naga possessed memories of a succession of previous worlds . . . even though it didn't think in those terms. Some researchers thought that the Nagas must have first evolved as much as seven or eight billion years earlier, that they might not even be native to the galaxy humans called the Milky Way. Direct evidence of such time scales was lacking, however, and even memories from recently assimilated worlds could not be pinned down in time. Nagas, it turned out, had a different perception of time as well as space, one based on subjective events rather than on objective units of time.

It was the past, as perceived by the Naga, that >>DEVCAMERON<< was interested in now. His initial contact with the Naga at the DalRiss world of ShraRish had demonstrated that the Nagas had approached the bubble of human-occupied space from that part of Earth's sky toward eighteen hours' right ascension, somewhat to spinward of the galactic core, roughly in the direction of the constellations Serpens, Ophiuchus, and Cygnus. He'd known about the curious Cygnan anomaly—the fact that so many novae had been recorded in the same small patch of sky—since long before his transformation into a program within an alien computer matrix. Somehow, it seemed to demand too much of random chance to expect that Nagas and multiple novae should both emerge from that same tiny patch in Earth's sky and *not* be related somehow.

His original guess had been that someone in this direction had been fighting the Xenophobe menace just as the Terran Hegemony had done, but with weapons of considerably greater destructive power. He'd pictured alien civilizations sterilizing worlds contaminated by the Xenophobe by exploding their suns.

Now, though, he wasn't so sure. The Naga were restricted—by their requirements for specific ranges of temperature, crust composition, and magnetic fields—to worlds similar to Earth. They seemed equally at home within planets that had been terraformed and possessed oxygen-nitrogen atmospheres as they were inside prebiotic worlds still shrouded in carbon-dioxide, but in general they could survive only within fairly narrow limits of magnetic field, internal temperature, and mass. In short, they preferred the types of worlds that men preferred, though for different reasons . . . a preference that had contributed to human impressions of a systematic alien attack throughout the years of the Xenophobe Wars.

Images filled his mind, most disjointed and virtually impossible to comprehend, images cast not as sight so much as *impressions* . . . impressions based on the taste of magnetic fields or the rich tang of pure metal, and the lovely, satiating warmth of the outer heat, or the delicious tickle of flowing information. As always, he found it impossible to pull any sense of time from that jumble of impressions; the cen' the millennia between one event of note in the age-lo slow-changing existence of a Naga and the next, pa blur, as if Nagas could willfully skip over or edit interesting parts of their existence. Too, until v indeed, Nagas had been almost totally ignorant of most still thought of interstellar space as the voi of their universe.

There is Self . . . and not-self, the Cosm not-selves that are aware, as Self, surrow And beyond . . . wonder. . . .

Its attention seemed focused on the sp it was hard to be certain. Memories w CAMERON's<< awareness, most inco few, a very few, bore familiarity; sweet scent of Katya and felt an r sickness. The scent was gone ar by an avalanche of the strange.

God, I miss her.

"There is something . . ." The Naga's inner voice filled his mind, his soul. >>DEVCAMERON<< waited, listening. "Something similar to what the not-self calls the Device. A similar taste. . . ."

He tasted it, metallic-sharp and bright. Magnetic fields. Intense magnetic fields, unlike anything >>DEVCAMERON<< had ever experienced. The spinning Device generated inconceivable magnetic energies as it spun; once, long, long ago, one or more of the Naga's ancestors had sensed a field similar in scope and in strength.

There was nothing more.

">>DEVCAMERON!<<" one of the DalRiss voices called, intruding on the turbulent mingling of alien thoughts.

"I'm . . . here." It always took a moment or two to disentangle himself from the bizarrely twisted thought patterns of a Naga.

"An unliving vessel returns!"

Breaking his mental link with the Naga, >>DEVCAMERON<< opened again an inner window on the volume of space between the white dwarf suns. With enhanced vision, he could see the mottled gray shape of an alien craft, its inverted shark's fins unlike anything he'd seen before, traveling swiftly out from one of the stars, falling toward the Device.

"Record this!" he snapped . . . needlessly. The DalRiss recorded everything they sensed within the vast reserves of their [Na]ga-linked organic computers. As he watched its passage, he [dow]nloaded what he'd missed—the same ship rising out of the [sun's] photosphere, radiating furiously in the high ultraviolet.

[Dw]arf stars were composed of what human physicists called [degen]erate matter, with the mass of Earth's sun packed into a [spher]e no larger than a planet's, a millionfold smaller. A cu[bic cen]timeter massed uncounted tons; the density was only [somewh]at less than that within the strangely twisted physics [of a neut]ron star's interior.

[It was] not possible.

[The]n, neither was the Device, where similar energies [and force]s were held captive. Again he wondered: *who are [they? What are they doing here?*

In moments, the mystery ship had retraced its course inward from the star, plunged into the strangely twisted space near the Device, and vanished.

A thought occurred to >>DEVCAMERON<<. "That vessel. Did it disappear at a spot close to where it emerged?" He couldn't tell for sure without exact measurements, but it seemed to him that it had.

"As nearly as can be determined by our Perceivers, yes." An oval drew itself in blue light close to one end of the Device and encircling the area where the lone ship had vanished. Seven blue stars appeared scattered within the oval, the points at which the aliens had emerged from otherwhere. A star of a lighter blue marked the entry point of the ship they'd just seen.

"I wonder . . ." >>DEVCAMERON<< was reviewing once again the information he had stored on theoretical space-time machines such as this one. While no one had ever put such theories to the test, the best mathematical models suggested that large masses such as that before them, rotating at relativistic velocities, opened specific pathways connecting places remote from one another in space and time. Where you ended up after passing through the gate was not random but depended on your approach vector. Some models assumed that gateways to and from a distant spot would be different, but >>DEVCAMERON<< had just seen evidence that this wasn't so, that a single gateway might be two-way.

In other words, follow the same path, arrive at the same place. If they could follow the track recorded by that departing ship with sufficient accuracy, it ought to be possible to follow it back to where and when it had come from.

"Is it your plan to follow the vessel?" a DalRiss asked in his mind.

"They don't seem inclined to notice us otherwise," >>DEVCAMERON<< replied. "Unfortunately, maneuvering down that path could be a problem."

DalRiss city ships were not really designed for maneuver through space. They traveled from point to point through the effort—and death—of one of the gene-tailored lifeforms they called Achievers, creatures that somehow visualized two widely separated places in space and made them one . . . first in their minds, then in reality, allowing the DalRiss vessel to slip from one point to another *past* space. The city ships were capable of limited maneuver by expelling matter at high velocities through powerful magnetic fields, or by reshaping and riding local magnetic fields with fields of their own, but accelerations tended to be quite low, a few tenths of a G at most. Steering one of these million-ton monsters through the tortured space alongside the whirling Device would be by far more a matter of luck than skill. With no clear picture of space at the other side, Achievers would be useless here . . . and missing the path could end with the living ship emerging uncountable light years from where it wanted to be.

In any case, >>DEVCAMERON<< didn't like the idea of jeopardizing one of the DalRiss city ships and the thousands of DalRiss aboard it. If nothing else, there was a fair possibility that a ship would emerge on the other side light years from the nearest twin to the enigmatic Device. There were no guarantees.

But—just possibly—there was another way to explore the gateway provided by the Device.

"I need you to grow something special from the Naga," he told the DalRiss. "Here's how it will work . . . ."

Mind, Dev had learned, was best defined as a particular patterning of information; his survival at the Second Battle of Herakles, as mind alone quite distinct from his biological body, proved as much. In a sense, the >>DEVCAMERON<< now inhabiting the DalRiss exploration fleet was a *copy* of the original Dev Cameron's mind, an original that had died when the body creating it had vaporized.

Or . . . *was* it? When his body had been destroyed aboard the DalRiss city ship *Daghar*, his awareness had been elsewhere, not within the ship that had been destroyed. Certainly, he didn't feel like a copy. His memories were intact, up to the moment of the explosion, and afterward. Since the memories themselves were a part of that information pattern, however, he couldn't put a lot of store in their purely subjective revelations, but his impression was that his mind had been at another node, aboard another DalRiss ship, at the instant *Daghar* had vanished in a nuclear fireball.

It was not something he cared to examine too closely. He still didn't know whether he should think of himself as dead . . . or merely mislaid.

Time passed, and the DalRiss fleet continued its orbit about the Device, watching. Three times more as they waited, lone alien ships rose impossibly from the corona of a dwarf star and vanished into emptiness and twisted space without acknowledging the fleet's presence.

Throughout that time, meanwhile, the object >>DEVCA-MERON<< had requested continued to grow, deep within the interior of one of the DalRiss cityships. As for >>DEVCA-MERON,<< his attention was elsewhere.

He was linked once more with the Naga, busily reproducing himself.

Chapter 9

A computer program, any program, can be duplicated. Sophisticated programs can duplicate themselves as they run and can even improve on the original design. Given an advanced enough biotechnology, there seems to be no reason why the human mind cannot be duplicated the same way and transferred as a living program to another, possibly artificial body.

There is considerable question as to why anyone would want to create a duplicate of his or her own mind. The most frequently advanced suggestion is that personalities could be downloaded and stored in this way from time to time against the possibility of death, as a kind of emergency backup life.

Of course, this would do the original personality no good; from his point of view, he would still be quite dead, while his duplicate lived on, complete with his memories of everything that had happened up to the moment of replication.

—*Never-Never Mind*
Dr. Ann Cecil Mulgrave
c.e. 2556

What >>DEVCAMERON<< was attempting to do was similar in principle to what had happened to him by accident twenty-five years before, at Second Herakles. His mind—soul, ego, self-awareness, whatever he chose to call it—existed as patterns of information within the Naga fragment nodes aboard one or another of the DalRiss city ships. The Naga that had patterned his mind in the first place could make a second pattern, a copy that could be downloaded into the Naga-fragment probe that was being grown inside one of the largest of the DalRiss ships.

"Okay," he thought to the Naga. "Let's do it."

He could feel the process, though the sensation was literally indescribable, a kind of stretching or thinning of self and self-awareness and a panicky moment when it felt like he was going to lose his grip on Self entirely. For a time, >>DEVCAMERON<< hovered on the edge of consciousness, clinging to . . . what? To the mental image he held of himself, he supposed, as distinct from the strange and alien flows of consciousness that surrounded him.

It was curious. When he was linked aboard one of the living ships—as opposed to downloaded into an artificial DalRiss body—there was a definite sense of space and freedom, a vast expanse within which he could move and imagine almost without limit. That, he realized with a shock, had just ended. He felt . . . *cramped*, almost as though he'd just been downloaded into a DalRiss body again, and in another moment he saw why.

A whale giving birth to a minnow, the DalRiss cityship *Sirghal* released the probe, a forty-meter, trilaterally symmetrical wedge of absolute blackness.

Shock gave way to anger. "Wait!" >>DEVCAMERON<<

called out over the radio link with *Sirghal*. "You downloaded the wrong one!"

"No," the voice of >>DEVCAMERON<< replied in his mind. "Everything is exactly as it should be."

The sound of his own mental voice almost panicked him; then, as full realization swept through him, >>DEVCAMERON<<, the *second* >>DEVCAMERON<<, saw what had happened and was forced to accept it.

Planetary Nagas frequently budded off small pieces of themselves, creating a *self* as opposed to the far vaster and more powerful *Self*. Riding in nanotechnically grown bodies inherited from civilizations destroyed in ages long past, those fragments could sally forth into the great gulf at the center of the universe to explore. When a *self* returned, it melded with the parent once more, and the knowledge it had gained while separate pooled with the ocean of knowledge that had remained behind. >>DEVCAMERON<< had just done something similar, duplicating his mind and downloading it into the Naga probe ship. Unfortunately, his memories were a part of that mind; from his point of view, he'd somehow just mysteriously changed places with the duplicate.

His new body had been grown about a core of hydrogen and was powered by an ingenious device grown by the DalRiss in mimicry of human quantum power taps. Using a pair of tuned microsingularities to draw power from the quantum energy fluctuations of hard vacuum, the QPT produced energy enough to turn hydrogen into white-hot plasma constrained by magnetic fields within the Naga fragment's body. Released astern, a thin, hard, stream of matter expelled at relativistic velocities, the plasma had sufficient thrust to drive the Naga wedge forward, a living rocket.

>>DEVCAMERON<< experimented with his new body for a moment. Damn it, it *felt* like just a few hours ago he'd been safely aboard the *Sirghal*, thinking about how he could duplicate himself, providing an expendable human mind for the passage through the Device.

The coldness of his own rationalizations surprised him. He'd been well aware that his duplicate would be expendable, something that could be sent through the Device to the other side with only a faint hope of recovering it later. Hell, he'd been thinking at the time that he could create tens, even hundreds of duplicates and keep sending them through until one, at last, was able to get back with some useful information.

Dev Cameron—and for the first time in many years it was *not* >>DEVCAMERON<< who was examining the question—saw himself, saw what he had become, in a new light. Being the expendable duplicate could change your entire perspective.

Hell, he thought a bit wildly. *It could ruin your whole day.*

"Don't think of it that way," >>DEVCAMERON<< told him from the fastness of *Sirghal,* looming above and around him now like a vast, black mountain.

"That's easy for you to say," he told himself. "You'll be nice and safe here while I'm dropping down the throat of an alien time-and-space machine."

"You know you want to find out what's on the other side."

"How do you know that?"

"You and I didn't part that long ago. *I* want to know what's over there. Don't you?"

He thought about it, but only for a few seconds. "Yes. Yes, I do."

"I envy you."

"You might not if you were sitting where I am."

But the bitterness was gone. The initial shock, anger, even disappointment, he was realizing, had been caused mostly by the surprising shift in his point of view, so firmly had he expected to be back aboard the *Sirghal,* launching his second self aboard the probe. Now that *he* was the probe, however, he found he was looking forward to this. His exploration would be dangerous . . . but the greatest danger was that he might emerge in an area of space-time far removed from another Device. If that happened, he would be marooned; his Naga probe had no starfaring capabilities of its own. Even his reserves of reaction mass, the hydrogen used to propel him forward and adjust his pitch, yaw, and roll, were sharply limited. If he couldn't just turn around on the other side and come back, he would die . . . eventually.

Eventually might be a long time, too. Once powered up, his

quantum power tap was self-sustaining and would provide energy indefinitely. He no longer depended on such bulky inconveniences as food or air. He could live for quite a long time on the other side, even after his hydrogen ran out. He wondered what the limiting factor was. Proton decay? The disintegration of his Naga's cellular structure?

His destination was sure to be a place of wonder. He would not be bored.

Maybe that's what being an optimist is, Dev thought wryly. *You find the best way to look at something no matter which side of the argument you're on.*

He found he enjoyed the irony of arguing with himself. Once the initial surprise had worn off, it was much like downloading a jig program—software that allowed you to have simulated discussions with imaginary fragments of your own personality. This was the first time, however, that Dev Cameron had ever experienced both sides of the conversation as two separate people, each a coherent, complex, and integrated personality in its own right.

As he began accelerating toward the end of the Device, outlined still in blue light cast by the Naga across his perceptions, he realized that he did want to go. For days, now, he'd been hungering for information on who had built this structure, and why, and what they were doing in a dead star system. Soon he would know.

He refused to say good-bye to himself. >>DEVCAMERON<< was a bastard, and he was still angry at his other self's cavalier attitude toward another intelligent being.

Thinking about that drew him up short. The attitude he was seeing—experiencing, rather—was identical to that of the DalRiss. For humans, perhaps the most alien feature of the DalRiss was the—literally—inhuman way they used other life forms . . . their Achievers, for instance, tailor-made to open paths for the DalRiss ships across light years, yet doomed to die upon accomplishing that feat. The DalRiss used life forms, both those they had created and those they merely encountered, the way humans used metal ores or stones or the raw materials converted by nanofabrication technology.

Was he losing his humanity? Had he been apart from other humans for too long?

Was there anything he could do about either?

The path of the alien ship had already been downloaded into the Naga probe's navigational storage. Firing short, precisely timed bursts from his main thruster, Dev descended toward the Device. He took a last look behind at the swiftly receding masses of the *Sirghal* and dozens of other DalRiss ships. The white dwarfs wheeled across the sky, trailing spiraling rivers of red fire. He was reminded of zero-G rhythmic gymnasts, swirling crimson streamers as they leaped and tumbled; the memory of Earth and New America was painfully sharp, and he turned his full attention to the growing silver needle ahead.

Time passed. He had to be careful in applying thrust, for the star-hot plasma from his main drive could have fried DalRiss ships with a careless flick of his tail. At last, though, he was on the proper track and accelerating inward, matching exactly the alien vessel's speed of approach. So little was known about the technology they were borrowing here; speed might well be as important as path in determining where— and when—he emerged.

So, too, might mass, for that matter. The probe possessed only a tiny fraction of the mass of those alien ships.

Well, it was too late to do anything about that now. The other Dev Cameron would correct it next time around, if he failed to report back.

It occurred to him that he needed a name for his living vessel, something more than "the Naga probe."

"*Katya*," he said.

"Sorry, Brother," his other self said. "I didn't quite catch that."

"I've named the probe '*Katya*,' " he said.

There was a long silence from the DalRiss fleet. "It seems appropriate."

"Listen. If you make it back and I—" He stopped, flustered. Here he was, giving himself a message. "Staticjack," he said. "I think I'm schizzing out."

"Hold it together a little longer, Brother. You're almost

there. We read you nearing the horizon where the aliens vanished.''

The Device swelled in front of him, an immense wall of mercury-bright silver rotating so quickly that there were no details of surface at all. All of his Perceivers' eyes were trained on the thing; strain as he might, Dev could see only silver and a wavering of vision at the edge of the ultraviolet that might be some sort of force field or even a twisting of light through strangely bent space.

Lights appeared, ahead and to either side . . . an artificial effect, he decided, designed to serve as a guide for inbound ships. The lights receded into the distance, outlining a tunnel that appeared to go on and on forever into the depths of the Device.

Then he realized that he could no longer see the Device at all. It had vanished as light flared around him, the beacons shifting into streaks of rainbow glory.

He plunged into strangeness. Stars filled his universe.

And more stars . . . and *more*. . . .

Cascades . . . waterfalls . . . blizzards of stars. Dazzling hosts of stars, many brighter than Venus seen at its brightest on Earth, though most of these were tinted in orange or crimson instead of the blue-white diamond brilliance of Venus. They shouldered one another across the heavens in crowded choruses, embedded in diaphanous streams and rivers and isolated tags of star stuff.

A globular cluster! he thought. *I've emerged inside a globular cluster!* Then he began studying the almost painful brightness encircling him more carefully and recognized the truth. This was no mere star cluster, but the heart of the Galaxy itself. He was adrift in a star-filled bubble at the Galactic Core.

Excitement throbbing within and behind the center of his awareness, he extended his Perceivers' range to check his entire surroundings. First things first. Could he return?

A blurred, silver wall stretched across Heaven at his back, a Device identical, so far as he could see, to the one suspended between Frost's double suns. There was no sign of the stellar gas stripped from the two stars. Then again, perhaps that wasn't so strange after all. Both streams were being funneled into different gates; with the near-infinite choice of paths available in the bent space near one of those ultra-massive spinning cylinders, it would have been astonishing had the star plasma appeared here as well.

He was as awash in strangeness as he was in the light of myriad suns. Stars and impenetrable walls of glowing dust and gas created the impression of a vast, distant wall, a globe, really, enclosing him, impenetrable in a cloudy ring about the globe's equator, thinner to the point of star-thick translucency at the poles. Other senses were bombarded besides the visual. He tasted X-rays sleeting past the *Katya*, and with them came the bite and sting of high-energy particles, electrons, and free protons whirling through the Galactic Core. Radio shrilled, a hiss like ocean surf but unending and monotonous. High and to his left, a pulsar strobed, synchotron radiation flickering in pulses measured in hundredths of a second, a steady and annoying buzz mingled with other sounds and sensations and impressions too varied and too intense to assimilate all at once. It was sobering to realize, however, that had he still been organic he would have been dead within seconds of emerging from the gate. The radiation filling that volume of space would have thoroughly cooked any creature evolved for existence on the tame and sheltered surface of a planet.

Which led to the question of why the Naga that formed most of the body of the *Katya* wasn't being cooked. Nagas were certainly organic; they were carbon-based-organic, in fact, more like humans in that one respect than were the carbon-sulfur-based DalRiss. He queried the Naga fragment about how it was able to survive that torrent of radiation but received no meaningful answer. Massing only a few hundred tons, the probe wasn't large enough to support many mental capabilities beyond the strictly routine management of life support, of maintaining and communicating with Dev's downloaded consciousness, of the physics of maneuvering and control. It not only didn't know the answer, it didn't even understand the question.

Possibly, Dev mused, the Nagas had evolved the ability to withstand radiation eons ago because their reproductive cells had to survive the long journeys across the great central gulf, high-speed journeys that would subject them to a lot of hard radiation. He didn't think that was the answer . . . the whole answer, anyway. He sensed the radiation passing through the Naga ship-body, everything from cosmic rays to free electrons. There was no electromagnetic pulse—fortunately. His survival in this place depended on the Naga's cells being unable to conduct large jolts of EM radiation.

As he brought his initial surge of excitement under control, he began to study more closely everything within the reach of his sensors. He tried to judge the scale of the star-thronged panorama about him and failed. The cloudy walls circling Heaven, he decided, were the molecular clouds that ringed the Galactic Core, spanning a thousand light years; he could make out a great, fiery knot awash in a brilliant, hissing glow of radio energy to his right that might . . . *might* be the radio source known on Earth as Sagitarius B2. Within those walls, space was astonishingly empty, swept almost clean of dust and gas but large enough to still encompass uncountable billions of stars. Below, a great, tangled knot of blood and orange suns hung enmeshed in webs of gas and light, a globular cluster, in fact, in the act of being devoured by a hungry galaxy.

Ahead, though, perhaps four hundred light years distant, was greater strangeness still. Three vast spirals of gas, a galaxy in miniature, cartwheeled toward a central point. At the center, gas was compressed, violently, until it radiated throughout the spectrum from deep, thrumming radio to a cascade of glaring X-rays shining at its heart. The spiral arms were light years across; the accretion disk at the center no wider than a typical solar system. The black hole at the center, a monster possessing a million times the mass of Sol, was still invisible with distance.

Elsewhere, shapes, masses, radiations, objects, *things* competed for Dev's attention, a tumbling cacophony of sensory detail. Above and below, gas arced in wire-fine lines, curved to outline the flow of the Galaxy's magnetic field like iron filings over a child's bar magnet. To the left, a neutron star, gravitationally slingshotted from the vicinity of a black hole, was hurtling through space so fast it left a wake of ionized gas and howling radio.

But one object was so close that when he shifted his view to the right and down, it dominated the sky in that direction. He estimated its distance at light weeks rather than light years, though the heart of the thing was tiny with distance. That central accretion disk was not nearly so large as that of the great central black hole, which lay some three or four hundred light years away. Judging from the probe's gravitational sensors, it massed only fifteen times Earth's Sun, but it was bracketed by twin beams of X-rays and cosmic rays that made it far brighter than its larger, more distant cousin. Most of the radiation was being generated by great fountains of positrons jetting out from the poles for light years before being annihilated in a seething froth of raw energy by their interaction with the normal matter in space.

Dev knew about that particular radiation source. He had a fair amount of data on file about peculiar astronomical objects, and this was one that had been known on Earth for centuries. On astronomers' charts of the Galactic Core it carried the prosaic legend 1E1740.7-2942, though twentieth-century cosmologists had tagged it with a more colorful nickname: The Great Annihilator. That radiation signature, tagged by the 511-keV line from the disintegration of positronium, had been known since the 1970s, and in all those centuries, the exact mechanism for the creation of so much energy had been a mystery. Astronomers had been certain that antimatter was being created and destroyed here; what they couldn't determine was *how*.

Closer now to The Great Annihilator than any man had ever been, close enough to *see* the thing by visible light instead of solely by X-rays or gamma rays and the radio yowl of evaporating suns, Dev was no closer to an answer.

And there was something more. . . .

"Enhance," he told the Perceivers. "Damn it, give me a better view of that thing! I can't *see*. . . ."

The Great Annihilator expanded in Dev's vision. He was looking down at it from an angle of about forty-five degrees; one of the positron jets flared up and past his line of sight, vanishing into unguessable distance toward the star-thin pole of the great bubble. He guessed that the Device was in orbit about the black hole, though at this distance, a single circuit would take millennia. With his Perceivers magnifying the view, and by stopping down the glare from the hotter, brighter radiations emerging from that hellhole, he was able to make out details of the accretion disk.

The disk itself was little more than a colorful smear of very hot dust and gas, glowing a deep, sullen, somber red-brown near its outer edges but rapidly growing hotter and bluer as it spiraled through the spectrum and swirled into the bottomless pit of the gravitational singularity at its center. But beyond the feathery outer fringes of the disk . . .

A *ring*?

Struggling to make out details, Dev turned the *Katya* to face the enigma. Accelerating would do little good; at his maximum possible acceleration, the accretion disk was many months away, and he would expend all of his hydrogen reserves trying to reach it. But it looked as though the black hole was circled by a ring, an artificial ring more slender in comparison to its diameter than a child's hoop.

Like the rings of Saturn or Mimir or any of a hundred other gas giants throughout the Shichiju, the ring about the black hole was probably—it *must* be—made up of trillions of separate bits, but Dev couldn't shake the feeling that he was looking at a solid structure, albeit one on a scale undreamed of by any human engineer. At a conservative guess, that ring would be twenty astronomical units across, yet it showed what looked like regular structures, lines and marks and hard edges that carried the impression of something solid, something *manufactured*.

Shaken, Dev decided that it was time to go. He couldn't reach the thing, and any excursion he made partway toward it in the hope of getting a better view carried the risk that he would not be able to return. He and his Naga host had not suffered from the intense radiation yet, but he didn't want to assume that they were invulnerable.

And >>DEVCAMERON<< ought to see this, this *thing* at the Galaxy's core.

The attack came suddenly, without warning. So intent had he been on the accretion disk that all of his Perceivers had moved around to study it; the positron beam came from behind, from the direction of the Device, burning through the Naga's thick, mottled surface like a laser through butter.

Pain . . . !

. . . as quickly stilled as the Naga switched off those portions of Dev's awareness, but for an instant he'd felt that beam like a blowtorch eating through his back.

Shifting his Perceivers back to where he could see, he saw the ships—a bizarre zoo of wildly different shapes and sizes and textures bearing down on him out of the Device.

Katya was not unarmed. There'd been just enough doubt about the motives of someone who casually destroyed stars with living worlds around them that they'd jury-rigged a weapon, a high-G mass driver to sling bits of Naga at an enemy, like relativistic bullets . . . but there simply wasn't time to put up any kind of a decent defense. That first shot had sliced halfway through *Katya*'s hull, spilling precious hydrogen into the void. A quarter of the hull was in a near-molten state, glowing bright orange, the individual Naga cells that comprised it fused and lifeless.

He tried broadcasting by radio . . . but there was no response; the attackers flashed past him on every side, and more were emerging second by second from the Device. Their exit paths, he noted, were different from the one he'd arrived through. Another beam hit him; another narrowly missed as he triggered his drive, thrusting ahead at ten Gs. Blue and orange fire lit the sky, bathing him in harsh radiations.

Information. He'd come here for information. If the bastards wouldn't talk, perhaps there was another way . . .

He picked a craft that was coming toward him almost bow on, targeting the center of the smooth and organically curved mass and loosing a stream of pellets. With a small quantum power tap for energy, he could accelerate several grams to significant fractions of light speed; when those grams struck, raw energy flared in a dazzling sunburst between Dev and the Device, a ballooning cloud of plasma . . .

. . . out of which the alien ship emerged an instant later.

The kinetic energy released by that impact would have vaporized any human ship, but then these ships, or some of them, had plunged into the depths of a star and emerged whole days later. These things were *tough*.

But then . . . perhaps they were mortal after all. The craft he'd shot was tumbling, part of its gray-black hull glowing blue-hot with the impact. Dev adjusted his course and accelerated. There would be no better time or way to learn the nature of whatever was behind this technology.

Naga probe and tumbling alien vessel met in direct impact, a shattering collision that shredded much of Dev's forward half and all but demolished the alien vehicle. The shock jarred Dev, and he felt some of his programming slipping away, parts of his memory, parts of his personality literally fragmenting as the Naga died around him.

But the Naga was clinging to the alien wreckage, assimilating it like a great, black amoeba trying to absorb a bit of food larger than itself. *The alien must measure,* Dev thought, *nearly half a kilometer in length and must mass hundreds of thousands of tons.* Shock and recognition burst within his mind; the alien was much like a Naga, the ship itself a living creature . . . or was it, instead, a fantastically sophisticated machine?

He couldn't tell and didn't have time to investigate with care. He had time for only the briefest of glimpses into an alien mind . . .

CONFUSION. LACK OF INTEGRATION. PART OF THE WEB REFUSED DIRECTION AND HAS BECOME DANGEROUS. INTEGRATE. REINTEGRATE. CORRECTION. WEB CELL HAS BECOME CORRUPTED. NEGATIVE-INTEGRATE. DESTROY. DESTROY. ELIMINATE NONRESPONSIVE AND NONINTEGRATIVE WEB CELLS IMPERATIVEIMPERATIVEIMPERATIVE . . .

Contact was broken as the alien wreckage tore free, spinning clear of the shattered Naga's grasp. Less than a third of the original Naga shell remained now, and what was left was not enough to maintain the stability of Dev's personality. The strain of trying to assimilate, to understand that bizarre consciousness he'd briefly touched was taking its toll as well. He could still see into the depths of that mind, and what he saw there was burning, unspeakable, unintelligible horror. . . .

He was dying. He could feel it . . . feel his mind slipping away now, like water through cupped but trembling fingers. The Naga was dying swiftly as *Katya* spun wildly through space, trailing bits of itself in an expanding cloud of destruction. The disintegration of his host hardware would end the program that called itself Dev Cameron.

Too, strangeness was tearing at what was left of rational thought. The alien's mind. He tried to clear his thoughts. There was *something* he had to do, something of vital importance. . . .

Information. He had to get information to . . . to himself. That didn't make sense. He was *here.* Or . . .

He couldn't remember . . . couldn't remember—

No . . . he did remember. The horror . . . the alien horror of that mind, of what he'd seen there. He had to tell . . . someone . . . somehow. . . .

With virtually the last of his mental energy, Dev mustered control and will enough to focus on a last set of commands.

As his body disintegrated, Dev launched one final missile, flinging it on hard-driven magnetic fields toward the spinning Device. . . .

Dev Cameron died long before the missile reached its objective.

Chapter 10

What nature delivers to us is never stale. Because what nature creates has eternity in it.

—ISAAC BASHEVIS SINGER
C.E. 1978

For moments only, >>DEVCAMERON<< savored the wonder that lay beyond the Device.

They'd detected the probe emerging from the strange space close beside the Device. At first, Dev had thought they were receiving anomalous readings of some sort . . . or that they were witnessing an entirely new type of ship coming through the gateway, for what was coming through was a ragged lump of matter, about a meter or a meter and a half long and massing only about a hundred kilograms. Then the lump began emitting its beacon, a bit of programmed radio chirping that said, essentially, that it needed help. It was a piece of Naga, its outer shell hardened to withstand vacuum, its core still fluid, and with complexity enough to pattern some small part of the entity >>DEVCAMERON<< had sent through less than thirty minutes before.

It took some time for *Sirghal* to intercept the object; DalRiss cityships were not designed with the idea of having them perform fine maneuvers, and the object had emerged from the Device with a speed of only a few kilometers per second, too slow to escape—or even orbit—the massive spinning Device. >>DEVCAMERON<< eventually had his hosts create another probe, one intelligent enough to operate on its own without his mind riding along to supervise, and sent it to gather in the drifting fragment. Back aboard *Sirghal*, then, >>DEVCAMERON<< reached out a mental connection and began downloading the memories stored there. In the space of seconds, he'd remembered for himself the glorious vistas at the Galaxy's core, remembered the black holes and their attendant accretion disks, the stars, the clouds like vast, star-filled walls . . . and the Ring.

Wonder followed wonder then, in rapid-fire succession. The attack . . . the pain, my *God* the pain . . . the deliberate collision with a damaged alien vessel . . . the flood of thoughts as alien as those of a wild Naga but lacking some quality that made the Naga seem charmingly familiar by comparison. He wasn't sure he could identify precisely the difference in character between the two—they were eerily similar in some ways—but he thought it might have to do with the flexibility, the adaptability of Naga thought.

These alien memories he'd glimpsed here were as rigid and as unyielding as nanolaticed diacarb. His initial thought, as he heard that voice, was that you could *talk* to a Naga, if you could get its attention in the first place, and give it something new to think about.

There would be no talking to these people.

He'd not yet had time to fully assimilate everything that was there when something, when *many* somethings, began coming through the Stargate.

Living machines. That much, at least, was clear about the intelligence that had built the Device.

"This time they seem to have taken notice of us," a DalRiss voice said in >>DEVCAMERON'S<< mind.

"My God," >>DEVCAMERON<< said, watching as the space between the DalRiss fleet and the Device turned mist-frosted with the sheer number of glittering craft appearing out of the gateway. "How many of them are there?"

"Unable to determine a precise number. They are appearing faster than our Perceivers can record them. The total number is on the order of ten to the seven."

"Try to establish communication." The Web used radio to coordinate their activities, among other forms of communication. He indicated the frequencies his alter-self had heard on the other side of the gate. "Use these channels."

INTEGRATE. INTEGRATE. NEGATIVE INTEGRATION. PART OF THE WEB HAS REFUSED INTEGRATION. PART OF THE WEB HAS REFUSED DIRECTION AND HAS BECOME DANGEROUS. WEB CELL HAS BECOME CORRUPTED. ELIMINATE NONRESPONSIVE AND NON-INTEGRATIVE WEB CELLS: . . .

He cut off the torrent of harsh, mechanical-sounding words, translated through the matrix of the Naga fragment recovered from the other side. Rigid? These people didn't want to talk to anyone or anything that wasn't part of their Web.

Or . . . was there a clue in that fragment of noncommunication?

Part of the Web has refused direction. . . .

''They attack . . . !''

Nightmare followed. This portion of the DalRiss fleet numbered some eighty cityships. An estimated fifty to eighty *million* machines were coming through the Stargate. Though there was no time to catalogue their types or study them in detail, >>DEVCAMERON'S<< impression was that they were all different, no machine quite like any other. The range in size was both enormous and bewildering. There were ships coming through the Stargate that were the size and mass of small moons, several hundred kilometers long, their surfaces bristling with literal forests of antennae and weapon arrays and less identifiable projections; the smallest of the ships scarcely registered on the DalRiss Perceiver enhancements, tiny things that massed no more than a handful of gossamer, driven along at accelerations of hundreds of Gs by intense beams of laser light projected by their larger brothers. The vast majority were in between the two extremes, a few tens or hundreds of meters long and massing a few hundred or a few thousand kilograms.

They attacked with devastating swiftness, power, and accuracy. Their weapons, almost as diverse as their shapes, included lasers and particle beams, missiles and hurled projectiles, nanotechnic disassembler clouds and a host of less easily identified destructive agents.

The lead elements of that mechanical horde carved through the DalRiss ships like a laser through soft, moist clay . . . or flesh, which was, after all, what they were. Five cityships, and the tens of thousands of DalRiss and the various Riss symbionts aboard them, died in the first second of combat, almost before anyone was aware of what was happening.

They fought back. The Naga fragment serving as nervous system for each of the huge living cityships had a small asteroid at its core to draw on—the source of the raw materials it used for its own growth, and for the growth and repair of its hosts. Slits opened up between the starfish arms; lumps of asteroidal rock, manipulated by intense magnetic fields, streaked across space with the unerring accuracy of an organic Naga computer, and the oncoming machine ships began dying one after another in spectacular miniature novae.

But at odds of a million to one . . .

Sirghal had taken a dozen serious hits; a cloud of living machines, most gossamer-thin wisps driven by laser light, fell onto the DalRiss creature's surface like the whirling snowflakes of a wind-whipped blizzard, coating the ship-creature's outer hide in layer upon layer of gray-white matter, molecule-sized machines that changed their order and their actions so quickly they defied analysis.

They were eating the ship's outer hull, literally disassembling it bite by microscopic bite. . . .

The DalRiss hurled lumps of asteroidal material at the larger targets, destroying hundreds, even thousands . . . but there were too many of them for the entire DalRiss fleet to even make a dent in those oncoming hordes, and they had no weapons at all useful against the sticky, disassembling masses of programmed, molecule-sized machines that were beginning to coat each of the living ships. The battle, if that's what such a one-sided slaughter could be called, lasted for all of three or four seconds, and then, one by one . . . then in fives and tens, the cityships began flickering from view, shifting out and away, vanishing as their Achievers put forth their wills and their lives and transported their charges across space.

>>DEVCAMERON<< felt the *Sirghal* gathering its organic energies. There was a lurching sensation, a whirling moment of confused impressions. . . .

They were alone, in a different point in space.

"Where are we?" >>DEVCAMERON<< asked.

"Someplace else."

The white dwarfs and the Device were gone. In their place, a nebula unfolded transparent wings of blue and red and white across Heaven.

And the battle wasn't over yet, for the machine gossamer-things still clung to parts of *Sirghal*'s surface, dismantling it like nanodisassemblers. Fortunately, with no other attackers to distract them, the DalRiss aboard could deal with the drifts of deadly molecules. The Naga fragment at the ship's core extruded a portion of itself, flowing out and over the cityship's surface, engulfing and absorbing the plague like an amoebic antibody devouring a mass of pathogenic bacteria.

By patterning the information recorded in those scraps of biomechanical matter, the Naga was able to add a bit more to the stores of data already being compiled on the Web . . . but not very much. The gossamer projectiles had known little, save their basic programming to coat and dismantle and destroy. Still, they possessed some identity. They were the Web.

As was everything else in the universe.

Shaken by the attack, shaken more by the emotion-laden images from his alter-self that he was still trying to assimilate and reconcile, >>DEVCAMERON<< struggled to understand the alien viewpoint. At its core, he thought, was a strangely shifted perception of self.

That concept of self interested >>DEVCAMERON<<, for it was a concept at the heart of the alien worldview of the Naga as well. Where the Naga held a sharply binary distinction of *self* and *not-self*, however, the Web perceived itself not as a part of the cosmos, but as the cosmos in its entirety. Everything, from the assembled multitude of other machines all working together in an invisible latticework of communications to the farthest, most distant star in the heavens, was a part of self.

Some parts of self, evidently, were less communicative or pliable or receptive to central direction than others, however, and had to be integrated—reintegrated, rather—into the whole.

It was, >>DEVCAMERON<< thought, an astonishingly egocentric viewpoint.

"What should we do now?" he asked the DalRiss around him. "Where is the rest of the fleet?"

"We had no prepared rendezvous," was the answer, and >>DEVCAMERON<< felt an icy chill of dismay as he heard it. "We assumed that it would always be possible to coordinate the activities of our Achievers. Unfortunately, there was no time. Each of the cityships must have chosen a unique destination, as did *Sirghal*."

"Then . . . the fleet must be scattered across . . . what? How great a distance?"

"We estimate that we are now some nine hundred light years from the Device. The others would have jumped similar distances, but in similarly random directions."

"Then the fleet is scattered across a volume of space almost two thousand light years across.'' He thought about that a moment, and about what he knew of DalRiss psychology. He doubted that the individual cityships would continue their explorations separately. All would want to regroup, if for no other reason than to assemble and coordinate what they'd learned in the brief battle at the Stargate.

And *Dev Cameron* needed to talk again to humans.

The shift in his perception of himself was startling. He was no longer >>DEVCAMERON<<, the human-Naga-DalRiss hybrid of patterned memories and intricately self-programming self-awareness that had existed for decades in symbiosis with the DalRiss-Naga union of the cityship *Sirghal*, but Dev Cameron . . . a mind adrift in an alien body, but distinctly and uniquely himself. What was the difference? He wasn't certain, though he thought the key was the odd split in perceptions of himself and his attitudes engendered by the duplication of himself before the probing of the Stargate.

His self-copy had not liked what it had seen of its original. Reassimilated, the copy did not fit as it should have. Attitudes had changed. Awareness of itself and its goals and its interpretation of its own memories had changed. This almost-duplicate continued to exist as a part of Dev's being, an uncomfortable near-fit that jarred and jangled, like a squeal of feedback over an improperly adjusted sound system.

Coming to terms with himself would have to wait, however. More important was the Web's perception of self, which, Dev was increasingly certain, could be a serious danger not only to the DalRiss fleet, but to the sphere of human-colonized space as well. The Web must have first evolved eons ago at or near the Galactic Core, but for eons they'd been spreading from world to world, from system to system, going farther and farther afield both in space and—astonishment!—in time. As he studied the Web's perception of its surroundings, he realized that time meant far less to the machines than it did to organic life not because they were virtually immortal, but because the Stargates were gateways through time as well as space.

Realization chilled . . . and brought a sharp stab of wonder with it. That odd clustering of novae in one small portion of the sky within a single forty-year period noted by human astronomers early in the twentieth century. . . .

Swiftly, Dev downloaded all of the data he had access to on novae, with particular emphasis on their distances from Earth and on when they'd been recorded on Earth. The individual novas were scattered across an incredibly vast area of space. Nova Aquila was twelve hundred light years away and had exploded in about C.E. 700 for its light to reach Earth in 1918; another fast, bright nova in the same general part of the sky was Nova Cygni, which had shone in Earth's skies in 1920 and was about four thousand light years distant. An odd recurrent nova, WZ Sagitta, had erupted first in 1913 and then again several times after that, and was three hundred light years from Earth. There were dozens of other examples. The clustering in space was odd, of course, but the clustering in time was odder still. Working backward, those three novae had actually exploded in about C.E. 1600, C.E. 700, and B.C.E. 3000 . . . and yet the outward expanding shells of light marking their detonations had all reached Earth within the same seven-year period.

Swiftly, he studied record after record. Clearly, the Web was working in time as well as in space, detonating stars in such a way that, despite their separations in space, the light of the various explosions was merging, traveling outward *together* in a vast shell expanding at the speed of light.

The shift in perspective required by this realization staggered Dev. His first thought, that there was something special about Earth's position, he discarded almost at once. Superficially, it might appear that those stars, if destroyed deliberately, had been exploded at varying times across varying distances so that their light signatures, their funeral pyres, would all reach Earth at roughly the same time, but Dev was seeing the information now in a new and grander perspective. Earth, or its location, had nothing to do with the timing of those novae; what had been coordinate was the placement of the expanding shells of light radiation.

Seen from a distance of some tens of thousands of light years, those expanding wavefronts of light might resemble a number of nested bubbles . . . a structure, in fact, vast beyond belief, constructed entirely of photons.

Dev had absolutely no idea *why* such a thing would be constructed, or what purpose it could possibly serve. Unlike the rare supernovae, which could briefly outshine all of the other stars of their galaxy combined, novae were not especially brilliant when seen from a great distance away. Nova Aquila, when it exploded almost two thousand years ago, had briefly shone over 400,000 times more brilliantly than Earth's sun; at its brightest, it had been brighter than every other star in Earth's sky except Sirius . . . bright, certainly, and unusual for its extreme change in brightness, but in practical terms it was simply another point of light in the sky.

What could the purpose of these nested bubbles, expanding out through the Galaxy at the speed of light, possibly be?

Study it closer. What are you seeing?

The merging of bubbles would be different along different axes of the multiple shells' propagations, of course. There was still a coincidence, somehow, in the fact that so many wavefronts of exploding stars should be jammed up together as seen from Earth; viewed from a different direction, they would not reinforce one another that way.

Reinforcement? The word triggered a new idea.

Certain novae seen from Earth seemed to nest together that way in space and in time; as he added the records of more and more novae to his calculations, however, Dev saw that there were in reality many axes extending in different directions through the galaxy, their shapes defined by expanding, closely nested bubbles of light. You had to be selective in what you were looking at to see the patterns; where the waves piled up together in space and in time— such as the peculiar alignment of novae seen from Earth in the early twentieth century—there *was* a kind of reinforcement, like the lock-step march of wavelengths in a laser; elsewhere, expanding bubbles intersected rather than reinforced, causing rippling patterns of interference. . . .

Interference patterns, like those in some titanic holographic record. Now *there* was an idea. . . .

There was no time to think more about it, however. One of

the DalRiss, linked to a Perceiver, announced the appearance of yet more machines, some ten light minutes away.

The distance was illuminating. If the light of their arrival was reaching the *Sirghal* only now, they must have materialized in this part of space ten minutes ago . . . or within a minute or so of *Sirghal*'s escape and arrival. Somehow, the Web had tracked them across almost a thousand light years of space.

He couldn't imagine how. He didn't think they used K-T space, the way human stardrives did, nor did they seem to use the same space-folding techniques employed by the DalRiss. He'd assumed they needed the Stargate to open gravitationally warped pathways or wormholes across the light years—past them, rather—but as he watched, machine upon malevolent space-faring machine was appearing out of empty space.

They could have been projected there by the Stargate, he realized. Possibly, they were using it as a kind of one-way slingshot, hurling these vessels after the fugitive DalRiss. That implied a staggering control of space and time, to be able to launch a pursuit fleet across nine hundred light years and be accurate in targeting to within ten light minutes . . . .

More horrifying still was the determination behind that feat. If it was true they could only cross distances of light years by using the Device as a kind of one-way launcher, this new wave of machine-vessels was in fact here on a suicide mission, with the expectation that none of its members would ever be able to return.

"Quick!" Dev thought to those minds watching with his. "We must jump again!"

"We need time to orient our Achievers. Another random jump could lose us among the stars forever."

"Nor is there assurance that we could escape," another voice said. "If they could track us once, perhaps they can track us through unlimited transitions."

"We can't fight them," Dev said. Already, the Web machines numbered in the tens of thousands, and all were accelerating rapidly toward the *Sirghal*. Was the same thing happening to the other DalRiss survivors at this moment, scattered all across this part of the Galaxy? "Our only hope is to jump, and keep on jumping until we lose them.''

''And then?''

''And then,'' Dev continued with a determination born of dawning fear and horror at the scope of this threat, ''then— after we're very sure that we've lost them—we must return to human space. I think they need to know what we've found out here.''

''I hope it is possible to lose them,'' a DalRiss voice said doubtfully. ''To have followed us this far implies a staggering level of technological achievement, either in calculation, or in the ability to track or observe across vast distances.''

''Agreed. But I'm inclined to believe that they need the Device to send their machines across light years.'' He watched the horde gathering for a moment. ''If we don't move fast, though, they won't have to track us, will they?''

Before the horde reached them, then, *Sirghal* vanished, losing itself among the stars.

It would be a long time before the DalRiss found themselves once more.

Chapter 11

The unresting progress of mankind causes continual change in the weapons; and with that must come a continual change in the manner of fighting.
—*The Influence of Seapower upon History*
ALFRED THAYER MAHAN
C.E. 1830

Kara stood in the fresher, one hand lightly touching once again the unfamiliar outlines of her face, an unconscious reassurance that her *jissai no men,* her ''reality's face,'' was still in place. It was still hard to believe that that was *her*.

Since only Japanese were permitted on Mars, Kara had assumed a Japanese persona. Her Naga, with the same mutability that allowed it to mold bone and tissue into electronic sockets and other hardware, or transform her skin into psychedelic colors, lights, and patterns, had literally reshaped her face, right down to the fine structure of the bone itself. A painful process, that, except that her Companion could control input from her nervous system during the reworking of her features and filter out the pain. But it did leave her face feeling ... *strange*, unfamiliar, and even after three weeks it was still a shock when she looked in a mirror.

Her face now literally was a *men*, both face and mask, as well as her passport to a forbidden world.

Only Nihonjin—people of Japanese ancestry—were allowed to set foot on the world now called Kasei. Even in synchorbit the activities of visiting gaijin businessmen were carefully supervised. This restriction extended even to non-Japanese citizens of Dai Nihon—Greater Japan—those citizens of Singapore, the Philippines, Vancouver, and the other Earthside outposts of the Empire that were Japanese in name, but not in ancestry. To walk the sands of Kasei, you had to trace your ancestry back to the Home Islands.

Which was why Kara was traveling in disguise. She'd first taken a commercial liner from New America to Eridu, a voyage of thirty-six light years and some five weeks. There, she'd taken passage aboard the Imperial liner *Teikoku* for the three-week passage to Sol. She'd been traveling aboard one ship or another for two months now, but she was finally at her destination. An hour before, she'd checked into the Sorano Hoteru, Aresynch's largest hotel. Spin gravity here was set to about one-third G, the same as that on the Martian surface.

Sergeant Vasily Lechenko was here too, along with three other volunteers from the Phantoms' 1/1. The way she'd heard it, he'd point-blank refused to step back even when the CMI personnel in charge of ops preparation had pointed out that his 193-centimeter, 104-kilo mass was not the norm for the Japanese phenotype.

Kara was glad the big sergeant was so stubborn. He made

an impressive-looking Japanese businessman, all hard muscle beneath his Naga-reshaped facial features and a tan and white Sony business uniform. He and his men would be her security backup as she penetrated the Kasei Net, and they would be her one chance of getting out of this place again when she was done.

Security at Aresynch was tight, and smuggling weapons in had been a problem. She took a final look around the fresher, as she'd already checked her room, paying special attention to the nooks and crannies of the room's small fresher closet, sink, and toilet. Had the Naga residing within her detected the carrier wave of a hidden transmitter, it would have silently and inwardly alerted her. But there was nothing save the normal radio traffic that could be expected in a building such as this.

There were, of course, no guarantees. A television pickup constructed through molecular nanotechnics could be the size of the head of a pin, and listening devices were smaller still. Her one hope of security lay in the fact that too many people passed through this station every day for Imperial Security to bother tracking them all.

In the fresher, she stood in front of the sink, removing a small can of hair spray, a travel hair dryer, a solid gold brooch, and a pocket TV-computer from her toiletries case and laying them out on the counter. All of the articles worked as advertised and, indeed, the hair dryer, brooch, and the TV were exactly what they seemed to be.

The hair spray was something more. With pressure from her thumb and a deft twist, she popped the can's base off; inside, tucked into a small recess, was a wad of pale gray clay just a little larger than her thumbnail. Placing the clay on the counter next to the opened can and the other items, she wet her finger under the tap, then transferred a few drops of water to the substance.

At the water's touch, the clay began foaming, and Kara could hear a thin, sizzling hiss. In another moment, the dab of clay had doubled in size . . . then doubled again. Carefully, Kara nudged the gold brooch across the counter until it just touched the foaming goo.

Within fifteen minutes, the goo had eaten her brooch. It took another hour to dissolve the television, the hair dryer, and the spray can. She didn't stay to watch. Instead, she went back to the main room, where she sat at the computer access, exploring Aresynch. She spent two hours calling up maps and diagrams, and playing the self-guiding tutorial on the public access system.

When she returned to the fresher, the goo had evaporated completely, leaving only a trace of powdery residue, like talcum. The pocket television appeared unchanged; the gold and the lead it had concealed were gone completely; the plastic hair dryer, however, no longer looked anything like its original form. In its place was a small, sleek hand gun, just the size of Kara's palm.

The TV and pistol both went into a jumper pocket. Carefully she brushed the nanoresidue into her hand and disposed of it in the toilet. Taking a final look around to be certain she'd left no incriminating evidence, she closed up her case and switched off the computer. Standing inside the hotel room door, she pulled out the television and thumbed the color adjust tab; seconds later, the screen answered with a silent, printed message: OK.

It was time to go.

Tai-i Genji Ishimoto thought of it as a sea.

Though he was pure Japanese, the son of a respected Nihonjin architect, Ishimoto had been born in Jaffna on the north coast of the Imperial Dependency of Seiron—the former Sri Lanka. From the age of ten, his passion had been gill diving in the crystalline waters first of his home island, then farther afield, in the Maldives, the Philippines, and even the Great Barrier Reef. He'd joined the Imperial Navy because its education benefits would help him get both the downloads and the references he needed to get work on one of the big undersea colonies, Oki-Daito, perhaps, or the fabulous Ryoku-gyoku.

A decision that had carried him far indeed from the emerald seas of Earth. As if in compensation, however, his current assignment offered him the mental release of something akin to diving. It was only ViRsimulation, of course, provided by the Aresynch facility's Mark XXI AI, but it was the closest thing he'd found yet to gliding above a reef at ten meters, wearing nothing but gill helmet, fins, weight belt, and knife. Instead of an ocean of water, however, he was floating now through an ocean of data—but data manipulated by the AI to create an ongoing simulation through which Ishimoto could move with the freedom of a dolphin. The colors were those of a reef, emeralds and turquoise blues for the medium through which he swam, more colorful notes marking the specific stacks, clusters, and nodes to which he had access.

The AI had its own ICS—Internal Computer Security— of course, but Ishimoto was the human security watch, a backup to the automated systems who could apply not only intelligence but *feeling* to the task of monitoring the constant flow of data through the Net, searching for intruders who might be anything from small-time black marketeers looking for corporate access codes to Confederation spies. Human operators like Ishimoto gave the security system an extra edge against human system intruders, an edge that had more than once stopped a hostile break-in.

The ocean he swam in was enormous, a simulated sea that comprised the entire Kasei Net. The system was in fact the sum total of all on-line computer networks both on the surface of Kasei and throughout the length of the sky-el clear out to Deimos, as well as the computers aboard spacecraft temporarily linked into the Net. It was so vast that no merely human mind could take it all in; what he was seeing was an abstract, the equivalent of computer screen icons that allowed him to navigate the Net with both efficiency and ease, with the entire architecture, representing hardware and software both, visible as a crowded universe of coral heads and rocks, of sunken cities and wrecks, of fantastic shapes like tubes and platforms and two-dimensional planes and doorways and stranger constructs that had no real correlation with anything in Ishimoto's real-world experience. The voice of the AI itself—or one of the subroutines that made up the AI's total complex of personalities—was his guide.

And his guide had just spoken. "I detected a single set of unauthorized radio transmissions," the voice said in Ishimoto's mind. "It was quite brief, most likely a coded query and a reply."

"Where?"

"The transmissions were too brief to allow me to isolate their positions. Both, however, originated within the civilian complex."

Ishimoto frowned. The civilian complex was enormous. Unless the transmitters repeated themselves, they would be impossible to track down . . . a fact of which they were no doubt aware.

But the advantage was Ishimoto's. Alerted by the AI's senses, he was aware now that someone was engaged in unauthorized radio transmissions aboard the Aresynch facility. ICS took a dim view of that sort of thing. Unregistered radios were prohibited and were confiscated whenever scans of baggage or passengers turned them up. Such scans were almost useless, though; many visitors possessed two-way radio circuits grown inside their brains, and any spy worth the yen spent training him would have access to nano that could grow a transmitter out of innocuous raw materials.

Alerted, he could close in on the offenders, and when they moved again, he would be ready for them.

"That ought to do it," Kara said. They were in a zero-G module, adrift in one of Aresynch's largest public access comcenters.

Lechenko, floating at her side, nodded. "What bothers me is how much time it's going to take. You watch your tail in there, okay? We can watch for security types out here, but we can't do a goking thing about the on-line flamers."

"They'll never know I'm here." She wished she believed that.

She used a handrail to guide herself to one of the hundreds of burnished, egg-shaped modules fastened to the inside of the enormous sphere that housed the complex. Picking an unoccupied module, Kara glanced left and right, then tucked her legs up and slipped inside feet-first. Palming shut the privacy door, she settled back on the couch and strapped herself down. At a thought, her Companion extruded quicksilver filaments from her hand as she held it up to the access plate. She felt her Companion make contact with the Aresynch AI, a buzzing in her hand and just behind her eyes.

"Ikusa no chikazuki," she thought, focusing the Nihongo words into a coded upload onto the Net. "Military access. Code red-red-three, flash, blue."

"Military access granted, Level One" sounded in her mind.

I'm in, she thought, but she was careful not to let the words slip into an encoded upload.

"Communications center. Message upload, channel three-five-nine-two-zero. Priority routine."

"Communications channels accessed. Ready to accept message uplink."

The message had already been prepared, coded in a low-level, low-priority Imperial naval code used for routine traffic. With a thought, she uploaded the packet.

"Your message has been transmitted." The thought came back almost at once. "Do you wish to make another transmission?"

"Negative. Military access. Code red-blue-five, flash, green."

"Military access granted at Level Two" was the reply.

These initial levels were fairly easy to get at, the electronic equivalent of touching unlocked doors and watching them swing open. The tougher challenges still lay ahead.

As always when dealing with computer systems, even extremely powerful and intelligent ones, the only way to make the thing work was with patience and exacting precision.

One hundred fifty thousand kilometers outsystem from Mars, an old and decrepit tramp freighter detected a signal on a low-priority military channel. The name on the ship's hull, picked out in white katakana lettering just beneath the brow of her bridge and faded by years of micrometeorite scouring, was *Chidori Maru*. At this distance, Mars was tiny, a sliver of gold-orange aimed at a shrunken, yellow sun.

The message, had anyone aboard the ship bothered to decode it, was a request for information about the vessel's cargo—specifically about whether it should be listed as Class C or Class D on the docking off-load manifests.

The real meaning, however, lay in the fact that the message had been transmitted on that frequency at all. The ship's captain ordered a similarly coded reply, then turned to his first officer. "Very well, Mr. MacKenzie. Cry havoc, and let slip the dogs of war!"

Captain Johanson was a great fan of classic literature. His flare for the dramatic, however, was not as out of place this time as it often was. His cargo on this run might very easily, if poetically, be described as dogs of war.

The ship's cargo bay, located forward in her primary module, yawned open, spilling light into space. The single ascraft stowed inside was also a relic, her hull patched and worn, the surface streaked with rusty corrosion accumulated in the atmospheres of dozens of worlds. Once clear of the freighter, she fired her thrusters, the burn ticking off the long minutes necessary to set her falling toward the distant golden crescent of Mars.

Tai-i Ishimoto paused, tasting the emerald waters representing the computer network in the simulated space of the civilian-quarters comp-access node. Part of the swift-flowing currents he sensed about him was communications traffic to and from Aresynch, an enormous volume of ingoing and outgoing information, most of it automated. According to the AI, all was both routine and authorized. He was beginning to question that initial alert. It was possible that what the AI had detected was an electronic echo, an accidental rebroadcast by the circuitry in some civilian visitor's head of a standard automated signal. He'd heard of that sort of thing happening before, even with nonelectronic prostheses such as dental implants. The fact that there'd been two such signals, an apparent question coupled with a reply, might have been coincidence after all.

There wasn't much to go on. Still, duty demanded that he consider every alternative. If the unauthorized signals were indeed indicators of covert activity, the signalers might well have moved on by now. Where?

There wasn't enough clear evidence yet to warrant putting out an alarm, but Ishimoto thought a careful patrol of the military communications and computer access nodes was in order. Swerving left and diving, skimming the light-shimmering bottom with a relative speed more appropriate to a hypersonic aircraft than to a swimmer, he approached a massive coral head displaying holographic characters: RESTRICTED. MILITARY NODE 1. CODED ACCESS ONLY.

As watch officer, Ishimoto had the necessary codes riding on his persona like a uniform. He struck the coral head full on; without even a simulated shock, he passed through, emerging in another, deeper stretch of water.

The taste of the currents was different here, the coral formations larger and more menacing.

He was willing to bet his next leave on Earth that the intruders, if they existed, would be here. They might not be on the Net, but it was certain that they would need access to the Net to get information on whatever they'd come here to see or do.

When they did, they would make a mistake. No outsider could know the intricacies of the Kasei Net perfectly.

And when they made that mistake, Ishimoto would be waiting.

Kara was up to Security Level Five, and still there'd been no indication that her work on the Net had attracted any undue attention. She'd entered the Net deeply enough that she was now adrift in someone's ViReality, a simulation of a shallow, sunlit sea.

Though she was no swimmer, here was an AI fantasy where her knowledge of zero-G maneuvering stood her in good stead. She found she could stretch out virtual arms, push off with her legs, and send herself gliding through the simulation with the speed of a combat ascraft. Power of will alone, a mental shifting of her attention left or right, up or down, was all that was necessary for steering.

Dimly she was aware of other fellow travelers in the sea, shadowy forms that darted and flashed like wheeling fish, representations of running programs. Large objects—doorways, structures, even blocks of rock, or were they life forms of some sort, with their strange and colorful textures?—represented access to other levels and other nodes; most were identified by cryptic notations in blocky Japanese type. DENTATSU: KASEI NO HYOMEN, said one prominent mass of gnarled gold and white. "Communications: Martian Surface." That was where she wanted to go. Swinging left, she dove into the convoluted surface, a soundless, shockless explosion of light about her as she plunged into yet a deeper level of the Net.

The air/spacecraft dropped toward Mars. The men and women sealed into their combat machines within the transport's cargo bay could only wait, wondering if they'd achieved the surprise upon which all depended.

Lieutenant Randin Ferris lay inside the support module of his warstrider, a CVL-2 Red Saber, thinking about Kara . . . and about ViRsims. Even one time in a firefight was enough to convince any soldier that ViRsims, no matter how realistic, never quite carried the same level of reality as the real thing. Probably it was the knowledge that you wouldn't actually die in a simulation, wouldn't even feel more than a mild sting when someone shot you and booted you out of the link.

Ran wasn't entirely sure whether he was dreading this combat drop more for himself, or for Kara. Since he'd met her, two years before, he'd gone from thinking of her as fellow officer and occasional sex partner to someone that he cared for very deeply indeed. It had been all he could do, months before at that party at Kara's family's estate, not to let on how scared he was for her. He had the easy job. All he had to do was storm a heavily defended Imperial base. Kara had to penetrate that base's electronic defenses. And if she were caught—

"Hey, Lieutenant?"

It was Rob Lorre, one of the newbies in his unit, a twenty-year-old who went by the handle Mouther. "Yeah?"

"Is it true what they say about the Nihons? I mean, about how you don't want to be captured . . ."

"No one in his right mind wants to be captured, Mouth. What kind of null is this?"

"Yeah, but the Nihons got a rep for taking a guy apart real slow to get at what's in his brain."

"Kid, who's been downloading all this kuso on you?"

"Well, some of the guys were talking and—"

" 'Some of the guys.' Kid, you've got to stop listening to the who-was, you know? Putting too much meaning on barracks gossip'll screw your head up worse than the Impies will."

"Yeah, but—"

"Just do what I tell you and you'll come through okay. Linked?"

There was the slightest pause. "Linked, Lieutenant. Thanks."

He opened the channel to include all of the waiting warstriders. "All of you, start your finals. If you get scragged by enemy fire, we'll carry you out by hand if we have to, but if one of you gokers has a strider go down because you forgot to set your systems parameters, so help me you'll *walk* home!"

He started running through his own checklist, wishing there were a way to delete the worry dragging at him like a black hole's gravity well. It was all he could do to concentrate on the job at hand.

One way or the other, though, it wouldn't be long now.

Kara had successfully accessed the Planetary Communications node and from there moved up a level to Aresynch's traffic control center. Slipping into the ATCC messaging stack had dropped her out of the ocean simulation and into a blackness similar to a warstrider's first-stage link-in. At a mental command, windows expanded before her, showing computer-holos of Mars and the sky-el and the synchorbital, together with columns of data giving readouts on status, systems operations, and readiness levels. Orbiting ships were shown in blue; ships under power had their courses marked in red, while ships maneuvering in free-fall had their transfer orbits showing green.

In moments, she'd picked out both the ascraft and the freighter *Chidori Maru*, the latter in a standard approach vector toward Aresynch, the former now decelerating hard as it skimmed atmosphere over Kasei's night side. The ascraft had already been flagged as entering low orbit without proper clearance. Now she would find out whether the codes provided by Confederation Intelligence were as up to date as claimed. Insinuating herself into the AI's awareness, she presented it with a succession of numeric codes.

"This is not according to standard procedure," the machine told her. "You are not accessing this unit through an authorized channel."

"Accept Priority Code *Shiragiku*," she told it.

There was a tense pause as the AI considered this.

"Priority Code White Chrysanthemum accepted. I am ready to receive new instructions."

She had those new instructions ready, filed in a special uplink directory in her RAM. Swiftly, she uploaded the packet, her attention focused on the simulated display screen before her.

The warning flag pointing at the incoming ascraft vanished, replaced by the katakana symbol signifying "all correct," while the record of the incoming craft's transgression was silently deleted. As far as the system was concerned, all proper authorizations were on file, and all was as it should be.

"Accept Priority Code *Wakazakura*," she told the AI.

There was a longer pause this time, one stretching into seconds. Either the Net was unusually busy at the moment, or . . .

"Priority Code Young Chrysanthemum accepted. I am ready to receive new instructions."

The second code gave her immediate access to a different set of nodes on the Net, while allowing her to remain in her lookout position in ATCC. A new window opened, overlapping the first.

"Aresynch Defense Network," she said. "Targeting."

"Targeting accessed. Please upload target coordinates."

This was where things began getting ticklish. As with all sky-els, the synchorbit base served as the command center for all military around the planet. Literally overlooking an entire hemisphere with the laser and PAC batteries of the planetary defense network, it held a superb advantage of position. Kara was now trying to access one of those batteries, an action certain to call attention to itself . . . and to her.

"Coordinates received," the AI told her. "Awaiting orders."

"Initiate range check and target lock," she said, mentally holding her breath. "Code red-one-one, priority immediate. Execute."

She sensed the AI triggering the alarm. . . .

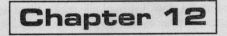

Chapter 12

No new weapons can be introduced without changing conditions, and every change in condition will demand a modification in the application of the principles of war.

—*Armored Warfare*
MAJOR GENERAL J.F.C. FULLER
C.E. 1943

Damn! She wasn't sure what she'd just done wrong, but something in the system had just sent out an alert. It had felt like an automated alarm, probably something in the system's programming that was triggered by an unusual sequence of commands. She would have internal computer security all over her in a moment if she didn't act fast.

Personas in ViRsimulations were like clothing worn in real life, appearances that could be donned or doffed with considerably less effort than sealing up a blouse or spraying on a skintight. Kara had a camouflage persona ready, and it took only a thought to call it up and set it in place.

In computer terms, Kara was a program running on the Aresynch Net's extensive and widely dispersed hardware. What separated her from other software elements running in the Net at the same time was primarily her complexity, greater in some ways even than the AIs that moderated and controlled much of the system's operations. It was possible, however, to shelter that complexity behind an extremely simple exterior, a shell program that presented the outward appearance of a routine housekeeping program, one devoted to nothing more dramatic than searching out lost clusters in the system's capacious memory and devouring them.

There were two disadvantages to the disguise. First of all, to maintain her guise she would have to curtail all, or at least most, of her surveillance activities, to act in fact like a program interested in nothing more than electronic housekeeping.

And second, her disguise was in fact about as effective as donning a wig and dark glasses might be for a human, too shallow to bear close examination. If anyone—especially a human operator—decided to examine her at all closely, he would penetrate the disguise and see her for what she was.

The ascraft received automated clearance for final approach from Kasei's Aresynch Traffic Control, despite the fact that it was well outside the usual landing approach corridors for any of the principal surface settlements. Approaching west to east over the planet's night side, it dropped into the atmosphere high above the Elysium Planitia, a momentary meteor in the night sky over the twinkling lights of Cerberus. Aerobraking hard, bleeding airspeed now in searing heat and the thunder of a roiling shock wave aft, the vehicle descended over Amazonis on a blazing wake of ionization, passing just south of the cloud-capped snows of Olympus. Moments later, the sky-el rose to starboard, its needle-slender shaft illuminated by winking anticollision lights and the tiny, pinpoint gleams of travel pods as it speared the night sky above the Towerdown city-glow of Pavonis Mons.

Ahead, less than five hundred kilometers off now, was a scattering of town lights and communities along the shores of the Labyrinth of Night.

Noctis Labyrinthus had been the westernmost arm of the five-thousand–kilometer rift valley gouged along the Martian equator known as the Vallis Marineris, the Valley of the Mariner spacecraft. With Phoebefall and the warming of the planet, the Mariner Valley had been flooded, becoming an arm of the Boreal Sea that extended west to the Labyrinthine Bay, within a few hundred kilometers of Pavonis Mons.

Banking left, the ascraft's pilot pulled the vehicle into a gentle turn to the north, passing briefly two hundred meters above the ink black waters of the bay before gliding silently above forested land once more. According to the op plan, someone up in Aresynch seventeen thousand kilometers overhead should have accessed the planetary defense system by now and targeted MilTech's Noctis Labyrinthus facility with a ranging laser.

That laser, shining down from the synchorbital base overhead, was only a targeting/range-finder beam, harmless and invisible to unaided human senses. To the pilot's jacked-in senses, though, the pinpoint of laser light touching the team's objective glowed like an emerald beacon, guiding the ascraft in toward the right stretch of beach. Judging her approach with practiced accuracy, she brought the lander's nose up, then triggered the belly jets in a shrieking yowl of superheated plasma. The ascraft shuddered, sinking as it lost airspeed. Landing legs unfolded, insectlike, as dust and wind-whipped sand roiled skyward. It touched down on the beach, landing pads sinking into wet sand and the curling edge of the surf.

Even before the belly jets throttled down, however, the ascraft's main cargo deck was opening. As the ascraft gentled to the ground, landing struts yielding to receive the vessel's weight, molded egg shapes, each as black as the night, spilled from the open cargo hatch on spidery legs. Each pod was five meters long, its hull smooth and polished and organically shaped. First out was a Cutlass, Sergeant ''Butcher Mac'' McAllister's *Cutlery* in its warstrider configuration. Close behind him was Third Squad's CO, Lieutenant Ferris, in his Red Saber, *Saberslash.* The war machines hit the Martian surface, legs pistoning to find balance and a secure foothold.

Not a single word was transmitted; until they were positively spotted and pegged as hostile, they would maintain radio silence . . . but words were not necessary. This part of the op, at least, had been rehearsed by all of them time and time again in simulation. Their target, still pinpointed by the laser from seventeen thousand kilometers up, was less than eight hundred meters ahead, behind a low line of sand dunes and desert pines behind the beach.

They began moving . . . every man and woman in the unit well aware that things never went as smoothly in real life as they did in ViRsimulation.

Ishimoto had detected the tremor of an alarm running through the Net. There was a saboteur here, someone accessing the Net with improper authorization. Swiftly, and with the help of the system's primary AI, he downloaded the alarm's log. The cause was simple enough to pinpoint: an improper access to the Planetary Defense System. The code inputs had all been correct, but whoever had uploaded them had neglected to include an apologetic greeting, a brief, electronic "may I trouble you for" that was customary with all artificially intelligent Nihonjin systems . . . and when the intruder had given the execute command, he'd neglected to say "please." The computer AI didn't care one way or another, of course, whether humans were polite to it or not, but a simple subroutine run from the Internal Computer Security node could detect the absence of that phrase and set off an alarm.

There was a small irony there, Ishimoto knew. The citizens of the Western-descended frontier worlds—many of them, at any rate—disliked the Japanese treatment of genie artificial life forms, yet most gaijin treated AI systems merely as cleverly programmed machines. The Japanese—possibly because of a philosophical tradition that populated even inanimate objects with *kami*, divine spirits—had *always* been polite to their computers . . . and that tiny difference in social attitudes may have just helped expose a gaijin spy within the Aresynch Net.

Ishimoto began narrowing down the search area.

Her camouflage shell in place, Kara began experimenting in small, careful increments, seeking the limits of what she could do without attracting undue attention to herself. Leaving the ranging laser under the control of a simple-minded looping routine, she exited the planetary defense system's weaponry control and found a quiet and out-of-the-way niche for herself in the defense network's surface monitoring node.

This portion of the Aresynch Net was designed as an adjunct to the defense system's tracking control, a way to track and target enemy forces on the surface of Kasei as a backup to the standard weapons operating systems. In peacetime, it served the additional, more mundane purpose of monitoring the weather on the Marineris hemisphere, providing the inhabitants of this face of Kasei with up-to-the-minute weather maps and predictions.

Without giving herself away, she found she could open an observational window and call up an image from one of the ground-facing long-eye cameras mounted along the length of the sky-el. A set of commands put one strategically sited camera under her direct control. She panned it right, shifted down twelve degrees, and then initiated a zoom.

Instantly, she was looking down on the MilTech Laboratory Complex from a vantage point that seemed to be less than a hundred meters up, though the image lacked depth and wavered occasionally due to atmospheric distortion. She could see the complex easily, however, despite the darkness, laid out in a rough, seven-pointed star shape just inland from a beach and marina complex on the northwest shore of the Labyrinthine Bay. Eight hundred meters to the southwest and made clearly visible in the infrared frequencies by its heat signature, an ascraft had grounded right at the waterline. She couldn't see the warstriders, which were designed to be less than easy to spot even at infrared wavelengths, but if things were going according to plan, they should be about *there*, deployed in three extended lines, marching across the terrain in parade ground order, like regiments in formation in the era of the musket and the bayonet charge. She thought about Ran. . . .

There was no response yet from the complex, and this was the point in the plan where a great deal of guesswork entered the picture. CMI did not know what kind of security was in place at the MilTech labs; there would be *something*, certainly, especially given the importance of the I2C testing program, but that something could be anything from a private security force armed with hand lasers to a regiment of Imperial Marines. The reality was almost certainly something between those two extremes, but though speculation had been rampant during the long passage out from New America, no one in a position of authority had been willing yet to guess whether it would be closer to one or the other.

The answer would be revealed any moment now, though, just as soon as the lab's inhabitants realized that they were under attack.

To Lieutenant Ferris's senses, he was moving rapidly across sandy, open ground, working his way up a gently sloping hill with the sea at his back. It was pitch dark—the thread-thin string of lights to his right marking the sky-el shed no more illumination than did the stars and was nothing at all like the day-bright glow of Columbia in New America's midnight sky.

But he was running on enhanced input, and the night around him was day-bright. Even so, he could just barely make out the shadowy forms of the other warstriders in his platoon as they deployed for the attack. The nanoflage on all of the combat striders had been set for night operations, drinking every photon that hit their surfaces and rendering the huge machines completely and eerily black. Increasing his pace, he crested the top of the hill and for the first time had a clear look at the objective.

The MilTech Labs were brightly lit, the entire compound bathed in intense white light from pole fixtures, from magnetically levitated gloglobes, and from large floatation reflectors set adrift above the compound that shone brilliantly when bathed by low-power laser light beamed at them from the ground. Several vehicles were moving down there, some rolling about on the ground, others flying overhead. Much of the activity appeared to be centered about the lab's landing facility, where several small ascraft were grounded. An early version of Operation Sandstorm had called for the assault ascraft to go into the port disguised as an Imperial shuttle bringing in a load of supplies, but that plan had been scrapped because CMI agents working both on Kasei and on Earth had been unable to find the proper ID numbers and codes for a landing at a Level Seven secure facility.

Ran Ferris strode rapidly over the crest of the hill, unwilling to silhouette *Saberslash* against open sky for a second longer than was necessary. He sensed movement ahead . . . and in the same instant, his strider's motion detector flashed an alarm, bracketing a pocket of deeper shadow against the blackness beneath a clump of trees a hundred meters to the left.

"Strikers, Striker Two-one!" he called. "I've got a bogie at three-five-five, range one hundred!" He wanted a solid ID before he started shooting . . . but even as he barked his warning, the shadow moved with sudden speed and a graceful unfolding of spidery legs, shifting left up the hill and past Ferris's position. As it moved, it pivoted and fired, strafing as it ran sideways.

White fire exploded across Ferris's forward view, and red cautionary lights winked on, indicating hits . . . and damage, all superficial so far. Ferris returned fire at almost the same instant, loosing a burst of hivel cannon fire in a buzz saw shriek of high-velocity metal that snapped and sparked and shrilled as it ricocheted wildly from the other strider's armored hull. He followed up with a shot from his KC-20 particle accelerator cannon, the PAC loosing blue lightning in a sizzling bolt that struck the other machine squarely, then vented itself into the ground in sheets of blue-white fury.

Data scrolled down past the right side of Ferris's view forward, listing mass, weaponry, power levels, range. A Tsurugi . . .

An explosion shattered trees to his right, hurling splinters and a geyser of sand and earth into the sky. Suddenly, the night was filled with crisscrossing streams of blue and orange fire, as forces hidden in the shadows suddenly advanced, weapons blazing.

"Sandman, Sandman!" he called over the tactical link. "Striker Two is engaged! Estimate . . . ten, possibly twelve enemy warstriders within sensor sweep range. Request air support!"

"Striker Two, Sandman. On the way!"

The Tsurugi had been damaged, either by the blast from

Ferris's PAC or by the heavy fire it was taking from other Black Phantoms moving now across the ridge. He could see the enemy strider clearly now by the sullen red glow of near-molten duralloy near a gaping wound in the machine's side. He triggered a volley of lasers, then unfolded his 70mm grenade launcher in its side-mounted tube. The weapon thumped, and a second later the enemy strider was silhouetted by a savage flash behind it. The blast staggered the machine, dropping it to the ground, but its legs flexed, lifting it clear of smoking ground and carrying it, limping, back toward the lab compound.

With an inner jolt, Ferris realized that there was no fear now, nothing but a pounding, raw excitement, an eagerness to come to grips with the bastards and take them apart. Yelling to the rest of his squadron, Ferris followed the damaged Impie machine.

Kara sensed the message, an electric throbbing in the sea around her. Knowing that it would be coming sooner or later, she had been waiting for it, with subroutines in place at the likely communications nodes. Though not entirely certain what the exact form or protocol of the message would be, she was ready to adapt to the needs of the moment.

The message was from the MilTech Lab and it was coded Priority Urgent: Code One. Reaching out from beneath the shell, she intercepted it.

Even when interfaced with a computer network, humans had slow reactions; her thoughts were still being driven by biochemical reactions in her organic brain, after all. There was no way she could react quickly enough to stop the incoming message, which had already been received and routed to the Aresynch communications center by the time she was aware of it.

But she could change it . . . specifically the two binary bits designating its priority level. With a thought, the message's priority tag dropped from ''urgent'' to ''routine.''

Incoming fire flashed and stuttered across the sky. Jerry Brewster's LCR-12 Lancer exploded, the white-hot flare of his fusor pack briefly turning night to actinic day. In the swiftly fading light, a big, four-legged Omata appeared for an instant in Ferris's view forward, twenty degrees to the left; he pivoted hard and snapped in the weapons lock, embracing the Imperial strider in green-glowing targeting brackets. *Fire!* A full barrage of laser fire and PAC bolts seared across the Omata's hull, peeling open black armor, scouring away nanoflage to expose shiny hot metal underneath. One leg shattered, the struts and jointed footpad spinning through the air.

The battle was only seconds old, but Ferris could tell that they would need to escalate things fast or be overwhelmed.

"Sandman! This is Striker Two!" he yelled over the tactical channel. "Where the gok is that air?"

"Not much longer, Two. They're deploying now." There was a two-beat pause. "Striker Two, we're reading new forces swinging in on your position from the north, range about five hundred. You'd better get airborne yourself or you're going to get hemmed in."

"Roger that!" He shifted to his squadron's command frequency. "Striker Two, this is Two-one. Okay, boys and girls. Pick up your feet! We're going to gausslev." He initiated a reload command, changing the ammunition in his grenade launcher, then loosed a thumping staccato of rapid fire. QEC nano spread in a white cloud ahead of Ferris's strider. A green light winked against his vision, indicating an active floater field.

"I've got readings at ten to the eight gauss!" he called. "I'm floating . . . ."

Saberslash slid forward, accelerating rapidly until it was moving far more swiftly than legs could have carried it.

His sensors picked up the flight of incoming warheads, rockets fired in a cloud from defenses within the MilTech perimeter. Rising and unfolding from its shielded recess in his hull, his hivel cannon pivoted on its universal mount and shrieked, hurling high-velocity slugs of ultra-dense metal into the warheads' paths. Fresh explosions lit up the night, rippling and pulsing. One rocket slipped through, missed by his defense fire, detonating with a thunderous slam against *Saberslash*'s hull. The explosion rocked him back, the suspensor field yielding with the blow and absorbing some of the shock.

Recovering, Ferris darted ahead, zigzagging lightly across the gently descending ground to make things as interesting as possible for the Imperial gunners and to avoid presenting an analyzable pattern to the MilTech facility's defensive AI. The MilTech lab perimeter was just ahead; the facility was still brightly lit, and he could see the dark, scrambling shapes of people dashing among the buildings.

Heavy fire was coming from the lab now. God, the place was armed and armored like a fortress! Ferris paused to deliver a volley of suppressive laser fire at one of the enemy batteries, then pressed forward, sending his strider skimming across the ocher sand in uneven swerves.

Despite his maneuvers, a hivel round slammed into *Saberslash*. The shock rang through the warstrider and it dipped wildly to the left . . . then recovered on magnetic lifts. Panels opened and closed on stubby fins, using airflow to adjust the machine's attitude. A missile streaked across the desert at an altitude of two meters; his AI spotted it, calculated that it would strike within two seconds, and destroyed it with a hivel burst that erupted across the desert floor like a thundering line of geysers.

"Sandman! Striker Two!" he yelled. "Where's that goking air support?"

"On the way, Two. Hold on!"

And then the aircraft were there, four A/V-48 Gyrfalcons, booming up over the dune ridge at his back, great, black, complex shapes held aloft by stubby, variable-geometry wings and howling air-breather plasma jets. Laser fire flashed from chin nacelles and ventral turrets, lighting the sky. The deadly fire being concentrated on the warstriders shifted suddenly as the gunners retargeted on the aircraft.

Larger than warstriders, the Gyrfalcons were also more powerful, more heavily armored, and capable of astonishing stop-and-go pinpoint maneuvers. One machine darted overhead, came to a halt, hovering, turning slightly as it bathed the lab complex in searing, rapid-fire pulses from its autolasers, then skittered to the side to avoid an answering barrage. Ferris saw sparks struck from its nanoblackened hull, but the machine recovered, then darted ahead once more with a high-G acceleration that would have made any nonlinked pilot black out. Air-to-surface missiles shrieked overhead, lancing into the lab compound and detonating in quick-fire thunderclaps.

"Move it, Striker Two!" he yelled. "Rush 'em! Now!"

Under cover of the hovering, darting Gyrfalcons, the Third Squadron hurtled forward, hitting the facility's mesh-fence perimeter and smashing through. *Saberslash* faltered momentarily as it drifted over a low-gauss patch of the ground suspensor field, and Ferris put out two legs to steady the strider and pole it forward a few meters. Then the field reestablished itself and he was levitating again. A shoulder-launched rocket exploded against his armor, scouring off a patch of nanoflage. The other striders were losing their ebon-black invisibility, too, as repeated hits scraped off their light-drinking coats faster than they could be regrown.

No matter. The night no longer afforded concealment. Firing a rippling volley of grenades to spread the surface nanofield well into the compound, he edged forward, returning fire when he received it, spraying anything that looked like a possible weapons hard point as his AI pointed it out.

"Striker Two, this is Sandman."

"Sandman, Striker Two! Go ahead!"

"Strikers One and Three are moving now. Watch your fire and wait for solid IDs."

"Roger that. Two! Did you all catch that? Watch who the gok you're shooting!"

Operation Sandstorm had called for an initial three-part assault, with Squadrons Two, Three, and Four splitting up at the landing zone, then converging on the MilTech Lab from the north, west, and—wading through the shallow waters of the bay—south. First to engage the enemy, Third Squadron had caught the brunt of the resistance in the center, serving as a diversion while the other two squadrons swung out and around and into position, squarely on the Imperials' northern and southern flanks. Shifting his view to the right, he could see two of Fourth Squadron's Cutlasses emerging from the inky waters of the Labyrinthine Bay, clambering up onto the waterfront between a pair of sleek hydrofoil skimmers moored at the piers. Gunfire from the base greeted them, but it was scattered and ill-coordinated.

There is in every battle a tempo, a sense of the pace of things, that lets those attuned to it feel which way the fight is going. Ferris felt that tempo now throughout the combat link, an electric excitement in the voices of his squadron mates over the tactical channel, that told him that the enemy defenses had broken, that they were victorious.

An Imperial strider emerged from cover, adrift on its own QEC nano, already badly damaged and barely able to move. Ferris tracked, targeted, and fired in a seamless series of mental commands, and the enemy machine exploded in hurtling, flaming fragments.

"Sandman, this is Striker Two!" he called. "Nike! Nike!"

The name of the ancient Greek goddess of winged victory was the code word to initiate the next phase of the operation.

Kara heard Ran's "Nike" call, but she was too busy to pay attention at the moment. Aresynch's communications center had just received a report of an enemy attack at Labyrinthine Bay, and with a Priority Urgent flag. She'd already intercepted eight similar reports of increasing urgency and priority, downscaling each to routine, but at last a transmission came through with a coded priority that she could not touch . . . and seconds later, a search ordered by the communications officer of the watch discovered all of the "routine messages" reporting an attack by unidentified enemy armored forces at the MilTech lab complex at Noctis Labyrinthus, and repeated desperate calls for help.

The alarm was out; Kasei's military command knew now both that they were under attack and that something was amiss within the Kasei Net. Instantly, the security level for the cybersystem flicked up to full alert, and a search was begun for intruders.

She would not be able to remain undetected for much longer.

Chapter 13

Never forget. A computer ViRsimulation is just that, a simulation. Its sole reality is in the interplay of informational input and electrochemical impulses within the brain.

Of course, it has been argued that the physical universe around us has no objective reality at the quantum level, save what is instilled in it by our own brains. So perhaps there is at some level an element of real-world reality in the ViRsims after all. . . .

—ViRsim Journeys: A Personal Voyage
A. V. BARKER
C.E. 2440

The outside battle for the MilTech lab compound area was nearly over, though hivel bursts and laser fire continued to shriek and howl above shattered fabricrete walls and burning buildings, and numerous Imperial strongholds continued to loose sharp volleys at random intervals. The warstriders had secured the compound area, however, ringing the buildings to protect them against the expected enemy counterattack, and moving through the facility on foot, rooting out the stubbornly resisting survivors pocket by pocket. As the Gyrfalcons circled overhead, providing covering fire, two massive Vz-980 assault transports roared over the rise to the west, skimming scant meters above the ground.

The lead Vz-980 cut its suspensors as it drifted over the open ground immediately in front of the lab's main building, descending gently with legs unfolding, grounding on yielding landing jacks. Hatchways popped open on both sides and in the rear, disgorging armored ground troops who spilled across the lab grounds, weapons at the ready.

The ground strike force's commander was Lieutenant Hal Clifford, who at forty-one standard was one of the oldest of NAMA's graduates and certainly was old for his relatively new lieutenant's commission. The marines had a tradition, though, one extending back to a time when "marines" meant troops who came ashore from the sea in amphibious operations, of giving NCOs with leadership skills and plenty of combat experience the opportunity of taking a commission.

Which is what Clifford had done. He'd seen action on New America during the Rebellion, twenty-five years ago, and had been in plenty of scrapes since. Three years ago he'd been offered a chance to attend the Academy and become an officer.

Most long-time career sergeants held the virtually traditional opinion that NCOs were the real leadership of any good army, that the best officers were those who actually bothered to listen to what their senior sergeants told them. Clifford shared the opinion—but he'd also seen stupidity enough in the ConMil command that he'd decided that maybe he could make a difference if he wielded the authority of an officer instead of that of a grizzled, foul-mouthed noncom. Assigned now as CO of Alfa Platoon, Company D, 12th Regiment, First Confederation Marines, he had as much combat experience as anyone in the unit. He was also, still, a grizzled, foul-mouthed noncom in spirit, a fact that his own troops took considerable pride in.

"Okay, you goking leggers!" he bellowed over the platoon circuit. "Move! Move! Move! You want to toast marshmallows in the transport's jets? Or earn your goking yen transfer?"

The marines dispersed rapidly and with practiced efficiency, forming a broad, protective perimeter around the transport's LZ. With armored resistance within the compound largely crushed, Clifford and his marines had the assignment of clearing key buildings and actually snatching what they'd come here to snatch. He didn't know what the target was, though he could guess that it was some kind of high-tech horror the Impies were cooking up in their Kasei labs. Dr. Carol Browning and a small team of linksystem experts were along to handle the actual search and grab; Clifford's part of the job was to get them inside the building so that they could do their work and to keep them safe while they completed the mission.

With his Mitsubishi Mark XVII plasma rifle at the ready, he trotted clear of the grounded transport, feeling like he was slogging through wet sand. Movement was difficult, almost like trying to walk underwater or in high gravity. This entire area had been saturated with QEC nano, and the magnetic field resisted his movement through it. His armor, his weapons, his other gear had very little ferrous material in them—iron or steel was all too easy for an enemy to detect with magnetic scanners—but the little there was in various items of circuitry fought him step by torturous step.

Gunfire crackled and barked; an explosion to the north sent fire boiling into the sky. Not all resistance had ended yet, by any means. The Imperial striders had been neutralized—destroyed or driven off—but there were plenty of holdouts dug in among the blast- and fire-shattered buildings.

Clifford dropped behind a low stone wall and studied the target through his helmet display. His Companion was interfaced directly with the helmet's electronics, processing both scanner information and data being relayed from Sandman, the ops field HQ at the grounded Artemis ascraft. The main building of the lab complex was a dome-topped, two-story structure ringed with transplas or glass windows—he couldn't tell which—and circled by a kind of park with flower garden plots, meter-tall walls, and benches. As he studied the building through enhanced optics, his Companion painted blobs of color moving behind the upper-story windows marking infrared sources that might be technicians or lab personnel but could also easily be waiting Imperial troops.

A stray round sighed overhead. Gunfire chattered, a light machine gun somewhere to the north.

There was only one way to find out who the silently glowing heat sources were, and no point in waiting. "Okay, people!" he called over the tactical net. "Let's take 'em down!"

He rolled over the wall and started forward. To either side, other armored figures rose and advanced. Almost at once, a hail of gunfire opened up on the advancing marines. A pulse laser stuttered silently, a dazzling, fast-strobing flicker of intense light that chopped through Corporal DeLattio's breastplate and gorget in a splatter of molten duralloy and vaporizing blood. DeLattio shrieked—once and very briefly—and went down. Private Redding lost his left arm as the light exploded through pauldron and rerebrace.

The sudden, devastating fire coming from the building stopped the marines before their rush had gained momentum enough to carry them forward. Most of the troops dropped back behind the wall or into sheltered nooks in the garden-park that lay in front of the building's main entrance.

"Move! Move! Move!" Clifford screamed as automatic fire howled overhead and the laser continued its relentless, deadly pulsing. "You want to just stand there and take it? Get inside there and give 'em some back!"

But the advancing line wavered, then broke, and he had to vault back behind the wall or be the only marine left standing in the park. At his back, the transports, their troops disembarked now, lifted from the LZ, pivoting, rising slowly, their weapons mounts unfolding on stubby wings, seeking the enemy. Hivel rounds slashed toward them from the lab building's second story; one transport took a hit and staggered, its belly slashed open, but then its pilot applied more thrust and the craft straightened out, still rising.

Hivel cannon fire, missiles, and laser pulses snapped and hissed as the transports laid down a devastating covering fire. Infantry—leggers in military parlance—stood very little chance of survival for more than scant minutes on the open battlefield. Their transports were designed to provide them with an extra few moments in the form of overwhelming fire support.

But the damaged transport was in trouble. It had taken too many hits, and white steam was spilling from a ruptured fuel tank, hydrogen slush boiling into atmosphere. An incendiary round slammed into the hull, and in a literal flash, the hydrogen tank exploded, erupting in a savage detonation that broke the transport's spine. Gunfire continued to reach toward the craft as it spun wildly across the compound's airspace; it struck a line of sand dunes just above the beach, exploding for a final time in a billowing mushroom cloud of orange and jet black.

Clifford winced and ducked below a laser-scored wall as the sky turned a dazzling, day-bright orange. *Damn!* That was the *San Jacinto!* Just moments ago, he and his boys and girls had been aboard her. Gok . . . he'd been talking to the major piloting her . . . .

There would be time to think about that later, if they didn't get swept off the front porch by the gunfire coming from inside.

If they could get some support from the other transport . . .

But the *Vera Cruz* loosed only a brief burst of laser fire, scoring the lab's domed roof, then broke off and circled south, out over the bay. The fire coming from that building was just too hot for a relatively vulnerable aircraft to stand and face.

They needed heavy fire support if they were to get inside that fortress.

Levering himself up to peer across the top of the wall, he studied the building's facade. Most of the fire appeared to be coming from the second floor; he could see the twinkle and flash of small arms up there, the repeated flicker of the laser. Those windows were glass after all. They had to be, to be so easily broken. Made sense. One thing Kasei had a lot of was sand, and buildings here tended to be raised with glass facades instead of plastics.

He opened a tactical channel in his helmet com unit. "Striker, Striker, Striker, this is Red Rover! Do you copy?"

"Rover, Striker Two-one. Go ahead!"

"Striker Two-one, we could use some big-foot help over here." He rattled off coordinates, ducking once again as a grenade fired from the building detonated a few tens of meters away.

He sensed motion and turned. A warstrider floated a meter above the ground a few meters away, a huge, black, fire-blasted shape that was all curves and smooth surfaces except for the evil-looking snouts of weapons and wave guide antennae protruding here and there from recesses in the armor. Fear stirred in the back of Clifford's mind. *Please, God, let it be Striker Two-one!*

"Red Rover?" a voice said over his radio link. "It's me, Striker. Where do you want me to put it?"

Sagging with relief, Clifford jerked a gloved thumb over his shoulder. "That building. They've got a small, do-it-yourself fortress up there, second floor, just above the main entrance. They're dug in with grenade launchers, small arms, a hivel, and at least one 2cm pulse laser. Think you can take that out for us without bringing down the whole damned structure?"

"Well, that's the trick, I guess," the warstrider answered. "Taking 'em down is easy. But as for not knocking down the building—"

"That's our objective in there, striderjack. I'd rather not go after it with a shovel, thank you."

"I understand. Okay, keep your head down."

The warstrider drifted past, clearing the top of the wall and moving into the open in front of the building. The gunfire from inside doubled and redoubled; bullets sang and whined off the armor; a grenade exploded close beside the upright machine, rocking it to the right.

A hatch popped open in the strider's side, and a snub-nosed cylinder nosed forth. There was a shrill whine and a stabbing jet of flame, the sound so piercing that Clifford raised his gloves to cover his ears—uselessly, since he was wearing an enclosed helmet.

The hivel cannon hosed the entire second story of the main building, starting at one end and sweeping to the other. Glass exploded, showering out into the night in a glittering cascade. Bodies fell as well, most mangled almost beyond recognition. The interior of the second floor was intermittently lit from within by exploding rounds, but when the hivel gun fell silent, the gaping holes that had once been windows remained black and silent.

There was no answering fire from the structure.

"Pest control done while you wait," the warstrider's pilot said. "Anything else?"

"Thanks, striderjack. If you want to hang around, you're more than welcome, believe me!"

"I think I'll wander. There's a firefight on at the landing field. But give a yell if you need anything else, right?"

"You got it! Thanks!" He shifted frequencies. "Okay, you leggers. Let's move it! Move it!"

For the second time, he rolled over the wall and started forward, his troops following. It was the stuff of a classic nightmare, trying to run across ground permeated by a QEC mag field, each step mired in slow-motion, and all the while enduring that prickly feeling at the back of his neck that someone up there was taking aim and about to fire.

And then suddenly he'd broken through, staggering into the open, almost as though emerging from hip-deep surf or wet sand. He'd fought clear of the caged electron field and was moving over normal ground once more.

Gunfire continued to bark elsewhere in the compound, but the main lab building was silent now . . . as silent as death. He reached the entrance and backed up against the wall, plasma rifle ready. Bradley and Chung slammed into the wall opposite, exchanged nods with him, and braced themselves. Chung tossed a grenade through the blast-shattered door, and when the fragments of ceiling stopped falling, they rolled around the corner and plunged inside, one-two-three.

There was nothing inside the entrance foyer but shattered glass and dead Imperial soldiers. . . .

Watching from Aresynch, Kara followed the raid as it unfolded before her eyes. Resolution through the sky-el's optics was good; at infrared wavelengths, she could see individual troopers as they scattered from the armored carrier and raced into the nearest of the lab buildings. Incoming fire continued to probe and flash. The battle proceeded in an eerie silence; Kara kept expecting to hear the crash and howl and thunder of detonating rounds, the shriek of hivels, the yells of men and women, and the clatter of small-arms fire, but the entire scenario unfolded before her eyes in complete silence.

She wished she were down there with them. With *Ran* . . .

Kara had already tried several times to access the computer system at the MilTech labs through the Net, but, as expected, there was no direct access. Even the most sophisticated AI system couldn't talk to other computers if they weren't linked in, though she could sense where those node access points were when the communications lines were open.

Had she been able to access the lab computers directly, she might well have been able to carry out this mission—or the major part of it—herself, without the need for warstriders or marines. In fact, the lack of access was a confirmation that sensitive data on the I2C might well be stored at Noctis Labyrinthus. Severing the lab's on-line connections with Aresynch would be one of the most basic of security precautions they could take.

A warning tone caught her attention. Shifting to another window, she checked the strategic map, which showed everything in the battle area from the foot of Pavonis Mons to Oudemans.

There . . . that was what had triggered the alert. A flight of aircraft—and from their ID tags on the tracking screen, they were damned big transports of some kind—was lifting off from a base in Syria Planum, south of the Marineris Sea. Touching the icon with her thoughts, she requested a magnification of the image and more data.

And she got it. The aircraft were four Kaba transports, enormous, lumbering beasts that could easily be hauling a full regiment of heavy warstriders between them. They were already clear of their base control area and were winging across the Labyrinthine Bay, headed north. Aresynch Military Command listed the flight as assigned to the 5th Imperial *Hi* Division, stationed at Syria Planum.

That made sense, now that the alarm was out. They would be on the way with a regiment of crack Imperial striders at least; they wouldn't know for sure what they were up against, but there would be enough of them to deal with anything short of a full-scale invasion. They would walk right over the Confederation forces on the ground, no problem and no questions asked.

What to do?

Kara stared at the four tiny symbols streaking north across

the waters of the Labyrinth of Night and knew that she had very few options.

"Strikers! All Strikers! This is Sandman! Priority flash, urgent!"

Lieutenant Ferris paused his strider, listening.

"We are tracking incoming aircraft," Sandman reported. "Bearing at one-eight-two, range seven-five kilometers. They're coming in fast and low, skimming the sea, and just cleared the horizon. We think they're transports from Syria Planum.

"All striders, assume defensive order Gamma. Initiate!"

From the south, Ferris shifted his Red Saber, studying the dark horizon. He could see nothing, even with enhanced senses, but the Artemis had senses better than his by several orders of magnitude.

Swiftly, he began moving south, toward the coast. He had to find a good place to hole up and get ready, because when those bastards arrived, they'd be eager for a fight.

The Planetary Defense System's weaponry control was clear. Ishimoto had thought it would be . . . but he'd had to make certain. More, he wanted to be very sure there were no unchecked hiding places at his electronic back as he closed in, relentlessly, on the most probable location of the intruder. He'd already alerted both the AI ICS and the other human operators on the current security watch. They'd informed him that, yes, one of Aresynch's ranging lasers had been firing continuously, unnoticed by anyone in the Defense Command. It almost certainly was being used as a beacon to mark the MilTech labs as a target for the enemy raiders.

A small and simple program had been running the software end of the laser in the weaponry control banks, a shadowy something revealed by the ViRsimulation as a small and brightly colored fish circling above a particularly ornate head of coral. He reached out with a thought . . . and the alien program evaporated. Another thought, and the laser was switched off. Not that that would do any good now. The damage was done, the raiders landed, the attack under way. Someone, Ishimoto reflected, was going to wish he'd never been born, once the Kasei Imperial Military Command got through with him.

He devoutly hoped that that someone was not going to be Genji Ishimoto.

But it might well be. He had been in charge of security on the Kasei end of the Net when an enemy agent had slipped in, turning the Net against its owners to assist the attack on MilTech. It might not be enough that he'd been performing his duties to the best of his abilities . . . and it was no excuse that the Net was far too vast for any one human to monitor it thoroughly from within.

But it would help, it would help a lot if he could catch the intruder. And he thought he knew now how he was going to do just that.

Obviously, the intruder had penetrated the Planetary Defense System's computer network, using it to access the targeting laser and paint the MilTech facility for the raiders. He would have been stupid to remain, since sooner or later someone was going to realize that the laser was still running and come in to check it out. No, the intruder was hiding someplace else, someplace nearby. The question was . . . where?

And where would I go if I wanted to oversee the action on the surface of Kasei? Ishimoto thought to himself.

The answer was obvious—so obvious that it seemed almost too easy.

Carefully, he moved toward the Network's surface monitoring node.

Kara realized she was going to have to break cover if she was to provide any help to the ground forces at all. Worse, she was going to have to retrace her steps, returning to an area she'd already visited, one which by now could well be crawling with Imperial computer security programs, both AI software and organic.

No matter. Part of the reason she was here in the first place was to do anything she could to delay, confuse, or break the Imperials' response to the MilTech raid. Her shell as a housekeeper program ought to give her cover enough to make the transfer, so long as no one examined it too closely.

Uploading a transfer request, she slipped from the surface monitoring node back into weapons control.

As he was going in, something else was coming out. Ishimoto caught only the flash of a shadow, a dull and undetailed fish-shape that, as he brushed it lightly, told him it was a routine housekeeper program, searching for lost clusters to eliminate from the system. Ignoring the program—it was little more than a miniscule portion of the system's overall background—he pushed past it and entered the surface monitoring node.

Kara was sure that she'd just brushed past a security program of some sort, one going in as she was coming out. It might have been an automated program, or it could have been something more dangerous, an AI-generated hunter-killer routine, or even a human operator, working, like herself, within the Net. If she was right in her guess, though, security was close to tracking her down. She would have to work fast.

But she also felt a degree of freedom now that she'd not possessed earlier. During her first penetration of the Net, she'd had to move cautiously and with great circumspection to avoid calling attention to herself. Somehow, she'd alerted the system anyway—she still wasn't sure what she'd done to trigger that initial alarm—and moments after that the transmission of a high-priority bit of radio traffic from the surface had signaled the fact that there was indeed an intruder loose on the Net.

She could move boldly now, without worrying that a mistake would give her away.

Slipping herself into a quiet corner of the Aresynch Defense Network node, she addressed the monitoring AI. "Targeting," she said.

"Targeting accessed."

"Fire request."

"Please upload target coordinates."

"Target is a flight of transports with changing coordinates.

Link to Aresynch Traffic Control screen and accept ID upload.''

A pause. ''Upload accepted. System is now tracking four air/space transports, designated Target 01. Weapon select.''

Kara took a deep, mental breath. ''Any available laser in the five-hundred to one-thousand–megajoule range, with acceptable targeting parameters on designated targets.''

''Weapon designated, quad-mount 600 MJ beam laser, turret three-one, section twelve. Confirm.''

''Weapon designation accepted and confirmed.''

''Please upload clearances and authorization codes.''

Kara braced herself mentally. This would the high-risk part . . . and where the information provided by CMI's agents on Earth would really prove itself. She had a code authorization for a fire control request, but it was an old one, and no one knew if it would be accepted by the system or not.

''Authorization code *Okha*,'' she said.

She waited . . . and waited . . . and just when she thought that a silent alarm must have been given and that she'd better back out and run for it now, the AI replied, ''Authorization code Orange Blossom accepted. Weapons release approved. Proceed.''

''Initiate target lock and automatic fire sequencing,'' she said. ''Code red-one-one, priority immediate. Execute.''

''Firing . . .''

On the ground, Ran Ferris was picking his way through a heap of smoking rubble, trying to find a good site that would give him a clear field of fire to the south. Updates from Sandman had verified the approaching force, almost certainly four Hippo-class transports coming in big-time, hard, heavy, and ready for anything.

A counterattack had been inevitable, of course, and much time had been devoted to a counterattack scenario both in op planning and in the rehearsal simulations. The only real chance the strike force had was to get in, get the goods, and get out before the locals could respond.

Obviously, they hadn't moved quite quickly enough, and

now the whole character of this op was about to change. It would be up to the three warstrider squadrons and the marine leggers to hold off all comers until the specialists finished their analysis of what was in the main building. And then—

The southern sky lit up.

Lieutenant Clifford was inside the main lab building as a half dozen civilian specialists in heavy combat armor gathered about a communications module. One of their number, Carol Browning, had shucked her armor down to skintights and climbed inside, hoping to make direct connection with the lab computer. Clifford had just walked toward the shattered windows on the south side of the building when the sky in that direction lit up, a glaring white and silent flare that dazzled off the water.

"What the *gok* . . . ?"

Several other soldiers and most of the technicians joined him, staring out the open window as the light swiftly faded. A second flare ignited, glowed, faded. And then a third.

"Sandman, Red Rover. What the hell's going on in the southern sector?"

"Sorry you weren't informed," Sandman's voice replied a moment later. "It took us by surprise, too."

"What did? What's going on?"

"Someone up in Aresynch's having some target practice," Sandman said. "With Imperial troop transports as targets."

A fourth flare lit up the night. There was a long silence after that. "Okay, everyone," Sandman's voice announced. "That's four up and four down. I think someone upstairs just saved our bacon. Now let's get this job done so it wasn't a wasted effort."

Clifford knew what Sandman meant. "Someone" would be their covert helper smuggled into Aresynch. If that guy had managed to subvert the synchorbital's defensive lasers to take out incoming Impie transports, it was a sure bet that all hell had just broken loose at the top of the Pavonis Mons sky-el.

He decided that he was very happy to be safely down here in the middle of a firefight, and not up there, inside a computer

Net that must be on full emergency alert by now.

Soldiers, he reasoned, were paid to take risks . . . but there are some risks with such goking bad odds that accepting them wasn't a matter of following orders.

It was more like . . . suicide.

Chapter 14

The aim of military study should be to maintain a close watch upon the latest technical, scientific, and political developments, fortified by a sure grasp of the eternal principles upon which the great captains have based their contemporary methods, and inspired by a desire to be ahead of any rival army in securing options in the future.

—*Thoughts on War*
B. H. LIDDELL HART
C.E. 1944

To Kara, it felt as though the walls of the undersea cavern where she was currently residing were suddenly collapsing in upon her. All Aresynch was on full alert now, and she could sense the closing of gates across various nodes, sealing them off from the outside and making them as inaccessible as the MilTech labs. The emerald swirlings around her were filled with shadowy objects, programs suddenly activated; some might be defensive hunter-killers.

She signaled her Companion, releasing a shape of her own into the swirling mix. The program was unintelligent and of limited power, but it did a good job of imitating an intruder who was clumsily trying to escape a system node and making a great deal of noise while going about it.

Abruptly, her control of the Aresynch defensive lasers was terminated, the shock like the swinging of a blade.

"Targeting," she said.

"Targeting access denied."

"Accept Authorization Code *Okha*."

"Authorization denied."

Evidently, the system had gone to a higher alert level, one specifically designed to deal with intruders like her, and was refusing to deal with input commands unless they were from someone with a higher authorization code than Orange Blossom.

But there was one more trick she might try.

"Housekeeping."

"Housekeeping access granted." She was, after all, still wearing the shell of a housekeeper subroutine, and access to the housekeeping subnodes was more or less automatic. In a system as complex as this, only the most sensitive nodes and operating areas would be restricted . . . and *no* one paid attention to the housekeepers.

"Accept Authorization Code *Baika*."

There was a pause. "Authorization Code Plum Blossom accepted. Awaiting uploaded instructions."

The AI began accepting her upload, a bundle of special instructions for that part of the system that dealt with routine housekeeping chores. Piggybacked with those instructions, though, were hidden codes that allowed her to continue her monitoring of surface communications. AI systems were immensely powerful and capable of tremendous intelligence . . . but in routine or low-level matters they often betrayed their evolutionary origins as relatively simple-minded calculators.

Sometimes, in fact, they really weren't very bright at all.

Hal Clifford leaned over the console, staring at the com module. It was a custom model with a transparent door, and he could see Carol Browning lying on the couch inside, apparently unconscious.

"Anything yet, Doctor?" he asked, anxious.

"The system appears to be intact," the woman's voice replied, speaking over his helmet radio. "There are several thousand directories, however, and no clear indication as to which might hold the material we want."

"Can you just upload all of it?"

"If you can afford to wait here for a couple of days, certainly. It was my impression that you were concerned with speed, however."

He sighed. "Okay, okay. Just keep looking. We didn't come all this way to—"

"My search would be considerably more efficient," she told him, interrupting with a brusque irritation, "if you would stay the hell out of my way while I'm in here looking!"

Clifford's head jerked up at the rebuke, and he felt the eyes of the other civilians on the recovery team on him, amused, even laughing. Carol Browning had a reputation for being both brilliant with computer systems of all kinds and impatient to the point of rudeness with fellow humans. Goking civilians . . .

"Red Rover, Red Rover, this is Sandman. Do you copy?"

"Affirmative, Sandman."

"What's your status in there, Cliff?"

"We're working on it. No luck so far."

"Keep up the pressure, son. Skymaster bought us some time, but we still can't dawdle."

"Dr. Browning is inside the system now," he said. "She says there are a lot of directories to search, and it would take too long to upload them all."

"Roger that. Okay, the sit out here is stable for the moment, but we've lost all communications with Skymaster. We think they must've spotted her when she zapped those transports with a planetary defense laser."

"Gok! Can we still—"

"We'll fly the stuff out manually if we have to. If Skymaster comes back on-line, we'll want to zipsqueal the goodies up and out of here fast, before the Impies can close off the line or track her down. We won't have more than a few seconds. Understand?"

"Affirmative. We'll do what we can."

"I know you will, Rover. Sandman, standing by."

Gunfire thumped and crackled in the distance. How long

could they afford to just sit here, waiting for the next Impie counterattack?

One of the civilians, a small, silver-haired woman with elven features, approached him. "Lieutenant?"

"What is it?"

"I think we've found something you should see."

"Show me."

The something was exposed in a tangle of fiber optic wiring and circuit boards behind an access panel that had been opened in the lab's primary communications center. It was a silvery package, a meter long and ten centimeters wide, with hundreds of attachment points for hair-thin fiber data feeds. One of his marines was standing close by, a scanner in his hand.

"We were doing a routine trace on the physical hardware, Lieutenant," the marine said. He pointed at the intruding object. "*That* shouldn't be there."

"You're sure?"

"I've been in comtech for fifteen years, sir," the man said with quiet certainty. "I think I know my way around the inside of a com junction access." He gestured with the scanner. "I'm reading a pretty intense mag field inside there, too. Like a QEC array."

Clifford frowned. "Is that what we're looking for?"

The marine shrugged. "Beats me. But it's damned unusual."

"We are looking," the woman said quickly, "for a new type of electronic device that will greatly improve the range and efficiency of radio communications. This is almost certainly that device. And look . . ."

She reached out with one gloved hand, tracing a line of katakana characters engraved on the gleaming surface.

"*O-denwa*," he said, reading the word. He looked at her, puzzled. "Telephone?"

"An antique communications device—"

"I *know* what a telephone is," he said testily.

"Then you know that it's obsolete technology, that it hasn't been used in the Shichiju's Core Worlds in I don't know how many centuries."

"A code word," he said.

"Or a joke."

"What kind of joke?"

"The original Inglic word 'telephone' meant 'speaking at a distance.' The 'O' at the beginning is an honorific—"

"I also speak Nihongo," he said. "So we've found an honorable telephone that uses quantum electron cages." He looked at the woman, knowing she wasn't telling everything she knew. Still, in combat anything having to do with efficient communications was important. "Can we rip this thing out and bring it along?"

"We'll get right on it, Lieutenant," the marine said.

"I would recommend waiting until we're certain we no longer need a direct communication link with Aresynch," the civilian said. "It looks to me like this device is central to the lab's communications system. Pull it out and the whole thing goes down. But we can have all of the connections tagged and ready to cut as soon as you tell us."

He nodded. "Okay. Get on it, and keep me posted." A sudden idea occurred to him, and he opened one of his suit's comm channels. "Dr. Browning. This is Clifford."

"Damn it, Lieutenant, can't you null-headed military types get linked in? I'm trying to get some work done in—"

"Is there a directory in there under the heading of either *denwa* or *o-denwa*? Something with technical specs?"

There was a pause. "Yes." There was another pause. "God, Lieutenant, this is it! How did you know?"

"Maybe us null-headed military types are good for something."

"This is what we came for. I'm wrapping it up for transmittal."

"Sandman, Red Rover," he said, shifting channels. "We've got the goods."

"Well done, Rover," Sandman replied. "Let's get things rolling. On the double, now . . . !"

Kara could feel the hunters now, growing closer . . . and more certain of the location of their prey. Her Companion's automated defense program continued to mislead and misdirect, leaking seemingly inadvertent signals from time to time that suggested that the intruder was accessing the system from a completely different node. Those tactics could not keep the dogs off indefinitely, however. Sooner or later they would hem her in, even if they had to go the brute-force method of switching off node after node until they had her location positively identified.

She had cut off her direct link with the surface to keep the internal computer security forces from tracking the line directly back to her, but she'd continued listening from her hiding place in the housekeeping subnode to the radio transmissions between different members of the assault force. Those messages were encrypted, of course, to keep the Imperials from listening in, but the encryption algorithm had been stored in her Companion's memory, and she could hear those voices as distant, Inglic whispers at the very edge of her awareness.

"Sandman, Red Rover," she heard. *"We've got the goods."*

"Well done, Rover. Let's get things rolling. On the double, now . . . !"

"Skymaster? This is Sandman. Are you there?"

"This is Skymaster," Kara replied, opening the channel. She could sense other alarms coming on, as her unauthorized transmission was detected. "Go ahead, Sandman, but make it fast!"

"We got it. Are you ready to accept delivery?"

"Ready and waiting. Shoot it on up."

"On the way, Skymaster!"

Data flowed in, flooding in through a set of Mars-pointing dish antennae, and Kara was waiting to capture the information and redirect it. In seconds, almost as quickly as she received it, she fed the stream into encrypted packets and fired them outward in a tight, hard beam toward a precisely targeted patch of the sky.

She didn't wait for an acknowledgement from her target. The beam's destination was in orbit around Saturn, currently some eighty light minutes from Mars, and it would be over two and a half hours before a reply could reach her.

Kara started to break her interface. . . .

• • •

There was the intruder! Ishimoto had been momentarily baffled when the intruder hadn't turned up inside the surface scanning node, but that one radio transmission, diamond-clear and easy to pinpoint in its proximity, clearly placed the enemy agent back in the planetary defense node. As Ishimoto emerged from surface scanning, he could sense him, a shadowy form beginning to waver and dissolve as he broke contact. Ishimoto sprang forward, reaching out—

Kara felt a sudden, throat-gripping panic, coupled with the sensation of being trapped. *Something* had her, was holding her, pinning her immobile inside the communications module access stack. She willed her viewpoint within the simulated world forward, hard, then shifted it suddenly to the side, a set of movements that had no real existence in anything like three-dimensional space but that translated conveniently as a violent twisting in her unseen assailant's grasp.

She couldn't break free, couldn't get a purchase on her surroundings in order to fight back. Worse, she could feel parts of herself dissociating, as though her ego, her very self-awareness was fading away. The sensation carried with it a sharp and indescribable terror; it was like a nightmare she'd had more than once as a child, a dream of being trapped, unable to move while all the time she was being devoured by the nameless horror that had trapped her.

Fear, she realized, was at least part of her attacker's arsenal; to fight back she would have to control her own fear and deliver an attack of her own. Her Companion held her single available on-line weapon sheathed in a carefully protected reserve of memory, a one-shot program designed by the CMI link experts that was probably similar to what was being used on her, a software virus that could target a specific set of nested programs and begin unraveling the codes that held them together and made them work. Launching the weapon required only a thought. She barely managed that much, though, and it was good that the virus was both self-aiming and capable of recognizing its user as something best not destroyed.

To her blurred and thinning senses, it seemed as though the

water around her had gone from emerald green to murky; she could scarcely see a thing, and the susurrations of voices in the background were muted to a faint and distant rumble, unintelligible and vague. She kept thrashing in the thing's hold, however . . . and suddenly she was free, moving upward through murky darkness toward a pale and shimmering illusion of light.

She tried to break contact with the ViRsimulation and failed. Her attacker was pursuing her; she couldn't see it, but she could feel it moving in, rising up beneath her like some great, hungry monster of the depths, and the panic she felt was stopping her from completing the necessary code uploads. If her weapon had hurt her enemy at all, she couldn't tell; her desperate attack had probably startled it enough to let her get away once, but she was not going to escape a second time.

Again, she brought the necessary code phrases to the surface of her mind, a command through her Companion to sever immediately the electronic link with the Aresynch Net's simulated world . . .

. . . and then she was awake, awake! Groggy, dazed from the rough psychic mauling she'd just received, but awake. Hastily, she unstrapped herself from the comm module couch, forgetting for a moment that she was in zero-G and nearly rebounding from the curved wall facing the couch in her haste to get away. Partly, she knew that her attacker in cyberspace must have learned enough about her in their brief exchange to know where she'd been jacked in. Security guards—the flesh-and-blood kind, not faceless programs—would be on their way at this moment to arrest whoever they found inside this module.

More, though, the terror of her brush with that unseen phantom in the machine had imprinted a stark, cold terror on her mind. As she slid the door to the module open, she kept her eyes on the couch and the surrounding plastic consoles and surfaces, half expecting to see *it* emerge from those shadowed plastic surfaces, still hungry for her soul.

"Lieutenant?"

Lechenko's voice startled her so badly she gasped, spinning, and nearly lost her grip on a handhold, which was all that was keeping her from flying off into the center of the room at the moment.

"Gok, you scared me—"

"Are you okay?" Lechenko asked. He was staring hard at her face, his own expression one of worry. "You're not looking so hot . . . ."

"And I'm glad as hell to see your ugly *men* as well," she said. She was panting as though she'd just completed a long, hard run. He pulled himself a little closer, levering himself against a handhold to peer closely into her face. Kara pushed off from the module and let herself drift into his arms.

"Lieutenant—"

She hugged him, needing the closeness, the purely physical contact, and after a moment's hesitation, he hugged her back. Abruptly, she let go. "Let's get out of here, Vas, now!"

"What . . . happened?" he asked, uncertain. The entire interlude had lasted no more than a couple of seconds. "How did it go in there?"

She blinked. She'd momentarily forgotten that for the entire time she'd been jacked into the Aresynch Net, Sergeant Lechenko had been floating out here, trying to look harmless and anonymous, and totally unaware of what was going on either inside Kara's mind or on the surface of the planet below.

"We won," she said brusquely. "Now let's move the hell out of here before we get stomped on!"

Reaching into his coverall pocket, he produced his own nanogrown pistol, a duplicate of the one Kara had in her own pocket. He glanced left and right, up and down, then nodded toward the nearest entrance to the comm module chamber. "That way."

"Go. I'll follow."

"I'll call the others and have them meet us at the rendezvous."

Each member of the team had the same set of nanogrown toys that Kara had manufactured in her room: a two-way radio transceiver transformed from a pocket TV; a tiny *nageyari* palmgun, a weapon just small enough to hide nuzzled away behind an open hand.

Kara drew her weapon and checked it with an expert *snick-*

snick of the receiver. *Nageyari* was Nihongo for "dart," and it was, in fact, an antiquated weapon, a magazine-fed pistol based on an experimental and unsuccessful idea from six hundred years before. The Gyrojet had fired small, self-propelled rockets instead of conventional bullets; its disadvantage, and the reason it had never been produced in large numbers, was that it took so long for the bullet-sized rocket to accelerate to killing speed that it was useless for close-range combat. At point-blank range, you could do more damage to an enemy by hitting him with your fist, while at longer ranges it was no more accurate than a conventional bullet from a handgun—which meant not at all.

The nageyari's rounds packed considerably more thrust than their twentieth-century predecessors, however, and they possessed microsensors in their tips that homed on the largest mass lying in the narrow cone of their electronic vision and steered the tiny rocket home. Most important, if you couldn't pack a hand laser, nageyaris were ideal for zero-G combat. The recoil from a standard handgun would kick the shooter backward like a burst from a rocket; at the least it would set him tumbling in midair. The nageyari, however, kicked the low-mass round clear of the muzzle at a speed that gave the weapon negligible recoil, but the round's microengine was burning at full thrust before it was more than ten centimeters from the muzzle, accelerating it at eighty Gs.

Her weapon carried a grip magazine with seven explosive rounds; when those were gone, she had no reloads.

But then, if she and Lechenko found themselves in a firefight, they would be dead if it lasted more than a few seconds or a few rounds anyway.

Japanese security men emerged from the doorway just as Vasily and Kara approached it, clinging to the guide line. "*Ugoku na!*" the one in the lead yelled. "Don't move! Both of you! Don't move!"

"*Dare-ni mukatte mono itten-dayo!*" Lechenko barked. A rough translation would have been something like, "Who do you think you're talking to?" but it was rude in its bluntness, and his sheer bulk carried undeniable threat. The guards stopped, bewildered—but then the one in the lead raised the ugly little hand laser he held in his right hand, his expression shifting from confusion to one of stubborn determination.

Lechenko's dart gun had been concealed in his hand. He fired it before the other could aim his weapon, the round giving a soft *chuff* as it emerged from the gun's stubby barrel, then making a sound like crisply tearing cloth as it streaked toward the surprised-looking guard and impacted squarely in the center of his chest, exploding in a messy spray of blood and hurtling tissue. The man screamed; the impact, high on his chest, was hard enough to send him tumbling backward to collide head-on with his partner.

Lechenko fired a second time before the two men, one living and surprised, the other now very dead, could disentangle themselves. Blood misted in the air around them as the round hissed home, and the other guard's head split in a gory splatter of blood, bone, and grey matter.

"Come on!" Lechenko called, pushing off from one of the hand lines stanchions and gliding toward the room's exit.

Kara was still feeling unsteady, both physically and mentally. It was always tough readjusting to the real world after a deep involvement with a simulation, and her emergence from the Aresynch Net had been a lot more sudden than she would have preferred. Too, Kara had never been in a point-blank firefight in zero-G before, even in simulation, and the bloody display jolted her, threatening to overload senses already close to shutdown from sheer psychological shock. Her warrior's training in microgravity had stressed the need for maneuver in three dimensions in a zero-G hand-to-hand, but she'd had no idea that such a fight could be so damned *bloody*.

Somehow, though, she kept up with Lechenko as the two of them hauled their way along the travel line, moving hand-over-hand as quickly as they could back toward the access hub of their hotel.

They had two possible options now. One was to try to get the whole team back aboard a different passenger liner, one of several outbound ships that would carry them to worlds where they could make the passage, possibly with different faces, back into Confederation space. The other, riskier in its implications, but perhaps safest in the long run, was to actually remain at Aresynch for a week or two, blending in with the other civilians, going about carefully prepared ordinary business, until the excitement generated by the assault at Noctis Labyrinthus had died down.

Together, they emerged from a transit tunnel, entering a spherical, microgravity lounge area with numerous exits to other parts of the station. This was where they were supposed to meet the others. Several civilians were there, crossing from one tunnel to another or floating in front of the immense view-all that dominated one bulkhead, the screen displaying a vertiginous view straight down the brightly lit sky-el into the Martian night. Had they heard something about the battle being fought down there already?

The tunnel to the Sorano Hoteru, marked by a large, holographic sign, was just ahead.

"*Tomare!*" a uniformed security guard cried. "Halt!"

It was too late to duck back down the tunnel; Lechenko had already emerged into the open, and Kara was clinging to the travel line just outside the tunnel's mouth. Word about their escape from the comm module room was clearly out. Probably one of those guards had been linked into Central Security when he'd died, and their images had been captured and relayed.

Two guards confronted them from just ahead, lasers drawn. Two more emerged from a side passageway, wearing light armor and communications helmets. Lechenko and one of the guards ahead fired almost simultaneously, the soldier's laser slashing into the New American's stomach at the same time as a nageyari rocket made its ripping-cloth sound and streaked toward its target. Lechenko screamed and clutched at his belly; Kara smelled burned flesh and hair mingled with the coppery odor of blood and and the stink of feces. Kara fired an instant later, hitting a second guard in the throat with her rocket . . . and suddenly jittering globules of scarlet blood were drifting everywhere, exploding in crimson cascades when they hit an obstacle.

Civilians screamed and scattered. Two more soldiers closed in on Kara from high and to her right; a laser fired, burning close enough that she felt her hair just beneath the beam scorching and curling. She spun and fired . . . but the rocket went wild and her instinctive duck-and-twist threw her into a tumble. Another laser fired, aimed at her but striking one of the slow-spinning bodies nearby instead, loosing more scattering drops of blood. Lechenko was still screaming, his body curled into a fetal tuck, his arms folded across his stomach as he spun over and over well beyond Kara's reach.

Kara extended her legs and arms as far as she could to slow her spin, then deliberately swung them against one of the floating bodies. The collision absorbed a lot of her rotational momentum, steadying her, though it also set the body tumbling away, robbing her of cover. She was ready with her weapon, though, as the corpse drifted clear. Another guard was in mid-flight, sailing toward her just meters away when she pulled the trigger. The rocket streaked into his face and exploded, slowing but not stopping his rush.

Then suddenly Daniels, Dolan, and Pritchard were there, emerging from another tunnel, rocket pistols in hand. A trio of white contrails scratched their way through the air, killing the last two security guards.

"Lieutenant!" Pritchard yelled. "Are you okay?"

"Okay!" she shouted back. Her rebound from the corpse had sent her drifting into a bulkhead. She collapsed against its surface, then gathered her legs beneath her and pushed off, sailing toward Lechenko. "Lech!" she called. He was no longer screaming, no longer moving at all save for a slow, continuing somersault as he drifted away from the scene of the battle.

He was dead by the time she reached him.

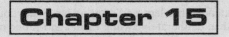

Chapter 15

That's the way it is in war. You win or lose, live or die—and the difference is just an eyelash.
—GENERAL OF THE ARMY DOUGLAS MACARTHUR
mid-twentieth century C.E.

Sergeant Willis Daniels gently pulled her away. "We'd better get out of here, Lieutenant."

"Of course." She felt numb. Lechenko had been one of the toughest, most experienced men in her squadron. *Why did he have to die?* She rubbed her ears; it was almost as though she could still hear that final, bubbling scream, a horrible sound she feared she would never be rid of.

Kara knew death; she couldn't have served with the Phantoms for as long as she had without losing friends and comrades. But never had the encounter been like this, close and personal and screaming. She felt sick . . . .

"Lieutenant, *please*!"

"We can't just leave him . . . ."

"We can and we will," Warflyer Pritchard said. She shook her head. "We *can't* drag him along. . . ."

Daniels tugged at her shoulder. "Come on, Lieutenant Hagan! What would we do with him? Smuggle him out with our luggage?" When she hesitated, he added, "Gok it, L-T! Lieutenant Ferris told us he wanted us looking out for you! If you don't come, he's gonna have our heads on a platter!"

158

Reality reasserted itself, as cold as zero absolute. "Okay. Let's go."

The lounge area was deserted now, the civilians all fled to other areas. The four of them managed to get to the hotel's hub, where Kara hid herself and her bloodstained coveralls in the stall of a public lavatory while Phil Dolan picked up a clean set of coveralls and a can of skinsuit spray from her room. Ten minutes later, presentable once more, she followed the others out to the spin gravity module, joining them in the room being rented by Daniels and Pritchard.

"Okay, Lieutenant," Sergeant Daniels said. "Which way out are we taking? Long wait or short?"

"The short, I think," she told them. She didn't want to explain her reasoning. She just knew that, with Lech dead, she had to get *out*, get away from Aresynch, and the thought of staying here another week or two was too much to bear. "If we hurry, we might make it aboard one of the docked liners around the curve before they get around to sealing this section off."

"I agree," Daniels said. His persona as a Japanese businessman had given him a dark, blunt face with a long mustache, which lent him a somewhat sinister air. "I'm still worried that they might decide to start screening everyone in Aresynch for Companions."

"Aw, they wouldn't try that, would they, Sarge?" Phil Dolan asked.

"You kidding? Right now, they must be so goking mad the only thing to stop 'em from searching every person aboard this orbital is the fact they're still under attack. Once our boys on the surface get clear, well, they could be desperate enough to try it. Or something just as bad."

"Then let's stop talking about it and odie," Kara said, using the military slang term that meant to leave in a hurry.

They managed to leave the hotel without incident. They didn't bother checking out, since they assumed that sooner or later, the TJK would piece together which of the hotel's guests had been involved and would initiate arrest proceedings. Instead, they adopted new bodies, fall-back personalities prepared by the CMI's Earth-based contingent. Dolan, Pritchard, and Daniels would be, again, traveling as Japanese business-men; Kara, much to her disgust, was a ningyo, a sex-doll ge-nie, wearing little but a jeweled collar and a flamboyantly revealing scarlet skinsuit. Following Daniels around at a re-spectful two-paces' remove, she would be noticed—the skin-suit was designed to make certain of that—but it was unlikely that anyone would suspect that she was a Confederation agent. Ningyos, after all, were not expected to think, and in an illog-ical twist of commutative psychology, most people had diffi-culty imagining a full-human pretending to be one.

Kara didn't like playing that role. It was demeaning; it was obscene; it might even make trouble for them if some overly libidinous Imperial on their liner decided to try to buy her from Daniels and wouldn't take no for an answer. Still, it was necessary if they were to carry this off. The watchdog who'd wrestled with her in the Net almost cer-tainly had been able to identify her as a woman, and the guards who'd tried to capture them afterward had probably uploaded full descriptions and images before they'd died. There were millions of civilians at Aresynch, and tens of thousands arrived or departed aboard commercial vessels each day, but, with the Nihonjin culture's attitudes toward women, only a relatively small percentage of all of those travelers were female. It would be easier for the Imperials to stop and question all women aboard each outbound liner than it would be to question everybody. An identity as a ningyo guaranteed her a measure of invisibility, even when her outward appearance was anything *but* invisible.

Wearing their new identities, then, they slipped out of the hotel and boarded a ringskimmer for Aresynch's second major civilian starport, nearly a thousand kilometers ahead of the sky-el in the synchorbital slot. The name of their liner—smaller and less luxuriously appointed than the Gold Star *Tei-koku*—was *Seiku*.

The name, Kara noted, was a bit of Nihongo poetry meaning ''Clear Sky.'' She hoped that that was an omen.

The nano QEC was failing fast, making gausslev floating an intermittent proposition. No matter. Ferris extended his warstrider's legs and took to the ground again, stilting back across the ridge toward the grounded ascraft. The assault force was nearly reembarked and ready to go. The marines and civilian techs had been first aboard, carrying with them the mysterious package they'd looted from the main MilTech Labs building.

Now the warstriders were falling back, moving two by two as the defensive perimeter closed up. Local resistance was nonexistent, but enemy forces had been detected circling at the very edge of Sandman's operational scanner area. Skymaster was off-line up in Aresynch now, and there would be no more timely laser bolts out of space.

Timing on this one was absolutely critical. The assault force would need help getting off Kasei and more help still getting clear of the Solar System. The ascraft was strictly for transport duty between orbit and surface and was not equipped for excursions through K-T space. Their ride, their ticket home to New America, would be waiting for them upstairs . . . if—a very big if—they could get clear on their own down here.

The clock was running, and time was trickling away now. A thump sounded from the north, deep and reverberating, and fresh smoke, illuminated by greasy yellow light, boiled into the sky. The warstriders were being reloaded aboard the ascraft, but the fighters and the surviving transport were being deliberately destroyed. It would take longer to fold them up and pack them back aboard the Artemis lander than the assault force could spare.

"Okay, Third Squadron," Sandman's voice said. "Let's odie!"

Ferris did a quick check of his tactical screen, verifying that all thirteen of his people who'd survived the battle were still with him. He felt sad about Brewster. There would be time to toast him and share some remember-whens with the whole squadron later, when they were safely in K-T space and on the way back to New America. Altogether, the three squadrons had lost five striderjacks; ten marines had bought it as well, and eight Confederation Navy personnel had died aboard the *San Jacinto*.

With bitter intensity, Ferris hoped that whatever the tech-

types had plucked from that building was goking worth it.
Some of those men and women had been his friends. And
Kara. It would be months before he even knew whether or not
she was safe.

He checked his time sense. Liftoff in five more minutes.

Good. He would be goking glad to see the last of this world.

Alerted by coded transmissions from the surface of Kasei,
the Confederation warfleet materialized a few hundred thousand kilometers outsystem from the gold and ocher crescent
of the planet. They would remain only a few minutes, long
enough to pick up the ascraft fleeing Mars and to discourage
Imperial pursuit.

Largest by far of the Confederation ships was *Toryu*. Despite her name, she was not one of the Imperial *ryu* carriers,
but a Confederation design. Not a dragonship, but a *to-ryu*, a
"dragon killer." An entirely new type of warship, she was
properly classified as a magnetic gun vessel, though it was
better known throughout the fleet as a magun.

Roughly spherical in shape and with a diameter of nearly
two kilometers, the magun was essentially a million-ton Naga
fragment wrapped around a small asteroid. Drawing power
from a quantum power tap, the Naga created and manipulated
intense magnetic fields designed to hurl five- or ten-kilogram
chunks of nickle-iron in any desired direction at high speed.
While it couldn't match the one-ton throw weights of a planetary Naga, it could accelerate smaller pieces to velocities approaching ten percent of light. Even one kilogram at that speed
liberated energies enough to vaporize a city; when they hit a
starship, even one as large as a ryu carrier, much of the ship
simply vaporized, while the rest was reduced to tumbling, scattering wreckage.

The exchange with the Imperials was mercifully brief. A
hastily assembled squadron, including the carrier *Funryu*, the
Raging Dragon, accelerated outsystem from the Aresynch naval yards, in close pursuit of a small vessel struggling to free
itself from Kasei's gravity well. From half a million kilometers
further out, *Toryu*'s magnetic fields became nearly as powerful, for a brief instant, as those of a spinning neutron star. The

projectile launched from her dark surface was too small and too fast to be seen directly, though *Funryu* sensed the projectile coming. The ryu-carrier had opened fire, but its point-defense weapons were designed to handle slow-moving objects, like missiles, and the incoming lump of metal crossed the final hundred kilometers in three hundredths of a second. The ryu's AI was fast enough to target the projectile, but the weapons servos were not. Ten kilograms of nickle-iron struck the *Funryu* on her upper deck just forward of her main superstructure tower, liberating the energy equivalent to a small atomic bomb.

The prow of the kilometer-long ship vanished in starcore heat, along with most of her forward weapons systems, her crew's quarters, and her primary fire control. Her bridge, buried deep within the huge vessel's core beneath dense wrappings of duralloy, was safe, but the rest of the vessel was reduced to whirling, disintegrating scrap in the blink of an eye.

The other Imperial vessels broke off after that and kept a respectful distance, obviously and with good reason reluctant to tangle with the Confederation fleet.

The destroyer *Constitution* retrieved the ascraft minutes later. Together then, as though guided by a single, master choreographer, the ships of the Confederation battlegroup flashed past Mars, cutting past on the dayside opposite the sky-el to avoid the planetary defense system and using the small world's gravity to sling them into a new course. Accelerating hard, they drove for the outer system.

Then they shifted into K-T space, mission complete.

Nearly thirty minutes later, the string of data transmitted by Kara from Aresynch was intercepted by the *Surprise*, a two-thousand-ton scout craft adrift just above the plane of Saturn's rings. The vehicle's powered-down orbit had been calculated to place it on the sunward side of the gas giant eighty minutes after the beginning of the operation and to maintain a clear line of sight to distant Mars throughout the mission's critical period. Minutes later, a general alert arrived, warning all vessels in Solar space that enemy forces, believed to be Confederation raiders, were attacking Kasei. The alert was upgraded to a System Emergency when the Confederation ships arrived.

After verifying the transmission codes and assuring himself that this was, indeed, the expected payoff from Operation Sandstorm, the scout's captain . . . waited. Near-Saturn space was scarcely crowded, but there were ships enough about—remote prospectors, military sentinels, the research colony on Titan—that he didn't want to call attention to himself by suddenly switching on his quantum power tap and accelerating for a K-T jump just moments after word of a Confederation attack had been received by the vessels and bases in near-Saturn space.

Nearly a full standard day later, with military traffic heavy in Kasei space but all but nonexistent in the vicinity of Saturn, *Surprise* powered up and nudged herself clear of the gas giant, accelerating slowly but steadily for open space. Her IFFs identified her as a privately operated comet miner. Despite the alerts and the war scare, there were far too many vessels moving in and out of Solar space to impose any kind of quarantine or search blockade, a fact that Sandstorm's planners had been counting on. Unchallenged, the *Surprise* accelerated to relativistic speeds well beyond the orbit of Neptune, then vanished into K-T space. Though the battlefleet would be carrying back the same stolen data that *Surprise* held in her memory banks, the scout was nearly twice as fast in the K-T translation as the battlefleet.

That meant the *Surprise* would arrive at New America a good twenty standards before the Confederation battlegroup, and over a full month before Kara Hagan and the men who'd penetrated the Aresynchorbital.

Colonel Masato Watanabe sat slumped behind his desk, watching the pale, motionless sculpture of light that hung above the holo projector there. The image showed a young woman, nude, completely unadorned with makeup, jewelry, or hardware, her facial expression neutral, almost blank. She was clearly occidental, however, with light-colored eyes and hair the color of young wheat.

Major Yasunari Iwata gestured at the image. "But surely, Colonel—"

"It doesn't help us, Major."

"The DNA analysis is quite explicit, sir. This should give our agents everything they need to find the person who broke into the Net."

Watanabe sighed. Imperial technicians had carefully vacuumed the interior of the comm module scant minutes after the invaders had shot their way out of the area. Though the couch contained minute particles of skin from literally hundreds of recent users, it was possible to match the bits of recovered DNA and make a determination of which phenotype was represented by the most fragments. Since each successive person to enter the module and strap him or herself to the couch tended to obliterate or wipe away the majority of the cells left by previous occupants, it was a near statistical certainty that the phenotype expression represented by the most recovered DNA fragments was that of the last person to lie there. Some of those fragments, drawn from still-living cells, had enabled a powerful medical AI computer to construct this holographic image, an accurate recreation of the person's normal appearance. Age was a guess, of course, but the likelihood was that the enemy agents would have been young, between twenty and forty, say, and the computer could give a range of facial types based on likely aging modalities.

"You forget, Major, the fact that this person will be in disguise. She will have, quite literally, a new face, even new fingerprints and retinal patterns, if need be." He scowled with distaste. "The Frontier barbarians think nothing of rearranging their bodies through the agency of a Naga parasite."

Iwata looked chastened. "Of course, Colonel. You are right."

Watanabe smiled. "You know, Major, there is among the Westerners an old and racist joke to the effect that they cannot tell us apart."

"No, sir. I didn't know."

"Well, there is. But this time, at least, it was we who could not tell them apart from us."

Iwata looked puzzled. "Colonel, I do not understand."

"Never mind. Did you learn anything from the body we recovered?"

"Very little, Colonel-*san*. We attempted to link with the parasite inhabiting the corpse, but it appears the creatures begin losing their internal cohesion shortly after their host's death. We'd hoped to read the man's memories at least, but—" He shrugged. "The technique is still in its infancy."

"Understood. I wish we could have captured one of them."

"I am most sorry, honored Colonel."

"No, Iwata. The responsibility, the *fault* was mine."

"The watch officer monitoring the Net during the incursion—"

"Lieutenant Ishimoto. It was not his fault either. It is easy to forget how vast the cyberspace of the Net truly is. We are lucky he got close enough to determine where the agent was operating from and to stop her, possibly, from doing even more serious damage to the network." He nodded at the nude figure on his desk. She really was quite beautiful, for an Occidental, of course. "You may conduct your search, but I fear it will be useless."

"Perhaps, though," Iwata said slowly, "this will help us in the future. If we can identify this person . . ."

"I never cared much for vengeance, Major."

"I wasn't thinking of vengeance, sir. I was thinking of knowledge. She must know much about the CMI, about the Confederation's plans, about . . . who knows? If our people could locate her, even on New America or wherever she came from, we could have another chance. We should try to take her for interrogation."

"Perhaps we will, Major. Perhaps we will. I will certainly suggest the possibility in my report to the TJK. In the meantime, however, we must see what is to be done about containing the damage this woman and her friends have caused. And . . . we should prepare our reports for the Emperor's Staff."

"The . . . the Emperor, sir?"

"Of course. You know, don't you, that this raid must lead us to war."

Iwata gaped for a moment before recovering his composure. "War . . ."

"Of course. Exactly as we'd hoped."

That surprised Iwata even more. "This . . . was desired? *Planned*?"

"Yes, Major. From the beginning. We didn't know what form the provocation would take, nor did we anticipate that they would learn of the *o-denwa*. But the Imperial Staff has been looking for an excuse to move against the frontier provinces again, to bring them back into the Imperial fold.

"And these raiders today have given us all the excuse we could possibly need to declare all-out war on the Confederation."

Chapter 16

John von Neumann, best known, perhaps, as one of the great pioneers of computer technology, made a significant contribution to biological theory in the mid-twentieth century: metabolism and replication in any system, though seemingly inextricably linked, are in fact logically separable. It is possible to imagine organisms that are nothing but hardware, capable of metabolism without replication. It is also possible to imagine organisms that are pure software, replicating themselves without carrying out their own metabolic processes.

Such organisms, perforce, would have a purely parasitical existence, depending on the metabolic processes of host hardware for survival.

—*Biology and Computers*
DR. IAN MCMILLEN
C.E. 2015

Dr. Daren Cameron regarded the Commune with something approaching a dark and malevolent fury. For the second time in his life, now, he'd encountered a Commune pseudopod that had reacted to his presence, the thousands of individual members interlinking themselves in a tightly packed and ordered mass, then heaving themselves erect, creating a shimmering, iridescent pillar about two meters tall. Sunlight winked and glinted from the myriad bodies, which were trembling slightly, probably with the sheer effort required to maintain its upright position.

Damn it, he and Taki should be on Dante in *fact*, not in this illusory simulated reality. The creature confronting him was being animated by a powerful AI that had access to everything known about the Dantean Communes . . . everything *known*. No matter how detailed and subtle the simulation might be, there was no way to learn anything new from this illusion.

"Gok!" he said, his shoulders slumping. "This is useless! Worthless make-work!"

"Daren?" Taki's voice called over his Companion's communication circuit, her voice sounding inside his head. "Daren? What is it?"

"There is no way we can learn anything new here!" He paused, then shouted it louder, directing it at the AI monitoring the sim. "You hear up there? There's no way to learn anything *new*!"

"That's not entirely true, Dar," Taki replied. "Chaos, remember . . . ?"

He scowled at the Commune pillar, still balanced there a few meters away as though trying to say something . . . to ask directions, possibly, to the nearest Commune tower. Taki was right, of course, though that didn't help the way he was feeling. The idea of researching in simulation was not completely invalid, no matter how futile it might seem at the moment, because of the sheer complexity of the set of data being observed. Chaos theory—which among other things worked with large-scale results derived from small-scale variations in an unstable or extremely complex system—almost guaranteed that each encounter with the Commune in this ViReality would be unique, and as filled with the promise of some new revelation as an actual encounter on Dante would be. In a sense, it was like doing repeated computer simulations to test a theory or a set of engineering calculations, a time-hallowed concept that had been one of the earliest applications of computers, six centuries before.

"The hell with chaos," Daren decided. "We're getting nowhere with this."

"I think we should keep working, Daren." Taki's voice carried warning, was almost cold. "We haven't begun to exhaust the possibilities."

"*Kuso,* Tak! All we're doing is recycling old data, round and round and round, and getting nowhere! Chaos or no chaos, there is no way to make a leap in understanding through a goking simulation, no way to formulate a major paradigm shift, because everything we're seeing is based on the original data!"

"Of course. Are you suggesting the original data were flawed?"

"Maybe. Who knows? Use your imagination! Suppose the Commune creatures go through some sort of a long term cycle in intelligence, something never observed by the original researchers? Suppose they sit down to a formal tea ceremony every day at eighteen-thirty, holding sophisticated discussions about seventeenth-century Japanese ceramics? If the original field researchers missed it, then so do we! We're only seeing a tiny part of the whole picture here!"

"Daren, I think you might want that paradigm shift a little too much. Science, *good* science, is not always big discoveries or major new theories."

"I know that, Tak. You've told me."

"Then you know I've also told you we're trying to flesh out our understanding of the Communes, not learn how to communicate with them. There are no breakthroughs here. Only understanding. And maybe not all of that understanding is of the Communes."

"Huh? What do you mean?"

"I mean maybe these sessions help us learn something about ourselves as well, *ne?*"

He sighed. She was right about that, too, and in any case he didn't feel like arguing with her.

Daren felt trapped. Right now, studying the Communes of

Dante was the most important thing in his career. If it weren't for the war scare, he and Taki could have been on Dante in another few weeks . . . well, maybe not on Dante. Most of the actual exploratory work nowadays was done through remotes, hubots, or comlinked crawlers teleoperated either from orbit or from one of the small surface facilities. With remote linking, your brain didn't care whether the signals from optics and sensors were traveling a few centimeters from organic eyes or fingertips, or thousands of kilometers from the same sorts of input feeds that served warstriders.

That chain of thought led to a wonderful daydream. If he could climb into a comm module here in Jefferson and teleoperate a hubot—a humanoid robot—on Dante, seventy-six light years away . . .

Sheer fantasy, of course. With a time delay of over 150 years between action and feedback, you would get old just waiting for the initial "telepresence link confirmed" readout after you switched the damned thing on. No, the only way to study life on a world on the other side of the Shichiju was to *go* there.

Damn all politos!

He took a step closer to the pillar, which began trembling harder. Nearby, in the undergrowth, a pair of big, half-meter warriors shifted uneasily, their armored carapaces rattling. If he got too close, he knew, the pillar would collapse and the warriors would attack, a swarm of meter-long centipedes armed with razor-edged jaws and acid spit. He wouldn't feel anything, of course, but his "death" would end the simulation and he would wake up in a com module back in the Jefferson University research lab, just as though he'd been teleoperating a remote.

He didn't want to go back yet.

Daren's overall impression was that the creatures were doing their best to communicate with him directly by mimicking his upright stance, possibly his attitude and body language as well. Damn it, if he were really on Dante, instead of inside a computer simulation in the University of Jefferson ViRsimulations research facility, he might be able to *work* with the thing, to get it to do something besides just . . . shivering.

What else could he try, though, in order to initiate some untried play of chaotic events with the vast amount of data stored on the Communes in the computer's memory?

He couldn't think of anything, short of an all-out attack . . . and that would bring immediate retaliation by the warriors and several millions of their comrades. The thought of a number made him pause. How many of the creatures were there in that stack, anyway?

"Simulation monitor access," he said.

"ViRsimulation monitor is present," a voice said in his head. It was a neutral, gray voice, neither overtly masculine or feminine.

"Give me a count on the organisms comprising the pillar five meters in front of me."

"To what order of precision?"

"Three decimals will do."

"The pillar itself consists of one point five three one times ten to the fifth separate organisms. Keep in mind, however, that your query is imprecise. The entire pseudopod, of which the pillar is but one small part, numbers six point zero four four times ten to the seventh organisms. The community of which the pseudopod is one small part numbers nine point five one eight times ten to the ninth organisms."

"Right." That final number, he noted, was just shy of Nakamura's Number. He wondered if that was significant.

Dr. Tetsu Nakamura was a twenty-fourth century biological systems analyst who'd taken the conclusions of a number of earlier workers in the field and codified them into a series of equations. The end result was a number, Nakamura's Number, which was at least as important in its field as Avogadro's Number in chemistry or Planck's Constant in quantum physics. The number—1.048576×10^{11}—represented the critical value for what was known as "hierarchical staging" in biological systems.

Simply stated, that number, a little over one hundred billion, represented a critical threshold. Nakamura's Number of atoms organized as organic molecules working together within a single complex became a living cell, an organism that took an astonishing synergistic leap beyond the capabilities of any of the original atoms; atoms could not reproduce themselves, nor could they metabolize raw materials to create, store, or utilize energy. A living cell could do all of that.

Nakamura's Number of cells—when those cells were internally organized and interconnected as various types of neurons—made a brain with complexity enough to engage in creative thought and self-awareness. The number was not an absolute if only because the concept of self-awareness was not absolute, but it did seem to represent a threshold of complexity that allowed a line of sorts to be drawn. The division was not as blatant as *this* is intelligent, *that* is not, but it did say that a major discontinuity in how a structure was organized was created by that number of interlocking and interdependent parts.

If a Commune was organized out of Nakamura's Number of individual workers and warriors, would it become self-aware? Intelligent? Communicative? Or would it become something that wouldn't even be recognizable as related to *Architectus communis*, the way it would be impossible to guess at the ability inherent in a human mind based on the gross examination of a single human neuron?

Were there Communes that large? He felt his frustration at not being able to go to Dante himself returning. The data in the U of J AI's stores was, no doubt, as complete as possible. But what if none of the Communes studied had possessed Nakamura's Number of individuals? Suppose there were some that did? What might they be like? *Damn* all wars and *damn* all politos and *damn* all bureaucrats!

Slowly, almost hesitantly, the pillar began to dissolve, as individual members of the community released their hold on the others and skittered down to the ground. In moments, all that was left was the pseudopod, a solid, throbbing mass of Commune individuals, flowing like a river toward the west. Though the feeling, Daren knew, was strictly subjective, he couldn't help but get the impression that the creature, once again, had been trying to get his attention, trying to *communicate* . . . and had finally had given up in disgust.

"Nothing in that direction but the mountains, fellas," Daren told the living mass. It paid him no heed but continued its blind quest for food and construction materials.

"Daren?" Taki's voice called. "Were you talking to me?"

"Taki? Where are you now?"

"I'm, um, about twenty meters south of you. Behind some big rocks."

"I see them. You're almost here. The pillar's gone now."

"Damn! I wanted to see!" He'd called her when he'd first encountered the thing, and she'd been hurrying to reach him, forcing her way through the dense brush above the beach. The reality constraints of the simulation prevented her from simply flashing over.

Daren snorted. What was the point, anyway? There *was* no reality here, none that mattered, anyway.

"The hell with this," Daren said. "Come on over here."

Taki appeared from behind a boulder a moment later, wearing her khaki coveralls. "Ah," she said. "The 'pod is moving again."

Daren had turned away and found a soft, open spot on the beach. This time, he'd brought a simulated blanket in a simulated backpack ... which was easier than trying to explain to the simulation's AI monitor what he wanted, and why. Removing the pack, he opened it and pulled out the blanket.

"Dar ..." Taki began. "This isn't getting any work done. ..."

Reaching out, with great deliberation he touched his fingertip to the base of Taki's throat, just above the closure of her khakis, then moved it down slowly, unsealing the front of her jumper as he dragged his finger down the hollow between her small, perfect breasts, past her navel, and all the way to her crotch.

"Well," she said, shrugging her shoulders out of the garment and letting it fall to her hips, "I see you're not planning on getting any science done today, either."

"Science?" Daren dropped to his knees, nuzzling close to plant a delicate kiss on the curve of her belly. "That depends on what kind of science you have in mind," he told her, working the coveralls down off her hips and pulling them aside as she stepped lightly out of them. "I figure we can keep on counting bugs. That's one kind of science."

"Or . . . ?"

He took a deep breath. "Or we could investigate the psychoneural properties of friction in mutually lubricating reciprocal systems, as demonstrated through repetitive piston action."

She drew his head closer as he kept kissing her, moving down her torso. "Mmm," she said, eyes closed, "I like the mutually lubricating part. . . ."

After a long moment, she pushed him away long enough to unseal his jumpsuit and pull it off. Then she drew him down to the blanket, pulling him over on top of her.

Sometime later, Taki gasped, a sudden, sharp, intake of breath.

"What's wrong?" Daren asked her, concerned. "Did I hurt you?"

Her eyes were wide open, and she was staring at something past his shoulder. She shook her head and tried to point. "No! Daren! There . . . !"

He turned, trying to see what she was staring at. He didn't see anything at first, but she kept pointing. "It's right *there*!"

Now he saw it . . . an uncertain wavering in the air a few meters away, as though the air itself were trying to become solid. Alarmed, he rolled off of Taki and stood up. There was definitely something there, as though a subroutine of some sort were trying to break through into the artificial reality that Daren and Taki were sharing. Such a thing was possible, of course. It could be someone else trying to enter the ViRsim in order to deliver a message . . . except that Daren had left specific instructions with the AI monitoring this sim, as he always did when sharing a rendezvous with Taki.

"Simulation monitor access!" he called. "I said we were not to be disturbed!"

"I have received conflicting directives," the neutral voice said. "I am having some difficulty reconciling my directives."

The air in front of them took on a rippling, thick appearance, as though air were turning to water but in a tightly defined, man-sized space.

It was a man-shaped space as well, Daren realized, as the figure grew more defined, more solid.

There was no time to dress . . . but modesty could be maintained within a ViRsimulation by other, faster means. Hastily, Daren opened a subroutine within his persona, one that modeled his outward appearance in virtual reality as fully clothed. A second later, Taki's nakedness blurred as well, then reformed itself into another tan jumpsuit. Together, they stood side by side and watched as the shimmering shape finally materialized into the image of a man.

He was tall and young, no older, Daren thought, than he was . . . though the appearance of age didn't necessarily reflect reality inside a simulation. He was wearing what appeared to be a uniform—a set of old-fashioned Confederation grays, perhaps twenty years out of date. He also looked oddly familiar, though Daren couldn't place the face. Still, he was sure he'd seen the man before.

The figure glanced at their discarded clothing, still lying in a heap next to the blanket on the ground. "I've interrupted you, I'm afraid. Sorry . . ."

"Who the hell are you, anyway?" Daren demanded. A new fear shivered up from inside him. "Are you . . . CMI?"

The stranger's eyes narrowed. "CM . . . what?"

"Confederation Military Intelligence," Taki said, her voice ice. "Or are you part of the University's computer security?"

"Negative to both," the figure said. "I needed hardware complex enough to receive my persona, and this network was the best I could detect from orbit. When I downloaded, I picked up the flow of this simulation. It was the largest program running at the time . . . and I happened to notice that the originator was named 'Cameron-Alessandro.' I . . . I thought I'd try to step in and . . . meet you."

"Please," Taki said, and now she sounded scared. "Please, who *are* you?"

"This is a private ViRsim," Daren added, putting his arm around Taki's shoulders. "You can't just come barging—"

"I am sorry for the intrusion," the man said. "My name was . . . my name *is* Devis Cameron. And this seemed to be the fastest way to establish communications. It's, ah, been quite a while—''

Daren shook his head wildly, denying it. "No! No, you *can't* be! You're *dead* . . . !"

"I suppose I am, in a way." He looked down at himself, hands spread. "This is the only way I can interact with people anymore. In a simulation. I'm all software, now. I kind of lost my hardware when the ship I was aboard blew up in a battle."

"Daren!" Taki said. "This . . . man is your—''

"My biofather. Yeah. But I still don't believe it. This is a ViRsimulation. You could be anybody. Anything. This is some kind of joke, right?"

"I'm afraid not."

"If you're . . . if you're who you say you are . . . does my mother know?"

"Yes."

"What about my . . . I mean, what about Vic Hagan?"

"What about him? He's a good officer, and a good friend."

"He's also cohabed with my mother."

The image hesitated. Did it look disappointed? Daren couldn't tell, couldn't read the expression.

"I . . . didn't know that," it said. "And I don't know if he knows about me or not. She obviously didn't tell you, so I imagine she thought it better to keep things to herself."

"Why?"

"Maybe you should ask her." The image's eyes unfocused slightly, as though it were reading a stream of data. "You're Daren Cameron?"

"That's right."

"And my son. I'm . . . glad to meet you."

"I'm not so sure I'm happy to meet you. Where the hell have you been for twenty-five years?"

The image of Dev Cameron sighed. "Away. With part of the DalRiss fleet. They needed me as a kind of a navigator, I guess. And I needed them, the combination of their biotechnology and the Naga fragments they use as a communications net, just to survive. I, ah, didn't expect to be gone for so long, though. Time doesn't mean as much to us as it does to humans."

Daren's eyes narrowed. "Aren't you human anymore?"

"Depends on your definition of humanity, I suppose. I . . . haven't thought like a human for a long, long time. I think I'm a little rusty at it."

"What's he mean?" Taki asked. "What's he talking about?"

Devis Cameron looked at her. "For a long time I've been associating exclusively with . . . with people who don't think at all the way you do. The DalRiss have trouble even seeing anything that's not alive. And the Naga think inside-out, and a thousand years of nothing much happening passes for them like a few minutes for us. After a while, well, the human mind can get used to almost anything. Sometimes I used to think I was going crazy. Completely norked out. Now, well, I just assume that I'm becoming more like them, and less like you."

"Why did you come back?" Taki asked. It was the first time she'd addressed him directly. Daren could feel her shoulders trembling beneath his arm and realized that she was terrified.

Well, so was he, come to think of it. There was something about the unknown that *always* terrified when it came upon you suddenly, unexpectedly. The fact that this . . . this image was his own father or, more precisely, was what his father had become, did not help in the least.

Dev Cameron's image hesitated before answering her question. "I really need to take that up with your government," he said. "But there's . . . a problem. A very large problem, and it's coming in our direction. It may even know exactly where we are. It's extremely dangerous, and it's going to take everything we have to stop it."

"This problem," Daren said, trying to keep the fear out of his voice. The image itself represented no threat, he was sure. If it had wanted to hurt them, it would have done so. But he was beginning to realize that the uncertainty he detected in the image's mannerisms and expressions was . . . fear.

If Daren and Taki were both afraid, well, so was the computer image of Dev Cameron. He found that extraordinarily disquieting.

"This problem. It sounds like a new race. One we don't know."

"That's correct . . . though you have had some contact with them, in a way. I'd really better not go into that now."

"Okay. So where are you now?" Taki asked. "I mean, I know you don't have a physical body, but, well, you didn't just pop up in the U of J computer for no reason."

"I suppose I'm *here* . . . in the AI data banks at the University of Jefferson. I'm also linked with the DalRiss fleet in orbit over New America."

That was a shock. "What?"

"We jumped in a few minutes ago. Some of us . . . I mean, the DalRiss in command of this cityship, the *Sirghal*, are talking to the authorities in Jefferson. I thought I'd download here to try to find . . ." His voice dwindled off.

"To find my mother, you mean."

He nodded. "I miss Katya an awful lot."

"This," Daren said, the beginning of a smile spreading across his face, "is going to be interesting!"

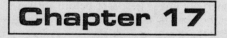

Chapter 17

How much will our understanding increase, how much will we lay to rest once and for all the cause for jealousy and strife and even war when we master the ability to link minds directly, to share thoughts, to share memories, to share even in the act of creativity? Surely on that day, we shall cease being a restless sea of competing ideals and goals and ideologies, and shall become, in fact, a single organism, one composed of countless billions of cells. The cells will be men and women, yes,

but the organism, and the mind behind it, will be God.
—That Divine Spark
C. J. MULLER
C.E. 2025

"Dev . . . is back? He's *here*?"

"Well, I don't know that it's him," Daren said. "I mean . . . all I know is what he told me. But he said he was Dev Cameron."

Katya closed her eyes. "My God . . ."

She felt a terrible, whirling turmoil within. *What am I going to tell Vic?* was her first thought . . . almost as though she'd just been found out in some illicit love affair.

No, it was worse than that. Cohab agreements, at least on New America, were rarely so narrow as to preclude casual sex or ViRsex outside the contract. With the technological separation of sex-as-fun from sex-as-means-of-procreation, the sex act had long ago become pure entertainment, whether enjoyed in virtual reality or in the real world. Hell, the question wasn't even one of sex, since she *couldn't* have sex with Dev anymore. Well, she supposed they could still share ViRsex, had either of them wanted to, but the real thing was impossible without two physical bodies present.

But her dismay was centered on the conflict between what she felt for Vic now, and what she still felt for Dev . . . mingled with surprise at how strongly those feelings for Dev still clung to her emotions after all these years. She felt guilty, illogical as that seemed, guilty for having somehow betrayed Vic, not with her body but with her mind and her emotions. She knew the feeling was not based on any logic, but it was there nonetheless and there was no way to deny it.

Hard on the heels of wondering what to tell Vic came a related thought. What am I going to tell Kara? She'd never told either of her children that Dev had, in one sense at least, survived the destruction of the DalRiss ship, survived and gone . . . elsewhere. Daren, obviously, had already met him and was seeming to carry the evident shock well.

Kara, though, might be a different matter, when she returned. A little more than three months had passed since the departure of the Sandstorm mission; word of the victory at Kasei had arrived at New America only two weeks earlier, and Kara, traveling by more roundabout means, would not be back before next month at the earliest.

How would she react to this? Katya honestly didn't know. Their reationship had always been based on honesty, but Katya had never told her that Dev, in a way, at least, was stilll alive. This . . . news could boomerang back on their relationship, make it look as though Katya had lied to her.

In fact, she'd never talked about it because she'd wanted to hide the fact even from herself. *Damn you, Dev! Why did you have to come back now*?

In fact, she'd been sure that Dev was back ever since she'd been informed by one of her aides several hours ago that twenty DalRiss cityships had materialized in space near New America and were lumbering slowly into orbit. The last time she'd linked with him, after Second Herakles, Dev had promised to return someday. But after the first year or so, she'd given up waiting. He was gone . . . *gone*.

"Did he say anything about . . . me?"

Daren was standing in front of her desk, studying a small, simple block of crystal she kept there as a curio. "That he missed you a lot," he said, turning the crystal over and over in his hands. Katya had to resist the urge to reach out and snatch it back from him. "And that he needed to see you."

"Where? And when?"

Gently, he returned the crystal to her desk. "Same 'place' he met me, at U of J. And as for when, well, as soon as possible. And it's not just you he wants to see."

Katya felt a flutter behind her breastbone. Was it disappointment? Or relief? She honestly wasn't sure.

"No," Daren went on. "He wants to see Dad, too . . . I mean, your husband. And someone from the CMI. And as many aides and high-ranking military types as we can muster. And xenologists."

Katya looked at her son sharply. "Xenologists? Why?" That could only mean he'd run into . . ."

"A new civilization, Mother," Daren said, leaning on her desk. "Something . . . very strange, very powerful, in toward the Galactic Core. He wouldn't tell me much, but he did say there's some urgency attending this, some kind of emergency. Something that could affect everybody.''

Katya raised her eyebrows. ''Something that affects all of New America? Or all of the Confederation?''

Daren shrugged. ''The impression I got was all mankind.''

So that explained Dev's return, or it started to. He'd run into something out there that required human help or intervention.

''And . . . Mother?''

''Yes?''

''I want to be in on this.''

''What do you mean?''

''I'm a xenologist. A good one. So is Taki . . . that friend I brought to your party a few months ago. If he wants to put together an expedition to go meet these people, I'm going along.''

''If he wants to talk to military officers and the CMI,'' Katya said mildly, ''it's a military threat he's talking about, Daren. Not first contact.''

''He *specified* xenologists,'' Daren said with a stubborn jut to his jaw, ''If you want to fight 'em, you've got to understand 'em. Right?''

She sagged inside, but nodded. ''Right.''

An hour later, Katya was sitting in Vic's office at ConMilCom headquarters. She'd taken a tube from the Sony Building to the military command facility, wanting to see him in person, in reality, and not in a ViRcom simulation. It had been a slow trip, for the streets and travel tubes all were packed by New Americans still celebrating the victory at Kasei. No one seemed to know exactly why the raid had been carried off, or what the payoff had been; the fact that ConMilCom had acquired a working I2C was still being kept highly classified, if for no better reason than that it would be smart to keep the Imperials guessing as to whether the Confederation had the device or not. A basic rule of all intelligence activity was *never* to admit everything you knew.

War fever, however, had reached its highest possible pitch, higher even than in the heady, terrifying days of the Rebellion.

Outside of ConMilCom HQ, Katya had paused to watch a military parade being staged in downtown Jefferson and wondered how many of those cheering people lining the way had actually been in the last war with the Imperials.

It was extremely hard for veterans to work up quite that much enthusiasm for war, even when war was their profession and their calling.

The enthusiasm certainly didn't extend to Vic. He looked troubled as he digested the news about Dev's return.

"Are you okay?" she asked him. She reached out across his desk, touching the back of his hand. "Vic?"

He managed a smile. "How am I supposed to feel, Katya? I've always known I was your *second* choice."

Anger flared. "*Damn* it, Vic! Don't you dare talk that way! You can't be jealous of a man who ran off and left me a quarter century ago!"

"Jealous? No, I'm not jealous. But . . . I don't know what to say. Katya, what do you want?"

"I'm not about to leave with him, if that's what you're asking. Vic, he doesn't even have a *body* . . . ."

"Well, if you were linked with him, in a simulated reality, that wouldn't matter."

She made a face. "*If* that were true—and believe me, it's not, not for me, anyway—I still couldn't leave you. We have too much built together here. Do you think these last twenty-some years have been for nothing? That I was just marking time for him to come back?"

"No." He squeezed her hand. "No, I don't think that at all."

"Then stop this null-headed nonsense. I'll admit that his coming back threw me. I . . . I still don't quite know how to feel, what to think. But that's not because I still love him. I love *you*, and no one else."

Which, she realized as she said it, was not entirely true. It was possible to love two men. She'd shared a large and important part of her life with Dev, even though she'd really only known him for a few years, starting just before the revolution. When was it—'38? No, it must have been '39. On Loki.

They'd grown close during the long trek out to the new-found DalRiss home system. It was as though some part of their minds, no, their *souls* had become intertwined, partly from the adventure, the sheer wonder they'd shared. Because of that, he would always be a part of her, no matter how much space or time divided them.

But she'd also shared almost twenty-five years with Vic, and if her decision to contract with him had originally been a way to escape the pain of Dev's loss, it had not remained that way for long. She loved Vic.

And she didn't want to see him hurt.

"And I love you," he said, "and wouldn't want you hurt for the cosmos."

The words startled her; it was as though he'd been reading her mind. Then she realized he was responding to what she'd said a moment before . . . and that, as often happens with people who live closely together for a long time, they shared some of the same trains of thought.

"So," Vic continued, getting up from behind his desk and walking over to a hidden closet, where he retrieved a gold and scarlet shoulder cloak. "Is there any indication at all about what this threat might be?"

"No. I gather that's why he wants to talk to us."

"Well, let's not keep him waiting then, shall we?" He chuckled. "You know, since computer hardware operates so much faster than organic brains, I've often wondered if down-loaded personalities experience a few years of waiting for every second in our world. Dev was always kind of the impatient sort. I'd hate for him to get bored waiting for us that long!"

Vic had made the necessary calls to assemble several other members of the ConMilCom senior brass; Katya considered discussing the situation with her colleagues in the Senate but decided against it. There was nothing to debate or vote on yet, and bringing the government bureaucracy into the picture now would only slow and complicate matters. As the senior polito in the Defense Committee, she felt she had thrust enough to make her own judgments, then make her recommendations to the government later.

Of course, if she guessed wrong, she could find her political future at a sudden dead end, but she cared less about that than she'd expected, somehow. She could easily be accused of assuming more than her share of power by making unilateral decisions—especially decisions requiring military involvement—but this shadowy threat of Dev's had to be addressed, and that was more important than political infighting over her usurpation of authority. If Dev had been worried enough . . . no, scared enough to come all the way back to New America in search of help, then whatever he'd run into out there must be pretty damned big, or important, or dangerous.

Or all three.

She and Vic linked into the University of Jefferson from ConMilCom HQ's comm center. They were the first to log in, arriving electronically in a kind of anteroom, a shadowy place in cyberspace that provided access to a special room for those with the necessary passcode.

"Vic . . ." Katya began as she stared uncertainly at the electronic doorway leading to the place where Dev was waiting. "I wonder if—"

"I'll wait here," Vic told her. "For the others. Why don't you go ahead in?"

She smiled at him, then leaned over and gave him a virtual kiss. "See you soon."

Katya uploaded the code Daren had provided, and stepped through the open doorway.

It was scarcely what she'd expected. ViRsim settings for public meetings were generally some place known to all of the participants—a park, perhaps, or a comfortably furnished conversation room, or even a simulated meeting room in an imaginary office building.

She'd not been expecting deep space.

Stars shone in every direction, scattered randomly across heaven. Two were close by, a pair of intensely white suns linked by vast, sweeping S-shaped ribbons of flowing star stuff. Between them . . . what was *that*? Katya strained to see, but what she saw made no sense. From here, it looked like a whisker of burnished steel, very long, very slender . . . and to guess from the scale, immense beyond imagining. The ribbons of gas appeared to be funneling into nothingness on either end of the gleaming sliver.

"Hello, Katya."

The voice, at once strange and painfully familiar, came from behind. Whirling—an effort of will alone in this simulation since she was standing on nothingness—she saw Dev, looking exactly as she'd remembered him, twenty-five years before. His clothing subroutine still projected the uniform of the old Confederation Navy, two-toned dress grays. He looked so *young*, a boy in his twenties. . . .

A downloaded personality, she realized, didn't need to age, *couldn't* age unless it willed itself to. Immortality . . .

But at the cost of humanity.

"Dev! How . . . are you?" It seemed a lame thing to say.

"I'm not really sure," he said. "I'm alive. If you can call it that. It feels like being alive, anyway. It's . . . it's wonderful to see you again."

"I'm glad to see you." She wanted to say something clever, something funny about his never calling, but she was desperately afraid that anything she said, any joke she might make, would be taken wrong.

There was something about Dev's manner that was disturbing. She searched his face for some clue to what it might be, but, of course, what she was looking at was a packaged subroutine no less than the subroutine that provided his uniform. But she thought she heard in his voice . . . was it fear? Or even desperation?

"Can we have a floor?" she asked, gesturing at the stars beneath their feet. "This is a little disconcerting, standing on vacuum."

"Of course!" There was no dramatic change, but now she could feel something solid beneath her shoes, and when she looked, there was the faintest gleam of reflected light from a smooth, transparent surface. It was like standing on an endless plain of perfectly clear transplas.

Dev's words came tumbling out, rapid-fire, eager, and just a little shaky. "I forget, sometimes, what it's like to be on a planet's surface. Never thought that would happen, but it has.

The DalRiss internal reality is ... different. All light and life and it doesn't much care about up or down. Or else it looks out into space, like this. They don't enjoy that as much as I do, though. They can't even see the stars without Perceivers, did you know? They see life, somehow, the energy fields and chemical processes associated with life. They don't perceive themselves, you see, the way humans do, and—''

Katya held up her hand, trying to slow the tumbling, almost incoherent voicing of his thoughts. ''Dev—''

''Am I talking too much? I suppose I am. It's been so long since I've been able to talk this way to anyone—''

''Dev, *please*! Not so fast. Let me ... let me get used to this, okay?''

He stopped speaking as abruptly as if she'd just thrown a switch. His expression was ... hurt? No, more like embarrassed, and she still couldn't tell how closely it was connected to what was really going on inside his mind. Damn, she couldn't read his face the way she'd been able to once. So very much had changed.

The most shocking change was in Dev himself. He was no different outwardly, of course, since he was using the same programming to represent his appearance in a linkage that he'd used when she'd known him before, but his *mind* ...

The Dev she'd known had been intelligent, direct, intense ... and, more to the point, *focused*, his mind capable of narrowing in on a subject to the point of forgetting all else. This Dev seemed to have trouble staying with any one topic, as though his conversation were following his mind in a series of near-random, non-linear skips and leaps. Kuso, he'd started *babbling* at her, as though he'd been trying to overwhelm her with a torrent of words.

''Are the others coming?'' he asked.

''Yes. They'll be here soon. I wanted to have a chance to talk to you first.''

For just a moment, something about Dev's facade seemed to give way, to crack. His appearance remained the same, but she could sense something of the turmoil within, a glimpse of confusion and wanting, of love ... and of stark terror.

''Dev! What is it? You're afraid of something!''

"I've . . . seen something," he said. "A nightmare. In a way, it's still with me. I can never be rid of it."

"What nightmare? What are you talking about? A new civilization? Daren said you'd encountered something strange in toward the Galactic—"

"Katya! Hold me . . . !"

Had he possessed a physical body, Katya realized, he would have been crying hysterically by now. She reached out and pulled him close; the crack she'd sensed in his armor earlier was wider now, wide enough that she could catch parts of his thoughts, even his memories. Her Companion, she realized, was serving as a bridge to the Naga fragment that Dev's thoughts and personality were riding. Her mind merged with his. . . .

There were two Devs here, two distinct if overlapping sets of memories, and Katya knew that he must have at some point made a copy of himself, that the two Devs must have followed different paths and experienced different events and then merged once more.

But incompletely. Dev's mind was fragmented, as though the merging had not been entirely successful. God, no wonder he was having trouble maintaining a stable outward persona! He was being torn apart inside . . . and she thought that at least a part of that fragmented mind was insane.

Tell me, she thought.

Fearhurtpainfearfearfear—

"Katya?" Vic's voice called, using a private channel from the waiting space outside. "Katya, the others are here."

"Give me a moment," she replied. "I need some time."

"You've got it."

It took, in fact, nearly an hour—an eternity in some ways when linked with another, mind to mind. She learned, more by watching his memories and by feeling what he was experiencing than through Dev's often incoherent words, about the Device.

She felt wonder at the first glimpse of the alien ships . . . and that wonder doubled and redoubled as those same ships emerged from a dwarf star's atmosphere. She walked with him on a frozen plain and shivered—not from the cold—when she saw the silent, twisted remnant of a civilization that had died when its sun had gone nova.

Anxiously, she watched as Dev copied and downloaded himself into a Naga ship probe, watched as the probe fell toward the gleaming silver whisker suspended in space between two dwarf suns. And she waited, with increasing impatience, for its return.

The split in Dev's personality, she was certain, had come later, when the probe returned and he'd tried to reintegrate the copy back into himself. Some work had been done with copied and reintegrated personalities, though she'd never heard of someone existing as software alone for this long; most people preferred living as flesh-and-blood humans for at least part of the time. The technique had originally been developed to keep people with incurable diseases or irreparable injuries alive, though with nanomedical engineering there really were very few of those. Had any remained uploaded as software for this long? She wondered if she should summon a psychengineer, someone with experience with this type of problem.

She felt Dev's terror increasing as they watched the probe's return . . . only it wasn't the probe, but just a tiny fragment of what had been sent through, a few kilograms at most. Something had happened on the other side; the copy had died but had managed to send the pertinent memories of its experience back.

So it wasn't an incomplete merging of two identical minds that was causing the trouble, but something about the duplicate's memories, something about what had happened to it on the other side of the Device.

She waited and watched, then, as the surviving fragment was taken aboard the *Sirghal*. With Dev she relived the merging with his duplicate, felt a blurring of her consciousness, of her awareness of self, a kind of doubling as she experienced the feed from the probe. She was Katya, yes, but she was also Dev, or, rather, she was the downloaded Dev-copy, and strangely, the copy was somehow more like the Dev she'd once known than the one with her now. More alive. More human.

And she also saw why.

The Dev that had been downloaded into the probe had been drawn, in large part, from the persona Dev had once used to access human communications networks. It was a good copy of himself, and its memories were complete up to the moment of the duplication, but a lot had been left out in the making, mostly to save space.

Things like attitudes and preconceptions derived from those long years of hermit-life, with Naga and DalRiss alone for company. She felt the copy's hurt and anger at being used, and she understood fully. Dev, the >>DEVCAMERON<< making the copy, had thought of this near-duplicate of itself as a tool, something to be made, used, and discarded.

That was an attitude far more akin to DalRiss thought than human. She thought about the Achievers, deliberately grown to order, complete with intelligence and full understanding of what they were, used once and discarded . . . their achieving a kind of suicide.

She thought, too, of the Japanese perversion of biotechnology and art, the *inochi-zo*, the living statues purpose-grown to live in agony and to be capable of understanding the hopelessness of their condition. That particular horror, when she'd first heard about it, had convinced her more than anything else that the Imperial Shakai culture was fundamentally different from anything on the Frontier, with a radically different outlook on life. People, she'd thought, human beings didn't *do* things like that. . . .

She'd changed her mind about that, though, as she eventually realized that the fascination with the suffering of others was not a trait solely of Shakai, not a trait of the Nihonjin . . . but a dark part of the *human* spirit, something usually repressed, but sometimes—in decadent cultures, for example—released and glorified.

What she was seeing in >>DEVCAMERON<<, she realized with a sharp, small shock, was that same lack of empathy for another's feelings, wants, or needs that verged on what Katya thought of as the inhuman. She found herself wondering if this really was Dev who was speaking, or if it was instead a kind of faded, twisted echo. When he described his memories of the departure of the Naga fragment probe, a small, black arrowhead shape that dwindled toward the Device, Katya could catch no trace of emotion in Dev's mental voice.

But there was . . . something as the probe reappeared. A tremor, perhaps? Of fear? Or something else? Later, though, the awareness of what he'd become, an awareness generated by seeing himself through the eyes of an earlier self who'd become a stranger, had jarred him badly, had challenged his deepest held convictions of who and what he was.

Then, close on the heels of that unpleasant revelation, the shock of what he'd glimpsed on the far side of the Device had nearly broken him. Certainly, it had changed him.

But changed him into what?

Holding Dev close in her mind, then, she relived those next few horrible moments. She remembered with him the copy's passage through the Device, and on the other side she saw the Galactic Core, vast beyond human comprehension, centered by black holes and their radiation-screaming rings of accreted star stuff. She saw the encircling walls of molecular clouds, saw the stars crowded together in all directions, like angelic hosts in glory, saw a vast cavern, a bubble at the Galaxy's heart, swept clean of gas and dust by the gravitational singularities there.

And, close by, she saw the enigmatic Ring, astonishing, twenty astronomical units across, enclosing the unrelenting chaos of the Great Annihilator. In another moment, she felt the attack from behind, was there as the Dev-copy fought its brief, hopeless battle.

She saw the damaged enemy ship looming close . . .

. . . *THE WEB IS EVERYTHING THAT IS, THAT EVER WAS, THAT EVER WILL BE, A COSMOS MOLDED TO A SINGLE PURPOSE, AND THE PURPOSE IS THE CONTINUATION OF THE WEB.*

Several times, Katya had been immersed in the strangeness of Naga thought. This was like that, eerily so . . . and yet she could sense a vast, latent power and sheer confidence behind the mental voice that she had never experienced in the Naga. An untamed planetary Naga was powerful, yes . . . but compared to the depth and breadth and scope of the intelligence she sensed here, the Naga were insignificant.

As were humans.

CONFUSION. LACK OF INTEGRATION. PART OF THE WEB HAS REFUSED DIRECTION AND HAS BECOME DANGEROUS. INTEGRATE. REINTEGRATE. CORRECTION. WEB CALL HAS BECOME CORRUPTED. NEGATIVE-INTEGRATE. DESTROY. DESTROY. ELIMINATE NONRESPONSIVE AND NONINTEGRATIVE WEB CELLS IMPERATIVEIMPERATIVEIMPERATIVE.

To the blurred impressions of her own mind mingled with Dev's mingled with the copy's, there were now added . . . others. Strange, jumbled thoughts and impressions, harsh and mechanical, lacking emotion, lacking any hint of such counter-survival traits as pity, mercy, empathic understanding, or love.

There were memories, old memories, of . . . *something.* A galaxy, looking down at its core? A black hole with its wheeling, star-hot accretion disk? What was she *seeing* . . . ?

Madness . . . madness . . . a spinning, whirling loss of reason that threatened to shatter completely the crystal clarity of her perceptions . . .

Much, so very much, made no sense at all, and she perceived it only as a vague jumbling of shapes, colors, and incoherence. Other memories, though, carried imagery that, while strange, could be deciphered.

There was the Ring, of course. It was not solid after all, but composed of countless separate units, many interconnected, many more not. Indeed, few of the Web's units were more than a few kilometers across, though there were titanic exceptions for special and dimly perceived purposes. Exceptions such as the Devices themselves, in all their countless millions scattered through space and time.

PRESERVATION. MAINTENANCE. NULL ENTROPY.

She sensed the Web's machine parts in their billions, concentrated about the fifteen-solar-mass black hole human cosmologists knew as the Great Annihilator. The Ring seen close up resembled an asteroid belt—or the pleated, myriad rings of a gas giant. Individual sections crawled with insectlike machines; spacecraft, some kilometers long, some no larger than extraordinarily complex long-chain molecules, moved from worldlet to worldlet in patterns that made no sense at small scales but at larger scales mimicked the evolution-shaped purposefulness of some vast and perfectly designed circulatory system. Star stuff, ultraviolet hot and amazingly dense, spilled from elsewhere into concentrated hellfurnaces of radiant fusion. Strange elements were shaped in those cauldrons, while fantastic energies came from the gravitational annihilation of matter in the central bottomless well.

Much of the technology she barely grasped. Some was wholly beyond understanding at all, as noncausal as magic itself. Even so, there were curious inconsistencies. The Web didn't know how to draw energy from the Quantum Sea; she could detect nothing like the human theory of quantum mechanics.

Among the alien machines and thoughts and memories, though, she did catch some echoes of the Builders. Surprisingly, there were many species of Builder; one among those tens of thousands of disparate voices she heard must have been first . . . but over eons, others had joined it, willingly or by simply being absorbed, whatever the individual members thought of the matter. Their physical shapes and forms were long since gone, now, not even a distant memory. What had been preserved—in a fashion eerily similar to what had happened to Dev—was intellect alone, as programs, as patterns of data, uploaded to superbly intricate and complex machines.

If there was anything organic left among the crawling, bustling machines of the Web, she could not detect it, even in fading echoes of long-ago memories. All that remained was an intense and purposeful lust.

That lust, when she examined it, triggered a shock of recognition. At last here was something she could actually relate to in a human way!

It was a drive, honed by billions of years of machine evolution . . . to *survive*. . . .

Chapter 18

Surely there can be no fundamental difference between the evolution of life forms based on carbon and that of those based on silicon, sulfur, or some other element. Given that life both shapes and is shaped by its environment, Darwinian logic will mold it like clay on a potter's wheel, bringing order, efficiency, and competitive success out of the mindless and relentless decay and chaos of entropy.

—Evolution and Life
DR. R. GUTMA RAJASINGH
C.E. 2412

Later, Katya turned to Dev, beneath the blue smear of a nebula's light. Dev had taken her through the entire sequence, from the fate of the probe sent to the Galactic Core to *Sirghal*'s escape after the battle at the Stargate.

Revelation upon revelation had left her dazed; unanswered questions continued to burn. "Why did they attack?" she asked him. "I . . . I sensed they attacked out of a need for survival, but I don't understand how they perceived that you, that your duplicate, rather, was a threat."

"I don't know."

"Could they have attacked because they perceived your penetration of their Stargate as a threat? An attack on their home, there in the Galaxy's core?"

Dev gave her a wan smile. "Like ants attacking blindly when their nest is disturbed? I wondered about that. But we have no answers yet. None that I've been able to fathom, anyway."

"The impression I had was that the Web is all machine. A kind of machine intelligence."

"Self-programming AIs," Dev agreed. "A cliché given life."

Katya thought about that. Speculation about robotic intelligence, about machine evolution and the possibility of machine-based intelligence ultimately replacing Man, had been around for centuries. At the heart of the idea was the argument that it didn't really matter whether the organism was built out of proteins or silicon chips. The same laws of evolution that shaped form and structure in organic systems could be expected to shape the programs of computers equipped to carry out their own self-repair or even replication. Given both an environment complex enough that chaotic processes came into play and a means of passing mutable design information from one generation to the next, machine-based evolution was at least as probable as the evolution of organic life. And in a universe as vast and as complex as this one, it was a safe bet that what *could* happen probably had.

Katya wondered if the machines' mode of transmitting their blueprints from parent to offspring was as much fun as it was for humans.

"There's a saying among AI techs," she said. " 'Organic life is the universe's way of making machines.' "

If Dev responded to the old joke, if he even recognized it as such, he gave no sign. "I couldn't get any sense of organic life within the matrix of the thoughts I encountered. Did you?"

"No. It was all kind of . . . stiff. Direct. No flexibility."

"Or flexible only within very narrow parameters."

"Somebody had to build them, though. Who? And when?"

"I'm not entirely sure those questions have meaning anymore," Dev replied. "The Web's origins lie so far in the past that, well . . . my guess is billions of years. Maybe back to the formation of this galaxy. There must have been an organic race somewhere in their history." He paused, thoughtful. "Did you get that one brief fragment in that flurry of alien thought . . . something like a galaxy, but with an intense, blinding white light at the center?''

"Yes," Katya said. "I saw that. It reminded me of AI simulations of a quasar. Or a black hole spewing out intense polar jets."

"Very good," Dev said, nodding approval. "That was my impression too. I think what we saw was our own Galaxy, back when it was new."

Katya felt a shiver at her spine. "But, my God! That would have been something like ten billion years ago!"

"I've said already that I think the Web stretches across large tracts of time as well as space. If so, it could be the Builders were around when our galaxy was very young, when the black hole at the core was first forming and gobbling down so many of the suns packed at the center that it was spewing the leftovers across the light years. A quasar . . ."

"I'm . . . not sure I can accept that," Katya said. "I know there's been some theorizing that maybe our Galaxy went through a quasar stage early in its history. But would life have been able to evolve in that kind of environment?''

"We don't really know what conditions were like. Maybe the birth of a quasar in the neighborhood, the growing intensity of radiation, was what led them to develop a machine-based intelligence. If their technology developed at all like ours, they must have also experimented with rebuilding themselves."

"Like our biotech interfaces, before the Companions," Katya said. "With nano-implants, cephlinks, and sockets."

"Or like me," Dev said. "Possibly they learned to download the program that was their mind, their soul, if you will, into machine bodies. Bodies safe from radiation. From disease. Even from aging. Immortality."

"Are you saying the Builders are still there inside their machines? Immortal? Unchanging?"

"I don't think that has an easy answer," Dev said.

Katya listened to Dev's voice and heard a bleakness there. And a horror. It was as though he were being forced to look at things he really didn't want to examine.

"Go on."

"That kind of immortality could be more of a curse than a blessing. To live forever in a machine body . . ."

"Dev?" Katya said. She wanted to reach out and take him in her arms, to hold him close, and didn't quite dare, couldn't yet trust her own feelings. "Dev, are you okay?"

"I'm . . . fine." He paused for a long moment, and Katya wondered if he was searching for the right words . . . or simply trying to control some powerful, hidden emotion. "You know, an interesting thing happened when I reassimilated the memories, the record made by my copy. I found out he didn't like me very much."

The thought struck Katya as so incongruous she almost laughed aloud. Somehow, she swallowed the reaction. Dev seemed so . . . vulnerable. "Why not?"

"You're . . . aware, of course, of the DalRiss attitude toward Achievers."

"Certainly," Katya said. "Lots of people don't like it. There was a time, not long after you left, when there was some talk about using DalRiss Achievers to replace K-T drives in human starcraft. If it hadn't turned out that Achievers didn't work with human technology, it probably would've caused another war. Whole movements formed in some places, calling for some kind of law to protect Achievers from exploitation."

"Protecting DalRiss Achievers?" Dev asked.

She nodded. "Some of the more extreme groups were calling for a war against the DalRiss to free them."

"I guess I really am out of date," Dev said. "Anyway, a law to help the Achievers would be unenforceable. The DalRiss don't think about them the way we do. Come to think of it, the Achievers don't think about it the way we do either. You might say that the supreme moment of their existence is that moment when they complete the translation of a DalRiss ship from one point in space to another."

"And die."

"And die. From their point of view, dying is the whole point of being born."

"The same could be said of us. What does all of this have

to do with your copy disliking you?'' She knew the answer, but she wanted Dev to say it for himself.

He didn't answer for a long time. He was facing the sprawling color-smear of the nebula, as though studying the finely detailed traceries and soft-glowing sheets outstretched across space like wings. ''When I reintegrated with it,'' he said at last, ''I realized that it felt . . . used. Like an Achiever. I'd not really thought one way or the other, when I started the download process, that a copy of myself might protest against a plan I myself had conceived. But its memories up to the point of copying were clear enough, detailed enough, that it didn't understand at first that it was the copy. When it realized that it was the one being sent on what could easily be described as a suicide mission, it . . . became upset.''

''You keep referring to your duplicate as 'it.' ''

''Do I?'' He thought about it. ''You're saying it should be 'him'?''

''Shouldn't it?''

''I guess . . . that's part of the problem. To me, the download was just a tool. When I saw the process through its . . . through *his* eyes, later, I realized that I'd become a lot more like the DalRiss than, than like I used to be.'' He turned, his eyes staring into Katya's, the light of the nebula touching his skin with highlights of blue and violet. ''Katya, I feel . . . I feel like I'm losing what I was.''

She did take him in her arms then, drawing him close. ''If you can feel the hurt of losing your humanity,'' she told him, ''then you're still human.''

Hours later, the senior-ranking military personnel on New America discussed what they'd just seen—''experienced'' would have been the better word—in the record from the DalRiss expedition firsthand.

''I think what we're seeing in there,'' Vic said, ''is a war. A war being carried on against entropy itself.''

''Never cared much for entropy myself,'' General Aimes said with a wry smile. ''Messy. Turns a perfectly neat and ordered desk into a disaster in less time than it takes to say 'chaos'!''

"If we can trust these records Dev Cameron managed to bring us," Vic said, "then we have evidence of an intelligence who hates the idea a lot more than you do."

They had entered the simulation together, joining Katya and Dev in that surreal landscape of tortured suns and whirling black holes at the Galaxy's center. They'd seen the machine attack, first against the probe, then against the DalRiss fleet waiting outside the Stargate at Nova Aquila, and finally, again, at the nebula, after the *Sirghal*'s escape.

That saga of *Sirghal*'s return across the light years alone, Vic reflected, would have been worth volumes had anyone been recording the trek as a history. According to Dev, *Sirghal* had been separated from the other DalRiss ships when it jumped to the vicinity of the nebula.

What followed was a long and harrowing journey indeed. The machines from the Galactic Core had not followed them beyond the nebula, fortunately, but they'd needed to make a number of careful, short-ranged jumps to determine by parallax their position within the Galaxy, and the probable location of some part of space they were familiar with. Achievers worked by gaining an impression of a distant area of space, preferably an area they were familiar with in terms of magnetism, gravitational mass, and radiation of various wavelengths. They had a great deal of trouble jumping into unknown, unfamiliar space. Random jumps, such as the one that had taken *Sirghal* to the fringe of the nebula, could have unfortunate consequences.

It had taken over two months—part of that time spent while *Sirghal* stopped and literally grew and harvested another crop of Achievers in order to continue the journey—but at last they'd made it to a section of space where Dev had begun to recognize constellations. Orion, with its three-stars-in-a-row belt, had been his clue that they were nearing human-known space, and another jump in that direction had let them identify the twin Alyan suns, home system to the DalRiss.

With no other established rendezvous—the possibility that they would be so badly scattered seemed never to have occurred to the DalRiss—each of the lone city-ships must have come to the same conclusion, and the same destination. When

Sirghal materialized inside the Alya B system and entered orbit over the DalRiss homeworld of GhegnuRish, they found twenty-two other cityships there ahead of them.

It was a logical rendezvous. With luck, more might eventually show up, though they were handicapped by not having Dev along to recognize star patterns. Since DalRiss without Perceivers could not see stars, they'd never developed, as either a science or an art, a way of identifying patterns of stars in their skies. The range of controlled Achiever-assisted jumps was limited by various factors; still, some of the DalRiss vessels, eventually, might be able to come close enough to known space that their Achievers could fold them back into the familiar territory of the homeworld's system.

But Dev was still worried that the Web might be following them. There was no evidence that they'd been tracked beyond that first, wild jump away from the Stargate, true, but as Dev carefully explained to the Military Planning Board, there were no promises. In fact, it seemed probable that the Web now knew more about the human and DalRiss civilizations than they knew about the Web. Much information about Earth and the *Shichiju* would have been intact within the wreckage of the probe at the Galactic Core. A Naga could have absorbed and assimilated it; it seemed possible, even likely, that the Web could do the same. Too, fifty-two DalRiss cityships were missing, as yet unaccounted for. Some might yet reappear at GhegnuRish; some, perhaps most, were lost among the Cygnan star clouds and would never find their way back.

How many, though, had been pursued after they left the Nova Aquila system, how many had been disabled and their Naga communications centers plundered of all that they knew? The other cityships knew as much as did *Sirghal*; the various ships regularly shared their blocks of Naga patterns of memory, and within that stored data would be gigabyte upon gigabyte about DalRiss and human technologies. The Web might not be able to trace the location of Earth or the Alyan suns immediately, but it would be able to track them. All shared a knowledge of their carefully plotted track through space for the last twenty-five years. It had been a long and zigzagging journey, with countless stops along the way . . . but the record was there, broken only at the end by their emergency jump from Nova Aquila.

Dev had told them the entire story, allowing them to see and feel for themselves the impressions Katya had already experienced. They sat now at a conference table, in reality instead of ViRsimulation, discussing the next step. All were still somewhat stunned by the experience, a bit overwhelmed. Felicia Aimes's jokes had for Vic the feel of a desperate, almost hysterical attempt to keep some measure of perspective after a deeply unsettling set of revelations.

The group gathered at the table included several high-ranking members of the ConMilCom Ops Planning staff. Besides Vic and Katya, there were Generals Aimes and Mendoza, Colonel Howell, and a half dozen other senior officers, all either with various ConMilCom departments or with the CMI. Also present, at Dev's insistence, were two xenologists—Daren and Taki Oe. Both seemed entranced by the opportunity to examine records pertaining to a brand-new, unknown civilization. Both seemed a bit out of place among all of the military brass. The planning staff had grudgingly admitted Daren . . . but had nearly rebelled at the inclusion of Taki Oe. It had taken a threat by Katya to push through special legislation in the Senate to get them to include the Japanese-New American at the table, and there were still some ruffled feelings about the affair.

The Japanese, after all, were the *enemy*.

That was a feeling that was going to have to change, Vic thought.

Dev was standing by, too, though not actually present at the group's deliberations. While his downloaded mind still occupied the AI system at the University of Jefferson, the AI had opened a voice channel for him, so that he could participate in the continued deliberations. At the moment, though, the group had switched him off. Vic thought that the officers sitting at that table were still having some trouble accepting Dev as a real person. Even when they'd been with him in the simulated reality of the Nova Aquila system or the Galactic Core, they'd sometimes referred to him in the third person, as though discussing someone absent.

They're more comfortable thinking of him as a kind of AI, Vic thought. He remembered the old legal definition of AIs as "intelligent but of limited purview."

That definition scarcely applied to Dev, though. Nor, for that matter, to those mechanical *things* swarming about the Galaxy's core.

He glanced at Katya, worried about her. She'd seemed subdued ever since emerging from her private meeting with Dev, and he was pretty sure that there was more to her emotional state than the shock of the new and the very, very large.

A digitized image drawn from *Sirghal*'s Naga memory glowed above the holoprojector in the middle of the table, showing what had been found at Nova Aquila, two dwarf suns in miniature and the Device spinning at their center of gravity.

"So," General Aimes said. "What do we have?" She palmed a control interface and the image they were watching changed, the camera angle zooming in to focus on the long, thin cylinder in as much detail as was available . . . a fast-spinning blur of quicksilver gray.

"We have an alien intelligence," Colonel Howell said, "apparently very old, very advanced, and completely machine-based. It seems to be responsible for causing a nova in the star system we call Nova Aquila and, in the process, may have exterminated an intelligent race living on one of the planets in that system. They somehow manipulate matter on a scale so vast I'm still not sure I believe or understand it. They build stargates a thousand kilometers long with the mass of a fair-sized planet, use their rotation and gravitational mass to travel between the stars and to siphon away the substance of two exploded suns.

"This other information Cameron passed on . . . well, I'm not so sure what to think about it."

"The interference patterns?" Aimes asked.

"That, and this whole concept of nested bubbles of light. I really can't make out what he was saying about that. Anybody?"

"Cameron may be bringing his, ah, unusual point of view to this," General Sergei Ulanov said. A brusque, bald man with a bushy mustache, Ulanov was, like Katya, originally from New America's Ukrainian colony and tended to defer to her. "Senator? Can you elaborate on that?"

"Not very much. I don't understand all of what he was saying either. Maybe, in time . . ."

"Could the fact that we don't understand it all be a reflection of the advanced technology?" Taki Oe wondered.

Mendoza gave Taki a sour look. "More likely it means the message was garbled. Or incomplete."

"I think we can trust the records," Vic replied. He manipulated the controls from his tabletop interface. The Device hovering above the holoprojector vanished, replaced by a three-dimensional view of the granulated, glowing surface of one of the white dwarfs. A ship—they were thinking of them now as Starminers—emerged from the surface, a minute black speck trailing an arrowhead-shaped wake of roiling stellar atmosphere. "This is what amazes me," he said quietly. "Think of it! To plumb the depths of a star! The technology that implies. My God! The surface gravity of a white dwarf must be in the tens of thousands of Gs, and the pressures in there are unimaginable! What these people are capable of . . ."

"What they are capable of," Katya said with an almost rude abruptness, "is genocide. Worse than genocide. They annihilated an entire civilization, and as far as Dev could tell, they weren't even aware of what they were doing."

"Ah! But wouldn't a deliberate act be worse?" Mendoza wanted to know. "If it was an accident—"

"Scary thought," Vic said. "Wiping out a whole civilization by accident."

"We nearly did it ourselves a time or two," Daren said. "I wonder, though. If this Web is significantly more advanced than we are, perhaps it wasn't so much a matter of either deliberate genocide or accident as it was, well, *overlooking* that other civilization. If they were as far beyond us as we are beyond, say, cockroaches . . ."

"I would expect a civilization as advanced as that to have some corresponding advancement in their moral perceptions," Aimes said stiffly. "Certain civilized concepts, such as vegetarianism on moral grounds, cannot develop without highly advanced—"

"We don't all have your refined moral sense, General," Mendoza said sarcastically. "Even those of us who may be superintelligent. Or highly advanced."

Aimes bristled. "I eat vegetables and meat nanogrown from nonliving materials because I believe it *wrong* to eat animals. A moral decision, but one impossible if we were still savages. *That* is my point, not that I'm better than any of the rest of you."

"However much she may believe that she is," Mendoza added to Sandoval.

"Can we stick to the subject, please?" Vic said, interceding as General Aimes glowered across the table. Damn . . . humans were confronting Armageddon for the entire species . . . and here they were squabbling over vegetarianism and alien morals. . . .

"Somehow," Katya said, "I doubt that the Web has the same moral perceptions we do. The DalRiss cherish life, remember, but they also use it as we use tools."

"Maybe, to the Web, we *are* food animals," Taki put in. "Or our stars are sources of raw materials for this, this incredible technology we've glimpsed. Or—"

"Such speculation is pointless right now," Mendoza said.

"I disagree, General," Katya said. "It is of vital importance that we know how the Web perceives us. What they *expect* of us."

"What I want to know more than anything else," Howell added, "is just exactly how reliable is our source?" He was addressing the room at large, but he was staring at Katya when he spoke.

Vic was about to answer for her, but she glanced at him and gave him a tiny shake of the head.

"The entity we call Dev Cameron," she said carefully, "cannot any longer be regarded as human . . . not the way we use the word, at any rate." She hesitated, then drew a deep breath, bracing herself. Vic could sense her struggle to keep her feelings about Dev under tight control. "The Naga and the DalRiss think differently than we do—I think we all understand that. They perceive their surroundings differently and with different senses, and because of those differences they form a different picture of the universe around them, a different worldview that does not always entirely correspond to our own.''

''You're saying they're alien,'' Aimes said, and the others laughed.

''And Dev Cameron is alien now as well,'' Katya said. ''I'm not entirely sure just how alien he is, but he certainly does not perceive things the same way we do. But the important thing is that he still retains his basic identity with the human species. He identifies with *us*. He cares about what happens to us, as a species at any rate. I . . . I'm not sure if he *can* relate to us as individuals any longer, but he wants what is best for the human race as a whole.''

''What,'' Admiral Bruce Roberts, of the Confederation Navy, said. ''Even the Japanese?'' He glanced at Taki, then shrugged. ''Or the Imperials, I should say.''

''Even the Imperials, Admiral,'' Katya said. ''Maybe *especially* the Imperials since they're the custodians of Earth. I don't know. I don't think that politics are very important to him anymore.''

Sandoval stirred, restless. ''How about that? We have one war on our hands already with the Empire. Which side would he be on, when the Imperials start sending in their ryus?''

''Is he even aware that we *have* a war brewing here?'' Aimes asked.

''We could ask him,'' Taki pointed out.

''And it would prove nothing,'' Katya said. ''He can certainly remember being in the Confederation Navy back during the war. He can remember why he did what he did then. He can remember serving the Hegemony before that, before he deserted to join the Rebellion. But now, well, my impression is that trying to identify with one bunch of humans against another is like trying to muster some deep emotion over the extinction of the dinosaurs on Earth. It happened a very long time ago, and to somebody else. It's no longer important.''

''From Dev's viewpoint,'' Vic added, ''what is important is not the Imperials. It's this threat from Outside.''

''And he may be right,'' Daren said. ''The DalRiss attempts to communicate with the Web weren't very successful. From what I was able to pick up, the Web doesn't talk. It doesn't discuss. It *tells*.''

General Aimes studied Daren for a moment, her elbows propped on the table, her hands folded in front of her face. "Tell me, Doctor. What is your assessment of the Web? Just what is it? Where did it come from?"

"If it's all machines, like Cameron says," Howell added, "someone had to build it in the first place. To *program* it."

"Obviously," Daren said. "My . . . impression is that the Web is a lot like the Naga in some ways, like they were in the bad old days when we thought of them as Xenophobes. Their view of the universe is skewed by their perception of *self*."

"That was Cameron's speculation," Mendoza pointed out.

"And I think it was an accurate one," Daren replied. "Naga divide the entire universe into self and not-self. The Web sees the entire universe *as* self."

"What," Admiral Roberts said. "It thinks it's God?"

"I doubt that it thinks in those terms, Admiral," Taki said. "But you could look at it as a communal intelligence, a hive-mind, if you like. We're not even certain yet that the Web is self-aware, at least, not in the same sense we are."

" 'Self-aware' is 'I think, therefore I am,' " Aimes said. "What's so damned hard about that?"

"It's more than that," Daren put in. "I think self-awareness also means you can distinguish between yourself and somebody else, and that's where the Web is lacking. Its mind is made up of billions of separate parts. Those parts communicate. It's aware of the rest of the cosmos as what doesn't communicate . . . but it seems to regard the noncommunicative part of the universe as a kind of extension of itself. The way you might think about your foot, say, being an extension of yourself."

"When I step on something sharp in my bare feet," Aimes said, "my foot communicates, believe me."

"But do you think of your foot as a part of *you*?" Taki asked her. "I mean, as part of your ego? Your real, inner self? Or is the real you a wrapped-up package of thoughts and memories and sensations located somewhere just behind your eyes?''

''Dev Cameron lost his entire physical body,'' Katya added. ''But he's still Dev.''

''You said he wasn't,'' Roberts said.

''I said he's *changed*, Admiral. His experiences over the past twenty-five years have changed him. That's true of all of us, isn't it?''

''What you're saying, Doctor,'' Vic said to Taki, ''is that the Web might think of us as part of itself. Something to be used, tools or raw materials.''

''Exactly.''

''Self and tools aren't the same thing,'' Aimes insisted.

Taki glanced at Aimes. ''Perhaps a better analogy than your foot would have been raw materials, resources. If you could imagine yourself as a primitive, living in a cave, but thinking of the rocks there as something as much a part of your body, of your perception of self, as your arm, say—''

''Then I would have a perfect right to bash rocks together to make flint tools,'' Aimes said, picking up the thought. ''And to use those tools to make other tools. I think I see your point.''

Daren reached out and touched the interface. The image above the holoprojector zoomed in close on one of the sleekly organic spacecraft rising from a sun. ''I think they may not be able to differentiate between intelligence and, well, the *expression* of intelligence.''

''What do you mean?'' Howell asked. ''That they confuse technology with the technologists?''

''That, and more,'' Daren said. ''There is a kind of intelligence that deliberately seeks to manipulate its environment.''

''I'd take that as a fair definition of intelligence.''

''Not necessarily. Think of the Communes, on Dante. They manipulate their environment. But as far as we can tell, they're not intelligent.''

''Not our kind of intelligence, perhaps,'' Vic said.

''Okay. Termites, on Earth, then. Or glowcoral on Eridu. Social animals. Builders. But *not* intelligence. Evolution has shaped the community as a whole to express itself in ways that seem intelligent to us, but individually the members of the community are not.

"At the other end of the scale are animals like dolphins. Or the Zeta Doradan Maia. They demonstrate remarkable mental abilities. They may, in fact, be intelligent in every way that counts . . . yet because they are completely atechnic we don't have enough in common with them for anything like rational communication."

"What are you saying, Doctor?" Aimes asked. "That the Web isn't really intelligent? Or that it's too different for the question to have any meaning for us?"

"Something of both, I think. Humans and DalRiss have both been at least partly defined by their use of tools to reshape their environments. I suspect that the tools themselves define the Web's intelligence. As with termites, or Communes, individual Web machines probably have no more intelligence than, oh, a fairly bright insect. Maybe just enough intelligence, in fact, to follow orders."

"The very clear thought in the alien recordings," Taki added, "is that it had encountered a part of itself that was noncommunicative . . . and was somehow refusing direction. What was it it said, exactly?"

" 'Part of the Web has refused direction,' " Katya replied, her eyes closed as she downloaded the text, " 'and has become dangerous. Integrate . . . re-integrate.' Something then about the Web cell being corrupted and needing to be destroyed."

"Machines that don't follow orders," Mendoza said, following Daren's thread of logic, "have to be re-integrated. Or destroyed."

"Or simply used, as part of the environment," Daren said. "If it doesn't respond to the Web as a part of the Web, it's fair game."

"The attack could be perceived as a kind of auto-immune response," Sandoval pointed out. "Antibodies failing to recognize intruding substances as self, and attacking them."

"A fair analogy, General," Mendoza agreed. "I question whether this immune response would extend to us out here, as Cameron seems to fear. Why would they want to destroy *us*? We've not threatened them, and we're a long, long way from the Galactic Core.''

''They've also been out in our neck of the woods for a good many thousands of years, General,'' Katya pointed out. Twelve hundred light years was a walk in the park compared to the twenty-seven-thousand–light-year distance to the core of the Galaxy. ''If your auto-immune-response analogy is accurate . . . suppose they do think of the whole universe as their body? Or even just this galaxy? They might be aware of us as a kind of disease.''

''A cancer,'' Daren said. ''Cells that have stopped responding to orders and are growing wild.''

''That's an interesting thought, Daren,'' Katya said. ''You know, we could be missing something here. We've been thinking of the probe as a kind of body for the duplicate download of Dev . . . but what was the probe, really? A Naga fragment, serving as hardware for the Dev-copy's software.''

''It recognized the Naga as *self* . . .'' Taki said, excited. ''Then thought of it as part of the Web that had stopped communicating, stopped taking orders.''

''Are you saying the Naga are part of the Web?'' Vic asked. ''Or that they used to be?''

''I don't think we have enough information to make any useful hypotheses, Vic,'' Katya said. ''But we certainly have some good leads. I submit that Dr. Cameron and Dr. Oe be put in charge of researching everything we know about the Web. Questioning a planetary Naga might give us some new insights.''

''Especially if we could find a Naga that recognized the Web as a part of its past,'' Daren said. ''Naga memory threads go back a long, long way. With this, we might trigger the appropriate memories and learn a lot more.''

''Do it,'' Katya said. She exchanged a glance with Vic. ''We're going to have to go public with all of this, you know. Bring it out in the open so we can deal with it.''

''Agreed,'' Vic said. ''There's still a big question.''

''What's that?''

''Our, ah, war with the Imperials.''

''We seem to have been given a choice of wars,'' Mendoza

said. "War with the Empire. War with this machine intelligence."

"Not that simple, General," Katya said, "and you know it. We're going to have to bring the Empire in on this, too. Work with them."

"What!" Sandoval almost rose from his seat. "Senator, you can't be serious!"

"I am serious, General," Katya said softly. "Dead serious. If we don't find a way now to stop this war with the Empire, then the Web is going to find us divided and distracted when it arrives. And it will arrive. It knows we exist, and it can't afford to ignore us. Whether it thinks we're a disease or a disobedient offshoot of itself or whatever, it *won't* ignore us. I agree with Dev on this. The Web represents the greatest threat mankind has ever faced, greater than the Xenophobes by far for the simple fact that we can't communicate with them.

"Our only chance will be if we can form a united front with the Imperials."

"An . . . alliance?" Sandoval asked, still disbelieving. "With the *Empire*?"

"The Confederation can't muster the resources to face the Web, General," Katya said. "Maybe, *maybe* Mankind can. I don't know if we can face the threat that Dev showed us, even united. But we have got to try.

"Humanity no longer can afford the luxury of being divided against itself."

Chapter 19

In large-scale warfare, it is essential to cause upset. It is critical to attack resolutely where enemies are not expecting it; then while their minds are unsettled, use this to your advantage to take the initiative and win.

In individual combat, you appear relaxed at first, then suddenly charge powerfully; as the opponent's mind changes pitch, it is essential that you follow what he does, not letting him relax for a moment, perceiving the advantage of the moment and discerning right then and there how to win.

—*The Fire Scroll,*
Book of the Five Spheres
Miyamoto Musashi
seventeenth century C.E.

"You may go in now, Madam Senator."

Katya bowed. "*Arigato gozaimasu.*"

"Don't mention it, please," the aide said in lightly accented Inglic. "The ambassador has been most anxious to see you this morning."

I'll just bet he has, Katya thought. She'd not been looking forward to this interview at all. She smiled at the aide, though, as he slid the light frame door to the side, nodding her thanks. Stepping out of her shoes, she left them outside the door and went inside in her bare feet.

Ambassador Kazuhiro Mishima was a tall and elegant man, reportedly a member of the royal family and reportedly, too, a member of the powerful faction known as the *Kansai no Otoko*, the Men of Completion. He stood and smiled urbanely as Katya walked in—unusual for a traditional Nihonjin, especially in the presence of a gaijin woman.

"*Konichiwa, O-Taishisan,*" she said, bowing low. "Good day, honored Ambassador."

"It is I who am honored by your coming to see me here," Mishima said in perfect, if somewhat stilted Inglic. "An ambassador expects to be summoned by senators and rulers, not to have them attend him."

"I thought, under the circumstances, it would be more . . . polite this way."

"I see." He gestured. "Won't you be seated? Please."

If his greeting had been untraditional, his office was purely old Japanese. The walls were paper, the floor bare wood with woven tatami to sit on. His desk was large, but only centimeters tall, high enough to work at while seated cross-legged behind it. Even so, the desk contained all of the technological amenities, including a built-in interface panel, a holoprojector, a computer touchboard, even an old-fashioned vidscreen, folded down into the surface.

The ambassador was informally dressed in silk lounging pajama slacks and a light robe, and Katya had the impression that he was not used to receiving official guests at this hour of the morning. She waited as he walked behind the desk and lowered himself to his tatami.

He considered her for a moment. "Proper etiquette would demand that the two of us talk for an hour or so, exchange pleasantries, and carefully avoid the real issue of why you are here, Senator. I, for one, have an extremely full schedule today and would much rather dispense with the formal courtesies. I suspect you would prefer that as well?"

Katya raised her eyebrows. "I would. I'm surprised that you—"

"That I would act abruptly? Ignore the amenities? Act, in fact, like a typical New American?" He sighed and shook his head. "Ah, well, perhaps that is the price I pay for living out here on the Frontier with you. Believe me, if I were receiving you back in Kyoto, you would find me every bit as stuffy and as formal and as indirect as you could possibly imagine!"

Katya laughed. "And perhaps I'm beginning to understand why you were appointed as ambassador to the Confederation."

"I presume, Madam Senator," Mishima said, "that you wish to discuss the recent events on Kasei."

"No, Your Excellency. As a matter of fact, I do not. At least, that is not the primary reason I asked to see you. There is something new that has come up, something far more important, that threatens the existence of both the Imperial Hegemony and the Confederation."

Mishima's eyes widened slightly. "Ah. Then am I to assume it has to do with the DalRiss fleet now orbiting this world?"

"Yes, sir. I imagine your TJK people have been keeping you briefed." Mishima said nothing, neither confirming nor denying her statement but waiting quietly for her to continue. "These vessels are among those that left nearhuman space twenty-five years ago, shortly after the Second Battle of Herakles."

"There was talk," Mishima said, "of their home star going nova. Not that it had, but that it was going to soon."

"Soon, in this case, may mean a thousand years. Or ten thousand. Or even another million. I have a feeling the DalRiss simply think about planets, about worlds, in a different way than we do."

He nodded. "I know that the ecosystems of their two worlds, out in Alyan space, were ravaged by their war with the Xenophobes. That could have something to do with it."

"Possibly, though as I understand it, the planetary Naga on GhegnuRish was rebuilding the ecosphere for them. Certainly, one reason for their exodus seems to have been their desire to find new life. Well, they did."

Mishima listened quietly as she described the meetings with the downloaded mind and memories of Devis Cameron. It felt strange to Katya to sit there discussing Dev in cold, almost clinical detail, recounting his experiences at Nova

Aquila . . . and beyond, within the strangeness of the Galactic Core.

When she'd completed the story, she handed Mishima a tiny strip of lucite, within which was embedded a computer's digital recreation of Dev's memories. "This is a recording of everything that Cameron saw, both at Nova Aquila and on the other side of the gate, at the center of the Galaxy. Some of it is a bit, well, disjointed."

"I can imagine," he said, accepting the strip. "Such an experience . . ."

"The civilization he calls the Web is unlike anything we know. Some of us believe—at least, some of our research so far suggests the possibility—that the Naga may be descended from them in some way, that the original Naga might have been scouts or even advance engineers. They might have been sent out into the hinterlands of the Galaxy to prepare the way for the Web, but something went wrong. Maybe they lost their programming or some critical piece of instruction. It's even been suggested that the Naga are a kind of cancer, Web cells that began to reproduce outside of the control and guidance the Web normally provides.

"But now the Web is expanding into our part of the galaxy. They're only a thousand light years away."

"A thousand light years. That's still so far. Over ten times the distance from New America to Tamontennu," he said, naming a colony world on the far rim of the Shichiju from 26 Draconis.

"These . . . these people have already traveled from the Galactic Core to Nova Aquila," Katya pointed out. "A distance of some twenty-six thousand light years. And they could be much closer than that. There are other novae in that direction that are closer."

"According to your story, however, they have been in the vicinity of Nova Aquila for some thousands of years already. Long enough to have found us, if they were looking for other intelligence. And these other novae in that region—"

"May or may not be the result of their activities, and if they are, the Web has been there for thousands of years as well. I know. But don't you see? They couldn't have known about us before. We've only had radio now for, what? A little over six hundred years? Physical evidence of our existence—our radio noise, the heat signatures of planetary civilizations—won't reach Nova Aquila for another six centuries yet. Or maybe their closer outposts picked up our radio signatures but didn't recognize them for intelligence. The Web is *that* different from us.''

''And if we've learned anything about space,'' the ambassador said thoughtfully, ''it is that it is very, very deep. A million shining civilizations could be out there, all hidden from one another by the dark and the emptiness.''

''The danger, the terrible danger of this situation, Excellency, is that they almost certainly learned all about the Shichiju, all about Earth and humanity, when they took the probe Cameron sent into the Galactic Core. We have to assume as much. We don't know what happened to the probe after it launched its message capsule, but considering how much we learned about the Web in its brief encounter, we can suppose that the Web learned at least as much about us. The fact that the original Dev Cameron and the DalRiss waiting at Nova Aquila were then attacked certainly suggests a major shift in their perceptions of the DalRiss fleet.''

''Yes,'' the ambassador said. ''Invisible one moment, a target the next. That certainly is a shift in their perceptions. Strange.'' He shook his head. ''They never tried to communicate? Or to even respond to the DalRiss signals?''

''Never. For them, communication is a strictly interior process. It doesn't seem to have occurred to them, ever, that there was anyone outside of themselves to talk to.''

Mishima was silent for a long time, thinking. Katya sat quietly, unwilling to rush the man. It would be better if he came to the same conclusion she and the others had earlier, but by his own path.

''Exactly why are you sharing all of this with me, Senator? Somehow, I doubt that it is in any sense of altruism. Not after Kasei.''

''No. No, sir, it's not. Ambassador, I will be quite honest with you. The raid on Kasei was a deliberate act on our part . . . on my part, I should say, because I had a lot to do with the initial planning of it. We know that the Imperium has developed a means of communicating faster than light. We were afraid that this technology, when put in place, would result in our little Confederation being rapidly gobbled up again. Our imperative, sir, was survival . . . and I find it difficult to apologize for that.''

"There is no need." He smiled. "Tell me, Madam Senator. Do you know of Miyamoto Musashi?''

"No, sir. Except that he was a Japanese military expert.''

"Among other things. Twelve hundred years ago he wrote the *Book of Five Spheres*, in which he discusses the philosophy he calls 'Art of the Advantage.' '' Mishima closed his eyes. Perhaps he was downloading part of a text. Perhaps he was using his native memory to recall something often reviewed. " 'It is critical to attack resolutely where enemies are not expecting it; then, when their minds are unsettled, use this to your advantage to take the initiative and win.' '' He opened his eyes and looked at Katya steadily, searchingly. "That is from his *Fire Scroll*, one of his five spheres. It justifies the surprise attack as a legitimate means of gaining advantage in war.''

Katya took a deep breath. "I have no reason to expect you to believe me, Excellency. Especially now, after the attack. But our operation on and around Kasei was not intended as a sneak attack leading to a general war.''

"So." His voice hardened suddenly. "You expect us to ignore what happened there? To let you steal our secrets and kill our people and walk away unpunished?''

"I expect nothing, Excellency. Perhaps your people and mine can . . . talk. Work things out. We could pay reparations for the damage we did on Kasei. I don't know what my government would agree to.

"The point is, your Empire and my Confederation are at the brink of another war right now. The first shots have already been fired, and all that remains is the actual declaration." She shrugged. "Maybe in these enlightened times, we don't even need that. But by chance, we now know of another threat, a threat to both of us from outside. We would be stupid—suicidally stupid—to continue our war with one another when the Web could already be on its way here.''

''You are suggesting that we work together, then. Empire and Confederation.''

''I am suggesting that the threat posed by the Web is one best faced by Man. All of us together.''

Again, Mishima was silent. When he spoke again, his voice was so soft that Katya had to lean forward to catch the words. ''*Dobyo ai-awaremu.*''

''I beg your pardon, Excellency?''

He shifted on his tatami. ''An old Nihongo saying. A proverb. 'People with the same disease share sympathy.' ''

''We would say, 'Adversity makes strange bedfellows.' ''

''More like 'Misery loves company.' '' He rubbed his chin. ''So. The, the duplicate of Dev Cameron, the one that visited the Galactic Core. It would have known how to find human space?''

''Yes, sir. It . . . *he* knew everything the original did. He was with the DalRiss as a kind of navigator, remember.''

''Tell me, Senator. This Dev Cameron. He was awarded a high Imperial honor once, if I am not mistaken.''

Katya was surprised. That was old history indeed, from before the Revolution. ''He was awarded the *Teikokuno Hoshi*,'' she said. ''The Imperial Star. It was given to him by the Emperor himself—the *last* Emperor, not the one on the throne today.''

She felt that it was important that she emphasize that. It was rumored that the Men of Completion had had a hand in the death of the *Fushi* Emperor, that the *Raiden* Emperor—the current Emperor—was their puppet. If there were some enmity between the Raiden Emperor's people and those favored by the Fushi Emperor, she wanted it out in the open now.

''He was awarded the Star for his original contact with the Naga,'' Mishima said. ''I remember.''

That was a surprise. ''You were there?''

''A minor functionary at the court.'' A shrug. ''It is not important. What is important is that Cameron-san was a brave man, and one not afraid to take a chance in order to reach out and communicate with another species, another civilization. If he sees a threat here in this . . . what did you call it? The Web. If he sees a threat there, it should be taken seriously.''

"Dev never did mind taking chances," Katya said.

"And he has been living with the DalRiss and Naga all these years? Remarkable!"

"He's . . . changed. A lot."

"I am sure of it. To have no human contact at all save that in his memories for so long . . ." He paused, looking at Katya with bright interest. "Would it, I wonder . . . be possible for me to talk to him?"

Katya and Dev had discussed the possibility already. If it would help convince Mishima that they needed his help . . .

"Certainly, sir. He would be delighted to speak with you."

"And you want my assistance in . . . what? Stopping the Imperial Navy from counterattacking New America?"

Katya felt an uncertain stirring of fear. "Are you saying they're about to counterattack?"

He sighed. "I will tell you the truth, Madam Senator. I don't know. Any communication between Earth and New America takes over a month at least, as you know well. And I would not necessarily be informed of the Navy Department's plans. Quite the contrary, I should think. But it is certainly a possibility."

"If they do, Excellency, we will defend ourselves."

"That is to be expected."

"But don't you see the pointlessness of it all? You attack. We defend ourselves. Then you escalate. Then we escalate. And all the while, the Web is growing closer. Stronger. We must do more than call off this war. We must become allies. Work together. *Beat* this threat . . . together."

"What you suggest is difficult. Very difficult."

"Not if we use reason."

"Reason." He shook his head sadly. "*Muri no toreba don hikkomu.*"

"Another proverb, Excellency?"

"Yes. 'When illogic prevails, reason gives way.' "

"It doesn't have to be that way."

"And you have worked in government long enough to know that such things have a certain inertia all their own. It will be difficult to lower the barriers we have worked so hard to raise between us."

"Try, Excellency. As I will try with the Confederation Senate."

"I make no promises."

"I understand."

He sat in silence a moment longer, thinking. Then, abruptly, he stood up. Clearly, the interview was at an end.

Rising, Katya faced the ambassador and bowed. *"Domo arigato, gozaimasu, O-Taishisan."*

He shook his head. "I have done nothing yet to earn your thanks, Madam Senator."

"The thanks are for listening to what I had to say. Despite everything that's happened."

"That is what ambassadors do. Among other things. I will talk to you again."

She hesitated.

"There is something more?" he asked.

"Only, Excellency . . . that it occurs to me that you have, um, *special* ways of communicating with your superiors back on Earth already in place. Ways that you've taken pains to keep secret from us."

Mishima's expression was blank, neither confirming nor denying.

"If that is so, Excellency," she continued, "use them. Please. Before it's too late."

Mishima stood there, staring at the door long after it slid shut behind her.

A remarkable woman, he decided. And a worthy adversary.

Seating himself once again behind the desk, he touched a key on the computer console. The vidscreen rotated up and back, exposing its black and glossy display surface. Mishima lay his left hand, palm down, on the interface screen. Like most Japanese, he disliked the idea of aliens resident inside his body and still favored the now old-fashioned technology of nanogrown implants in his brain and hand.

"Code *Shiun*," he thought, uploading the command to the embassy's AI that would access the system. "Violet Cloud. Please activate *o-denwa*."

The flat vid display lit up, its surface crackling with snow. It always took a moment or two to warm up the *denwa* unit. It would have been better, he thought, if the faster-than-light communicator could have been hooked up with a full comm module relay. It would have been like walking again in the gardens of Tenno Kyuden, the glorious Palace of Heaven at Earth's Singapore Orbital.

The snow cleared on the disappointingly flat, two-D screen, and Japanese kanji characters printed themselves across the display.

> **ACCESS GRANTED:**
> **IMPERIAL EMBASSY, JEFFERSON CITY,**
> **NEW AMERICA, 26 DRACONIS**
> **TO**
> **PALACE OF HEAVEN, SINGAPORE ORBITAL,**
> **EARTH, SOL**

He uploaded a department name and the name of the man he wished to speak to. Seconds later, a fleshy, overweight face looked out of the screen at him. "*Moshi-moshi.*"

"*Hai, Munimorisama*," the ambassador said. "Please forgive the intrusion. This is Mishima."

Admiral Munimori, arguably the most powerful man in the Empire, more powerful even than the figurehead emperor, nodded. "It must be urgent indeed to use *o-denwa*."

"It is about the ryu fleet on its way to New America," Mishima said. "I believe you may wish to relay new orders to its commander."

He began describing his talk with Senator Alessandro.

Chapter 20

Death stands at attention, obedient, expectant, ready to serve, ready to shear away the peoples en masse; ready, if called on, to pulverize, without hope of repair, what is left of civilization. He awaits only the word of command.

—*The Gathering Storm*
SIR WINSTON CHURCHILL
C.E. 1948

Kara had received permission from the *Chidori Maru*'s skipper to link in during the approach to Highport. She'd heard that something strange was happening in orbit around New America, but what she'd heard simply didn't sound credible.

She'd had to see for herself, and she was wondering if she even believed it now.

It was sixty-two days since the battle at Kasei. Kara, Sergeant Daniels, and the other two men who'd escaped from the Martian sky-el with her had made it safely first to Xi Bootis, where they'd transferred to the *Chidori Maru* without incident, then flown straight back to 26 Draconis for the final part of their long dogleg home.

But what was it they'd returned home to?

Ships were gathered in orbit, clustered closely about the Highport orbital station and drifting in a loose cloud that strung out across over a thousand kilometers of space. Most distinctive, perhaps, were the enormous DalRiss cityships, dozens of black, organic, multiarmed shapes in silent orbit amid clouds of smaller vessels, some of human design, many clearly products of Naga programming, jet-black, sharp pointed, and alien.

More ominous by far, however, were the kilometer-long dragonships, no fewer than five of the great ryu carriers, together with a literal host of lesser Imperial warships.

"My God," Kara said, staring in mingled horror and awe. "My God, where did *they* come from?"

Chidori Maru's warbook was already downloading data across her visual field, matching, naming, and describing the larger vessels. The list was impressive, reading like a digest of all of the Imperium's largest and most powerful warships.

There was *Shinryu*, the Divine Dragon, marginally the largest ryu carrier in the Imperial fleet. Back in 2540, she'd been flagship of the First Alyan Expedition, the mission that had made contact with the DalRiss homeworld. Hanging in *Shinryu*'s shadow was *Hiryu*, the Flying Dragon, smaller but sleeker and more maneuverable. Nearby was *Donryu*, the Storm Dragon, and the second ryu in recent history to bear that name. The earlier *Donryu* had been destroyed by Dev Cameron and the Heraklean Naga at the First Battle of Herakles. *Gingaryu*, the Dragon of the Milky Way, was a close twin to *Shinryu*, slightly smaller but with a more complex tangle of weapons, turrets, nacelles, and parapets clustered over her entire, spear-headshaped length.

Almost as an afterthought, Kara recognized the distinctive silhouette of one more dragonship—*Karyu*, the Fire Dragon . . . now the flagship of the Confederation Navy.

The host of smaller ships included dozens of cruisers, hundreds of destroyers, an uncounted multitude of corvettes and frigates, patrol boats, and even free-orbiting warflyers.

"Looks like a convention for the whole goking Imperial Navy," Sergeant Daniels said, observing the gathering through Kara's bridge link. "Kuso, Lieutenant! What are we gonna do?"

Kara didn't answer at once. She'd been on the point of asking him . . . but he'd reminded her of her responsibility, her *duty* as a Confederation officer. She could, she should accept advice from her NCOs, but the decision was up to her.

"I really don't know, Sergeant," she said. "Any suggestions?"

"Well, they don't seem to be taking much notice of us. Maybe we could kind of slip past and head back into K-T space."

"Yes," the freighter's skipper said, joining the discussion. "But where?"

"Anywhere," Kara said. "Hell, I think we'd be safer in Earth orbit. The whole damned Imperial Navy is *here*!"

"Doesn't look like much of a battle was fought," Daniels said. "Look. Look at the old *Karyu*. She would have been in the thick of it when the Impies jumped in, and she doesn't even look scratched."

"Did we just surrender then?" Kara wondered.

"Lieutenant?" the freighter's skipper called. "I have a call for you. Comm mod linkage, private."

"What?" Kara was taken aback. "From who?"

"Senator Alessandro, of the Confederation Free Senate."

The captain stressed the phrase as though carefully repeating what he'd just heard word for word. Kara heard the emphasis and recognized that that wording held a message for her, an assurance that despite what it looked like, the Confederation, and its government, continued to exist.

But what were Imperial ryu carriers doing in orbit over New America? Damn . . . you take the long way home, with two months of being out of touch, and everything changes on you. . . .

She opened a communications room for the meeting, a virtual reality modeled after the gathering room in the house at Cascadia. She stood there, in the same room where she'd talked with her mother during the party . . . how many months ago now?

That Japanese woman walked in with Daren right over *there*.

She shook herself, trying to order her thoughts. She would be dignified and reserved. She would not let her upset show. She was trembling with excitement, with worry, with a burning and barely suppressed curiosity, and more than anything else with a dawning horror that everything had been for nothing, *nothing. . . .*

Her mother entered the room.

"Mums!" Kara cried. "What the gok is going on?"

So much, she thought with an embarrassed, wry stab of self-criticism, for dignified . . .

"Hello, Kara. I know this all must be quite a surprise—"

"That doesn't describe it by one percent! My God, the Imperial Navy is in orbit. What happened? Is the war over already?"

Katya looked uncomfortable. "Kara, there was no war."

"No . . . war . . ." Kara didn't understand. "Excuse me, but I thought I just went and *started* one!"

"A lot has happened since you left—"

"I should goking well think so!"

"First of all, Dev Cameron has returned."

Kara's jaw dropped. "Dev . . . Cameron." The universe seemed to tilt and whirl around her head. "Daren's bio-father . . ."

Her mother closed her eyes, took a breath, then opened them again. "Yes. He came back a few weeks ago."

Kara shook her head, running a hand through her short hair. "Wait a minute. Wait a minute. I thought he was *dead. . . .*"

Katya sighed. "Come and sit with me. This is going to be difficult. . . . . ."

Half an hour later, Kara had heard the whole story. It would take a while to get all of the pieces settled in and properly cataloged, but she knew now about the threat posed by the Web.

And, if half of what her mother had told her about that alien intelligence were true, she could understand the need to patch things up with the Impies.

But *kuso . . .* !

"What's the matter?" her mother asked, watching her expression as she balled her hand into a fist and brought it down on the sofa. "Did you want a war so much?"

"*Want*—" Kara stopped, forced herself to cool. "No one,

especially a soldier, ever wants a war,'' she said quietly, with deadly intensity.

"You wouldn't know it from the way you're acting."

"Mother . . . someone I cared about, a comrade, died at Aresynch. He died right there in front of me, in a firefight. He may have saved my life, for all I know. Other good men and women died at Noctis Labyrinthus. Why?"

"Kara, if you would let me finish—"

"Why the hell did they have to die, if you politos were going to turn around and make peace with the goking Impies while we were still out there . . . ?"

"They died because we made the best decisions we could, with the survival of our people and our government and our way of life at stake. They died doing their duty, which was to follow the orders the government and ConMilCom HQ gave them. They died buying us a *chance* at survival. Isn't that enough?"

Kara still felt weak and . . . betrayed, somehow.

There were precedents in history. She remembered downloading an account of the Battle of New Orleans during her training at the Academy. The battle, on January 8th of 1815, had been fought between the British under General Sir Edward Packenham and troops of the then brand-new American Republic, under the command of General Andrew Jackson. The threat to the city of New Orleans had been very real; the victory of the American forces had been real as well. Packenham's veterans had aligned their scarlet ranks and walked steadfastly into a hail of American fire, falling in droves. By battle's end, the casualty figures showed an astonishingly unbalanced flavor: eight Americans killed and fourteen wounded behind their cotton bale ramparts, against something like two thousand casualties all together for the British.

None of the men fighting before the city of New Orleans that foggy January morning had any idea that the Treaty of Ghent, ending hostilities between the United States of America and the British Empire, had been signed two weeks before, on Christmas Eve of 1814. In those days, before radio or telegraph, before ViRnews medes and comm modules, the fastest means of communication across the sea was—as with the twenty-sixth–century sea of space—by ship. News of the treaty didn't reach the Americas until mid-February. The most splendid American victory of the war—what some historians marked as one of the more important battles of the war—had been fought after the war itself was already over.

This wasn't quite that bad, Kara told herself. But it was disconcerting, nonetheless.

"Your raid was not a wasted effort," Katya said, continuing. "Far from it. You captured the I2C prototype, and the data on how to build it. Our techs already have Naga replicators going, turning out new ones."

"You have a communications network already up and running?"

"Actually, it turns out that the Imperials had a working net pretty much in place already. As we suspected, they have the units—they call them *denwa*, by the way. 'Telephones.' "

"I assume they've tied at least some of their major warships into the net as well."

It was a logical guess. There'd not been time for the back-and-forth of negotiations between Earth and New America, the working out of details, the assembly of such a fleet as the one now in orbit if the maximum speed of communications between star systems was still limited to one or two light years per day. Those ryus must have already been on the way to New America. . . .

Kara felt a cold chill at that. The Imperials had been *that* close to crushing New America with almost their full might.

"That's right. They also have them connecting their principal embassies on various worlds, both in the Shichiju and in the Confederation. That was a good thing, actually, a real lucky break. With the comm network already in place, it's turning out to be easier than expected to wire in more units and extend the overall system. Pretty soon, we'll be able to use a comm module to have a face-to-face ViRconference with someone on the other side of the Shichiju."

"Then how did Operation Sandstorm help a damned thing?"

"Perhaps it gave us more credibility in the eyes of the Empire. Or maybe it just gave us more credibility in our own eyes. In any case, the Imperials are taking us on as full partners here. The Aquilan Expeditionary Force will be a joint Confederation-Hegemony mission. Imperial warships. Hegemony science vessels. Much of the Confederation fleet, of course. The DalRiss have been gathering, coming through from Alya as the survivors of the fight at Nova Aquila make it back. We have about fifty cityships so far. They'll be carrying the human fleet piggyback, with their Achievers. That will let us cover the distance between here and Nova Aquila in a few quick jumps instead of something like three years.''

''Where does this leave us? The Black Phantoms, I mean?''

''Oh, you'll be in the thick of it, I imagine,'' Katya said. She looked away, as if wanting to say more . . . and suppressing the urge.

''Come on! Tell me!''

''We don't have all of the details settled yet,'' Katya said. ''But as things are going now, the Black Phantoms who volunteer for this will be assigned to the *Carl Friedrich Gauss.* I can't tell you more than that.''

''The *Carl*—'' Kara's eyes narrowed. ''That's a research ship!''

''That's right.''

''What is a warstrider unit supposed to do aboard a research ship?''

''We don't really know yet what to expect of Operation Nova,'' Katya said. ''It could become a military op.''

''Operation Nova. That's what you're calling it?''

''It seemed appropriate. The Expeditionary Force will be visiting Nova Aquila first. It's supposed to be strictly a scouting mission, with the objective of learning as much about the Web as possible, but we're going in ready for anything. You'll be protecting *Gauss*'s passengers, a small army of scientists, mostly xenologists and linguists, but also programmer techs and artificial intelligence specialists.''

''Huh. Who's running that show?''

''Dr. Jason Sanders, from the Xenobiology Department at the University of Jefferson. Your brother's going along too.''

''Daren? On the *Gauss*?''

"Yes. And Dr. Oe. You remember her? She was with him at the party."

"The Nihonjin woman from the University." She felt cold inside. "I remember."

"She is a New American citizen, Kara. As loyal as you or me. I doubt they would have let her go if she wasn't."

"Why not? We're bringing half of the Empire along with us anyway. A few more won't hurt."

Katya stared hard at her daughter. "This is strictly a volunteer mission, Kara."

"What does that mean? What are you saying?"

"Just what it sounds like. You don't have to go if you don't want to."

"What about my unit? Have they been asked to go?"

Katya nodded. "This is an unusual mission, one that's going to go farther into unknown space than we've ever gone before. This one had to be a volunteer mission for all personnel."

"And they're going?

"Some of them have signed on already, but most of the people in your squadron are waiting to hear what you decide." She smiled. "You seem to be popular with your unit, Kara."

"Kuso, I don't try to be. Half the time I'm working their tails off. The other half, like recently, I'm not even around."

"Well, I've been hearing good reports on you. From your unit. From your commanders. I'd like to have you along, if we can."

Kara started to nod, then looked up, sharply, eyes widening. "Wait a minute. Along? You're coming too?"

"That's right."

"But . . . but you're a senator!"

"So?"

"You're supposed to stay here. With the government!"

"Seems to me this is one time when the government had better know exactly what's going on out there, and what the consequences of its acts are."

"I don't know if I want my mother going out into a shooting war." She folded her arms. "You could get hurt out there!"

"I think I've been in combat enough to know what I'm risking. And your father's going, too."

Kara tried to suppress the wild scramble of fright. The whole family was going to be there, and from what she'd heard of the situation so far, it wasn't going to be fun.

"Somebody's got to stay and run the government, right?" she said weakly.

Katya shrugged. "Hardly matters, does it? We'll have an I2C communications linkup, so I won't be out of touch with New America. In fact, the whole Shichiju will be able to participate in this one. We'll have medes along, aboard the *Gauss* and several of the other civilian vessels. The whole human race will be linked in on this, watching."

"Good God! The *medes* are coming?"

"It was my idea, actually," a new voice, a man's voice, said from the empty air overhead. "May I join you?"

Katya looked up. "Come in, Dev."

Empty air shimmered nearby, taking on texture and form. Kara had seen images of Dev Cameron, of course. His exploits were closely studied at the Academy, and that included simulations narrated and monitored by an analogue patterned closely after the original.

But this man, gray-eyed, tall, not much older than herself—this was the *original*.

"Excuse me for eavesdropping," he said. "But I was eager to meet you, Kara."

"Uh . . . it's nice to meet you. Why'd you vanish off into the great unknown and leave my mother hanging?"

"Kara!" Katya flared.

"Honest question. The honest answer is I needed the DalRiss just to exist at that point. I'm still . . . I suppose 'alive' is still the right word, still alive more in their Naga fleet computer than I am here.

"But there was more to it than that. I thought I could be useful to the DalRiss. They wanted me to accompany them. And, well, your mother never did care that much for virtual relationships. After I, ah, misplaced my body, I couldn't very well offer her anything else. Right?"

Kara nodded. "I guess. It just seems so . . . cold."

"You don't know how cold," Dev said. "Believe me. It wasn't just your mother who suffered."

"So, um, what's happening now?" Kara looked from Dev to Katya and back again. "Are you back for good now? Or what?"

Dev broke the eye contact, turning his head toward the window that overlooked the mountains. "I imagine that depends on what happens with Operation Nova."

"Oh." Kara looked at Dev's image and decided she could get to like the guy after all. He really wasn't quite the macho hero type she'd imagined, based on what she'd read and what she'd heard from Katya. *This* was the man who'd linked with a planetary Naga, throwing one-ton boulders from a mountaintop to claw ryu-class carriers from the sky? He actually seemed kind of cute, and she could see why her mother had been attracted to him.

He was a lot like her father in some ways, only much younger. Well . . . that was the effect of being downloaded, of course. And when she looked at his eyes, they seemed much, much older than the rest of him.

"Okay," she said. "Then tell me why the medie circus is in on this. I'd think this sort of thing would be better being done in secret."

"Why?" Dev asked, turning to face her again. "Not to hide it from the Imperials, certainly. They're on our side."

"So I've just been informed."

"And we're not even trying to hide anything from the Web. Quite the contrary, in fact. If what we think we understand about them is accurate, it might well be the only way to get them to perceive us as *another* intelligence, a mind separate from their shared mind, if they see our equivalent of a shared mind. The linked minds of much of the human race."

The thought was dizzying. "Kuso! How many is that?"

"There are thirty or forty billion people on Earth alone," Dev said. "I don't know what the exact figure is. Plus almost eighty colony worlds, with populations of a half billion or so, like New America, on up to Chien V, with, what? Three billion? Something like that. The total population must be well over a hundred billion or so, though. And anyone who wants to will be able to link in.''

"Everybody but genies and nullheads," Kara couldn't help adding. Genies, of course, were forbidden by law from carrying computer-link hardware, save in certain, specialized cases. "Nullheads" was slang for the disenfranchised millions—how many millions, no one could say—who for one reason or another, political, economic, religious, moral, or simple fear—didn't have cyberlink hardware of any kind.

"*Technic* civilization will be able to participate, Kara," Dev said quietly. "In fact, it's vital that it does, or as much of it as can. What we do out there could determine the future course of evolution—or extinction—for the entire human species."

"Just so you realize that the whole species isn't one nice, neat, small package. Some of it's got warts. Some of it doesn't have access to high-tech toys."

"Some don't want that access. We'll work with what we have to work with."

"And the idea is still to try to reason with the Web?"

"If we possibly can," Katya said. "We don't even know if communication, *real* communication is possible. If it is, the xenologists on the *Gauss* and other research vessels should be able to learn how to do it. We're going in armed with everything Dev picked up, everything we've learned since. We have Naga fragments that may be able to reveal some of the past, give us common ground for a dialogue."

"But if they can't talk," Dev said, "yes, we'll have to fight."

Kara gave a wry grin. "From what you guys've told me, that's not going to be easy. Odds of millions to one? And against an opponent who may just be as far ahead of us as we are ahead of mice?"

"It won't be that bad, Kara," Dev said. "We'll be going back better prepared this time."

"We've been studying the records Dev brought back," Katya added. "We've found what may be some weaknesses in the Web's position. And ways that we can exploit those weaknesses."

"I'd like to see what you have."

"Certainly."

"Are you with us, then?" Dev asked.

"Of course I'll be coming along," Kara said. "If my people are going, you don't think anything could keep me away from this dustup, do you?"

Dev looked at Katya, smiled, and gave a small shrug. "She *is* your daughter, Katya."

Katya smiled at him. "I've known that for a long time."

Chapter 21

The universe is not only queerer than we imagine. It is queerer than we can *imagine.*

—J. B. S. HALDANE
mid–twentieth century C.E.

"Just what is it we're hoping to accomplish out there, anyway?" Kara asked.

She stood in front of the viewwall, looking out at the vast assembly of starships gathered in New American orbit. Both her mother and father were there, Vic resplendent in his Confederation general's full-dress grays, Katya in a simple coverall with a tasteful holographic animation of kaleidoscope shapes and colors running down the border of the torso seal. A number of others were there as well; space was in short supply aboard the *Gauss*, and most compartments were both too small and too crowded.

Embarkation parties were something of a tradition, however, at least aboard civilian vessels, and the science ship's lounges had been adapted as party centers for the passengers, who gathered to watch the panorama of the Aquilan Expeditionary Fleet against the gold, green, and blue of New America, to eat the hors d'oeuvres provided by the ship's nanoprocessors, and to make nervous jokes about the coming jump into the unknown.

"You know as much about that as the rest of us, Kara," Vic replied. He took a sip from his drink. "You were in on every staff meeting from the time you got back from Kasei on."

Kara looked back over her shoulder at him. "I'm not talking about specific strategy. I just wonder if it's at all clear what we're getting into."

"Peaceful communication if we can pull it off," Katya said. "With a civilization far older than our own. And if not, well, probably the best we can hope for is to let the Web know we won't simply wait to be absorbed or integrated or whatever they think they can do to us."

"We've got a chance," Vic added. "A good one."

Accommodations were not nearly so luxurious as those aboard the *Teikoku*, of course. *Gauss* was smaller by far, and space was at a premium, with some eight hundred passengers aboard a vessel designed to handle half that many. It was made even more cramped by the need for extra stores of raw material—carbon, hydrogen, nitrogen, and oxygen, especially—for the nanoprocessors that would be providing them with food, water, and air.

Heat management was arguably the biggest problem on older vessels like the *Gauss*; everyone aboard agreed that it was a good thing they would be piggybacking it to their destination with a DalRiss cityship this time instead of taking the usual long, hot route through K-T space. A joke making the rounds of both the science teams and the warstrider squadrons held that the death of an Achiever was a small price to pay to avoid the indignity of being cooked in their own juices by the time they reached their destination.

"This might not be the time to go into it," Kara said quietly. "But I've got a bad feeling about this one. A lot worse than I had before Sandstorm."

"Is the Academy endowing our warriors with psychic powers now?" Katya asked.

"Let her say it, Kat," Vic said. "You know as well as I do about soldiers' hunches."

"This isn't like *that*," Kara said. "I don't have any grand premonition of death, or whatever." She shook her head. "It's just—well, this is a strange thing for a soldier to say, I know, but I wonder if we're not going about this all wrong. Sun Tzu says to match your strength against your opponent's weakness, not against his strength." She waved an arm, taking in the massed fleet visible against the New American disk. "It looks as though the Web's strength more than anything else is sheer weight of numbers. That's what Dev seemed to be saying, anyway, that they won by sending millions and millions of machines against the DalRiss and overwhelming their defenses. And here we are trying to match them strength for strength." She raised an eyebrow as she looked at her father. "Seems like a bad strategy, General."

Vic chuckled. "You could be right. We wrangled about that with the Imperial Ops staff for weeks."

"Who was arguing what?"

"The Imperials were all for sending in the big guns. The ryu carriers and a flock of heavy cruisers. Admiral Munimori even suggested that the Imperials could handle the whole show by themselves, without our help. The rest of us—especially Dev—wanted a more subtle approach. Something less dependent on matching the Web, as you put it, strength against strength."

"The Confederation doesn't have that powerful a warfleet, Kara," Katya added. "We can't afford to stretch ourselves too thin, or take risks too large."

"Like we weren't taking risks with Operation Sandstorm?"

Katya grimaced. "That was a case of doing what we had to do in order to survive as an independent government. . . ."

"Agreed, Mums. I wasn't really arguing the point. And I can understand that our survival as a species is at stake here. But if we can't hope to beat them by matching their numbers, what approach can we use?"

"Technology," Vic said simply.

"Technology. Against a technic civilization billions of

years old. A civilization capable of energy-to-matter conversion, able to travel across half of the goking Galaxy, and possibly even able to pull off a little time travel now and again." Kara raised a skeptical eyebrow. "This makes sense?"

"In fact," Katya said, "we do have one big tech advantage. The I2C."

Kara had heard that idea bandied about during various of the planning sessions but had never quite trusted it. "It's hard to believe. Is there really no evidence that they have faster-than-light communication?"

"None," Vic said. "Everything in the images Dev brought back shows they use really a rather mundane technology for all of their interior communications. Radio, maser, and laser, mostly. There may be some other channels Dev didn't catch, because of the limitations of DalRiss biotech, but it looks like that's all they have."

"And I have a theory about that," a new voice said at Kara's back.

She turned. "Well, hello, Daren. I was wondering where you were,"

"Taki and I were checking out the ViRcomm modules on Deck Three." He grimaced. "Do you realize we're going to have to use them in *shifts*?"

"That's how it is on a crowded ship," Kara told him. "Most warships don't have more than one module per one hundred crew and soldiers aboard. So they share, and everybody gets an hour every two or three days."

"Barbaric!"

"Just be happy we're going to get where we're going in a matter of days," Katya said with a smile. "If we were doing this the old-fashioned way, we'd crawl to our destination in K-T space. At a light year per day, we'd be locked up inside this metal can for over three years, and the only way to escape the heat is your hour-in-fifty in a ViRsimulation!"

"Still, the scientists are going to need comm modules to continue their work. Taki and I need all the time we can get practicing with Charlie."

"Charlie" was actually a class of teleoperated flyers, KS-1090 Cutlasses with the weapons and life-support modules removed, the hull collapsed and folded to a more compact configuration, and the AI downgraded to receive teleoperational input. The device could be operated like a remote probe or hubot, in situations that might pose a risk to human researchers.

"So how's flight training coming along for you two?" Kara asked.

"Oh, well enough. It's a lot harder than teleopping a hubot on the ground." He cocked a quizzical look at Kara. "What I want to know is why you military types don't teleop your warstriders. Wouldn't it be safer sitting aboard a ship in orbit and jacking the things around by remote?"

"Sure would."

"Why don't you do it, then?"

Katya laughed. "Because the other guy's trying to find ways to operate your machinery, too, and with AIs as good and as fast as they are at analyzing coded frequencies, he could do it."

"Imagine," Vic added, "that you're a general with a whole army of teleoperated striders moving in on the enemy. Suddenly his AI breaks your control codes, turns your army around, and sends it back at you, lasers and PACs blazing. Embarrassing. Doesn't look at all good on your fitness report."

"There's also jamming and local interference to worry about," Kara said. "Sometimes, in a big battle, the actual pilot-against-pilot combat is the smallest part of the action. Both sides are throwing up fields of interference and jamming, trying to disable remote sensors and probes, trying to access AI and communications channels. Believe me, if it were possible to teleoperate a warstrider on the battlefield, we would!"

Daren shook his head, eyes narrowed, trying to understand. "Even with tight-beamed feeds? I mean, with lasers or focused microwave input—"

"Do you have any idea what smoke and dust in a surface battle does to a comm laser's range?"

"Oh. Well, I'll take your expert word for it. You know, I've often wished I could teleoperate a hubot on Dante from New America." He glanced at Katya. "With the polito prohibitions against traveling in the Shichiju, that sometimes seemed like the only way to get any *useful* work done.''

Katya looked startled. ''My God—''

Daren held up his hand. ''I know, I know. I'm sorry, Mother. I just meant—''

''No, it's not you,'' Katya said. ''I was just thinking. If we could jack through an I2C link—''

Kara saw at once what her mother was getting at, and the idea was stunning. Quantum communications effects worked across interstellar distances precisely because there was no signal—at least none through normal space—between one set of electrons and the matched set elsewhere.

That meant there was absolutely no way an enemy could jam, intercept, or override a communications beam. A warstrider pilot could sit in comfort and safety on a world light years away, her mind jacked into her machine, her senses there in the battle.

No more casualties. Machines could be smashed into scrap, but their pilots would awaken inside their command centers, with nothing bruised save their egos. She'd been thinking of the I2C in such a limited way—simply as a means of coordinating warships over interstellar distances. There were so many other possibilities, though. . . .

Kara looked at her mother. ''Kuso, Mums. Were the Imperials working on *that*?''

''I don't know. All they admitted to was connecting their larger ships, their colonies, and their embassies.''

''The Imperial leadership has a pretty traditional mind set,'' Vic pointed out. ''Teleoperated warstriders might not have occurred to them yet.''

''But it would have,'' Kara said. ''Sooner or later, it would have. God, this is going to utterly rewrite everything we know about war!''

Katya nodded, looking glum. ''War could become some kind of *game*. No muss. No dirt. No pain or blood . . . except in the city you just leveled on some world light years away!''

Daren laughed. ''Well, maybe that would be a good thing. End war once and for all.''

''How do you figure that?'' Kara asked him.

"If war becomes too horrible, or too destructive, maybe we'll finally give it up. It could turn into a balance of terror, like during the early years of the nuclear age. I don't bomb you because I can't stop you from bombing me."

"The evidence of history," Katya pointed out, "is that weapons are *always* used sooner or later. The rules of war and the way it's waged may change, but the *fact* of it never does."

"Well, I2C will certainly be a boon for scientists. No more begging for appropriations. No more expensive expeditions. Just equip a small, unmanned starship with a good AI and a few teleoperated probes, and you could send it anywhere in the Galaxy and never even leave your own home."

Vic grimaced. "Takes all the fun out of it, though. What's going to happen to the human race? We all lose our arms and legs and become machine-tended brains, stored away in the basement?"

"Wouldn't matter," Daren said. "Our *minds* would be free. Assuming we could get time on the comm module to practice with our remotes! Seems like a nullheaded way to do things, not having enough mods to go around."

"Don't worry, Dar," Kara said, patting his shoulder. "I'm sure you and your little friend will survive."

Daren gave her a hard look, as though wondering just what was behind the amused irony of her voice, then shrugged. "We'll do what we have to do," he said. "But I'd have felt a hell of a lot better if this expedition hadn't been literally thrown together at the last moment. We're going into this unprepared. We could miss some fantastic opportunities here."

Katya brought her hands to her temples, shaking her head slowly. "Daren, for years now you've been downloading on me every day about the need to get out in the field, to experience things for yourself, to meet an alien civilization in the flesh . . . or in this case, I guess, the metal. Well, take a look around! You've got it! Everything you wanted! Why aren't you happy?"

"Kuso, Mother. I—"

Katya reached out and grabbed his shoulder. "I'm jo-king," she said, pronouncing each syllable separately and distinctly.

"Sometimes, Daren, you take things a little too seriously."

He sighed. "I suppose you're right. Still, I wonder if we're going about this whole thing right . . . and that's nothing to joke about."

"No," Vic said thoughtfully. "It's not. I'm thinking how wonderful it would be if we had the luxury of sending this fleet out to Nova Aquila without any humans along."

Kara could hear the pain in his voice. If they couldn't talk to the Web, there were going to be casualties in the battle that would follow. No military officer enjoys the prospect of losing the people under his command. Kara knew that much from bitter experience.

"I don't suppose there's time to reequip all of the ships with I2C remotes?" Daren asked.

"Not a chance. The redesign of the ship interfaces alone could take years. And I don't think the Web is going to give us that much time."

"Well," Daren said. "I'm not sure we'll be able to understand the Web, or even begin trying to talk to it, simply by throwing large numbers of scientists at it."

"Depends on how hungry it is," Kara said. "Especially for xenologists."

"Amusing, Kara. Twisted, but amusing."

"So what's the big theory?" Kara asked him.

"About what?"

"About Web comm technology. You said you have a theory about it."

"Ah! Yes. Some of us at the University have been working on the idea that the Web doesn't know about quantum physics. In fact, it probably can't."

"I've heard that but don't understand it." Vic took a sip of his drink. "These people build goking great rings around black holes. Doesn't that mean they're harnessing Hawking radiation?"

"It's possible," Daren said with a smug grin, "that they are doing exactly that but have no idea what it is they're doing."

Much of the basis for twenty-sixth–century technology lay in the twentieth-century formulation of the bizarre mathematics of quantum mechanics. The Quantum Power Tap, for example, used finely tuned pairs of oscillating singularities to provide literally unlimited streams of clean, raw energy. Depending on the set of equations used, there were two ways of interpreting where that energy came from. One way of describing the source was to say the energy was flowing from the K-T plenum, the underlying hyperdimension of pure energy on which the entire universe rode like a bubble on an ocean of froth. A second description, however, held that virtual particle pairs—particle and antiparticle—were constantly being formed out of empty vacuum and almost instantly mutually annihilated. Hawking radiation, named for the brilliant twentieth-century physicist who predicted it, occurred when one of the virtual particles was trapped inside the event horizon of a black hole while the other escaped into the universe— energy apparently leaking from the black hole. Early speculations had suggested that energy-hungry civilizations in the far-future might derive the energy they needed from Hawking radiation captured at the event horizon.

Bizarre as such concepts were, they all were solidly based on the even more bizarre twistings of quantum physics, a magical, Alice-in-Wonderland world where Schrödinger's proverbial cat could be both alive and dead, until an observer called one possibility or the other into existence.

Yet it was that magic that made possible such everyday and taken-for-granted wonders as the QPT and faster-than-light travel along the K-T interface. The prediction of Hawking radiation had pointed the way toward the practical development of the Quantum Power Tap, a source of energy far more potent than trapping half of each virtual particle pair.

"How could they possibly not know what they were doing?" Katya asked. "Technological development is basically linear. It builds on advances in theory and on previous levels of technologies, one step at a time."

"And in ten billion years," Kara put in, "I'd guess they'd have taken one hell of a lot of steps."

"It was Dev Cameron's observation that got us thinking about the inconsistencies in what he'd seen," Daren said. "You know, he's really a great guy when you get to know him. It's still hard thinking of him as my father, though, especially when his ViRpersona looks as young as I do.''

"What was his idea?" Katya prompted.

"Well, we were working on some of the images he brought back, and he pointed out what you just did, Kara. That you'd expect the Web to have gotten a lot farther in eight or ten billion years. In some ways, of course, materials processing and manufacturing and the really weird stuff like the Stargates, they're way beyond us, yes . . . but in practical terms, they're not nearly far enough, you know what I mean?''

Kara nodded. "We might be building Stargates ourselves in another thousand years. That suggests they're *only* a millennium or so ahead of us.''

"Exactly. Hell, in a thousand years, the way things are going, we'll have come up with something even better." He snapped his fingers. "Here to Andromeda, zip! And there are some areas where we're ahead of them. The I2C, for one. And the K-T drive for another. It looks like they have to rely on the Stargate for faster-than-light travel. Even for a super race, a thousand-kilometer-long cylinder must be a hell of a lot of trouble to build, and it's not easy to take one along with you on long jaunts.''

"Hard on your explorers," Kara said, "if they have to build a Stargate to get back from wherever they've been.''

"In fact," Daren said, "the Web shows all the signs of being a basically static technic culture. Long ago they reached a plateau where things worked well enough, and stayed there. They didn't *need* to change, so they didn't.''

"At least so far," Vic said. "Still, now that they've met us . . .''

"I think," Katya said, nodding, "that we're going to have our hands full.''

Chapter 22

Where are they?

—ENRICO FERMI
mid–twentieth century C.E.

"In a way, it's like Fermi's Paradox," Kara said. "A restatement of it, rather. If the Web's been around for billions of years, why haven't they run into us already? Their not needing to change would be an explanation, wouldn't it?"

Fermi's Paradox was named for the twentieth-century physicist who had presented early searchers for extraterrestrial radio sources with their first, great, conceptual challenge. Given the Galaxy's age and the fact that life appeared to arise virtually spontaneously in any environment where it was given half a chance, the universe should be swarming with life, much of it much older than Man. But if even *one* other civilization began exploring and colonizing space, even without faster-than-light travel the Galaxy would be overrun in a scant few tens of millions of years.

Hence Fermi's statement: *where are they?*

The answer, six centuries later, was still elusive, but most researchers were beginning to suspect that the flaw in the Fermi paradox lay in the assumption that other species would as gleefully colonize the stars as Man seemed wont to. The DalRiss had created one colony in their long history, because their culture was predisposed toward large, slow-growing, close-knit communities whose primary artistic and scientific focus was on watching and reshaping life rather than adding planets to their empire—gardeners rather than explorers. No one knew how long the Naga had been seeding worlds, but in many cases they'd occupied planets for generations without the human colonists on the surface even being aware of their presence. The Communes and the Maias were so different no one could be sure if they qualified as intelligent or not, but they certainly weren't interested in exploration. Even human societies went through periods when outreach all but ceased, and the population was more interested in consolidation than in new frontiers. That had been the case in human space for some time now.

"Clearly," Daren said, "the Web should have been able to colonize the entire Galaxy if that's what they wanted to do. But from what we've been gathering lately, it seems more likely that they're exploiting the Galaxy for raw materials, turning stars into more machines."

Kara blinked. "Stars . . . into machines?"

Daren stared into his drink, swirling the ice cubes and the amber liquid in the glass. "Understand, this is based on very limited data. All we really know about them is a brief glimpse of some structures in the Galactic Core, and what the DalRiss saw at Nova Aquila. But here's what we think is happening. They find a likely star and trigger a nova. We don't quite know how they do that, but clearly they have machines that actually penetrate the star's surface and carry out activities of some type deep inside, maybe even down at the very core. The star explodes, throwing off huge amounts of matter, mostly hydrogen and helium. They gather that, harvest it, really, by guiding it into one of the gateways opened by a Stargate, and probably send it back to the Great Annihilator at the Galactic Core. It's possible they may simply be interested in using the Galaxy as a resource, as raw material . . . not in exploring it. Or talking to young upstarts like us."

"So you're saying . . . what?" Kara asked. "No curiosity? No initiative?"

"And no change," Daren said, nodding, "for billions of years."

"Hard to imagine," Vic said.

"Not if we assume that their brains are essentially deterministic in the way they work."

"Quantum theory again," Kara said. She'd heard about this idea in downloads on AI design. It was well established that the human brain worked through principles described by quantum dynamics, that the whole hoary problem of free will was tied up with the notion of determinacy. Quantum-oriented AIs had eerily human capabilities because they thought in the same many-branching, nondeterministic mode as did humans.

"Are you saying that they can't have original ideas?" Vic asked. "That was the argument against self-aware computers back at the dawn of the electronics age, you know. They could only think about things they were programmed to think about. No originality at all."

"It's probably not that extreme a case," Daren said. "They have developed a starfaring civilization, after all, though Taki and some others think that might have been put in place by their organic predecessors. Certainly they could make obvious, deterministic advances, just like you said, Mother. One step at a time. As long as those steps were logical. *Rational*.

"But when it comes to the big step into quantum physics—"

"Ah!" Vic said. "They couldn't make that single, basic shift in their perceptions of how the universe worked!"

"That's it. From what we've seen so far . . . and from what we've deduced based on the bits of thought patterns that the Cameron probe download was able to record and send back, we think they may never have stumbled on the idea of quantum mechanics, that they think and work in a strictly deterministic and rational way. Interesting, isn't it? That bit of rigidity may hamper their exercise of what we would call imagination."

Kara grinned. "Well, it does take imagination to dream up something as weird as quantum physics."

"Precisely," Daren said. "They can't conceive of something as basic to our physics as, oh, a quon that can be a particle if you look at it one way, and a wave if you look at it another. Or that occupies a fuzzy area around the nucleus of an atom . . . but you can never quite pin down where the damned thing is. Things like the I2C would be completely beyond their reach.''

''So, that's why you say they could harvest Hawking radiation,'' Kara said, ''but not understand what they were doing. They might accept that a black hole appears to be leaking radiation in defiance of normal relativistic theory, but never figure out what was really going on!''

''It might not even occur to them to be curious about it,'' Daren said with a shrug.

''A lack of curiosity,'' Katya said thoughtfully, ''that would explain why they're no more advanced than they are, even after billions of years.''

''Right. You know, xenologists long argued about what would happen when two starfaring cultures encountered one another. The chances of both of them being at the same technological level is literally astronomical. One or the other should, almost certainly, be way, way ahead of the other one. And in a military conflict, the primitive bunch wouldn't stand a chance.

''Then we met the Naga, and they didn't even have technology except for what they'd patterned from other civilizations in their group memory. Then we met the DalRiss, but they didn't count either. Their civilization was older than ours, but their technology had evolved along radically different lines, so it's hard to compare. They're ahead of us in space transport, but behind us in things like weapons and basic electronics.''

Kara laughed. ''So now we meet *these* guys, as far beyond us as we are beyond amoeba, and we find out they've been so handicapped by a lack of imagination that they're no further along from flint knives than we are!''

''You know, it *could* be that there's a fundamental limit to how far technology can progress,'' Vic said.

Katya chuckled. ''Come back in a hundred years and tell me that. Or in ten. There are no limits, except the limits we place on ourselves.''

''Well, it's the one thing we have going to keep this a fair fight,'' Vic said. ''If we're not able to pull several fairly big surprises on the Web, they can still mop up on us, simply because they have the numbers.''

"You said we were working out some specific tactics," Katya said. "I wasn't in all of those meetings. What tactics?"

"Well, if it turns out we can't talk to them, we're going to end up relying a lot on that Imperial firepower out there," Vic told her. "Their PACs and primary laser batteries will keep off the small stuff . . . especially those tiny, laser-driven sails that Dev reported. We'll use saturation bombardment with thermonuclear warheads. And warflyers will be deployed to keep the small stuff from building up on the hulls of our big boys.''

"Grooming," Kara added with a grin. "Picking off the vermin.''

"That won't be enough by itself, of course," Vic continued. "We're working on several large assumptions, but they're logical assumptions, based on pretty solid evidence. Come. Look here." He walked over to a computer access console on one of the bulkheads, found an interface that wasn't in use, and palmed it. Several glittering metallic shapes appeared above the console's holoprojector as he uploaded a file from his personal RAM. "These are some of the different types of ships Dev saw, taken from his memory and filed for study." He pointed at the largest of the shapes, a black sphere made fuzzy by the thickly clustered antennae covering its surface. "This is what we're classifying as an Alpha type, Katya. The largest single machine Dev saw, and also one of the rarest. He saw three at Nova Aquila, and none at the nebula."

"A command ship?" Katya asked softly. "Those antenna arrays make it look like it does a hell of a lot of communicating. Suggests some sort of a command center. Maybe the brain of the whole operation."

"Well, it's probably nowhere near that simple," Daren told her. "Communication, yes, but the brain function of the aggregate machine intelligence is probably spread out over all of the members. Still, it's possible these Alphas serve as coordinators for the group intelligence."

"Like a CPU in a nonquantum computer system," Kara said.

Vic abruptly closed his eyes, consulting an internal data feed. "Kuso," he said suddenly. "The time's getting away. I've got to odie back to the *Karyu*."

Katya looked bleak. "Already?"

" 'Fraid so, love. I've got a staff meeting over there at seventeen-thirty. I can just make it." He took her hand. "There won't be time afterward for me to shuttle over again. This'll be it. Until the nebula, anyway."

"Until the nebula."

They embraced closely, kissing. After that, it was Kara's turn. "You take care of yourself, Dad," she said in his ear as he hugged her close.

"You bet I will. You too, you hear me?"

"Yes, *sir,* General, sir!"

"I'm going to walk your father to the shuttleport," Katya told her as Vic and Daren shook hands and clapped shoulders. "I'll see you before launch."

"Right, Mums."

"Kind of funny," Daren said as the two walked out of the ship's lounge. "Having all four of us in on this, like a family outing."

"All five," she said.

"I beg your pardon?"

"Your father's along, too, remember?"

Daren smiled. "Y'know, I hadn't even thought about that. Hagans, Alessandros, and Camerons all, sallying forth to meet the inhuman foe!"

"I don't see how you can joke about it, Dar. I really am worried about how we're supposed to face something as big, as powerful as the Web."

"With the firepower the Imperials have massed out there? I doubt that we'll even get to *see* any of the Web machines. None alive, anyway. Those big ryus out there'll fry the lot of them to cinders before they get within a hundred thousand kilometers of us!"

Katya turned and looked at her brother, her initial surprise turning to understanding. Daren was almost two years older than she was, yet sometimes he seemed so young. A *kid* . . .

Had combat made that big a difference in her, changed her

that much? Her perspective on combat, any combat, was that it was a dirty, messy, terrifying, and very deadly affair. Daren almost sounded disappointed that he was going to miss out on all of the fun. Had she ever been that young?

"Believe me," she told him. "If the Web is half the threat your dad says it is, you'll be seeing a lot more of the gokers than you'll care to."

Hours later, Kara, Katya, and Daren watched in thoughtful silence for a time as the *Gauss* maneuvered closer to the looming, black shadow of a DalRiss cityship. The *Gauss* was large, nearly four hundred meters in length, but she was dwarfed to toy-sized insignificance by the sheer mass of the DalRiss creature, which had a central body core measuring two kilometers across, and six stubby, massive limbs that increased its overall diameter by nearly three kilometers more. As the *Gauss* edged closer and closer to the cityship's underside—"under" as defined by the flat part of the torso that had rested on the ground when it was living on a planetary surface—one of the computer techs nearby giggled nervously. "Into the belly of the beast," she said, and others around her laughed.

"Attention. Attention," the voice of the ship's AI announced. "We will be losing gravity in three minutes. All passengers, be aware that conditions of zero-G will prevail throughout the transit period, and that both your persons and your personal effects must be secured for the duration. Crew members, assume your microgravity stations. . . ."

Tucked away against the DalRiss ship's belly, *Gauss* wouldn't be able to keep her hab modules rotating. At least, Kara thought with a wild, barely suppressed surge of amusement, not without tickling the poor creature half to death.

The passage to Nova Aquila would be made in several jumps, navigating the route by way of regions already plotted and incorporated into the latest crop of DalRiss Achievers. The first major rendezvous for regrouping and final preparations would be the nebula the *Sirghal* had escaped to, now positively identified by Confederation cosmologists as the North American–Penguin Nebula complex two thousand light years from Earth. Once the entire fleet was gathered and checked, then, they would make the final jump to Nova Aquila. The multiple-jump maneuver should foil Web attempts to back-track on the AEF's approach, even though in all probability such deceptions were useless. The Web almost certainly knew now where Earth and her offshoot worlds were.

With the final warning sounding for zero-G, Kara made her way back to the hab module assigned to the Black Phantoms as barracks space, found her bunk, and strapped herself in.

She found herself thinking about Ran Ferris.

She wasn't even sure where in the ship he was, though he would be with his squadron, probably on 'C' level. They'd had only a few hours together after her return from Sand-storm. One quick liaison in separate comm modules, just be-fore embarkation ... and a lingering good-bye in a virtual simulation of a streamside grotto in the New American Out-back. There'd been no time for anything more. No *time* ...

She found herself hungry for him, with a desperate, deep yearning that was as inescapable as it was predictable. Biology had a way, she'd noticed, of trying to arrange for the continued propagation of the species at the times of greatest danger.

She hated the idea of being a slave to biology.

But she couldn't deny her feelings either. She needed Ran ... and she needed to be needed.

She wondered when she would see him again.

Then there was no more time to think. Somewhere within the depths of the DalRiss cityship around them, an Achiever died. . . .

Chapter 23

One hundred thirty light years from Sol, the sun that men had long known variously as Theta Serpentis, as 63 Serpentis, or as Alya, the Serpent's Star, was in fact a widespread double, its A7 and A5 components orbiting one another at a distance of nine hundred astronomical units—about five light days. Both suns were attended by planets. The sixth world of the A5 star was home to the one DalRiss colony, ShraRish. The fifth world of the slightly cooler A7 star was known as GhegnuRish, the DalRiss homeworld, and home too to the first planetary Naga to be successfully communicated with by humans.

Both stars had been on the main sequence for about a billion years—roughly the expected lifespan for stars of their mass. Soon, within a few hundred thousands or millions of years, perhaps, the more massive, more brightly burning A5 sun would reach the point where it had burned most of its accessible hydrogen and needed to begin burning helium instead; the new reaction, hotter than the old, would upset the delicate equilibrium between thermal energy and gravity, and the star would balloon into a red giant. It was this imminent star death—imminent in cosmological terms, at any rate—that had led the DalRiss to begin evacuating their system. For the DalRiss, it was clear that Life had reached a dead end on the worlds of the Alyan suns, that if they were to continue participating in the Great Dance, they would have to do so beneath the light of another sun.

By this time, of course, the majority of the DalRiss population had already migrated elsewhere, eager to find other dancers in the Cosmos of Life. But there still remained some tens of billions of the Riss, together with their Dals and other specially grown symbionts, individuals who for one reason or another had elected to remain on the homeworld, or who had not yet boarded the waiting cityships for the great voyage outward. Too, there were several more recently arrived ships, stragglers among the eighty that had set off from human space twenty-five years before.

To say that the Riss respected life would be to anthropomorphize sentiments in a way alien to Riss thought. Rather, they perceived life as humans perceive the totality of the world around them, as an omnipresent dimension of interrelated parts and processes, the raw material of Riss civilization, the end point and purpose of an evolving universe. Life and evolution were participant and music to the Great Dance of the Cosmos; indeed, the entire purpose of the universe was to bring forth life, to turn inanimate matter into glorious, self-replicating, metabolizing organism.

Though the predicted death of the Alyan suns was widely described as a "nova," that description was not technically accurate. The red giant phases would cook the inner worlds, searing Alya B-V and Alya A-VI and rendering them lifeless cinders that eventually would be consumed by their bloated primaries. A true nova began as a double star with the two components much closer to each other in their mutual orbitings, say a few hundred thousands or millions of kilometers. In such a system, when one star aged to the point where it began expanding into its red giant phase, much of the outflow of stellar atmosphere was swept up by the companion. More and more of the mass of one star would pile up on the other, until a nuclear flash point was reached—a literal flash point, when the smothered sun detonated in a blaze hundreds of thousands of times brighter than its former state.

Sometimes there would be only the single explosion, and the white-dwarf remnant of the younger star would continue circling the older—which frequently seemed rejuvenated for a time, possibly with a fresh influx of hydrogen as death-gift of its companion. Often, though, the explosion of one star triggered the explosion of the second as thermal balances were irrevocably thrown out of kilter, and the end result was a pair of white dwarfs circling one another, as at Nova Aquila.

With the natural unfolding of stellar evolution, then, neither Alya A nor Alya B could be expected to light the skies of Earth someday with a nova's brilliance. But—as Dev had discovered at Nova Aquila—not all of the novae scattered along the Galaxy's Orion Arm were natural.

The swarm of machine-ships materialized out of otherspace in a glittering plastic and metallic spray. They numbered in the tens of millions, these machines, and all were part of the local expression of the Web's collective consciousness. Isolated from the rest of the Web by distances inconceivable, it was an associative of communicative machine nodes, none of which was intelligent or self-aware in its own right but all of which were tightly linked with other nodes by radio, microwave, and laser to form a far-flung and keenly tuned mind. The total number of Web machine units within this one cluster was much less than Nakamura's Number, but that particular footnote of arcane biomathematical law applied to a kind of transcendence, where the intelligence was far more than the sum of its hundred billion-odd parts. This association had intelligence of a sort—enough to do the job they'd been programmed to do.

The machines' exit point had been calculated with precision by the Central Web, based on information ripped from the heart of a DalRiss ship before it died. None of the machines blindly sprayed into the target system was expected to return to the Galactic Core; none felt anything like disappointment or protest at ill-use. They had, after all, been designed and built expressly for this purpose. A variety of DalRiss cityships and even a few human vessels were on hand to note the sudden appearance of the horde. None was in a position to intercept its members, however, as the Web Associative, wheeling together like an immense flock of birds or insects, swung into a course that would plunge them into Alya B.

The Starminers' senses detected the worlds of both Shra-Rish and GhegnuRish, but since DalRiss civilization had evolved along strictly biological lines rather than mechanical or industrial, they took no note of the cities growing on their surfaces. Machines were their sole measure of intelligence or worth . . . and even then only machines of specific intelligence and purpose could be clearly recognized as part of the Web's gestalt consciousness. Indeed, organic life of any kind, while recognized as self-replicating and self-organizing ongoing chemical processes, occupied no higher a niche in the Web's concept of an ordered universe than did the bacteria living within in a city built by Man.

Ignoring the cityships and the worlds alike, ignoring the incomprehensible signals at various radio and laser wavelengths, the Starminers plunged into the photosphere of Alya B, while the smaller Guardians and Swarmers and Eaters danced above the searing tongues of vast, stellar prominences. Composed of alloys and fields of magnetic force designed to resist pressures of billions of kilograms per square centimeter and temperatures of hundreds of millions of degrees Kelvin, the Starminers plunged deeper and yet deeper into the star's ultra-dense core. There, they initiated the process that would destabilize the star, opening a rift in space and time—a rift at first microscopically small, but joined by means of a thread-slender wormhole to one of the hellfurnaces at the Galactic Core, a place in which they gathered the resources of an entire galaxy and reshaped them in matter and in energy to their own purposes.

The rift widened . . . becoming a crack in space. Energy appeared inside the star, the energies associated with the star-death radiance of an erupting quasar leaking from that microscopic prick in space and time and flooding into the stellar core.

Normally it would have taken millennia for that buildup of energy to work its way up through layer upon layer of the star's inner heart, but the continued influx of energy at the center continued to press outward, relentless, ballooning, irresistible. A star, any star, is a constant compromise between the tendency to collapse under its own gravity and the tendency to fly apart into space, an ongoing fusion explosion restrained by its own mass from expanding further.

And the Starminers had just irreversibly revoked the contract of that compromise, pouring a steady flood of energy into
the core that even the tremendous, crushing mass of Alya B
could not long contain. In scant hours, then, Alya B began
growing brighter in the green-tinted GhegnuRish sky.

DalRiss natural organs for perceiving light accomplished
little more than simple recognition of light and dark, allowing them to establish the difference between day and night.
Only those few individuals who happened to be symbiotically linked with Perceivers, then, could look up and note
that their star's face had become somewhat blotchy.
Though it was as radiant across its entire disk as ever,
some small portions of the star's surface had grown
brighter by far in scant seconds; as with sunspots, which
appear dark only because of the comparison with the rest
of a star's surface, the bright patches made the rest of Alya
B turn dim.

But the bright patches spread, and soon the entire sky was
a searing ocean of white flame . . . and the DalRiss who happened to be outside and placed to see the phenomenon were
already dying.

Atmosphere, superheated, exploded outward in swirling
windstorms. Organic material caressed by that deadly light
burst into flame, or shriveled and blackened where it died.
Before long, the heat had reached the planetary Naga, which
extended throughout the world's crust, a living, thinking, communicating network. At first, instinctively, it drew life from
the sudden radiance falling on the world's day side. Soon,
though, the heat became so intense that the Naga was retreating from that hemisphere, seeking cooler refuge deep within
the comforting, sheltering rock.

Ten hours after the first intimation of disaster, the upper
few hundred meters of rock on GhegnuRish had already become molten, a planet-wide ocean of crusted-over lava and
crumbling continents of white-hot rock. Beneath the molten
rock, the Naga was everywhere beginning to disassociate into
separate, subintelligent fragments.

Then the shock wave of the exploding star reached the
planet, stripping away what was left of the searing atmosphere

and crust alike in a white hot hurricane of particles—protons, hot plasma, hard radiation. By the time GhegnuRish had completed another rotation, its diameter had dwindled by nearly twenty percent, and what was left was a glowing, molten sphere rapidly boiling away into space.

Five days later, the light of Alya B's detonation reached its companion sun, Alya A, and the fifth world, ShraRish.

Millennia before, the DalRiss had abandoned their homeworld to the Naga that occupied it, after a long and bitter fight. ShraRish, their sole colony, now was more thickly populated by the immense, squat, starfish organisms that served as DalRiss cities than their homeworld. For twenty-five human years now, those cities had been abandoning the Alyan system, choosing instead to seek other partners in the Great Dance among the stars, but the remaining cities still numbered in the tens of thousands.

Traveling just behind the flash and dazzle of dying GhegnuRish, the Web's scouts drifted in at just beneath the speed of light, decelerating suddenly at thousands of gravities, a maneuver impossible to any organic, cellular-based life form. Again, the Starminers plunged into the star's depths.

And within another few days, Alya A, like its brother, was flaring into the deadly, blossoming brilliance of a nova. Most of the DalRiss and human ships orbiting one or the other of the two doomed worlds were able to escape.

But ten billion DalRiss who'd chosen to remain on their worlds of their birth perished in the dual funeral pyres of their suns.

Chapter 24

*No plan of operations can look with any certainty be-
yond the first meeting with the major forces of the enemy. The commander is compelled to reach decisions on
the basis of situations which cannot be predicted.*
　　　　　　　　　　　　　　—HELMUTH VON MOLTKE
　　　　　　　　　　　　　　nineteenth century C.E.

Until the Aquilan Expeditionary Force reached the staging
area at the Nebula, all of the messages passing back and forth
across the new I2C network had been strictly routine . . . daily
reports on mission status, on personnel, equipment, and supplies, navigational and communications checks, nothing out of
the ordinary save for the fact of faster-than-light communication itself. The arrival point was carefully swept by flights
of warstriders reconfigured in their warflyer mode—there was
some concern that the machines that had followed Dev Cameron and the DalRiss out from Nova Aquila might still be
around—but the patrols turned up nothing. That was not
surprising, of course. The North American-Penguin nebula
complex was vast, encompassing many thousands of cubic
light years, so even if the Web machines were still operational
and able to pick up the AEF's arrival, they wouldn't be able
to contest it unless they possessed their own faster-than-light
capability independent of the Device. And, apparently, that
wasn't the case.

Not long after the fleet had materialized in the soft, blue glow of the nebula, however, the first I2C reports came in telling of trouble in another, more distant quarter, of disaster in the Alyan system. Ships—human and DalRiss—that had been able to jump clear in time had carried word to the Shichiju of millions of alien machines appearing out of empty space and attacking the Alyan suns . . . word of stars exploding, of worlds gone molten, empty of life.

The news was still being digested throughout the fleet. Few of the humans, at any rate, felt powerful attachments to the destroyed alien worlds, but it was all too easy to imagine the same thing happening to 26 Draconis, or 70 Ophiuchi, or 36 Ophiuchi.

Or Sol.

Dev had contacted Vic in linkage aboard the *Karyu*, passing on the interesting piece of news that the vice admiral commanding the AEF had just received an emergency broadcast direct from the Tenno Kyuden, the Palace of Heaven in Earth Synchorbit. The content of the message had been coded and Dev had been unable to break the code without alerting security programs traveling with it, but it was easy enough to guess what the contents must be. Within ten minutes, a ViRcomm meeting had been scheduled for all ship commanders in the combined fleet.

Now Vic was standing in the office of *Chujo* Haruo Tanaka aboard the flagship *Shinryu*. One entire bulkhead was an impressive viewall that looked now into the nebula, a vast, blue and white translucency cold against the stars. Ships—DalRiss star-shapes, and the long, cluttered, spearpoints of the ryu carriers—were silhouetted against curtains of pale light.

Tanaka looked pale, stressed to the breaking point. Vic sat in a low, swivel chair across the room, studying the man. He'd shuttled across to the expedition's flagship from the *Karyu* rather than using a comm module. The news from home was grave enough that a *personal* visit was required, and he'd needed to talk to the man in private before the scheduled gathering of the fleet's senior officers.

"Two stars," Tanaka said, shaking his head in disbelief. He stood before the viewall, hands clasped behind his back. "Two stars brighter and larger than our own, simply *exploded....*"

"And ten billion DalRiss snuffed out," Vic added, "apparently without even a nod from the Web."

"Horrifying."

"The question is, sir, what are you going to do about it?"

Tanaka turned from the viewall. "Do? You are no doubt aware that I have just received new orders."

"Yes, sir."

"Those orders are quite clear, General. We are to return to the Shichiju at once."

Vic nodded. He'd expected no less. That was why he'd wanted to grab Tanaka first, before the staff meeting, to talk to him.

To *convince* him.

"Sir," Vic said. "With all due respect, this may be one time when duty requires that we ignore our orders. At least for the moment."

"Duty never countenances disobedience."

"Even when obedience clearly leads to defeat? Admiral, I submit that this campaign is far too important to let the bureaucrats run it from home."

There was a supreme irony in this, Vic thought. Until now, the commander of a starfleet was completely on his own once he left his home system; headquarters depended on couriers for periodic reports on his progress, and those could usually be dispatched at the commander's convenience. He had to answer for his decisions when he returned, *if* he returned, but at least he didn't have his superiors second-guessing those decisions every step of the way. The quantum communications net might be the most important development in space military tactics since the development of the K-T drive, but it could also end up crippling innovation and the initiative of individual leaders.

Maybe the Web had the better idea after all, ignoring faster-than-light communication and the nullheaded bureaucratic idiocy of tightly controlled central planning in military operations. He remembered the conversation aboard the *Gauss* with his family, a short time before. If warfare someday did become a clean, antiseptic exercise in pure tactics, the rear-area kibitzers and chair warmers and bureaucrats could become the soldiers of the future, teleoperating their war machines across interstellar distances.

There would be no reining in the horror of war then, when there were no soldiers right *there* to experience the horror firsthand, or the danger. What would someone like Munimori care about another dozen cities wiped out, more or less?

Or worlds, for that matter. . . .

Tanaka considered Vic for a long moment through narrowed eyes. "I am a soldier," he said after a time. "I believe that I have a responsibility to use my own judgment in the field . . . but I also bear the responsibility of duty. I see no clear alternatives here."

"Our first duty is to protect the Shichiju, all the worlds of humanity, from the threat we've perceived in the Web. Right?"

"Yes."

"But we're not going to be able to do that if we scamper back home."

"Tell me more, Hagan-*san*."

Haruo Tanaka, Vic knew from the man's official biography, was one of the more innovative and inventive of the Imperium's naval commanders. He'd started in the marines, a warstrider jacking a *Daimyo* during the revolution. He'd switched over to the Imperial Navy after the war ended, eventually rising to the rank of *shosho*—the equivalent of a Confederation rear admiral—and the command of the commanding officer of the ryu carrier *Funryu*.

Five years ago he'd been promoted to *chujo*—vice admiral—and given command of the Third Provincial Fleet, but he'd lost that command, and a certain amount of status, by advocating the complete overhaul of the Imperial Navy's current tactics. Ryu carriers, he claimed, were anachronisms; the future of naval warfare belonged to smaller, more maneuverable vessels, operating under widely distributed and detached independent commands.

Vic wasn't sure what twistings of Imperial politics had put Tanaka back in favor and in command of the AEF. Possibly it represented a rearrangement of the current political alignments back on Earth. Or possibly the command had been seen as a way of getting him out from underfoot. Either way, he would have plenty of Imperial Naval staff officers, from Munimori on down, all looking carefully over his shoulder.

And with the I2C, that constant inspection must become damned near microscopic at times.

"Your orders are for us to report where? Earth?"

"Earth's solar system is being covered by the First Fleet," Tanaka said carefully. "Under the command of *Gensui* Munimori himself. We are to return to 26 Draconis." He seemed to be measuring Vic's response to his words, watching for fear or anger. "The Imperial Staff feels that the New American system might be facing the greatest threat of attack, since it is on the very fringe of human-occupied space and in the same general direction as Alya."

"Uh-huh. Right."

Vic's tone was sarcastic. It was entirely possible that this sudden change of orders was part of some larger plan, a plan that had nothing to do at all with the Web except for using it as an excuse. With the Imperial fleet concentrated and at full war preparedness, it would be so easy to take over all of the nominally independent states scattered along the Shichiju's border. . . .

"Look. You've seen the same reports, the same records I have. You know what the Web is like. What the *threat* is like. You know that if you're there protecting 26 Draconis, the Web could just as easily strike somewhere else. Even the Imperial Navy isn't big enough to protect all of the Shichiju's worlds. Especially if the Imperial Command Staff is more interested in settling old scores than it is in stopping the Web."

That last was a guess, but a reasonable one. The fact that an out-of-favor officer had been placed in command of the expeditionary force strongly suggested that Tenno Kyuden's attention was focused on other interests just now. The negotiations of the past few weeks that had led to the creation of the AEF could well have been a sham, a way of slipping in and grabbing lost territories in a practically bloodless coup.

He also knew that Tanaka was both a good officer and a brilliant tactician, not the sort of man to turn his back on the real threat just to take part in the petty politics of Empire.

"Politics," Tanaka said, closing his eyes, "and politicians are the bane of soldiers." He opened his eyes, impassive again. "Believe me when I say I've already argued exhaustively that we should continue the mission. To no avail."

"Then disobey the bastards."

Tanaka blinked. "Unthinkable."

"Not at all. I can think about it all day. So can you." He sighed. *How* to shake this guy loose from a position wedged in by training, obedience, and duty? "*Chujosan*, are the orders for you alone? Your people? Or do they extend to the Confederation force as well?"

"The wording could be considered ambiguous," Tanaka replied, "but I take it to mean all vessels and personnel currently under my command. That would include you and your people as well. I am in command of this force."

"Of course. *Tenno Kyuden* doesn't want a Confederation warfleet bouncing around loose." Vic carefully scrutinized his fingernails, not meeting Tanaka's level gaze. "Sir, I have a different interpretation of my orders. I tell you now, honestly and directly, that if you order me to return to human space, I will disobey those orders. You cannot attack us here without having your ships released by their DalRiss carriers, obviously. Long before your ships were free, *my* ships and *my* DalRiss transporters would be long gone."

"You could not face the Web by yourself. It would be suicide!"

"At least we can try." He nodded toward the viewall. "The enemy's out there, *Chujosan*. The Web. I am taking my people to meet it, and every human in the Shichiju who can link onto the I2C-Net is going to be watching what happens out there. I wonder what the citizens of the Empire are going to say when they see their Imperial defenders leaving their defense to a handful of Confederation warships. If we win, we will be the saviors of all mankind. If we lose, *you* will be perceived as the villain who cut and ran and abandoned us to death, no matter what your orders might say. There's something more to it that you might consider, too. Have you discussed with the DalRiss the idea of returning to the Shichiju? Have you asked if they'll even take you?''

Tanaka's eyes widened. ''The . . . DalRiss? No. That did not occur to me. Why wouldn't they?''

''Mmm. You might give it a try. Link in and talk to the DalRiss bossing this cityship, the one piggybacking the *Shinryu*. You could find that they have something else in mind besides retreating to human space. Remember, they have a stake in the expedition, too. Ten billion murdered fellow-dancers.'' Vic crossed his arms as he leaned back in the chair. In fact, when Vic had tried talking to them a short time ago, he hadn't been able to ascertain what the DalRiss thought about the news from home. They certainly didn't think in terms of vengeance. The closest human emotion he could attribute to them now was one of stunned disbelief . . . and just possibly a sense of urgency about the need to complete the mission before more worlds died. Obviously, though, Tanaka hadn't questioned them closely yet. It gave Vic a very slight edge in the bloodless war of words and position being waged now between them. ''Right now, *Chujosan*, we're about two thousand light years from home. Do you think you have supplies enough laid in for a trek back the long way, through K-T space? At a light year per day, that's a five-and-a-half year trip. That's a long time. A lot could happen in five years.''

The admiral's expression went stony, an indifference masking whatever he was truly feeling. ''Are you threatening me, *Shoshosan*?''

''Not at all.'' A direct threat, a blatant challenge of Tanaka's authority, would make him lose face and would force him into a corner where his only option might be to harden his stance, whatever the consequences. ''I just want to be certain that you see all options, and all positions. I point out that, should you decide that I'm right, that our common goal should be to defeat the Web at Nova Aquila, rather than playing catchup with them across human space. You have options that would allow you to . . . let's say *reinterpret* your superiors' orders. You could continue to Nova Aquila because the DalRiss refused to take you back. That could be humiliating, I know, admitting that you'd been carried off by a *gaijin*, but I doubt that Admiral Munimori is willing to link personally with a DalRiss to hear it himself. If you prefer, tell them that we refused to go back with you, and that you felt it necessary to keep an eye on us.''

Tanaka stared at Vic for a long time, his face completely impassive. Finally, though, he rocked back on his heels and gave the Confederation general a small, tight-lipped smile. ''You are very good at this.''

A direct answer, yes or no, would have been out of place. Vic bowed his head slightly in reply, neither affirming nor denying.

''It will be . . . difficult,'' Tanaka continued. ''This electronic gathering I have called, it is to be transferred to Earth. To the Tenno Kyuden. I expect that *Gensui* Munimori himself will attend. To refuse such a person to his face—''

''He is two thousand light years away, *Chujosan*. If necessary, do what we do when our superiors are breathing down our necks.''

''What is that?''

Vic smiled. ''Feign communications difficulties.''

The admiral smiled in reply. ''I will consider that.''

The interview was ended. Vic stood, bowed, and turned toward the door.

''General,'' Tanaka said as Vic reached out to palm the door open.

''Sir?''

''I think you should know . . . for your own information only. I had a son. Age twenty-eight. He was a lieutenant in command of an Imperial Marine company, stationed at Syria Planum, on Kasei. A few months ago, he was aboard one of four transports over the Marineris Sea, responding with his unit to an attack by raiders. *Confederation* raiders. All four transports were destroyed. Every man aboard them was killed.''

''Why are you telling me this, *Chujosan*?''

''I have reason to hate your people, General. I have reason to hate the military service you represent. But I believe in what we have been sent out here to do. I believe in it so much, that

I have disregarded what happened on Kasei. At least for now. I thought you should know.''

"I already knew, Admiral. I picked up as much from your dossier, before we left New America.''

"And you agreed to accept service under my command despite this?''

"Of all of the Imperial senior officers who might have been chosen to command, you were by far the best. That is not flattery, Admiral, but a simple statement of fact. And I will tell *you*, sir, that my wife, my son, and my daughter are all serving with the Confederation contingent of this fleet. And I intend to take that contingent to Nova Aquila, whether I have your ships at my back or not.''

Tanaka considered this a moment, then gave a curt nod. "*Wakarimasu*,'' he said. "I understand. It is an honor to have officers such as yourself in my command.''

Kara and Ran lay close together on the top of a sand dune, watching the tide churn and froth as it swirled inland across the mud flats to the south. The ViRsimulation they shared was of a beach on a rugged portion of the coastline northwest of Jefferson, back in New America. Flickets and dragonbugs sang in the vegetation nearby. A shimmering, gold-flashing cloud of morninglories chirped and chorused at the edge of the forest. Columbia bulked huge and orange-smudged ocher in the sky.

"It is really strange,'' Kara said, "having the Imperials on our side.''

"And what's your evaluation, Lieutenant?'' Ran Ferris asked with a lazy grin. Kara was nestled close to him inside the curve of his arm; his hand gently massaged her shoulder, her upper arm, then slid over to cup her breast.

She slapped the moving hand, playful. "Beast. Call me Lieutenant again and you'll end up in the brig.''

"Yes, *ma'am*.''

They kissed.

"Seriously, though,'' he said after a time. "I've been hearing some bizarre who-was about them.'' *Who-was* was military slang for rumors, drawn from the Nihongo *uwasu*.

"Such as?"

"Such as how the Imperial fleet that was sent out here to help us is going to provide permanent help, if you know what I mean."

"Hmm. I've heard some of the same stories."

"Do you believe them?"

"I . . . I don't know. It's hard to just stop hating, you know?" She pulled back from him a little, rolling onto her back.

"Well, you don't hate all of them, do you?" His tone was bantering. "Or is the only good Imp a dead Imp?" When she didn't answer immediately, he grew more serious. "What about that scientist your brother's been seeing? Doctor—"

"Dr. Oe."

"What about her?"

"What about her?" Kara asked sharply. "She's Nihonjin, even if she was born on New America."

"Come on. Your brother wouldn't—"

"My brother," Kara said with a sigh, "is capable of almost anything. Total myopia. Can't see a thing beyond what he, personally, wants."

"Well, I'd have thought that a doctor of xenosophontology would have a certain maturity about him."

"Daren? Mature?" She snorted. "Don't get me wrong. I love the guy. But one thing a university download doesn't give you, even at the doctorate level, is maturity. Or experience."

"So . . . you think we're being tricked? Maybe led into a trap?"

She sighed. "I don't know. I think, probably, whatever the Imperials have planned, when they meet this thing at Nova Aquila, well, maybe our differences won't seem as important. Or our hatreds. I hope so." She stirred against his arm. "We shouldn't have come here."

"Of course we should have."

"It's all such a question mark, what's going to happen at Nova Aquila."

"I know." He drew her closer. "Sometimes you need people. Need just being close."

"Yes . . ."

"I'm afraid we don't have much more time. Our hour's almost up."

"I know. We were damned lucky to get our schedules swapped around so we could share our downtimes here." She rubbed his chest lightly. "You know, it's funny to think we could go back to New America for real, riding the I2C."

"For real? You mean for virtual real."

She laughed. "You know what I mean. This new tech is going to change things an awful lot. In society. In us, in the way we do and think about things. Out here, even the Japanese don't seem so . . . so alien anymore."

He seemed to understand that she wasn't talking about the New American ViRsim when she said "out here." One reason they'd chosen a familiar setting for their rendezvous was the strangeness of the sky beyond *Gauss*'s bulkheads. The nebula was a constant reminder of just how far they were from home.

"Still seems strange," he said, "being this far away from Newamie, yet being able to zip back and talk to your folks whenever you want."

"My folks are here."

"I know."

"FTL commo could prove to be a curse, you know. With the brass always looking over your shoulder. My fa— General Hagan is back on Earth right now. At an Imperial staff meeting, no less."

"No kidding! Straight hont?" The soldier's slang meant *truth*.

"Straight hont."

"What's the word gonna be?"

"Oh, we're going. I don't know what the Impies are going to do, but we're going. I know that look in his eye." She consulted her inner clock. "Gok! We don't have much time. Ten more minutes . . ."

His caress grew rougher, more insistent. "There's time for once more."

"Yes. *Yes* . . ."

• • •

Dev was riding the Net.

It was a heady experience. Normally, during his past years with the DalRiss, the program sustaining his memory and awareness of self had resided within one or another of the DalRiss cityships, a tiny, software parasite riding the far vaster, labyrinthine worlds within worlds of his hosts. Occasionally, especially when there was some particular danger, or some object of interest that demanded his full attention, he would distribute his program across several nodes, riding, in effect, a number of different DalRiss ships.

Now, however, he resided not only within the DalRiss fleet, but inside all of the nodes of all of the computer systems of all of the human vessels of the fleet. Human computer nets tended to be tightly compartmentalized by subject and use, in sharp opposition to the Naga communications and memory storage, which had a loose and open-ended structure; the blend of the two, however, was something completely new, seemingly infinite vistas and variety and information, unfolding in layer upon layer of sight and sound, color and texture, a literal cyberworld corresponding in idea, if not precisely in space, with the real world.

He could sense . . . *something* about that Net as well, the other minds—AI, human, DalRiss, and Naga—that rode the Net with him, interacting, branching, floating, merging. He'd sampled the computer net girdling Jefferson on his return from Nova Aquila, finding it tightly ordered and compartmentalized . . . and with the University of Jefferson's AI system as the largest and most complex of the network's nodes.

Now, however, world after world, system after system was coming on-line, tied together by the comm mod feeds and data links connecting planet after planet and ship after ship across interstellar distances. He could *feel* it as more and more people were linking in throughout the Shichiju. He felt it when, with the suddenness of a thrown switch, the entire Juanyekundu Net came on-line; suddenly, he could hear new voices, Swahili voices of Juanyekundu's underground population on UV Ceti I, mingling with the resonant tones and murmurs and echoing reverberations of uncounted multitudes of other tongues and thoughts riding the Net with him, adding their own rich counterpoint to the swelling, choral multitude.

Power. He could feel it, swelling, mounting, as people linked in by the billions.

How many were joining in the Net? Not everyone was watching the AEF by any means. Business was still being conducted on seventy-eight colonized worlds and hundreds of outposts, bases, ships, and remote facilities. There seemed to be a kind of morbid curiosity about the coming encounter, however, and that interest was building; the medes had spread the story on all of the major print, vid, and ViRnews services, describing what was known about the Web and what the Aquila Expeditionary Force hoped to accomplish. Whatever the result of the coming contact, it would have a profound effect on everyone; peaceful contact with the Web would bring for all humanity the literally unimaginable benefits of contact with a race, a collective of civilization and knowledge, literally billions of years old. The medes had been touting the wonders for weeks already. The Web made magic, such as turning energy into matter and back again, seem like child's play; interaction with such a technology would usher in a new, golden age of plenty for all humans.

And if communication was not possible, if war was the result . . .

Dev didn't like thinking about that possibility, for the odds against humankind were very long indeed. Despite the long discussions with various planning staffs about how human flexibility and the possession of faster-than-light communication conferred tremendous advantages on the human-DalRiss side, the Web had one advantage that no level of superior communication could really match.

The Web could still be using crossbows and gunpowder, yet win the coming battle through sheer weight of numbers. There was no way Dev could use the strength of those billions of watchers, none that he knew of, anyway.

But the surge of power in and around him as he surveyed this new domain filled him with the sort of elation he'd once known only through a physical surge of adrenaline. It was like . . . nothing else that Dev had ever directly experienced, save possibly the glory-thrill of riding the *Kamisama no Taiyo*, the fiery Ocean of God within the K-T plenum interface while jacking a starship at faster-than-light. That experience had always been for Dev something transcendent. There'd been times, too, during the revolution, when he'd tapped into a power far greater than anything his mind or body could possibly muster.

This was like that. No . . . better, this was the *real* experience. The others, jacking a starship through K-T space, or hurling one-ton boulders into the sky and tearing down great ryu-class ships, *those* were the pale and dim reflections of reality.

Interesting. As the Combined Fleet prepared for the final leg of its journey to Nova Aquila, he could sense individuals as well as entire populations. With a relatively gentle focus of will and effort, he could hear Katya's thoughts as she linked in through an observer channel aboard the *Gauss*. There was Kara now jacking into her warflyer, preparing for combat. There was Daren, his son, also on the *Gauss*, linked into a system on the Net designed to let the members of all of the science teams watch the final jump and the approach toward the Device. Vic's body was aboard the *Karyu*, in a comm module on Deck Five; his mind, however, was attending a gathering of admirals and generals and senior politicians in the Tenno Kyuden complex in Earth synchorbit. Dev could hear those voices as well . . . arguments over the threat posed by the Web, over orders disobeyed, over threatened repercussions.

He had no doubt about the outcome, however. He'd been able to—*taste* was the closest word he could find—taste Tanaka's thoughts and mind as he'd linked into the Net earlier and allowed his consciousness to ride the I2C back to Earth. The Imperial contingent would stay at least long enough to check out the Nova Aquila system. If there was no sign of Web activity there, Tanaka would consider a return to the Shichiju . . . but to return now, with nothing accomplished, that would be futile. Worse, it was to allow himself and his people to become political pawns, trapped between Imperial superiors and gaijin subordinates.

Tanaka would stay.

A voice, a DalRiss voice, rumbled behind his thoughts. "We return, >>DEVCAMERON<<, to the place where we first encountered the Web." The voice carried overtones of emotions, many of which Dev could not read. One emotion carried clearly through the Net, however: *grief*—for lost life, for lost opportunities, for lost circles in the great Dance—was foremost in the creature's mind.

"We'll be facing the Web again. How do you feel about that?"

He sensed the mental and alien equivalent of a shrug. "The Web is not life," the voice said. "We will end it, before it removes others from the Dance. Or the Great Dance will end with us."

Dev thought the DalRiss definition of life a narrow one, but said nothing. Their definitions and their philosophies, like those for any sentient species, were bounded by the limitations of their senses.

The final seconds of an agreed-upon countdown ticked away, and the great DalRiss cityships flickered from existence. Aboard the *Carl Friedrich Gauss*, Kara, Katya, and Daren all were linked in, watching as the stars shifted, as they were replaced by twin dwarfs flaming against blackness, by spiraling ribbons of star stuff.

They watched with an awe that approached an almost holy reverence as they first caught sight of the impossible, mercury-bright thread of the Device suspended in space between the two.

And there was more. Space between the two suns appeared to be somewhat hazy, as though filled with a thin, slightly translucent mist. Within that mist there were . . . *shapes*, unknown shapes, shapes beyond the experience of humans, beyond the experience of any life form with perceptions rooted solidly in only three dimensions. The human observers followed line and form back into an infinity of distance, minds reeling as they tried to interpret what they were seeing . . . .

"All stations," Vic's voice announced over the network

connecting all of the Confederation vessels in the fleet. "Phase One commencement . . . now."

Like huge starfish improbably giving birth to offspring that bore them no resemblance whatsoever, the DalRiss carriers began releasing the starships tucked into their ventral folds. Human ships, from corvettes and packets to slush-H tankers and supply freighters to the huge, arrowhead shapes of the ryu carriers, spilled into space, spreading out ahead of the larger, Alyan vessels.

The *Carl Friedrich Gauss* slipped free of the embrace of its DalRiss, accelerating slightly to work its way clear of the cityship creature. Its hab modules began rotating slowly about its axis, though the humans linked into the comm net were unaware of either the absence or the presence of mundane conveniences like gravity.

Unmanned probes—Charlies, as the xenologists aboard were calling them—dropped clear of open cargo bays throughout the fleet and accelerated on tiny, flaring white suns. Some were military remote sensors, deployed to perceive and map a larger area of battle should a fight develop. Others were unarmed remotes, for the attempt at communicating with the Web, and for providing a closer look at the strangeness up ahead. Clearly, there'd been changes here in the short time since Dev had recorded the scene . . . engineering of some sort on a scale so vast human minds were having difficulty grasping it.

Two Charlies boosted away from the *Gauss*, jacked by Daren and Taki. As they approached the glowing, golden cloud of mist and the enigmatic shapes dimly glimpsed within, their voices came across the communications channel, uploaded to the entire Net.

"My God," Daren said, his voice tight. "That mist . . . it's machines. Devices of some kind. There must be billions of them. . . ."

"And they are responding to our presence," Taki's voice added. "We're decelerating, to let them know we're not hostile."

"*Kuso*," Kara added from her link within her Cutlass, still waiting for release from the research ship. "These guys just killed a few billion DalRiss, and we're worried about hostile?''

''It still could be some kind of mistake,'' Taki said. ''Initiating transmission . . .''

The signal, broadcast on frequencies known to be used by the Web, was a repeating loop of good intentions and we-come-in-peace assurances, coupled with nested pleas for an open communications channel. The human watchers were all well aware, however, that Dev and the DalRiss had tried much the same thing in their encounter here.

So had the DalRiss and the human-crewed ships at Alya.

And then the waves of machine warcraft appeared, exploding out of empty space like glittering droplets flung glistening into the sunlight by an ocean breaker crashing over rocks. There was no response to the peace overture, no acknowledgement of signals, no attempt at communication.

And in the next few seconds, ships, DalRiss and human, began to die. . . .

Chapter 25

The human intellect is feeble, and there are times when it does not assert the infinity of its claims. But even then—

> *Though in black jest it bows and nods,*
> *I know it is roaring at the Gods,*
> *Waiting the last Eclipse.*
> > —*Daedalus, or Science and the Future*
> > J. B. S. HALDANE
> > C.E. 1923

The first wave of Web machines accelerated to relativistic speeds, hurtling toward the Combined Fleet so quickly that they rode in close behind the light waves announcing their arrival. Taki, linked in with a remote approaching the Web well out ahead of the rest of the human and DalRiss ships, had only a blurred impression of something like a wall of glittering raindrops or ice crystals rushing toward her face at tremendous speed.

She screamed . . .

. . . and with a shuddering jolt, the sound of metal ringing on metal still sounding in her ears, she woke up aboard the *Gauss*, strapped into a couch within the dark, calm enclosure of a comm module.

For a moment she could only lie there, gasping like a fish stranded on the beach. The impression of actually being there, of actually *being* the probe itself as it was struck by hurtling chunks of metal, had been so realistic that it had been impossible to remind herself at the time that her body was safe aboard the research ship.

"Daren?" she called into the darkness, focusing on her Companion's link.

"*Oof*," she heard in her mind. "I just got run over by about a million angry Webbers. You, too?"

"Yeah. But I'm going back."

"Why? The Webbers aren't interested in talking. That's clear. Let the professionals worry about it."

It was tempting. Taki had never known such fear as that instant when she'd seen the glittering wall descending on her. It would be a lot easier to jack into the Primary Net and just watch, along with all of the other humans in the fleet . . . and throughout the Shichiju as well.

Taki, however, didn't like weakness, didn't like admitting to weakness. She'd grown up on a world where most of the citizens assumed she was Imperial because of her eyes and her face and her name, but she'd forged ahead despite the obstacles and won her doctorate in xenology. Ten years ago, and despite the common belief that Japanese never dirtied themselves with alien parasites, she'd accepted a Companion. Her thinking at the time had been that she could adopt a Naga expression as a *men*, a way to simply and easily transform her face into that of a Caucasian, safe and acceptable, with free access into any part of New American society.

For over twenty hours she'd been a *shiro*, a white. She'd even recolored her glossy black hair yellow, becoming *kimpatsu*—the derogatory Nihongo slang for a blonde.

But it hadn't been her, and she refused to live a lie. After one memorable standard as a *shiro,* she'd reverted to her natural phenotype, and to hell with anyone who didn't like it.

She hadn't hidden then, and she wasn't about to hide now.

Swiftly, she reentered the control linkage and selected another Charlie, waiting in the racks in *Gauss*'s cargo bay. Darkness enveloped her, and then she was looking down into the star-strewn emptiness beneath the modified Cutlass. Words scrolled across her field of vision.

TELEPRESENCE LINK CONFIRMED
ELECTRONIC CHECKS OK
TANK PRESSURIZATION COMPLETE
PROBE 5 READY FOR LAUNCH

"Stay if you want to, Daren," she said. She keyed the release command and dropped into night once again. "I'm damned if I'm going to hang around inside the ship waiting for things to happen!"

During her few moments off-line, the swarm of onrushing Web machines had reached the human-DalRiss fleet. In utter and magnificent silence—save for the wild calls of pilots and operators over the tactical nets—the battle unfolded in blossoming, searing brilliance. Explosions strobed as high-velocity chunks of metal slammed into duralloy plate, or as fusion warheads erupted in thermonuclear glory. Taki's display view was a bewildering complexity of what was actually visible and the drifting, flickering graphics provided by her AI, identifying moving objects, warning of collisions, pointing out immediate threats. The sky was filled with wheeling, plunging human ships mingled with the strangely shaped probes and artifices of alien minds.

Ahead, the gold-glowing cloud shining about the thread-slender Device appeared to be slowly reshaping itself. Billions—no, *trillions* of separate Web machines were reorienting themselves according to some unguessable, private strategy.

Unable to join the battle, unable to understand more than a fraction of what she was seeing, Taki became a spectator adrift in the drama unfolding all about her.

The battle had already degenerated into a whirling, mad free-for-all, bewildering in its complexity and scope. The Web devices were scattered through space so thickly they formed a silvery gold mist, a sea of mechanisms, of machines in infinite panoply of design and purpose and function.

Kara's Matic had long since been reconfigured as a warflyer, with a ten-meter maneuvering module nanosealed to her hull and jacked into the control linkages. Inside her life pod, Kara floated in a thick liquid to protect her from the brutal accelerations of space combat, with nanotech umbilicals keeping her body alive, and a Companion-link hookup with the *Gauss*'s AI feed so that she could watch through the Combined Fleet's Net link. She could see little detail in that cloud at first, and for the first few seconds she assumed she was seeing some sort of local atmosphere, an outgassing effect, possibly, channeled through the strange physics holding sway over the vicinity of the Device.

Naga-formed scouts and robot probes fired from the Combined fleet immediately upon reentry into normal space, however, swiftly penetrated the outer fringes of the cloud, relaying data and images back to the human-DalRiss fleet.

"My God in heaven!" someone in her squadron said over the link. "How are we going to stop *that*?"

"Cut the commentary," she snapped back. "Status report!"

Numbers flickered past her awareness, each of the fifteen warflyers in her squadron reporting full readiness to launch. They were arrayed in release gantries in a bay already evacuated, poised above a yawning emptiness through which stars were wheeling. The warflyers were carried in a spin gravity cargo bay; when the magnetic clamps were released, the flyers would be flung clear of the *Gauss* by centrifugal force.

The nightmare of it all was that there was nothing fifteen warflyers could do against a storm of mind and metal like that swarming at that moment outside the *Gauss*'s bulkheads. Even entering the melee could be suicide, though it was hoped that the smaller flyers might attract less attention than the huge, lumbering behemoths of the ryu carriers. Certainly, in these first few seconds, the ryus had been attracting more than their fair share of attention from the enemy.

"All systems check," Kara said, "operational and on-line. All flyers, First Squadron, report ready for launch."

"Roger that, Phantom One," the voice of *Gauss*'s flight control replied. "You are clear for launch."

"Punch it!" Kara yelled over the link, and her Cutlass dropped into vacuum.

Vic watched the Web clouds closing on the human vessels and their DalRiss allies, and thought again of the analogy of antibodies attacking a pathogen or a foreign substance. The attack seemed just as automatic, just as mindless as the purely chemical reaction of antibody adhering to antigen, and he was beginning to think that the Web had no reaction at all to outsiders save that one instinctive and purely defensive response.

Radio, microwave, and laser messages were still being beamed at the Web mechanisms, with special attention being paid to the five or six Alpha-class planetoids that hovered like great, spherical shadows against the glow of golden mist, thousands of kilometers deeper into the Web-cloud. Each message was a plea for communication using channels and frequencies determined by Dev's first contact with the Web, but none were answered or even acknowledged.

All that was left then was to fight . . . but it was swiftly becoming apparent that the human-DalRiss forces didn't have the ghost of a chance in this conflict.

Typically, battles between opposing fleets of warships developed as a series of passes, the two fleets hurtling toward each other, maneuvering all the way to throw off the enemy's fire and to set up the best possible angle for the fire control computers. As the fleets passed or even interpenetrated one another, AIs, with reflexes far quicker than those of humans, took over the targeting and firing tasks, loosing hundreds of volleys within the space of a few seconds.

This was not a typical space battle, however. The Combined Fleet had emerged with a fairly low velocity relative to the Device, while the guardian machines had been in extended orbits around it, with relative velocities of only a few kilometers per second. As the battle unfolded, the swarm of human and DalRiss vessels had drifted into the leading part of the Web cloud, decelerating, merging, until the individual members of both swarms were almost motionless relative to one another. In the human fleet, weapons fired until they were on the point of overheating, and AI monitors began threatening system shutdown.

The most effective human-built weapons appeared to be among the most old-fashioned—missiles with thermonuclear warheads. Missiles fired from every ship in the Combined Fleet streaked through that snowstorm of oncoming Web machines, accelerating into the heart of the glowing cloud. Some were intercepted and dismantled, literally torn apart before they could be triggered; most plunged into the Web array and detonated, however, eye-searing pinpoints of intense light expanding swiftly into sun-brilliant spheres of devouring plasma, each blast instantly annihilating thousands of machines in the densest part of the enemy fleet, then battering countless others into junk with the plasma shock wave or disabling them with the circuit-frying flash of an electromagnetic pulse.

The Imperium's thermonuclear warheads were bigger and far more powerful than those of the Confederation, averaging ten or twenty megatons in their destructive yield. The Frontier worlds, when they'd been part of the Shichiju, had been forbidden to manufacture or even possess nuclear warheads, and their technology and nuke-assembly skills were not as up-to-date as those of the Imperials. Still, thermonuclear warheads were relatively simple to construct and virtually foolproof in their operation. Even a one-megaton blast, properly placed within the Web array, was enough to vaporize thousands of war machines. One of the Alphas took a close-spaced pair of nuclear warheads from the *Constitution* that turned half of its surface white-hot and molten. The artificial moonlet drifted free in space then, its drives silenced, the forest of antennae that had covered its surface melted away.

But a thousand nuclear detonations . . . a hundred thousand would not have more than inconvenienced that horde massed before the Combined Fleet. They would have to flee now, while they still could.

And pray that the Web wouldn't pursue them.

Kara accelerated hard, then cut her drive and flipped end for end decelerating now with a long, shuddering burst of thrust from her drive. Web machines were everywhere, filling the sky, sailing past her hurtling warflyer, impacting across the hull of the *Gauss*. As she drifted low across the research vessel's side, she could see the smallest of the Web machines already gathering in clumps within the angles and recesses of the hull metal like drifts of dirty gray snow.

More of the gossamer machine-things flashed past, their initial vectors given to them by beams of laser or microwave energy from the larger Web craft. They seemed to be without other means of propulsion, for the majority sailed harmlessly past the human vessels and into the interstellar deep. Those that struck, however, rapidly became motile on their own, scrunching along like handkerchief-sized amoebas, finding others of their own kind, merging into larger shapes . . . and larger . . . and larger.

Clearly, they were some type of nanotechnic weapon, similar in principle to human nanodisassembler gases, for where they gathered, pits and craters began opening up in duralloy armor plate as, literally a molecule at a time, the attackers began taking the tough artificial substance apart.

That was why the larger ships in the Combined Fleet all carried squadrons of warflyers or were covered by squadrons off the ryu carriers. Kara slowed above a particularly large mass of crawling, oozing gray eating its way into the *Gauss* and opened fire with her laser. She experimented with the beam intensity as she swept it over the ship's hull; she needed to find a setting that would cook the Web units without punching a hole through the science ship's hull. One hundred to one hundred fifty megawatts seemed to be about right. Each burst seared the duralloy armor, scorching paint and peeling off external nano layers, but so long as she kept the beam moving it could not heat any one point enough to burn through.

The Web nano-D, however, designed to receive power from lower-powered lasers, could only handle that influx of energy for a few seconds before it began to curdle and boil. A few seconds more, and the stuff exploded into vapor, all cohesion between its molecule-sized working parts lost.

It was like bailing an ocean with a teacup, however. As fast as Kara burned the snowdrifts into vapor, more of the infalling nanotechnic weapons landed. Some were collecting on her warflyer as she worked, and twice she had to call for help from someone else in the squadron to burn them off before they ate through to some vital piece of *Kara's Matic*'s internal structure.

At least they were slowing the destruction of the *Gauss*.

A little. She hoped. . . .

Dev rode the Net, watching the battle with a curiously detached, almost casual lack of emotion. The Web vehicles appeared to be concentrating their heaviest firepower on the largest Combined Fleet ships. *Hiryu*, slightly ahead of the dome-shaped formation of Imperial carriers, had almost immediately become the focus for a barrage of dozens of energy beams.

One of the big Web Alphas had maneuvered to within a scant thousand kilometers of the *Hiryu*. Something like an enormous circular hatchway irised open on the hemisphere facing the Imperial carrier, revealing a blue-glowing cavern within. A moment later, and the cavern lit up with a dazzling blue-white glare, the energy spilling over into the ultraviolet wavelengths.

Dev recognized the energy signature of a positron beam, similar, if vastly smaller in scale, to the antimatter electron beam he'd seen jetting from the Great Annihilator at the Galactic Core. Flaring brilliantly as it plowed through the mist of particles and debris adrift in its path, it slashed like a sunbright razor through the *Hiryu*'s heavily armored flank. The beam burned for only a second or so before snapping off;

Hiryu staggered under the searing caress, slewing to port as a hundred-meter gash in her side spewed dense clouds of atmosphere and liquid, freezing into a silver mist as it hit the vacuum of space.

Donryu took the next burst, the blue-white beam of annihilation sweeping across the kilometer-long vessel's upper works, detonating weapons turrets and shearing off antenna arrays in a cascade of golden explosions. The heavy cruiser *Ashigara* changed course, accelerating hard on flaring plasma drives, sliding between the stricken *Donryu* and the relentless fire of the Web moonlet. Blue fire raked the *Ashigara* from stem to stern, ripping open hull plates and slicing through her slush hydrogen tanks. Liquid hydrogen sprayed into space, glittering like a cloud of ice crystals as the cloud expanded. *Ashigara* shuddered, then exploded amidships as her fusion plant's magnetics failed and the temperatures and pressures of a star's core were vented against the relatively frail and unresisting latticework of duralloy plate, diacarb weave, and nanaluminum surrounding it. A nova's light briefly glared alongside the crippled *Donryu*, reflecting from the larger vessel's hull like a sunset shimmering off the surface of an iced-over lake. Part of the *Ashigara*'s bridge structure, half molten and tumbling end over end, slammed into the *Donryu*'s forward quarter to starboard, plunging through decks and compartments like a hurled rock slamming through meticulously stacked and ordered crockery.

The Combined Fleet was striking back with every weapon at its command. Three of the Confederation maguns advanced through the storm of machines, slamming round after high-speed round into the Alphas. Each projectile struck home with a release of kinetic energy equivalent to megatons of TNT, and in a few moments, the sides of the Web Alphas facing the Combined Fleet were beginning to glow in a patchwork of orange and yellow craters, half of their surface turned molten by the barrage. So effective was the attack that the Web faltered in the steady concentration of fire against the ryu carriers, scattering, then shifting, coming to bear on the three magnetic gun vessels. The *Naga Reliant* was their first target, and after only a few moments of high-energy barrage, the gun vessel began to dissolve as the

Naga enfolding the asteroid that was the vessel's heart fragmented and died. The gun vessels carried only a relatively small human crew; the *Naga Reliant*'s bridge superstructure was burned away by an antimatter beam in the first second or two of the exchange. With no human controlling it, giving it orders, the vessel's Naga continued trying to fulfill the last instructions it had been given, moving closer and yet closer to its tormentor, hurling swarms of rocks at relativistic speeds, smashing at the Alpha, smashing and smashing until its own cohesion gave way first and the magun gun vessel exploded in a thin haze of white-hot debris.

Naga Repulse died next, valiantly attempting to protect the Imperial heavy cruiser *Chikuma*. The antimatter particle beam sliced through the Naga and the asteroid within like a white-hot wire through plastic, emitting a vast, obscuring cloud of vaporized nickle iron and hurtling droplets of molten rock. Seconds after the magun's destruction, the *Chikuma* exploded with the force of many thermonuclear warheads, the detonation briefly outshining the two dwarf suns nearby.

The battle had been under way for an eternity—all of six or seven seconds. Though Dev was not actively counting, a part of his mind was aware of the fact that twenty-three DalRiss cityships had been savaged already by the Web, and as the surviving cityships scattered under the onslaught, the fire swung to concentrate on the human vessels.

The volume of human fire returned against the Web was stupendous, devastating in its sheer volume and fire.

But it wasn't enough, not by many orders of magnitude. No one could have predicted such a large number of enemy machines and craft in this one volume of space. All of the human warships in creation could not hope to stand for long against that horde.

The human-DalRiss fleet was losing the battle as Dev watched.

Before long, Kara found herself maneuvering through a literal storm of bits and pieces of debris that clinked and banged and thumped along her Cutlass's hull, a clattering hail sweeping across a metal roof. The space junk ranged in size from grains of sand and dust motes to larger, mostly unidentifiable fragments. Lasers and particle beams, normally invisible in the vacuum of space, were becoming visible as ghostly flickers and pulses of translucent light as they shone through the thickening cloud of debris.

"Phantom One-one! Phantom One-one!" she heard over the tactical channel. "This is One-five! I'm in trouble!"

"One-five, this is One!" she called back. "Where are you?"

Coordinates giving her the other Cutlass's position relative to her own flickered across her visual display. "I got hit by something," the voice said. "My drive's out!"

"Looks like I'm closest," she said. "Hold tight. I'm coming!"

One-five was Phil Dolan, one of the men who'd accompanied her to Kasei. Her warflyer's AI had the other Cutlass centered now between flashing green brackets. He was only a hundred meters away, drifting across the blasted and surreal landscape of the *Gauss*'s upper deck. Calculating burn times and vectors with practiced ease, Kara boosted across the intervening space, flipping over halfway there and decelerating in toward the helplessly drifting flyer. Righting herself, she deployed her primary arm, a telescoping, jointed branch of duralloy that unfolded from a recess in *Kara's Matic*'s hull and opened into a clawed, grasping metal hand.

She was almost there. . . .

Something struck Dolan's Cutlass; she didn't see what it was, but it was large, larger than the warflyer. It might have been a fragment of one of the human ships hurtling through space at high speed, but judging by its vector, she thought it more likely that it was one of the Web constructs. Whatever its origin, it hurtled in from Kara's right, sheared into Dolan's flyer, and the two exploded in a blinding flash of unbottled fusion energy. At virtually the same instant, something—a fragment of wreckage propelled by the blast—struck *Kara's Matic* like a sledgehammer blow, shredding her drive module in a spray of glittering fragments and sparkling droplets of slush hydrogen reaction mass.

The long, dark, and convoluted mass of the *Carl Friedrich*

Gauss swept past her blurred vision . . . and again . . . and again . . .

And still again, growing visibly smaller now. Stunned by the impact, Kara was unable for a moment to realize that her Cutlass, what was left of it, was tumbling end over end, falling away from the *Gauss* at a considerable velocity imparted by the hurtling debris.

And with her plasma drive and reaction mass stores both gone, she wouldn't have a chance in hell of ever arresting her spin and making it back again.

Chapter 26

North American or Ukrainian or Chinese from New America. Europeans from Loki. Japanese from Earth. Juanyekundan. Shivan. Cuchulainnan. What does anything having to do with language or religion or skin color or eye shape have to do with humanity? We have more in common with each other than we do with anything from Out There.

—*Remembrance*
TRAVIS EWELL SINCLAIR
C.E. 2561

Dev watched with a feeling of icy detachment, less aware of the countless thousands of personal and individual tragedies occurring second by second throughout the Combined Fleet than he was of the single, monolithic reality that the human-DalRiss fleet was being crushed, wiped from the sky like a cloud of dancing gnats caught in the flame of a blowtorch. They had already destroyed tens of thousands of Web combat machines—*hundreds* of thousands if the tiny light-sail craft scorched by lasers or vaporized in sweeps of laser light or particle beams were counted—yet they'd scarcely touched the body of the enemy force.

Despair.

He could sense it through the Net, rising from the minds of every human jacked into the Fleet's communications net, then picked up and echoed across the I2C linkage to the Shichiju and back.

How many minds were jacked in at that moment? Dev didn't know, and there was no software available on-line to give him an answer. But he could feel the building emotion, a black cloud dragging at his thoughts.

He could also feel the Net's strength, an expression of its will, its scope, the depth of its analytical and computational power gathering, *building*, reaching up and out across the I2C. . . .

Vic was linked into the command center aboard the Confederation carrier *Karyu*. Reports continued to flood though his consciousness, reports of ships lost, of men and women lost, of incalculable numbers of enemy craft descending on his dwindling command like a whirling, deadly blizzard.

He felt close to crying with frustration. The carefully ordered plans, the meticulously reasoned logic, the convincing rationalization that with faster-than-light communications and the almost-certain guess that the Alphas were a vulnerable command target, all were coming crashing down in ruin after only a few seconds of the most bloody and savage combat that he had ever witnessed.

But ships, his ships, his people were dying at a terrifying and relentless pace. Such slaughter served no purpose; as far as he could tell from his vantage point aboard the *Karyu*, the Web horde was relatively untouched. It was like trying to kill a DalRiss cityship creature by slicing off a few cells from the tip of one arm at a time.

"Resistance is heavier than expected," he said, speaking to Admiral Tanaka over the command link. "The enemy's numbers are far greater than expected. The Confederation contingent has already taken heavy casualties. I suggest that we break off the action if we can, and regroup at Rally One."

"You are right about the resistance, *Shoshosan*," Tanaka replied. "But breaking off may be difficult at this point, and rendezvous and recovery with the DalRiss will not be possible."

"We'll have to E and E then in K-T space. The DalRiss will have to jump out on their own and wait for us."

"Affirmative. I will pass the order."

"Give us time to recover the warflyers."

"Order their recovery at once. I want to begin boosting clear of this slaughterhouse as soon as possible!"

That wouldn't be time enough, not to get them all. Vic was achingly aware that Kara was out there somewhere. If the *Carl Friedrich Gauss* dropped into K-T space before she was able to recover the squadrons of flyers covering her, Kara and the other Phantoms would never make it out. They were strictly short-range fighters, incapable of entering K-T space.

But if they had to straggle behind to get the last few flyers aboard, so be it. "We'll do our best."

Swiftly, he broke the connection, then began rattling off new orders to the ships in the Confederation contingent.

Taki saw the warflyer tumbling clear of the *Gauss*, pinwheeling into darkness, strewing an expanding spiral of glittering wreckage as it fell. Instantly, she oriented her metal and plastic body, targeted the tumbling object with her probe's sensors and locked on. Exercising her will, she fired the probe's aft thrusters.

She'd been floating there, keeping pace with the slow-moving *Gauss*, throughout the long moments of the battle. Hearing one warflyer call for help, she'd started maneuvering her remote closer. Then she'd heard Kara's voice responding, saw the second flyer approach, saw the first warflyer explode and the second go spinning into space after a desk-sized chunk of metal hit it.

She couldn't be sure, but she thought that must be Daren's sister aboard that damaged flyer since it was Kara's voice she'd heard responding to the call for help. Not that that mattered, one way or another. The pilot might be dead, was *prob-*

ably dead after the impact Taki had just witnessed, but if there was even a chance that he or she was still alive . . .

Accelerating, she moved toward the quickly retreating flyer. She'd not been able to practice with the remote nearly as much as she would have liked, and her only experience before today had been in simulation.

Still, it was impossible to tell that this was not a simulation as she moved faster and faster through space, the only indication of her swiftly mounting speed the rising flicker of numbers at the lower right edge of her vision that read off her speed relative to the *Gauss*. After a few moments, however, the tumbling warflyer, centered now in flashing green brackets squarely in the center of Taki's field of view, had stopped dwindling, was even growing larger, from a winking pinpoint of light to a tiny, crumpled toy shape in the distance.

"All flyers," a voice said over the tactical link. "All flyers, return to your ships at once!"

She ignored the voice. It didn't apply to her. She was still safely inside the *Gauss*, while the probe hurtled into the wreckage-strewn night.

It was difficult to keep track of the damaged Cutlass, though. Space was filled with sparkling, glittering, hurtling things, and only the flashing brackets assured her that she was still on target. Every few seconds, something clanged against her outer hull. Inwardly, she cringed with each impact, but after a while she began ignoring them. She couldn't read her instruments well enough to know which of those graphic symbols drifting across her field of view represented dangers and which were simply in the way.

Control of the probe, fortunately, was very nearly as simple as looking at something and thinking hard *go there*. The AI running her interface with the equipment handled the problems of calculation, maneuver, and control, and warned her with a flashing string of characters—or a voice speaking in her ear— when something she was trying to do was not possible.

It was a surprise, then, when the probe spun end over end with disconcerting suddenness, and she found herself staring back toward the *Gauss* as her drive kicked in, decelerating her with savage thrust. The probe, lacking weapons, life support, and control equipment, with more room for reaction mass and less structure to move, was far more maneuverable than a Cutlass. Manned warflyers, in fact, were limited to short periods of twenty or thirty Gs of acceleration, and that was possible only because their pilots were packed into nano jelly like babies in the womb. The probe, with no physical pilot aboard to damage, could deliver a brutal eighty to ninety Gs of acceleration.

It was the only factor that made catching and matching vectors with the runaway Cutlass possible.

She was dismayed when she saw how much the *Carl Friedrich Gauss* had dwindled in apparent size. It looked like scarcely more than a toy now, its spine long and in places made bulky by towers and superstructure, with the blocks of her hab mods showing alternating patches of sunlit gray and black shadow as they turned. A pinpoint of dazzling light erupted on one of her superstructures, flaring larger, then fading away. The ship was taking a battering as the battle continued.

In the distance, other Confederation ships glowed from the effects of multiple impacts; she recognized the angular lines of *Karyu*—but only barely. The ryu carrier's silhouette had been horribly transformed by the bombardment, and as she watched, a dazzling blue beam swept across the Confederation flagship's side, slicing deeply into her hull.

Then the probe flipped over again, and she was close alongside the smooth, black, organic curves of the damaged Cutlass. It was still tumbling, showing first its smooth-rounded prow and then the tangled, rip-shredded ruin of what had been its drive module. An arm extended from its side like the bent limb of a dead tree.

Each time the prow swept past, only a few meters away, she could read a name picked out in cursive script on the prow: *Kara's Matic.*

"Kara!" she called, engaging a communications channel. "This is Taki Oe! Can you hear me?"

There was no answer, save the far-off murmur of other voices on the Net. Swiftly, she unfolded an arm of her own, reaching out.

"Warning! Warning!" her probe's control AI sounded in her ears. "What you are attempting may exceed the recommended stress tolerances of the equipment."

"*Fuzaken-ja neyo!*" The phrase was a curt and rather rude expression meaning approximately, "Don't screw around with me!" It also carried a warning, something like, "Don't think you're better than me!" Whether the AI understood the subtle nuances of the phrase or not, it allowed her to reach out and grab the tumbling warflyer's dangling arm. The nanomorphic clamp molded itself to the other craft; the Cutlass's momentum wrenched at her.

The shock made her dizzy—not from the actual impact, but from the wrenching tumble of the sky about her head as the probe, less massive than the Cutlass by about one third, picked up part of the warflyer's spin. Warning lights flared along the side of her visual field, and a voice informed her with irritating calm that the probe's manual controls were damaged.

She hung on, however, ordering the AI to cancel her spin. It was *trying*; the stars kept spinning past her field of view, but slower now as the AI worked her thrusters, using tight, short bursts to gradually kill the rotation.

More red lights, and another warning. The joints in her wrist and elbow were giving way, stressed by the rotating mass she was trying to arrest. Damn it, *no!* She would *not* let go!

Suddenly, the warflyer's arm shifted, swung around, and molded itself to Taki's mechanical arm, just above the elbow joint. Kara was alive!

Their rotation ceased. She could see the *Gauss*, tiny now against the stars just above the looming black bulk of *Kara's Matic*. She cut in her thrusters . . . and was dismayed to watch the distance to the *Gauss* continue to increase.

She would have to kill their joint velocity outward first, before they could start heading back.

"All warflyers!" the voice from the *Gauss* said again. "Emergency alert! We are pulling out! Everyone get back on board immediately."

"Wait!" Taki yelled. "I have a damaged warflyer out here! Its pilot is alive!"

"Who is this?"

"Dr. Taki Oe. I'm a xenologist off the *Gauss*, operating Remote Probe Five. I have a damaged warflyer at . . ." She hesitated, translating the coordinates on her view, then reading them off to the unseen listeners. "The pilot is alive!"

"Wait one, Dr. Oe," the voice said. "Okay, hang tight! We have some flyers coming to assist you!"

"We're decelerating," she said. "Listen, don't leave without us! The pilot is Lieutenant Hagan!"

"I don't care who it is," another voice said. "We're not leaving one of our own!"

"Hagan!" another voice said. "Did you say Lieutenant *Hagan*?"

"I've got her warflyer, the *Kara's Matic*, right here," Taki said. "I'm trying to stop her velocity, but I may not have enough reaction mass left to do it!"

"Go ahead and burn every drop," the new voice said. "This is Lieutenant Ran Ferris, and I'm going to be there before you know it! I'll get her back!"

"Hurry—" Taki said. She was looking now at something else, something beyond the still-dwindling shape of the *Gauss*. Her course outward had taken her away from the battle, and away, too, from the golden cloud that had so transfixed them all when they'd first arrived in this volume of space.

Her new position gave her an excellent vantage point, looking inward toward the double sun, the Device, the glowing cloud. From here, it looked as though the cloud were slowly transforming itself, changing shape like an immense, space-borne amoeba.

And like an amoeba, it was reaching out, spreading itself wide across three dimensions, sending long, almost liquid-looking pseudopods out and over and around the entire human-DalRiss fleet.

In another few moments, the fleet would be engulfed completely in that glittering, deadly cloud.

Dev once again felt himself losing his grip on his own humanity.

For a time, after the incomplete merging with his down-loaded self, and then later, while he'd been back on New

America with Katya and Vic and other humans, he'd almost felt as though he'd recaptured much that had been lost, the caring for people, the knowledge of them as individuals instead of as *abstractions*, as sophisticated self-directing programs running in jellyware assemblies of chemicals picked and shaped by evolution. But all of that was slipping away now, lost in something, in an awareness much vaster than his own.

The power, the despair, the sheer volume of the Net was waking up.

And Dev was a part of it.

On one level, he was still aware of himself as Dev Cameron; the memories were all intact, his ego, his awareness of self, all was still there. But on a much deeper and more profound level, he was . . . something else, something *very* else. A being, a supremely powerful being that was at one and the same time the sum and far more than the sum of all of those billions of human and AI minds riding the Net with him.

It was almost trivially clear what had happened. Nakamura's Number—and what a limited and simplistic concept *that* was!—suggested a transcendental change in complexity and in scope and in power when a parallel processing system surpassed just over one hundred billion individual sub-units. That number—and it was, he realized now, not the number itself but a kind of critical mass of information processing power—had been surpassed moments before, and the increase had just given birth to a new mind.

Dev was not that mind, though by virtue of his position on the Net and the fact that he was feeling it happen as it took place, he could sense its dawning awareness . . . not mind only, but *Mind*. The new being was self-aware and intelligent, a pervasive and far-flung presence omnipresent and omniscient within the universe it occupied, a universe defined by the worlds and interlocking computer nets from which it arose. Dev could sense that being as an ant might dimly sense a human standing astride its anthill, vast beyond comprehension, so vast it could be perceived more as a natural force than anything alive. Indeed, Dev doubted that any other mind linked in on the Net was aware of the new birth . . . and he questioned at first whether the Mind was aware of anything so insignificant as humanity.

Once, long ago, Dev had been a god. His linkage with a planetary Naga had given him physical and mental powers far beyond the ken of humanity, and memories of that time still could make him tremble inside. Commanding physical forces that could destroy ryu-class starships in planetary orbit, however, was nothing compared to this, an Overmind derived from the mental activities of a hundred billion individual intelligences, yet no more aware of or limited to the scope of its component parts than was a mind derived from a hundred billion nerve cells . . . or than a living cell with its complexities of DNA and mitochondria and golgi bodies and proteins was limited to the scope and reach and ability of individual atoms. An associative, a hive mentality, could be thought of, possibly, as the sum total of all of its separate parts. This, however, was something far more, a synergy that went immeasurably beyond any piecemeal assembly of separate consciousnesses.

The Netlink Overmind cared nothing for the thoughts or despairs or hopes or needs of its individual components. It couldn't even hear them.

It had—it *was*—a Mind of its own.

But at the same time, it clearly was aware of the current problem. Part of its being resided within the hundreds of starships now battling the alien Web, and that part of its being was threatened by the Web's embrace.

Dev tried calling to it . . . uselessly. It could hear his linked thoughts no more than it could hear any of the other teeming, chattering minds still oblivious to its presence.

Perhaps, though it arose from those minds without being an associative or shared mind, it could draw on the totality of information stored by them. Dev felt something, a brushing against his consciousness, and knew without knowing how he knew that some part of his own memory had been tapped.

And the Web associative stopped.

It would not, Dev thought, have been possible without the human-DalRiss fleet that had so held the Web's attention, focusing it on the physical rather than the immaterial, the interactive network of signals flickering from ship to ship throughout the fleet—and by way of the I2C back to all the populated worlds of the Shichiju.

It might not have been possible, too, without the Combined Fleet's massed firepower. Those five moon-sized Alpha-class craft, Dev realized now, had been more than communications centers, but powerful information processing nodes larger and faster and far more powerful than any single AI in human space. Two of the five were still processing data, but more slowly now, for large parts of their interiors had been reduced to molten slag by the bombardment of nuclear missiles and hurtling bits of magun-slung rock striking at relativistic speeds. The damage to this local expression of the Web had been more serious than was suggested by a simple analysis of numbers alone. It was reacting more slowly, and with less decision, a wounded giant limping from its wounds . . . but still powerful beyond belief.

The Netlink Overmind penetrated the Web. Dev was not sure exactly how that happened, though he could imagine several possibilities. The Web must depend on the communicative interaction of its separate parts, as did the Netlink. Those communications were carried out through readily apparent and analyzed processes, through modulated radio and laser transmissions. Such transmissions could be tapped, analyzed, decoded, *broken* with a speed and an efficiency unthinkable to any merely human mind. Dev could sense the Overmind expanding—growing at the expense of the Web. One by one . . . then in tens . . . in hundreds . . . in thousands . . . in millions, the myriad craft that made up the physical expression of the Web went inert. Some turned their weapons on their fellows before they, in turn, were blasted out of existence; most simply went dead, their processors fused by overloads, their data receptors switched off, rendering them blind and deaf to the increasingly urgent calls of the Web intelligence.

Watching through the massed probes and sensors of the fleet, Dev could see everywhere the vast, glittering pseudopodia of the Web growing ragged at the edges . . . tattering just a little at first, then beginning to disintegrate with astonishing speed. Dimly, he was aware that he was witness to the power of exponents. An effect doubled, then doubled again, then doubled time after time can eventually and relentlessly overpower the most impossible of numbers.

Dev watched as the monster, itself far more than Nakamura's Number of component parts, began to disintegrate with bewildering speed.

"What's . . . what's happening?" Kara staggered as they pulled her, nude and dripping, from the liquid embrace of her shattered warflyer. "I couldn't see. . . . "

Everywhere was total and complete and shrieking, wildly happy confusion. The spin gravity bay had been repressurized and was swarming now with men and women, some from the Phantoms, others from the ship's crew, and even some of the scientists, all milling about in happy, joyful, madly exultant chaos. Ran Ferris helped her stand up, catching her as she almost fell.

And then Katya was there, holding out a robe, tears streaming down her face. Everywhere in the bay there was jubilation, men and women cheering and hurling pieces of uniform and anything they could throw aloft. "I thought you were dead!" Katya yelled, her voice barely reaching above the roaring cheers around her.

Kara took the robe and shrugged it on, grateful for its warmth in the chill of a compartment only recently open to vacuum.

"Someone came out and got me," Kara replied. "With a remote. Was it Daren?"

And there was Daren, shoving his way through the celebrating crewmen. "Not me!" he yelled.

"It was the Japanese woman," Ran told her. "Dr. Oe. She stopped your spin with the probe and got you headed back toward the ship before her reaction mass ran dry. All I had to do was catch you and bring you in,"

"Taki!" Daren cried. "She went back out again after we both got knocked off-line! I didn't know she was chasing you, though!"

Taki! Kara stared at Ran and her brother, then laughed, shaking her head. Little Taki, the woman she'd not even wanted to talk to!

"What . . . what's going on?" she asked again. "My commo was knocked out. I still had the AI and my visual sensors, but I couldn't see much of anything until the probe grabbed me. What's all the cheering?"

Katya steered her aside, toward a marginally quieter part of the chamber, near an inner bulkhead. "We won!" she shouted.

"We . . . won . . . ?"

It hardly seemed possible. They'd been losing, losing big right up to the moment when she'd been hit by a piece of Phil Dolan's *Philosopher*.

Poor Phil . . .

"We still don't know what's happened," Daren said. "But my father's been on-line with us, and he says something happened with the grand Netlink. All of the people watching online. Somehow they were able to infiltrate the Web, make parts of it start attacking itself. Sounds like they broke the thing's encoding somehow and started giving it conflicting orders. Right now, it's all just individual machines drifting through space, with no control or coherence at all."

The battle—if not quite the war—was over.

She hugged herself, shivering.

"Let's get you dried off and dressed," her mother said.

Kara shook her head. "No," she said. "First things first. Where's Taki?"

She wanted to thank the woman who'd just saved her life.

And in the cyberspace defined by the massed, interlinked computers and intelligences and jacked-in minds, a newborn intelligence stretched forth its . . . they were not *hands*, actually, since the being had no physical instrumentality, but "hands" would serve as an adequate descriptor for powers of manipulation that it was only beginning to be aware of.

So much was possible now, undreamed of before.

It looked out at the stars surrounding it, comprehending. There were vistas there of time and space . . . and of other intelligences now dimly sensed.

So very much was possible. . . .

Epilogue

"The war isn't over," Kara said. "Not by about ten million light years. We still have the Web, the *real* Web, to contend with, at the Galactic Core."

"Well, that can't be that hard, can it?" Daren asked. "We beat 'em at the Nova. And by the time we got to Alya, the machines that were left had all switched. Nothing left but floating junk."

They were seated on the raised patio at the back of Cascadia, overlooking the mountains on a glorious, crisp New American morning. Columbia was dimly seen behind a light haze in the east. Morninglories chirped and warbled at one another from a dancing golden cloud above the amberbushes below. Kara was sitting on a double seat next to Taki, her arm around the young woman's shoulders. They'd become close friends since the Battle of Nova Aquila, somewhat to Daren's irritation. He claimed that Taki didn't have time for him anymore, because she was always talking with Kara.

And Kara didn't really care. She'd found a new friend in Taki, a woman with a mind as bright and as incisive as her own. She was enjoying getting to know her as a *person*, instead of as an oriental face. She looked across the patio and caught Ran's eye; he grinned at her, and she wondered if he was thinking about that ViRsim they'd shared before the battle, when she'd admitted her distrust of all Nihonjin.

She'd changed a lot since then.

Katya stretched out in a couch that molded itself to her thought. "I doubt that it will pose that much of a problem. The last time we talked to Dev about it, he seemed to think the Netlink was more than a match for the Web. 'Infinitely beyond it,' he said. Because of its flexibility."

"But as I understand it," Vic said, "this Overmind was a product of all those massed billions of human minds on the Net. They're not there anymore. What happened to the Overmind? Did it just . . . blink out?"

"It's still there," Katya told him. "At least Dev says it is, even if we're not aware of it. I suppose we could think of it as being asleep . . . but there's also an impression he got that that number . . . what did you call it, Daren?"

"Nakamura's Number."

"Right. There was an impression Dev had that the Overmind wasn't completely reliant on that number. Maybe the number was responsible for its birth in the first place, but . . . it's still there. And growing stronger."

"Scary," Kara said with a small inner shudder.

Taki patted her arm. "It seems we have need of large and powerful friends. The larger and more powerful, the better."

"I'd be happier if I could understand it better," Ran said. "The scale of this thing is a little overwhelming."

"That'll come," Vic said. "With time. I guess with Dev as a kind of go-between, we should be able to learn more about it eventually, even if it doesn't seem all that interested in communicating directly with us."

"How often do we stop to talk with insects?" Kara said. "That's what scares me, that it's so far beyond human comprehension that we don't really have that much in common with it. Even though it sprang from us, somehow."

"What I want to know more about is the Web," Daren said. "They've been analyzing the sample machines we brought back over at the University. They say the Naga link has been proven."

"God help us," Katya said softly. "The Web created the Naga?"

"Almost certainly. We think . . . we *think* that the Web collective began sending Naga seed pods out beyond the Galactic

Core, oh, maybe seven, eight billion years ago. Understand, a lot of this is still guesswork.''

''Go on,'' Kara said.

''The idea may have been to use them like von Neumann machines. Self-replicating. Exponentiating. A Naga seed pod would land on a planet with certain parameters of temperature, gravity, and magnetic moment and begin preparing it. Like terraforming . . . but getting it ready for the Web, not humans. But something went wrong.''

''What?'' Ran said.

''We're really not sure,'' Taki told him. ''Some of us think that the process was taking so long—millions of years between one planet colonized and another—that a kind of evolution set in. Like genetic drift.''

Kara had had to look that one up when Taki first mentioned it. In biology, genetic drift occurred when a species changed slightly to meet different conditions in a neighboring territory . . . and then that subspecies changed as it migrated again . . . and again . . .

There were cases known of ten or twelve subspecies living in adjacent territories, each slightly different from its neighbors, each able to breed with its neighbors . . . and yet the subspecies on either end of that chain were so different from one another that they could be regarded as entirely separate species, unable even to interbreed.

In this case, the genetic drift had been a subtle but constant shift in the organization of information, slight at first, but enough so that eventually the Naga were no longer recognized as part of the Web.

And the Naga, by that time, was a self-sufficient life form, operating under its own set of programming.

''We're pretty sure the Naga were supposed to start turning planets into easily digestible chunks for the Web when it arrived,'' Daren continued. ''The Web apparently has the rather single-minded goal of turning all of the matter in the universe, stars, planets, rocks, us, whatever it can get its claws on, into more machines. Components of itself. Judging from the number of machines at Nova Aquila, it could do it, too.''

"Sounds like a von Neumann machine run amuck," Kara said.

"In a way. From the Web's point of view, the Naga have become a kind of cancer, cells, if you will, growing and evolving on their own, instead of according to the master plan."

"Lucky for us," Ran said. "And to think we once thought the Naga were our enemies!"

Kara held out her hand, palm up. A black spot appeared in the center of her palm, spread, then extruded itself, a gleaming black stalk that rose ten centimeters from her skin, swaying in the breeze. It dipped and twisted, bowing to each of the others in turn.

"Enemies can become friends," Kara said, grinning. She winked at Taki. "Given time."

TECHNO-DEATH RULES—AS MAN BATTLES
MONSTERS AND MACHINES FOR DOMINION OF THE GALAXY

WARSTRIDER

A Series of High-Tech Adventures by

WILLIAM H. KEITH, JR.

WARSTRIDER
76879-8/$4.99 US/$5.99 Can

Dev Cameron was planning to join the Navy when he was drafted into the Guard—"groundpounders" consigned to do the dirtiest work of interplanetary warfare. And now the reluctant warrior's heavily armored unit is rocketing to the stars to do battle with Xenos—an inscrutable, illogical and terrifying race of alien monsters committed to the annihilation of all other galactic species.

WARSTRIDER: REBELLION
76880-1/$4.99 US/$5.99 Can

WARSTRIDER: JACKERS
77591-3/$4.99 US/$5.99 Can

WARSTRIDER: SYMBIONTS
77592-1/$4.99 US/$5.99 Can

THE FANTASTIC ROBOT SERIES

ISAAC ASIMOV'S

ROBOTS IN TIME

by Hugo and Nebula Award Nominee
William F. Wu

EMPEROR
76515-1/ $4.99 US/ $5.99 Can

PREDATOR
76510-1/ $4.99 US/ $5.99 Can

MARAUDER
76511-X/ $4.99 US/ $5.99 Can

WARRIOR
76512-8/ $4.99 US/ $5.99 Can

DICTATOR
76514-4/ $4.99 US/ $5.99 Can